SHADOWS OF WAR

MICHAEL RIDPATH is the author of eight financial thrillers and the Fire & Ice series of crime novels. He was born in Devon, brought up in Yorkshire, read History at Oxford University and now lives in North London. Before becoming a full-time writer, he worked in the City for twelve years as a bond trader and venture capitalist.

www.michaelridpath.com

REVIEWS FOR

MICHAEL RIDPATH

Also by Michael Ridpath

TRAITOR'S GATE

SHADOWS OF WAR

MICHAEL RIDPATH

HEAD
of ZEUS

First published in the UK in 2015 by Head of Zeus Ltd

This paperback edition first published in the UK in 2015
by Head of Zeus Ltd

9 7 5 3 1 2 4 6 8

A CIP catalogue record for this book is available
from the British Library.

Paperback ISBN 9781781853337
eBook ISBN 9781781853344

Printed in the UK by Clays Ltd, St Ives Plc

Head of Zeus Ltd
Clerkenwell House
45-47 Clerkenwell Green
London EC1R 0HT

WWW.HEADOFZEUS.COM

To Richenda

And we are here as on a darkling plain
Swept with confused alarms of struggle and flight,
Where ignorant armies clash by night.

From 'Dover Beach' by Matthew Arnold

SHADOWS OF WAR

The Western Front
1939–1940

PART ONE

September–November 1939

One

Chilton Coombe,
Somerset
3 September 1939

Dear Theo,
   War was declared this morning, at eleven o'clock. I am staying with my parents on weekend leave in Somerset, and we had just got back from church when we heard the Prime Minister announcing it on the wireless. They say there have already been air-raid warnings in London. Perhaps by the time you get this the streets of London will be rubble and men will have started dying in trenches in Flanders. Again. With all the modern killing machines mankind has developed, all the aeroplanes and the tanks, this one will be worse than the last one. Millions more will die.
   You and I are at war. I can't help thinking of the oath you made me swear that night eight years ago in my rooms in Oxford, that we would not let them tell us to go and kill each other. We were both tight on college port, but I meant it then, and I haven't forgotten it. Yet now I am in uniform and so are you. I feel guilty that I am breaking that oath. Not exactly guilty, but regretful, and I think you deserve an explanation.
   I have seen war for myself, in Spain, and I know it is hell. I voted at the Union not to fight for King and Country. And I have done my best to avoid this war; you know that. I am British, but my mother is German, and Father is as firmly opposed to war of any kind as he has always been. Yet when I was in Berlin with you last year I saw what evil the Nazi regime can do, will do, unless it is stopped.

3

That's why I joined the army, and why I will probably soon find myself in France in the mud shooting at your compatriots, maybe even shooting at you. It is a cause that is worth fighting for; not just worth fighting for, it must be fought for, and I must fight for it. I hope you understand that.

I am sending this via the safe address in Denmark you gave me. Despite that, it might not reach you, but even if it doesn't, at least I will have tried to get in touch.

I hope that in a year, or five years, or however long this damn war takes, we will be able to share a glass of port again. Make that a bottle.

Yours,
Conrad

Two

Zutphen, Holland, 21 October 1939

In a neutral waterlogged country on the edge of a war that was already becoming phoney, Captain Sigismund Payne Best sat in his American Lincoln Zephyr and waited. Beneath him, the broad powerful waters of the River IJssel rolled down to the North Sea. Ahead, across green damp meadows, the medieval towers of Zutphen scratched grey bellies of heavy cloud.

This was Payne Best's second war. He had been involved in intelligence in the last one, and made a decent fist of it, although he had lost some good agents along the way. But already, only six weeks into the rematch, he was on to something. Something big. Something that might, just might, bring this new war to a halt before it had even had a chance to get going.

An absurdly long barge, two hundred feet at least, nosed under the bridge, its bow and its stern visible on either side, carrying raw materials upstream to feed the German war machine.

He checked his wristwatch. They were late, over an hour. That wasn't yet a cause for alarm; there was plenty that could delay them on the border. Payne Best tapped his fingers on the steering wheel and lit yet another cigarette. Patience was a necessity for an agent, but Payne Best had little of it. He had the languages – his Dutch and his German were perfect – he had charm, an excellent memory and people trusted him. But he hated waiting.

Two cars approached, a Citroën followed by an Opel. The Citroën swished past, but the Opel slowed down and pulled over just on the Zutphen side of the river. A German number plate.

Stubbing out his cigarette, Payne Best stepped out of his car and stood on the bridge. He adjusted his monocle to examine the two men approaching. One of them, Lieutenant Grosch, Payne Best recognized. The other was young, about thirty, with a chubby face bearing nicks and cuts picked up from duels in a German student corps. He, too, was wearing a monocle, Payne Best was glad to see. Cut a bit of dash, a monocle, Payne Best thought.

Grosch greeted Payne Best and introduced his companion in German as Captain Schämmel. They shook hands, and Schämmel performed a little heel click.

Payne Best smiled at the stranger, but disappointment and frustration nagged at him.

He turned to Grosch. 'And the general? We were supposed to be meeting the general.'

'I am sorry the general could not be here,' said Schämmel. 'As you can imagine, it is very difficult for a serving general in the Wehrmacht to travel to a neutral country without permission. But he and I are close colleagues. He has asked me to open discussions on his behalf.'

Payne Best studied the German captain. Large brown eyes, a ready smile; his words were soft and precise. An intelligent man, not some lackey.

'And what do you wish to discuss?'

The German scanned the bridge and the road beyond it, empty now apart from their two vehicles, and then fixed Payne Best with those sharp eyes.

'Our plans to remove Hitler. And what peace settlement your government will agree to when we do.'

Three

Wiltshire, 5 November

'Chin chin.'

'Cheers.' Second Lieutenant Conrad de Lancey raised his glass to his company second-in-command and knocked back half his scotch and soda. 'I needed that.' They were alone in the ante-room of the mess in armchairs around a blazing fire.

'Your men did well, de Lancey,' Captain Burkett said.

'I heard the CO calling it a shambles.'

'Everything is a shambles to him,' said Burkett. 'It was raining; the visibility was perfectly bloody. We're getting better. You did a bloody good job considering you've only been with us a couple of months.'

They had spent the last thirty-six hours on exercise on Salisbury Plain with a cavalry regiment that to Conrad's eye had yet to grasp the difference between a Matilda tank and a horse. Conrad's battalion, however, had become adept at jumping in and out of lorries, as befitted its 'motorized' status, and Conrad himself could read a map and a compass and readily identify fields of fire and dead ground. He had spent enough time with his face pressed into Spanish dirt with live bullets whizzing over his head to get a feel for that kind of thing.

'We'll be doing it for real soon,' Burkett said.

Conrad's ears pricked up. 'Are we going to France? Have you heard something?'

'No, nothing specific. But they'll send us sooner or later. Probably sooner.'

'Good,' Conrad said.

Burkett's eyes darted up to Conrad and then away. 'Absolutely.' Despite being the senior officer, the recently promoted Burkett was three or four years younger than Conrad, probably in his mid twenties. He was a broad man, squat with a trim moustache and a pugnacious chin, but his eyes never stayed still. His father and grandfather had been in the regiment, and he had joined up himself straight from public school.

They drank their whiskies, thinking of France. Conrad genuinely wanted to go, not out of some kind of innocent gung-ho patriotism, but out of a desire to do his bit to stop Hitler. When Poland had been invaded and war declared, the whole country, Conrad included, had been grimly prepared for modern wholesale slaughter. Sirens had sounded, but no bombs had fallen on London or anywhere else. No German boots or tank tracks had crossed the French and Belgian borders. Given the lacklustre way the 'phoney war' was progressing, Conrad might just as well be drinking in a mess in Wiltshire as in northern France.

'Are they anything like real battle?' Burkett asked with a hint of anxiety. 'The exercises?'

Conrad was surprised by the question. He had spent eighteen months fighting for the International Brigade in Spain, a subject that his fellow officers usually avoided. On the one hand, the idea that one of their number had fought for the socialists was awkward; on the other, Conrad had experience of real fighting and they realized that could come in handy in a war.

'No,' Conrad said. 'Nothing at all.' He thought of Madrid, Jarama Valley, Guadalajara and of the final nightmare on the slopes of Mosquito Hill. It was nothing like sitting on a damp knoll in the middle of England deciding when to order a brew-up. But he couldn't explain all that to Burkett, so he tried to reassure him. 'The training will help, especially when we first go into battle.'

'Hmm.' Burkett looked into his whisky. He was nervous, thought Conrad. Scared even. Well, that was fair enough. Rational.

'Got any plans for next weekend?' Conrad asked.

Burkett straightened up. 'Meeting Angela in Winchester. We're going to the pictures. She wants to see *Gone with the Wind*, although I rather think she's been twice before.'

'I thought Angela was Dodds's girl? Or is that a different Angela?' Dodds was a young subaltern in Baker Company.

'Same Angela. He might think she is his girl, but she never was.' Burkett grinned. 'At least, not according to her. But he did introduce us. Which was very decent of him. All's fair in love and war, eh?' The captain winked.

Conrad didn't answer. He wasn't yet completely au fait with all the traditions of his regiment, but he was pretty sure that captains pinching second lieutenants' girlfriends wasn't one of them.

Burkett indicated that the mess orderly refill their glasses. 'What about you? Are you married?'

'Divorced,' said Conrad.

'Sorry to hear that, old man.'

'I'm sure it's for the best,' said Conrad. Veronica running off with a racing driver while Conrad was getting shot at in Spain had not been pleasant, but the divorce, when he had finally agreed to it, had been a relief.

'Do you have a girl?'

Conrad hesitated. Then smiled. He didn't want to keep her a secret. 'I do actually. In London.'

'What's her name?'

'Anneliese.'

'Pretty name,' Burkett said, and then frowned. 'Isn't it . . .'

'German?' Conrad said. 'Yes, it is. She got kicked out of Germany last year.'

'Jewish, is she?'

Conrad glanced at his fellow officer. The question was posed innocently enough. One eyebrow was slightly raised, but Burkett's face registered only mild curiosity. Yet Conrad realized he was being judged. Burkett knew Conrad was a leftie who had fought for the Bolshies in Spain. He knew Conrad spoke fluent German, although he didn't yet know that Conrad's mother was German herself. And now he had discovered that Conrad had a girlfriend who was not only German but possibly Jewish.

Conrad could deal with Burkett's ill-informed judgements about himself, but not about Anneliese. Anneliese and people like her were why Conrad had joined the army. Conrad knew, because he had seen it, that Anneliese had courage. For her, the war against Hitler had been going for years, and it was a war in which there had already been thousands of casualties.

'Sort of,' he answered.

Burkett thought better of asking what that meant and took another slug of whisky.

'There you are!' Conrad and Burkett turned to see a tall, lanky figure with fair hair and a flushed red face standing at the door of the ante-room. The figure moved towards them, his eyes on fire.

'Dodds! You are improperly dressed,' Burkett barked. 'We do not bring weapons into the mess. Go and hand it in to the armoury!' Second Lieutenant Dodds was indeed still wearing his Sam Browne and service revolver.

Burkett squinted at Dodds more closely. 'Are you drunk?'

At first Conrad thought Dodds was going to slug Burkett, or at least try to, but then he came to a halt in the middle of the room.

'I might be drunk. But you are dead.' He whipped out the revolver and pointed it at Burkett.

Colour drained from the captain's face. He opened his mouth but nothing came out.

'Put the gun down, Matthew,' said Conrad, getting to his feet. The end of the barrel of the revolver was unsteady, but not unsteady enough that it would miss at a range of five yards.

'Move out of the way, de Lancey. This has nothing to do with you.'

'If you press that trigger you will be court-martialled,' Conrad said. 'Your life will be over.'

'I don't care,' said the young subaltern. 'My life is over anyway.'

Dodds was only nineteen. Conrad rather liked him. His father was a vicar in a rural parish in Lincolnshire. Although naive, he was enthusiastic, good under pressure and he had a kind of innocent charm that won over fellow officers and his men alike. Conrad had seen him reading and rereading letters from Angela, and he knew the boy was smitten. But this?

He glanced at Burkett, whose face was now white. The mess orderly, a lance corporal and the only other man in the room, was rooted to the spot.

Conrad took a step forward.

'Stop, de Lancey! Or I'll shoot you and then I'll shoot Burkett.'

Conrad took a step to the left. He was as tall as Dodds, but had broader shoulders, so he hid Burkett from Dodds's view. 'Put the gun down now, Matthew.'

'Out of the way!' Dodds cried. He took a step back away from Conrad, his gun pointing straight at him. Conrad held Dodds's eyes. They were bright blue, glittering through moisture.

'Captain Burkett, I'm going to step twice to the left,' Conrad said. 'You stay behind me and then back off towards the door.' There was a door at the back of the ante-room, which led through to the dining room. 'Corporal O'Leary, stand back!' he called to the mess orderly.

Conrad took two slow steps to the left. Dodds's revolver followed him. Conrad could hear Burkett moving behind him.

'I will shoot you, de Lancey,' Dodds said.

'No you won't,' said Conrad. 'You might want to shoot Captain Burkett, but you don't want to shoot me.' He took a step forward.

He could see indecision replace anger for a moment in Dodds's eyes, but only for a moment, before it was replaced in turn by a new decision. In that instant Conrad knew what would happen next, but before he could move, Dodds had whipped the pistol round and pointed it at his own temple.

'Stop!' Conrad shouted. 'Don't do it, Matthew!'

'Why not?' said Dodds. 'I was going to kill myself after I had killed Burkett. I'm going to be court-martialled anyway – you said it. And now I've lost Angela, I may as well be dead.'

Conrad saw the boy's terrible logic. 'All right, Matthew, so you're going to die. You've lost Angela. But why don't you take a couple of the Hun with you? You're a good officer. We'll all be in France some time soon. You want to die, at least die fighting. Killing yourself now is the coward's way out. And you're no coward, Matthew. You are a soldier. A good soldier.'

Dodds was listening. 'But after this, they won't let me fight.'

'I won't say anything. Neither will Captain Burkett – will you, Captain Burkett?' Silence. 'Captain Burkett?'

'No.' Conrad heard a croak from behind him.

'And Corporal O'Leary didn't see anything, either, did you, O'Leary?'

'No, sir.'

Conrad took another step forward and held out his hand. A tear crept down Dodds's cheek. He let the gun fall to his side, and Conrad gently eased it out of his fingers.

Four

'What happened last night, Mr de Lancey?'

Lieutenant Colonel Rydal sat back in the chair behind his desk, his fingers steepled. Despite his grey hair, Rydal had a smooth face and an energetic air that suggested more youth than you would expect from a regular army colonel who had fought in the Great War.

'Lieutenant Dodds and Captain Burkett had an argument,' Conrad replied. 'Over a girl. It blew over.'

'Blew over?'

'Yes, sir.'

'I understand that Lieutenant Dodds drew his weapon?'

Conrad was silent. He wondered how the colonel had found out what had happened. Both Burkett and Lance Corporal O'Leary had promised to keep quiet. Conrad wasn't sure he could trust Burkett. And O'Leary might have told his fellow NCOs. Either way, it hadn't taken long to get back to the colonel.

'What happened, Mr de Lancey?'

'Lieutenant Dodds is a good officer, sir. It's my belief that he will turn into a very good officer.'

'Good officers don't get drunk and wave weapons around in the mess.'

'No, sir. But it's likely we are all going to be in France soon. And I know that I would rather have Mr Dodds behind me, or next to me, or leading a platoon coming to relieve me. Men like him are valuable.'

'Rather than Captain Burkett, you mean?'

That was what Conrad had meant but he couldn't admit it. 'In Spain I learned whom I could trust and whom I couldn't. There were men like Lieutenant Dodds in Spain who fought bravely; many of them died bravely. And yes some of them got drunk and behaved badly. But I spoke to Lieutenant Dodds for a long time last night. I really don't think he will cause trouble again.'

'You don't expect me to overlook this, Mr de Lancey? Without discipline this battalion would become a shambles.'

'That's right, sir. But with young officers like Lieutenant Dodds, this battalion will be able to fight and fight well.'

The colonel paused briefly, but only briefly. He was a decisive man.

'I can't risk Lieutenant Dodds and Captain Burkett being in the same company, can I?'

'No, sir. But perhaps Mr Dodds could be transferred to another company?'

The colonel reached into his in tray and pulled out a sheet of paper. 'I have a request here for the secondment of regular army officers to training camps for new recruits.'

'Lieutenant Dodds isn't experienced enough for that, though, is he, sir?'

'No. But Captain Burkett is.'

Conrad tried to repress a smile. 'I think Captain Burkett would be an excellent choice, sir.' Conrad considered his next words carefully. 'While I am sure that Captain Burkett would miss the opportunity for active duty, he would relish the chance to lick new recruits into shape.'

'My thoughts exactly.' The colonel tossed the sheet of paper on to his desk. 'You know I was fifteen when the last war started, nineteen when it finished? I served six months in the trenches.'

'Sir.'

Rydal examined Conrad. He saw a tall, fit officer in his late twenties, with fair hair and athletic build; the sort of man who could take care of himself and his men. 'You and I are the only two officers in the battalion with experience of real war.'

'Yes, sir.' The first two regiments Conrad had attempted to join had turned him down, almost certainly because of his time in the International Brigade. He had wondered why Colonel Rydal had been different.

'Once the last war got going, promotions accelerated, and I am sure it will be the same with this one. You haven't been with us long, Mr de Lancey, but I like what I have seen of you so far. I need men like you as my company commanders.'

Conrad gave up repressing his smile. 'I won't let you down, sir.'

'I'm sure you won't. Now, there's something else.' The colonel pulled out another sheet of paper and examined it. 'You have been ordered to report to Sir Robert Vansittart at the Foreign Office immediately.'

'Immediately?'

'Today,' said the colonel. 'I've no idea what it is about. Have you?'

'No idea at all, sir. Although I did come in contact with Sir Robert last year.'

The colonel frowned. 'Really? You have a shadowy past, Mr de Lancey.'

Whitehall, London

Conrad decided to walk from Waterloo Station to Whitehall. London was entering its third month of war, and Conrad did not feel at all out of place in his uniform. For over a year the city had been preparing, but now that war had actually arrived, there were some changes. Motor cars' bumps and prangs in the all-encompassing blackout had demonstrated a need for white stripes on lamp-posts, kerbs and crossings. Tops of pillar boxes were daubed with yellow paint which would supposedly detect poison gas. Brown paper strips criss-crossed shop windows to minimize blast damage. And up in the sky, over the Thames, barrage balloons dipped and bobbed, now daubed a murky green rather than the silver they had sported when they were first hoisted.

Conrad was pleased with his conversation with the CO. He knew that in most other regiments, Dodds would be up for a court martial. He was convinced that he was right: Dodds would make a better officer under fire than Burkett, and he was impressed that the colonel had agreed. But he was worried that Dodds had lost his head. Conrad's instinct was that the young lieutenant would come into his own when under the pressure of battle, but what if he was wrong?

Still, he was damned sure they would all be better off without Captain Burkett. And from what the colonel had said, Conrad might be commanding his own company in a year or two. If the war lasted that long, which Conrad feared it would.

He passed through Parliament Square and strode up Whitehall, glancing at the Cenotaph with its reminder of all those hundreds of thousands of young men, like Conrad, who had perished in the last diplomatic balls-up twenty years before. He turned left into Downing Street and, opposite Number 10, entered the grand palace that was the Foreign Office.

Conrad had met Sir Robert Vansittart, Chief Diplomatic Adviser, several times before, mostly over dinner at his parents' house. 'Van', as he was known, was a friend of Conrad's father from their school days at Eton. He was tall, almost as tall as Conrad, with square shoulders and a square jaw. He was known for his forthright opinions, especially on the subject of appeasement of Germany, and for that reason he had been shuffled out of his former position of Permanent Under-Secretary a couple of years before, although he still maintained the impressive office with its view over St James's Park.

'Ah, de Lancey, take a seat.' Van indicated one of the ornate chairs in front of his desk. 'Good to see you in uniform. How is soldiering?'

'I'm enjoying it, Sir Robert,' said Conrad. 'I seem to have a facility for it.'

'Well, let us hope you will not be called upon to fire a shot in anger.'

'Actually, I rather hoped I would. That was the point of joining up, after all.'

Van smiled. 'I trust your father hasn't heard you say that?'

Conrad admired his father both for his courage and for the strength of his convictions. Viscount Oakford's pacifism was well known. During the Great War, as Captain the Hon. Arthur de Lancey, he had won a Victoria Cross, lost an arm, and honed a determination to prevent his country's return to such wholesale slaughter ever again. Conrad's mother was from Hamburg. So the declaration of war two months before had been a personal disaster for Conrad's family.

But for Conrad it was a grim necessity. He smiled. 'Father and I differ on the subject of war and peace.'

'You don't have to tell me,' said Van. 'He never ceases to harangue me and Lord Halifax to bring this war to an early conclusion.'

'Which is impossible to do without giving in to tyranny,' Conrad said.

'Perhaps. But there might be a way.'

Conrad's pulse quickened. His suspicion as to why he had been summoned to Whitehall looked as if it was going to be confirmed. 'Are the German generals finally going to do something?'

'It's an eventuality that we cannot discount. It is for that reason I summoned you here. Have you had any communication recently with your German . . .' Van paused to reach for the correct word. '. . . friends?'

'Not since this time last year.' Conrad had received no reply to his letter to Theo on the first day of the war.

'And who were those friends, exactly?'

'You want names?'

Van nodded.

Conrad hesitated. When he had returned from Berlin the previous autumn, he had been determined not to betray Theo, who had warned him of leaks in the British secret service. But now Britain and Germany were at war, and Sir Robert Vansittart was at the centre of the government directing that war.

'My friend Lieutenant Theo von Hertenberg of the Abwehr.' The Abwehr was the German secret service. 'His boss, Colonel Oster. Captain Heinz, another Abwehr officer. Ewald von Kleist, a well-connected Prussian aristocrat. General Beck, the former Chief of the General Staff.'

'And who else was part of the conspiracy?'

Theo had known most of the conspirators, but had not passed their names on to Conrad. Some, though, had been obvious.

'Well, there's Admiral Canaris, the Chief of the Abwehr. Theo Kordt in the German Foreign Office. Count Helldorf, the Chief of the Berlin Police. General von Witzleben. General Halder, the current Chief of the General Staff. Hjalmar Schacht, the former President of the Reichsbank. Many others I don't know.' As he reeled off the names, Conrad was reminded how extraordinary it was that so many senior members of the German government had been willing to overthrow their leader. And had come so close.

'Have you come across a Captain Schämmel of the OKW Transport Division?'

Conrad frowned. 'No, I don't think so. There were a lot of people involved. Hertenberg may know him.'

Van was listening intently as he jotted the names Conrad mentioned on a pad of paper on his desk.

'Over the last few months we have been bombarded by peace initiatives from every quarter. Most are a waste of time.' Van grimaced. 'An enormous waste of time. But our people in Holland have come across one which seems promising. They have been approached by a certain Captain Schämmel to discuss possible peace terms following a successful attempt by unspecified generals to remove Hitler.'

Conrad grinned. 'I'm very glad to hear that.' They had come so close twelve months before; only the offer by Neville Chamberlain of peace talks at Munich had derailed their plans at the last minute, to Conrad's intense frustration. He had assumed that now war had been declared, all thoughts of removing Hitler would have been shelved. But apparently not.

'Schämmel seems genuine and the Cabinet have been discussing how to respond. But we need to be sure. Which is why I thought of you.'

'Me?'

'Yes. You are the only Briton who has had direct contact with a number of the conspirators. I want you to go to Holland at once and meet this Schämmel, with our people. I would also like you to make contact with your friend Hertenberg. We believe that he has been operating in Holland recently; as a neutral country directly between Germany and Britain, it has seen a good deal of intelligence activity. Ask him whether the generals really are planning to remove Hitler and whether this man Schämmel represents them.'

'Hertenberg might be unwilling to tell me,' Conrad said. 'He always made clear to me he was a patriot first and foremost, and his country is now at war with ours.'

'If indeed there is coup planned, and the potential new government wishes to open discussions with us, he'll tell you.'

Conrad considered Van's point. It made sense.

'Can you get in touch with him yourself?' Van said. 'Our people could no doubt help you, but it would probably be better all round if you could contact him independently.'

Conrad could hardly telephone him or send him a wire. But Denmark might work after all. 'I can't guarantee it, but I can have a go,' he said. 'When do I go to Holland?'

'You are booked on a flight to Amsterdam early tomorrow morning.'

Conrad felt a rush of excitement. After the tedium of all that training, finally a chance to do something that might make a difference. 'I'm due back at Tidworth this evening. Have you cleared it with my CO?'

'That will be done,' said Van.

Conrad smiled. 'Excellent,' he said. 'If the German generals are finally going to dump Hitler, I'm grateful for the chance to be a part of it.'

'Good. Mrs Dougherty outside will furnish you with the details.' Van stood up to usher Conrad out of his office. 'You will no doubt have contact with our people in Holland, but I would like you to report directly to me when you get back to London.' He smiled. 'I prefer to have direct access to sources of information. It gives me a much clearer picture.'

'Certainly, Sir Robert,' Conrad said as he shook the mandarin's proffered hand. 'One question?'

'Yes?'

'Have you discussed this with my father?'

Van smiled. 'In very general terms. He helped me track you down.' The smile disappeared. 'You raise a good point. I think it would be inadvisable to discuss the details of this with him. He may well press you on the issue, but you should be firm.'

'I will be,' said Conrad.

Conrad was damned sure his father would press him on the issue, and he wasn't looking forward to that at all.

Conrad didn't have much time. He arranged with Mrs Dougherty for his aeroplane ticket to be forwarded to his club, and went there himself to compose the telegram.

When he had last seen Theo, in Berlin over a year before, Theo had suggested a means of communication in emergencies. It involved an address in Copenhagen, and the use of certain codewords. These involved people and places from the Second Schleswig War of the 1860s, which was the subject of Conrad's unfinished thesis at Oxford. The idea was that these could credibly be buried in a letter to a Dane on the subject of his academic work.

It was the address Conrad had used for his letter in plain English in September. He didn't know why he hadn't received a reply. Perhaps Theo disapproved of the sentimentality, or the lack of professionalism, or, more worryingly, he had simply never received the message.

Anyway, there was no time for a letter now. Scarcely time for a telegram. It took Conrad several attempts before he was happy.

'PLEASE INFORM PROFESSOR MADVIG THAT I WISH TO MEET HIM IN LEIDEN 10 NOV STOP NEED TO DISCUSS DYBBOL STOP LEAVE MESSAGE AT HOTEL LEVEDAG STOP DE LANCEY'.

Johan Madvig had been a Danish liberal politician in the 1860s: the use of his name in the message meant 'meet me'. Dybbøl was the major battle of the war, and that meant 'emergency'. Three was subtracted from any dates and times, so '10 Nov' meant 7 November. And there was no way that Conrad could think of to hide the name of a rendezvous near The Hague. Leiden was a nearby university town, and the Hotel Levedag was one mentioned in the guidebook to Holland in the club library. He translated the draft telegram into Danish, addressed it to Anders Elkjaer at a house in a suburb of Copenhagen, and took it along to the Post Office to be sent right away.

It was the best he could do.

Fortunately, Conrad's passport was at his parents' house in Kensington Square, rather than the family home in Somerset. He would also need some civilian clothes: he could hardly travel in his uniform. Unfortunately it was likely that his father would be up in town. The most natural thing would be for Conrad to stay there that night and dine with his father, but Conrad thought Van had been absolutely correct in anticipating that Lord Oakford would want to interrogate him about his mission. Much better to sneak in, grab his things, sneak out, and stay at a hotel somewhere.

The plan worked. His father was out at the House of Lords, and Conrad left a message with his valet, Williamson, apologizing that he had missed him.

Telegram sent, travel documents in order, dressed in mufti and suitcase in hand, Conrad checked into a hotel in Bloomsbury.

Five

Paris

Major Edward 'Fruity' Metcalfe skipped up the steps of the imposing house on the boulevard Suchet out by the bois de Boulogne, and rang the doorbell. The gendarme on duty outside nodded to him in recognition. Lights peeped out beneath the curtains which barely covered the tall windows of the four-storey property. There would be no German bombers that night, and the inhabitants of Paris knew it.

The door was promptly opened by a footman, and inside a butler as tall as Fruity stepped forward.

'Good evening, Hale,' said Fruity, handing the man his coat and hat.

'Good evening, Major Metcalfe.'

'You know we are dining with your former employer this evening?'

'Please be sure to send my regards to Mr Bedaux, sir.'

'If you like, Hale. But I don't want to taunt him, what?'

Hale was the best butler in France. Everyone knew it, including both his former employer – Charles Bedaux, and his present employer – the Duke of Windsor.

'Tell His Royal Highness I'm here, would you? I'll wait.'

'Very good, sir.' Hale disappeared up the stairs, and Fruity settled in his favourite Louis the somethingth chair, crossed his long legs and lit up a cigarette. He stared at the absurdly ornate clock opposite him, its dial surrounded by an exploding sun of gold leaf, and listened to its familiar restful tick. One way or the

22

other he had spent a lot of time over the last month waiting for the duke in this hallway. The duke would either be late or very late. Fruity didn't mind: it was all part of the job.

Fruity was HRH the Duke of Windsor's aide-de-camp, or equerry or something. He wasn't quite sure what his official title was, which was fine, but he was becoming increasingly unsure whether he would even be paid for it, which wasn't. The duke had found himself in a pickle when war had broken out, and Fruity had been willing to step into the breach. The British government had tied itself in knots trying to work out how the king-in-exile should be treated in the new war. The duke and his wife had returned to England from their house in Antibes to be met with official indifference. Fruity had done his duty, inviting the duke to stay at his own modest house in Sussex, and then joining him when the powers that be had finally found a job for him in France. That's what friends were for. And whatever else he was, Fruity was the duke's friend. Sometimes he wondered whether he was his only friend.

He heard the scrabble of paws on the stairway and stood up. Pookie, Detto and Prisie tumbled down. Fruity bent down to scratch the ears of the largest of the cairn terriers, Detto, his favourite. Detto wagged his tail, as did the other two. The younger one, the puppy, started yapping. They were all pleased to see Fruity; animals usually were.

'Oh, Prisie, do be quiet!'

Fruity straightened up. 'Hello, Wallis.' He tried his best friendly smile, but it wasn't returned. The duchess was smartly dressed for a night in alone, in an elegant black dress with a giant diamond brooch in the shape of a star sparkling from her forbiddingly flat chest. On anyone else, Fruity would have assumed it was fake, but Wallis never wore costume jewellery. She was, after all, the woman for whom a king had given up his throne.

'Be sure to bring him back right away, Fruity.'

'Of course, Wallis.'

'No going on anywhere else?'

23

'Straight home for us,' Fruity said. Wallis's strictures were completely unnecessary, more was the pity. In the old days in London, when the duke was the Prince of Wales, he and Fruity would have gone on to the Embassy Club after dinner, and stayed up all night drinking and dancing. And of course there were plenty of tempting places to visit in Paris. But the duke was even more scared of Wallis than Fruity was; there was absolutely no chance of him going on anywhere afterwards.

'Fruity!' The duke himself bounded down the stairs, dressed in black tie and dinner jacket, his mane of thick blond hair carefully parted and combed. He smiled broadly at Fruity, showing off those perfect gleaming teeth, his blue eyes twinkling. 'Are you ready?'

Fruity grinned back. 'I certainly am.'

The duke turned to his wife.

'Give my love to Charles, Dave,' Wallis said. Fruity winced. The duke's family and his closest friends called him by the seventh of his many Christian names, 'David', instead of the first, 'Edward'. But Dave?

'And to Fern,' the duchess went on. 'I haven't seen her for years. See if you can arrange for all of us to meet up soon, will you, sweetheart?'

'I will, darling. Let's go, Fruity!'

The duke's Buick was waiting outside, piloted by his chauffeur Webster, with a former Scotland Yard detective in the front seat next to him. Fruity and the duke climbed in the back.

'I was just writing up my notes for the Wombat,' said the duke. 'The Wombat' was Major General Howard-Vyse, the senior British liaison officer at French headquarters.

'I'd say it was rather a successful trip,' Fruity said. They had just spent five days together touring a portion of the French lines.

'I suppose so,' said the duke. 'But they are a frightful shower, the French, aren't they? I've done my best to point it out tactfully, but it's damned difficult.'

It was their third trip. The duke had been given a job at the British Mission to the French headquarters at Vincennes, reporting to the Wombat. In that role he was to inspect the French lines in a series of tours, but he had also been given the task of reporting back to the Chief of the Imperial General Staff in London with an assessment of the strengths and especially weaknesses of the French defences.

They had started near the Channel, where the powerful French 7th Army was poised to speed north following a German invasion of Belgium, and then worked their way east. Their most recent trip had been to the French 2nd Army stationed along the Meuse in the Ardennes, at the hinge where the Maginot Line along the Franco-German border met neutral Luxembourg and Belgium.

The duke was right: the 2nd Army was a frightful shower led by a complacent idiot, a general named Huntziger. But Fruity enjoyed driving around the lines with the Little Man, hundreds of miles from Wallis. The further he strayed from her petticoats, the more the duke loosened up, the more fun he was.

The Buick cruised down the wide avenue du Président-Wilson towards the centre of Paris. Headlights of oncoming motor cars were barely covered; strips of light spilled out between inadequate blinds in the cafés. Where London was battened down under a grim black cloak, Paris at night was lifting its hem to show some garter.

The Little Man might have to rush back to Mrs Nibs after dinner, but that didn't mean Fruity had to.

'How was Bedaux?' the duke said. 'I haven't seen him for nearly two years now.'

'Back to his old self,' Fruity said. 'Has a finger in every pie. Knows everything. Dashing about the place: Holland, England. I even got the impression he was going to Germany.'

'Really? How the devil does he manage that?'

'He's a Yank, isn't he? Neutral passport.'

'He's a man of the world, if ever there was one,' the duke said. 'I look forward to seeing him again. That man certainly has imagination. And energy.'

'And he was very keen to see you.'

25

Very keen. Fruity was staying at the Ritz, and a few days before he had been accosted by Charles Bedaux, a fellow resident of the hotel. Bedaux was a Franco-American businessman, frightfully rich, who had amassed his pile from time-and-motion studies or something. He was a friend of a friend of Wallis's and had made his chateau available for her wedding to the duke. It was a fine place on the Loire, and Bedaux and his American wife Fern had been the perfect hosts.

It wasn't their fault that the wedding itself had been a cringe-making disaster. Almost no one from England had accepted their invitations, and those who had had pulled out once they had recognized their error. The disapproval of the new king and queen, and of society, was powerful and pervasive.

Of course, Fruity had done his duty to his old friend. He had been best man.

They pulled into the place Vendôme and drew up in front of the Ritz. The doorman recognized the car and leaped for the duke's door. Inside, the hotel was buzzing, but the chatter subsided a little as the former king entered the glittering lobby.

'Your Royal Highness!'

Fruity and the duke turned to see a short, powerfully built man with jug ears and thick black brilliantined hair bustling towards them.

'Charles! Good to see you again!' said the duke, holding out his hand. 'You're looking well.'

'I am well, sir, I am well,' Bedaux said in his European-film-star American accent, before turning to Fruity and shaking his hand. 'I've organized a private dining room. A lot has happened in the world since we last saw each other. There is much to discuss.'

Six

Schiphol Airport, Amsterdam, 7 November

Conrad found no difficulty spotting the Englishman waiting for him in the passenger terminal at Schiphol Airport. He was tall, wearing a check suit, a monocle and spats.

'Captain Payne Best?'

The man reached for Conrad's hand and shook it. 'The very same. Lieutenant de Lancey, I assume. Welcome to Holland. The car's right outside. Can I take your bag?'

'I'm all right,' said Conrad, gripping his suitcase.

'Follow me.'

Payne Best led Conrad out of the building to a car park and a sleek black American car.

'Good to be back?'

'Back?' said Conrad. 'I haven't spent much time in Holland. Once on holiday when I was a child. Other than that just en route to Germany.'

'But you do speak Dutch?' Payne Best said.

'Not as such, no,' said Conrad.

'I was told you speak Dutch.'

'Danish.'

Payne Best shook his head. 'Typical of them not to know the difference between Dutch and Danish.'

Conrad decided not to ask who 'they' were. The onset of war had led to a mushrooming of bureaucratic screw-ups, and this one didn't surprise him. 'Does it matter?'

They climbed into the car. 'My plan was that you should be

my chauffeur when we go to see the Hun officers. But if you don't speak Dutch, I'm not sure what we will do.'

'Teach me the Dutch for "yes, sir" and "certainly, sir",' said Conrad. 'I'm a good mimic.'

'Sprechen Sie Deutsch?' asked Payne Best.

'Oh, yes,' said Conrad in that language. 'My mother is from Hamburg and I was actually born there just before the last war.'

'Your accent is perfect,' said Payne Best, whose German was also pretty good. 'All right, we'll stick to the plan.' He guided the car out of the car park and followed a sign to 's Gravenhage, The Hague's official name. He glanced at Conrad's own suit. 'Savile Row?'

'Yes. Norton.'

'We must get you something much cheaper and more obviously Dutch. I have a man who drives for me occasionally, and we're going to make you look like him.'

Payne Best put his foot on the accelerator of the powerful car, a Lincoln Zephyr, and they roared past lesser vehicles on the highway.

'Can you tell me something about this Major Schämmel?' Conrad asked.

'We've met him three times,' Payne Best said. 'He seems genuine to me. Rhineland accent, I think. Intelligent. My only question is what someone of his calibre is doing in the Transport Division.'

'Transport is important for a modern army,' Conrad said. 'Especially a mobile one.' That was one thing that his regiment had drummed into its officers. Their battalion had been 'motorized' two years before, and had embraced mobility with enthusiasm.

'Perhaps,' said Payne Best. 'We have been supposed to meet a general, but Schämmel has some excuse about why he can't make it. Of course the excuses may be valid; I can understand how it is difficult to smuggle a general out in wartime. We were meant to meet him tomorrow, but Schämmel has postponed again until Thursday. The idea is to get the general to agree to fly to London.'

'Does this general have a name?' Conrad asked.

'Not yet,' said Payne Best. 'Look here. I'm not entirely ⸻
your role in this operation, de Lancey. I was told you woulc
be watching. You won't be involved in the negotiations, will yc

'No, I'll leave that to you,' said Conrad. 'My job is to make su.
that Major Schämmel is real.'

'Have you had contact with these generals, then?'

'Some,' said Conrad. 'But we don't want Major Schämmel to
know that.'

'Where? In Germany?'

'Rather not say, if that's all the same to you,' said Conrad with
a smile.

'Fair enough,' said Payne Best, nodding to himself with what
looked like approval. 'Or, as we say in Holland: *Zeker, meneer.*'

They spent the remaining half-hour driving very fast towards
The Hague going over the kind of phrases that a taciturn chauffeur
might say to his boss. Dutch pronunciation was tricky, but Conrad
quickly picked up Payne Best's accent. How good that was, he
didn't know, but to Conrad's ear it sounded the genuine article.

The countryside reminded Conrad a little of the levels near his
family's home in Somerset, which he knew had been shaped by
Dutch engineers a few centuries before. Green, flat, waterlogged,
criss-crossed with ditches and dykes, only the odd barn or copse
broke the monotony. And the windmills. Somerset didn't have
the windmills.

Once they reached The Hague, Payne Best drove to the C&A
department store in the centre of the city and found Conrad a
cheap off-the-peg suit and a flat cap. Not an actual chauffeur's
uniform, but rather the kind of thing that a mechanic might dress
up in to look smart on a driving job. Payne Best paid.

'Your name is Jan Lemmens,' he said.

'Do you have papers for me? What if I get stopped by the Dutch
police?'

'There's a fellow from Dutch military intelligence who they
insist comes along with us named Klop, although we pass him off
as a British officer. He's a good man. He'll square them.'

29

'All right. Where am I staying?'

'I'll take you there now. It's a bit of a dump, I'm afraid. Too risky to have you staying at a smart hotel. The Hague is crawling with spies, don't you know?'

True to his word, Payne Best dropped Conrad in a small scruffy hotel near the Hollands Spoor railway station. 'Lie low tomorrow. I'll pick you up at half past nine on Thursday morning. Wear your new suit – perhaps crumple it tonight if you can; put it under your mattress. The plan is to meet Schämmel at three o'clock near the border.'

Düsseldorf

The man whom Captain Payne Best knew as Captain Schämmel eased off his headphones and stared at the notepad on the desk in front of him. *Venlo. 3 pm. 9 November.*

He was in the small sitting room of a *pension* in Düsseldorf that had been turned into a communications room. Pride of place was given to the wireless transmitter which had been given to him by Payne Best and on which he had just confirmed the rendezvous. Accompanied by the general.

The British were pleased. He was pleased. He was getting somewhere.

He picked up one of the three telephones, the one with the direct line to Berlin. He was put through within a few seconds.

'Heydrich.'

'Herr Gruppenführer, this is Schellenberg.'

'Ah, Walter. How did it go?' The high-pitched voice of his superior immediately put Schämmel, whose real name and rank was SS Sturmbannführer Walter Schellenberg, on his guard, as it always did. You could never let your concentration slip for a moment in the presence of the head of the Gestapo.

'I have set up a meeting in two days at Venlo. And I have just the man to play the part of the general.'

'Do you think they suspect anything?'

'No. And once I produce a general they will be happy.'

'Good, good.'

Schellenberg, the head of the counter-intelligence section of the Gestapo, knew his chief. Heydrich's tone suggested that something was not in fact good. Schellenberg waited.

'I was speaking to the Führer about this,' Heydrich went on.

Here we go, thought Schellenberg.

'He is concerned about you flying to London.'

'But if we are to get the British to tell us what they know about a plot to overthrow him, then we have to get them to believe we are real! They have insisted that the general comes to London, and if he goes, I have to go with him.'

'I know that, Walter. But the Führer doesn't like talking about plots to overthrow him, even fictional ones. He is going to Munich tomorrow, and he is back on the ninth. He will confirm you can go ahead then.'

'Yes, Herr Gruppenführer!' said Schellenberg and hung up.

The whole plan had been Heydrich's idea, and now he was talking about pulling the plug on it at the very last minute, just as Schellenberg was getting somewhere.

But Schellenberg couldn't worry about that; he had to assume that the rendezvous was going ahead. He needed to brief his 'general' and work on his strategy to negotiate with the British.

And in a couple of days, with any luck, he would discover who among the German generals really were plotting to overthrow the Führer.

The Hague

Conrad waited in his pokey room for ten minutes and then headed back outside. The Hollands Spoor station was just around the corner and there were frequent trains to Leiden. It only took twenty minutes.

Conrad had picked Leiden because of its proximity to The Hague and the famous university there. It was the sort of place where a doctoral student might meet an academic. Even when the doctoral student was actually a serving officer in the British Army? An intelligent German censor with time to check up on Conrad's bona fides would never believe it. Conrad just had to hope that his telegram had been passed directly to the Abwehr and Theo.

It was a reasonable assumption.

Leiden reminded Conrad a little of Oxford. Lots of students acting as if they owned the place, lots of bicycles, lots of ancient buildings. But it was quieter, and prettier, and a network of canals threaded through the town. There was no war anywhere to be seen.

Despite the November breeze, it was a pleasant walk from the station to the city centre. The Hotel Levedag was on the Breestraat just past the town hall. Conrad decided to be himself as he approached the man behind the desk, whom he guessed was the hotel manager.

'Good afternoon,' he said in English. 'Are there any messages for me? My name is Conrad de Lancey, and I was intending to stay at this hotel tonight, but I had to change my plans and stay in The Hague.'

'Certainly, sir. Let me check,' the manager replied in good English. He studied a bank of pigeonholes and then rummaged around in a drawer beneath his desk. He pouted and grimaced. 'Nothing, sir, I am sorry.'

'Ah.' Conrad was disappointed, but he wasn't giving up. 'What about for Professor Madvig?'

'Is he a guest at the hotel?'

'I'm not sure,' said Conrad. 'I was supposed to meet him here.'

'Are you expecting a message *from* the professor?'

'Either from or to,' said Conrad.

The manager looked at Conrad doubtfully, but then turned to have another look at the pigeonholes and a large ledger. 'We have no record of Professor Madvig staying here or making a booking. Nor a message for him.'

Conrad smiled. 'I understand. I'm afraid there has been a frightful mix-up. I'll come back tomorrow. And if someone does leave a message, can you keep it for me?'

The hotel manager's doubts were rising. Conrad had a t͎
he wasn't doing the secret-agent thing very well. Theo was
professional. It was too much for Conrad to expect his friend to ͙
the message via Copenhagen to Berlin, and get to Leiden in a day

'Thank you,' said Conrad and beat a retreat.

He stood in the Breestraat and wondered what to do. A blue
tram rattled past. It was past two o'clock and he was hungry. He
spotted a café-restaurant, and crossed the street to examine the
menu in the window, dodging bicycles whizzing past.

'Don't look at me,' said a voice in German next to him. A
very familiar voice. 'The Diefsteeg, back towards the station. Ten
minutes.'

Conrad managed to suppress a smile, but showed no sign that
he had heard anything. After a minute or so, he moved on to
another café to inspect its menu. Then he strolled back along the
Breestraat the way he had come.

The Diefsteeg turned out to be a quiet narrow lane, paved with
red brick and squeezed between blind sides of houses on one side
and courtyard walls on the other. Conrad walked slowly down the
alley. He saw a tall familiar figure ahead, sauntering towards him.
Before Conrad reached him, the figure ducked into a little café.
Conrad examined the sparse menu in the window for a moment
and then followed him in.

Theo was sitting at a table, back to the window, facing the door.
He grinned when he saw Conrad. His dark hair had receded a little
in the year since Conrad had last seen him, but the duelling scar
along his jawline was still visible. And his smile was as charming
as ever.

'Professor Madvig, I presume,' Theo said in English. 'Or am
I Professor Madvig?'

'Sorry about that,' said Conrad, taking a seat opposite him. 'I
think technically we are both supposed to be meeting Professor
Madvig, whoever the hell he is. It was the best I could think of
in the time.'

'It worked,' said Theo. 'Fortunately I was in Holland anyway, so I could get here today. By the way, I think it's better we speak English than German. Fewer Dutch people understand it, and it's a little less suspicious.'

'I'm glad you got the message. I was worried when you didn't respond to the letter I sent you a few weeks ago. Did you receive it?'

'I did get it,' said Theo. 'I thought about replying, but I didn't know what to say. Because I didn't know what to think.'

'About the war?' Conrad asked.

'About the war. About you. About me.'

The barman approached, and they ordered pea soup and beer.

'I know what I think,' said Conrad. 'Hitler must be stopped. That's why I joined the army: to stop him.'

'It's easier for you than me,' said Theo.

'But you do still think Hitler must be stopped, don't you?' asked Conrad. It was an important question. If Theo had changed his mind about that, then Conrad should halt the conversation right there and then.

'Oh, yes,' said Theo. 'But I don't want to undermine my country in a war. Unlike you, for me those two things clash.'

'Yes, of course,' said Conrad. He had visited Theo's family seat in the heart of Prussian Pomerania. Theo's father had been a general, as had his father before him. Patriotism, duty, the obligation to fight for one's country: all these were bred deep into Theo's bones, despite the socialist ideals he had professed at Oxford in the early 1930s.

'You're still in the Abwehr?' Conrad asked.

Theo smiled. 'You know I shouldn't really answer that question.'

That was good enough for Conrad.

The soup came and they began eating. 'I have dropped everything to come here,' Theo said. 'And I'm curious why. What's an infantry officer doing in Holland? Shouldn't you be in France?'

Conrad scanned the café. There was one other customer, an old man reading a newspaper and drinking a small glass of beer. He looked very Dutch. He was also out of earshot, as was the barman.

34

'Do you know a Captain Schämmel? Of the OKW Transport Division?'

'I've never heard of him,' said Theo. 'Should I have?'

Conrad hesitated. Could he trust Theo? Of course he could. Theo knew the names of most of the people who had been involved in the previous year's conspiracy. One more name wouldn't make any difference.

'Perhaps,' said Conrad. 'He claims he is representing a group of German generals who intend to overthrow Hitler. Soon.'

Theo nodded. He was thinking. Conrad let him. 'And you are meeting him? Here in Holland?'

Now it was Conrad's turn to hesitate. But he had to trust Theo; he had already taken that decision. 'Yes.'

'And the British secret service sent you?'

'Sir Robert Vansittart. Chief Diplomatic Adviser. Personally.'

Van had been aware of the discussions with Theo's co-conspirators and the British government before the Munich peace conference the year before, and Theo knew that.

'I see.' Theo studied Conrad. 'I haven't heard of this Schämmel. Which is a little strange. I have spent a lot of time in Holland recently.'

'Is there an imminent plot?'

Theo hesitated. Then he nodded.

Conrad leaned forward. 'When?'

'Next week. The fifteenth of November to be precise. If the generals don't lose their nerve.'

Conrad felt a surge of excitement. 'Which generals?'

'Halder. And most of the others from last year.'

'Halder is still Chief of the General Staff?'

Theo nodded. 'Hitler intends to launch an offensive through Holland and Belgium next week.'

'Next week?' Conrad was stunned by what Theo had just told him. The date of a major offensive. In a lot of people's eyes that would be treachery of the highest order. He glanced at his friend. Theo knew what he was saying.

'That will turn the *Sitzkrieg* into a real war,' Theo said. 'Nineteen fourteen all over again. The generals think the German people won't like that. So it's the right time to strike.'

'So by next week Hitler will be overthrown and the war will be over?'

Theo grinned. 'That's the plan.'

It sounded too good to be true.

'Do you think they will go through with it?' Conrad asked.

'The offensive or the coup?'

'Both,' said Conrad.

'The Führer seems determined not to be put off from the date of the offensive. As for the coup? Halder has let us down before. He said he would act if Hitler invaded Poland and he didn't, so I can't be sure he won't let us down again. I hope he won't. I have to believe he won't.'

'I hope to God he does act this time,' said Conrad. 'Does that mean it's possible Halder could have sent someone to sound out the British government about peace terms if there is a coup?'

'Yes, it's possible. And I suppose it is possible I wouldn't know about it. But I can find out.'

'Ask Canaris?'

Admiral Canaris, the Chief of the Abwehr, had given his behind-the-scenes support to the planned coup. He knew everything.

Theo avoided answering the question directly. 'I'll have to go back to Berlin. I might not get you an answer for a couple of days.'

'That's all right. I expect there will be a number of meetings to discuss possible peace terms. Schämmel is supposed to be bringing one of the generals he is working for.'

'Do you know who that is?' asked Theo.

'No. Schämmel hasn't said yet. Which is understandable.'

'I suppose so.' Theo narrowed his eyes. 'Are you going with Major Stevens?'

'Who is Major Stevens?'

'He's the British Passport Control Officer in the Ha\
which means he is in charge of the British secret service in\
Netherlands. I know a lot about Major Stevens. In fact I know a l\
about everyone who works for him, and the people who work in\
the British Embassy. Your whole Dutch operation is full of holes.
You should be very careful.' He frowned. 'You haven't told them
about me, have you?'

'No,' said Conrad. 'I haven't met Major Stevens yet.'

'Good. Best not to mention me at all, and if you do, give me
a code name. Say I'm in the Luftwaffe and close to Göring. That
should confuse them.'

'You are asking me to confuse my own side?'

'You bet,' said Theo. 'Because if you don't, there is a good
chance that my side will find out that I have been talking to you.
And the wrong people on my side.'

'I understand,' said Conrad. 'But I *will* pass on what you said
about the offensive next week. You know that?'

'Yes,' said Theo. 'I know.' He mopped up the last of his soup
with some bread. 'How's Anneliese?'

'She's well,' said Conrad.

'How's she settling in to life in London? Do you still see her?'

Conrad took a spoonful of soup. 'I do, when I can,' he said. 'It's
difficult for the Jewish refugees in London. It's hard to find a job,
although she's just got something working as a nurse.'

'It's got to be easier than Berlin,' said Theo. 'At least she left
before Kristallnacht.'

Theo was referring to the wholesale beating-up of Jews and
smashing of their property twelve months before.

'That's certainly true.'

'I'm glad you are still seeing her. I admire Anneliese. She's a
strong woman. I've come across people who have spent time in
the concentration camps; they are not quite the same afterwards.'

Conrad smiled quickly. 'It was difficult for her,' he said.

Theo caught something in the tone of Conrad's voice, and
looked as if he was about to pursue it, before deciding not to.

Theo signalled for the bill. 'Oh, and please give your beautiful sister my regards when you can,' he said. 'Once this has all worked out as it should.'

'I will,' said Conrad. Theo and Millie had met briefly in Germany the previous year and Theo had clearly taken a shine to her. Although Theo had many strengths, the way he treated women wasn't one of them, so Conrad was quite happy that Theo had only met his sister the once.

'How will we meet next time?' Conrad asked.

'There's a chemistry professor at Leiden University: W. F. Hogendoorn. He's Dutch, but trustworthy. Leave a message with him, at the university, and he will tell you where and when.'

'W. F. Hogendoorn,' Conrad repeated. By 'trustworthy', Conrad wondered what Theo meant. Trustworthy for the Germans? The Abwehr? Theo? The cause of peace? 'I hope you are right about the coup.'

'So do I,' Theo said. 'So do I.'

Theo paid the bill and left the café walking up towards the Breestraat. Conrad waited a moment and then turned the other way.

He was still stunned by what Theo had told him. In a week's time the Germans would launch an offensive and General Halder would arrest Hitler. Or perhaps kill him. There was hope after all that Europe wouldn't tear itself apart again.

Conrad was looking forward to seeing Schämmel. As he had told Theo, he was prepared to fight. But much better if Theo, Schämmel and their friends could topple Hitler and sue for peace at the same time, avoiding the deaths of millions in the process. And Conrad was glad he might get to play his part in it after all.

His one regret was that he had brushed off Theo's questioning about Anneliese, or at least not told him the whole truth. Anneliese was not 'well'. Conrad was worried about her, very worried. He hadn't spoken to anyone about her, but Theo was an old friend. At Oxford they had shared their feelings about everything. And Theo actually knew Anneliese, and how important she was to Conrad. Perhaps he could help; perhaps Conrad should have let him help.

As he reached the end of the Diefsteeg, Conrad realized he was heading the wrong way for the station and turned on his heel. A man was walking alone down the lane towards Conrad, hands in his coat pockets, hat tilted down over his eyes. He looked Dutch, nondescript, forty perhaps, but there was something about his nose – a little long, an upward tilt at the end – that Conrad recognized. Conrad was pretty sure that he had passed the man leaving the lobby of the Hotel Levedag an hour before.

Despite all Theo's precautions, it looked as if someone had spotted Theo talking to Conrad after all.

Who was it? Conrad wondered.

Seven

Berlin, 8 November

'Ah, come in, Hertenberg. Sit down.'

'Thank you, excellency,' said Theo as he took a seat in front of the admiral's desk.

Admiral Canaris's office was on the top floor of the Abwehr building on the Tirpitzufer in Berlin, overlooking the chestnut trees lining the Landwehr Canal. The admiral was a small, neat man with light blue eyes and fine white hair. He was stroking a rough-haired dachshund nestled with its eyes closed on his lap. With him was Colonel Oster, a debonair cavalry officer and the man who had recruited Theo into the Abwehr. As a trainee lawyer, Theo had been introduced to Oster by his father, under whom Colonel Oster had served. Paradoxically for a former pacifist, the Wehrmacht and the Abwehr had seemed to Theo a good alternative to joining the Nazi Party, which Theo would have had to do if he wanted to pass his final assessor's exams. Officers in the Wehrmacht were still not required to become Party members.

Despite Canaris's rank, Theo felt at ease. The Abwehr was a haven of safety in a very dangerous Reich. Canaris led by example: he felt spying was the preserve of gentlemen, and honour and duty were more important than ideology. He looked after his own, and Theo was very much one of his own.

'What brings you to Berlin in such a hurry?' Canaris asked.

'A couple of things, excellency,' Theo began. 'I saw de Lancey yesterday.'

'Ah, de Lancey,' Canaris smiled. 'I wondered when he would

40

pop up again. I take it he is with the British secret service now

'Not directly, I think. He said he was sent to Holland by Si,
Robert Vansittart of the British Foreign Office. To meet a man
called Captain Schämmel of the OKW's Transport Division.
Schämmel is supposed to be representing leaders of a plot to
overthrow Hitler. I've never heard of him.'

'Neither have I,' said Canaris. 'Tell me what you know about him.'

Theo related all that Conrad had told him about Schämmel
and his generals.

Canaris listened closely. 'And de Lancey didn't say which
general this Schämmel was representing?'

'No.'

'What do you think, Hans? Have you heard of this person?'

Colonel Oster shook his head. 'Could he be one of Göring's men?'

'Possible,' said Canaris. 'I doubt it myself, but you never know.'

The senior echelons of the Nazi Party were by no means united;
it was Hitler's deliberate strategy to keep them rivals. Himmler's
SS, Heydrich's Gestapo, and Göring's little empire comprising the
Luftwaffe and the Prussian Interior Ministry were all separate
power blocks. Then there were the lesser Nazis like Ribbentrop
and his Foreign Ministry, Goebbels's Propaganda Ministry, Rudolf
Hess and Alfred Rosenberg. The stormtroopers of the SA, once
a force to be reckoned with, had been neutralized by Himmler
in the 'Night of the Long Knives' back in 1934. Outside the Nazi
Party were Canaris and the Abwehr, Schacht and the Finance
Ministry, Admiral Raeder's navy and, perhaps most powerful of
all, the army led by Generals von Brauchitsch and Halder.

The conspiracy that Canaris, Oster and Theo had been
involved in encompassed the army and Schacht, as well as one
or two other politicians and some elements of the police. Göring
was certainly not one of this group, but he was ambitious and
powerful, and perhaps the most likely of Hitler's friends to make
a move against him.

'Or it could be a trap,' said Canaris.

'A trap?' said Oster. 'Set by whom?'

41

'The Gestapo,' said Canaris. 'We know they suspect something. They could be trying tease out from the British who among us has been talking to them.' He gave a wry smile. 'It's what I would do. And it's the kind of idea Heydrich would love.'

Theo was yet again impressed by the subtlety of his chief's thought process. Not for him the simple giving and taking of orders. The admiral's escapades in the last war when, as an intelligence officer aboard the *Dresden* in the South Atlantic, he had used bluff and double bluff to stay one step ahead of the Royal Navy, were legendary. A model of the ship stood on his desk.

'I know there have been some Gestapo agents operating in Holland,' Theo said. 'Mörz, for one.'

'I'll talk to Schellenberg, see if he knows anything.' Canaris and the new young head of the foreign-intelligence section of the Gestapo were neighbours in the Berlin suburb of Schlachtensee, and occasionally rode together in the Tiergarten. Although Canaris held the Gestapo in contempt, he had some respect for Schellenberg. Theo had never met Schellenberg and found the Gestapo's efforts at spying frustrating.

'If it is a trap, we don't want de Lancey caught in it,' said Oster. 'He knows too much about us.'

'De Lancey won't talk,' Theo said. 'I mean, he will talk, but not about us. He has outwitted the Gestapo before.'

'That's true,' said the admiral. 'But we don't want to rely on anyone keeping quiet once Heydrich has his hands on them. Warn de Lancey to be careful, Theo, until we are sure who exactly this Schämmel is.'

'Certainly, your excellency.'

'And the other matter?'

'I have been having some very interesting conversations with Mr Bedaux ...'

After the meeting, Theo followed Oster to his office.

'Do you think Halder really will move on the fifteenth?' Theo asked the colonel.

'He's trying to persuade Hitler that the weather will be too bad to launch an offensive,' Oster said. 'But Hitler won't listen.'

'So the coup will go ahead?'

'I don't know,' said Oster. 'I mean, if Halder really wanted to overthrow Hitler he would be urging that Case Yellow would go ahead.' Case Yellow was the general staff's plan to invade the Low Countries and attack France from the north. 'That's what we were all hoping for last year.'

It was true. Theo remembered how the conspirators had prayed for Hitler to order the invasion of Czechoslovakia so they could launch their coup. When he had called it off at the last minute in response to Chamberlain's peace overtures, they had all been devastated.

'It's more difficult now we are at war,' Theo said.

'It is,' said Oster. 'You know, Theo, strictly between us, in my view it would be a disaster for our country if France was knocked out of the war.'

Theo trusted his superior. Oster was the driving force behind the conspiracy. Canaris left Oster, and through him Theo, to do the organizing. Canaris was careful to preserve the delicate balance of loyalty to the Fatherland and willingness to overthrow its leader. Oster had fewer qualms.

Theo nodded. 'I understand, Colonel.' He also understood how Oster's words would be seen as treason, not just by the Nazis, but by most German officers and by Admiral Canaris himself.

Theo had intended to tell no one what he had told Conrad. But somehow telling Oster made what Theo had done less treasonable. Like Theo, Oster believed that the most important thing for Germany, the only thing for Germany, was to get rid of Hitler by any possible means.

'I gave de Lancey the date of Case Yellow,' Theo said.

Oster looked at Theo gravely. And then a smile spread across his face. 'And I told the Dutch military attaché last night that we would be invading his country next week. But let's keep this to ourselves, eh, Theo? And now, isn't it about time you went back to Holland?'

Eight

Munich

Fräulein Peters stared down at the Bavarian countryside flickering beneath the clouds below her and marvelled at her good fortune. It was her first time in an aeroplane and it ranked as one of the most exciting days of her twenty years. Not only was she a thousand metres up in the sky, but she was there with the Führer! Six months before, she would never have believed it. Then she had been transferred to the Reich Chancellery secretariat, and for the last three weeks she had been working for the Führer himself.

Fräulein Peters was doing a good job; she was an efficient and competent secretary, quick thinking and able to see one step ahead. The only trouble was her nerves. On those occasions when the Führer spoke to her directly, she could sense herself blushing. She could almost feel her tongue swelling in her mouth and she was sure that at some point soon she would garble her words and make a fool of herself. Fortunately, the Führer seemed to enjoy her blushes. She had blond hair, blue eyes and a very clear complexion. She was, she knew, a true German, and she was proud of it.

They were on their way to Munich, where Hitler was giving a speech to mark the sixteenth anniversary of the 1923 Beer Hall Putsch, in which he had led his National Socialist comrades in a failed attempt to take over the city.

The ground was pressing up towards the underbelly of the aircraft. The machine juddered and Fräulein Peters was alarmed to see outside her window part of the wing detach itself and droop downwards. There was a grinding beneath her feet. She braced

herself as the runway rushed upwards beneath the wings, a.
then they were down with barely a bump.

The machine turned towards the airport terminal building and
jolted to a stop. The pilot came through to the cabin.

Hitler, who was sitting only two rows from Fräulein Peters,
greeted him. 'I need to be in Berlin tomorrow morning, Baur. Can
you guarantee we can leave early? What's the weather forecast?'

'At the moment they are saying visibility will be good, my
Führer, but it is November and fog is always a possibility. If that
was to happen, there's a chance we could be delayed for a few hours
until it clears. If you have to be sure of getting to Berlin tomorrow
morning I recommend you take the train tonight.'

Hitler nodded. 'Fräulein Peters,' he said. 'Please arrange a train
back to Berlin after the speech. It is imperative I am back there
tomorrow morning. I have a meeting at ten o'clock.'

'Certainly, my Führer,' said Fräulein Peters. She had no idea
how she would arrange it, but she was confident she would work
it out. If the Führer wanted something done, it was done.

She wondered what the meeting was. She knew it wasn't in his
diary, but the whole concept of a diary when it came to the Führer's
schedule was a joke. Flexibility was the watchword.

Düsseldorf

Schellenberg paced up and down the small lounge of the *pension*.
He had had virtually no sleep the night before. This was turning
into one of the most difficult operations in his short but eventful
career at the Gestapo. He was still only twenty-nine, but Heydrich
had just entrusted him with the new foreign-intelligence branch
of the organization, known as the Amt VI. He knew he was up
to the job, but he also knew that if he screwed this operation up,
it would be a high-profile failure.

Those were best avoided in Germany these days.

He heard a commotion and a familiar voice in the lobby of the
pension. Familiar, but unwelcome.

'Naujocks!' Schellenberg exclaimed. 'What the devil are you doing here?'

Alfred Naujocks was a colleague and rival to Schellenberg in Heydrich's intelligence-gathering apparatus. Where Schellenberg was subtle, Naujocks was brutal. Where Schellenberg could charm, Naujocks could intimidate. Which wasn't to say that Naujocks wasn't cunning. He was. Cunning and dangerous.

'The boss sent me to protect you,' Naujocks said. 'I've brought a dozen SS troopers with me.'

'I don't need a nursemaid!' protested Schellenberg. 'I've told Heydrich the British believe me. The last thing I want is a bunch of thugs watching my every move.'

'Heydrich thinks the Dutch might snatch you tomorrow,' said Naujocks. 'You are far too important for us to lose. At least that's what he says. We'll be watching the meeting from the border. If the Dutch try anything, we'll come and snatch you back.'

'Very well,' said Schellenberg. 'But don't do anything unless you are sure that there is trouble.'

Schellenberg left the *pension* and went for a stroll around the block. This latest development worried him. Did Heydrich know something he didn't? Heydrich usually knew something other people didn't. Perhaps the deception was blown. Or perhaps Heydrich just didn't trust Schellenberg not to negotiate his own deal with the British. If anything, that was more worrying.

You didn't want Heydrich to distrust you.

Schellenberg would just have to keep his eyes open and rely on his wits. They had served him well in the past and they would in the future.

He entered the front door of the *pension* and bumped into a Gestapo Kriminalassistent. 'Herr Sturmbannführer, Admiral Canaris has been trying to get hold of you in Berlin.'

What the hell did he want? The Abwehr was not a part of this operation, and Schellenberg knew that Heydrich would require it kept that way. But if Canaris had gone to the trouble to track Schellenberg down it must be important.

Schellenberg went to the room that served as a communications centre in the *pension* and put through a phone call to the Tirpitzufer.

'Ah, Walter, thank you for getting back to me,' Canaris said. 'How are you?'

'Very well, Herr Admiral. Our soldiers might be sitting on their arses, but there seems plenty for us to do.'

'That's certainly true,' said Canaris. 'I wonder if you can enlighten me? Our people in Holland have come across an army captain named Schämmel. Do you know him?'

Schellenberg thought quickly. If he denied knowledge of Schämmel and Canaris discovered later that the captain and Schellenberg were one and the same person, he would have blown his credibility with the Chief of the Abwehr. And that credibility was important. So he had to admit some knowledge.

'I do know of him,' Schellenberg said.

'Ah, good. He has apparently been claiming to be in touch with elements who wish to overthrow the Führer. Have you heard that?'

Now Schellenberg realized he would have to come clean, or else the Abwehr might disrupt the operation. Interesting they had found out. Never underestimate Canaris's sources of information.

'Actually, I know Schämmel well,' said Schellenberg. 'Extremely well.'

'Really?'

'In fact, he and I are the same man. We are running a little operation to draw out the English on whether they have been discussing such a plot with anyone within Germany.'

'Hah! I like it!' said Canaris. 'So it's you who has been in Holland talking to Payne Best and Stevens?'

'That's right. I've had several meetings with them, and in fact I am due to meet them tomorrow near the border. They appear to have fallen for it.'

'And have they admitted to discussions with any conspirators?'

'Not yet,' said Schellenberg. 'But they didn't seem surprised at the idea that there might be some out there. I'm hoping to press them tomorrow.'

'It's a bold move, Walter, and I congratulate you. But it would have been courteous to let us know what you were doing. It's dangerous to step on each other's toes in a neutral country: it will lead to trouble.'

'Of course, Herr Admiral.' Schellenberg would have to play this next part carefully. 'Heydrich was keen that this should be a Gestapo operation. Perhaps if we had bumped into each other in the Tiergarten, I might have mentioned something . . .'

'Yes, Walter. I enjoy our little chats. Good luck tomorrow, and please keep me informed of developments.'

Schellenberg replaced the receiver. He thought he had done a reasonable job. He was pretty sure he had retained Canaris's trust. And if he had denied all knowledge of Schämmel, the Abwehr would have taken action to find out about him of their own accord. It could all have turned very ugly.

Naujocks. Canaris. There were too many distractions. Schellenberg forced himself to focus on the task at hand, which was convincing the British that he and his general were genuine, and getting them to talk about other conspirators. He needed a good night's sleep.

Munich

Fräulein Peters could listen to the Führer speak for hours. He had been talking for fifty minutes and they had flown by. He had seemed tired at the beginning of his speech, but his words and the adulation of his audience had lifted his spirits, as they always did. Fräulein Peters felt jealous of those comrades who in 1923 had gathered in this very hall and marched out into the streets to try to reclaim Germany for the Germans. They had failed, of course, but it was the first brave step on a glorious path.

Hitler was talking about Providence, how Providence was with the German people and with the National Socialists, how

Providence was leading the German people – after centuries of bravery and spilling of blood – to their true destiny.

'Fräulein Peters.' It was Frau Kühn, the telephone operator. 'Reichsminister von Ribbentrop.'

Fräulein Peters tore herself away from the Führer's words and hurried to a small room just next to the hall.

'Herr Reichsminister!'

'Fräulein Peters, what time does the train leave for Berlin?'

'Nine thirty-one, Herr Reichsminister.'

'The Führer will want to talk, he always wants to talk. But it is essential that he is back in Berlin tonight. Give him a message from me to wind up his speech soon and make sure he catches that train. Put it under his nose.'

'Yes, Herr Reichsminister!'

Fräulein Peters quelled a moment of panic at how she could tell the Führer to do anything. She scribbled out the message, making clear that it was from Ribbentrop. Then she summoned an SS trooper to deliver it: she knew that would look much better to the crowd than if she were to do it.

The trooper placed the note in front of the Führer as he was speaking. He paused, and during the applause, glanced at it. He concluded his speech: 'Party Comrades! Long live National Socialism! Long live the German people! And especially today, long live our victorious army!'

The applause in the confines of the beer hall deafened her. Fräulein Peters checked her watch: 8.58 p.m. They would be all right so long as Hitler didn't linger chatting, which he was very capable of doing. But he shook only a few hands and by 9.09 they were out of the hall. Fräulein Peters had arranged for an extra carriage to be placed on the Number 71 train leaving at 9.31, and they were all aboard with three minutes to go.

Relieved, Fräulein Peters settled into her seat and at 9.31 p.m. precisely the train left the station.

Despite the slightly hurried departure, there was an air of gaiety in the saloon carriage and bottles of champagne were broken out. Fräulein Peters was given a glass by a handsome SS officer she hadn't seen before, who proceeded to strike up a conversation. The Führer was in a good mood and Goebbels was making him laugh. The relief and the champagne made Fräulein Peters feel giddy, and she was enjoying the attentions of the SS officer.

The train pulled into Nuremberg and Goebbels climbed out to see whether there were any messages. Fräulein Peters saw him return a few minutes later with a grave expression. The carriage quietened to hear what he had to say. Fräulein Peters wondered if it was some military disaster: a battleship sunk, perhaps, or a surprise Allied offensive.

She was totally unprepared for what Goebbels did say. 'My Führer, I have just heard that at nine-twenty this evening an enormous bomb went off in the beer hall. At least a dozen comrades were killed.'

The Führer didn't seem to take this in. Fräulein Peters refused to believe it until he believed it. All eyes were on him, waiting for a lead.

'It's true, my Führer,' said Goebbels. 'If you had not left early you would be dead.'

There was silence in the carriage. Then Hitler nodded to himself. 'Now I know,' he said in a low voice full of grim satisfaction. 'The fact that I left so soon shows that Providence *is* looking after me. Providence will ensure I fulfil my destiny.'

Fräulein Peters felt her whole body tingle. She knew that the Führer was right. She knew, right then, that she had just witnessed an important step in the destiny of the Führer, the destiny of the German people. *Her* destiny. She could feel her face flush with the emotion.

'So, Joseph,' he said, anger rising in his voice. 'Who is it who tried to assassinate me?'

Somehow, in the depths of a heavy slumber, Schellenberg heard the insistent ringing of the telephone. His body was thick with sleep; he had taken a pill to make sure he was rested for the morning. He checked his watch – 3.30 a.m. He climbed out of bed in his pyjamas and picked up the receiver.

'Hello?'

'What's that?'

Schellenberg didn't recognize the voice, but it sounded shaken. 'I haven't said anything,' he said. 'Who is speaking?'

The reply was clear and direct now, all nervousness gone. 'This is Reichsführer Himmler. Finally you answer. Is that you, Schellenberg?'

'Yes, Herr Reichsführer.'

'Have you heard the news?'

'No, Herr Reichsführer.'

'There was an explosion at the beer hall in Munich. Miraculously the Führer had just left the room, but several Party comrades were murdered. There is no doubt that this is the work of the British secret service. The Führer is convinced of this. He orders you to arrest the two British agents you are meeting tomorrow in Holland and bring them back over the German border. Use the SS detachment that arrived to protect you today. Do you understand?'

'Yes, Herr Reichsführer, but—'

'No buts. This is an order from the Führer. Do you understand now?'

Schellenberg realized there was no point arguing.

'Yes, Herr Reichsführer!'

Schellenberg put the phone down. It was going to be a long and dangerous day.

Nine

Conrad was waiting in the small lobby of his hotel in his freshly crumpled suit. He was nervous. There were a number of things that bothered him: the fact Theo didn't know this Major Schämmel, the leaks in the British operation in The Hague and how to get the message about the planned German offensive to Van. He hadn't agreed a means of communicating with Van directly, and the date of the offensive was less than a week away. He had just lost a day; he couldn't afford to lose another. After he had met Schämmel he would insist on returning to London to report to Van directly.

He had spent most of the last twenty-four hours kicking his heels in the hotel, lying low as Payne Best had suggested.

'Mr de Lancey, I have a telephone message for you, from a Professor Hogendoorn,' said the woman behind the reception desk in German, handing him a note. It too was in that language, with some spelling errors; not surprisingly, the hotel receptionist's German was not perfect. *Please meet me on Sunday if you can. Prof. Madvig with me. Ask for me at the university.*

That must be Theo, perhaps with some information on Schämmel. By 'Sunday', Theo meant that day, Thursday; he would be using the 'subtract three' code. But there was no chance of Conrad getting to Leiden that day. 'Did Professor Hogendoorn leave a telephone number?'

'I am afraid not, Mr de Lancey.'

Just then Payne Best's long low car drew up outside the hotel. Conrad had no time to find a Leiden telephone directory and leave a message with the professor that Conrad would be unable to see Theo that morning. It was a shame: it would have been extremely useful to hear what Theo had to say about Schämmel before Conrad met him for the first time.

Conrad folded the note, stuffed it in his pocket, and went outside to greet Payne Best.

'Not cancelled again?' he said.

'No. We're on. Hop in.'

They drove through the centre of The Hague. The city was full of peacetime bustle: trams, cars and swarms of bicycles fighting for road space, with policemen expertly directing things. The frantic traffic contrasted with the sedate, quietly opulent mansions that lined the city's streets. They passed the old Binnenhof, a complex of brown turrets and courtyards that housed the Dutch Parliament, and headed north through narrow streets to a peaceful little canal lined with bare trees and elegant townhouses.

Payne Best pulled up outside one of these, bearing a brass plate on which Conrad read the words *Handelsdienst voor het Continent*. They entered the building, which seemed to be a discreet office. Payne Best nodded to the man at reception, said something in Dutch to him, and led Conrad up a flight of stairs. 'This is my business in Holland,' Payne Best said. 'Continental Trading Services. Pharmaceuticals mostly these days.'

He greeted a secretary sitting at a desk outside an open door. Payne Best's office was large and comfortable with a good view down on to the canal and its little bridge outside. Bookcases and traditional Dutch landscapes lined the wall, together with a striking portrait of Payne Best himself.

A mild man with a trim, greying moustache was sitting in a leather chair by Payne Best's desk, reading *The Times*. He put down the newspaper and rose to his feet.

'De Lancey? I'm Major Stevens, the Passport Control Officer here in The Hague.'

Conrad shook Stevens's proffered hand. So this was the head of the British secret service in Holland Theo had warned him about.

'Major Stevens will be joining us,' said Payne Best. 'Isn't Klop here yet?'

'No sign of him,' Stevens said. 'In the meantime, I've got something for you, Best.' Stevens produce two Browning automatic pistols from a briefcase at his feet, and gave one to Payne Best, keeping the other for himself. 'Sorry, de Lancey, I don't have one for you.'

'We won't need them, will we?' Conrad said.

'We shouldn't,' said Payne Best. 'But we are going to be very close to the frontier, so it makes sense to be careful. Mind you, during the last show I used to meet people in a café in Limburg that was half in Holland and half in Germany. Can't get closer than that.'

Payne Best's secretary stuck her head around the door and said something to her boss. A moment later a tall, dashing Dutchman of about thirty appeared: Lieutenant Klop. Payne Best introduced him to Conrad in English. Klop's accent was indeed very good; he could easily pass for a British Army captain to a non-native speaker.

The four men climbed into the Zephyr and set off for Venlo, a small town 180 kilometres away on the German border. Payne Best was driving, and he drove fast. But there was a whole series of checkpoint and tank barriers to pass through. Given what Theo had told him, Conrad was pleased to see that the Dutch were expecting visitors. Klop sat in the front with Payne Best, and Conrad in the back with Major Stevens.

'I have a question for you, de Lancey,' Stevens said.

'Yes?' said Conrad. There was something about Major Stevens's tone that made him wary.

'Where did you go after Best dropped you off on Tuesday?'

'Leiden,' said Conrad.

'And why did you go there?' Stevens asked.

'To see an old friend.'

'An old friend?'

'Yes,' said Conrad, keeping his voice as natural as possible.

'And who was this old friend?'

'Someone I went to university with. I'd rather not say his name.'

'That's tosh,' said Stevens, staring hard at Conrad. 'His name is Lieutenant von Hertenberg of the German secret service.'

So that explained the man with the long nose Conrad had spotted in the Diefsteeg. On balance Conrad was happier that it was the British and not the Germans who had been following them. But there was no point now in trying to claim that Theo was a Luftwaffe officer.

'It's not tosh, actually. Hertenberg and I were good friends at Oxford.'

'You were seeing an enemy agent, de Lancey.'

'I'd rather not say any more.'

'In that case I'll get Best to stop the car at the next railway station and you can take the train back to The Hague.'

Conrad realized Stevens wasn't bluffing. He would have to give him something. 'All right. I saw Hertenberg when I was in Berlin last year.'

'Is he an agent of ours?' Stevens asked. 'A double agent?'

'No, he's not,' said Conrad. 'I can't tell you the details of our discussions. It was related to Schämmel.'

'Look here, de Lancey. If we are going to work together, we are going to have to trust each other.'

Stevens had a point, but then so did Theo. 'Do you know the other British Passport Control Officers in Europe?' Conrad asked.

'Yes,' said Stevens. 'I visited a number of them last year before I took up this post.'

'So you know Captain Foley who used to be in Berlin?'

'I do.'

'Ask him,' said Conrad. 'He can confirm my relationship with Lieutenant von Hertenberg.'

Stevens stared at Conrad. 'All right,' he said. 'That will do for now. But I will get in touch with Foley as soon as we are back in The Hague.'

'Thank you,' said Conrad.

They drove on in silence for a minute or so.

'Do you know Charles Bedaux?' Stevens asked.

Conrad shook his head. 'No, I've never heard of him. Who is he?'

'He's an American businessman based in France with operations in Amsterdam. A distinctly shady customer. Hertenberg has met him at least twice since the war began – we don't know why.'

'I have no idea why either,' Conrad said. 'But if Hertenberg has been meeting him, it is probably as part of his work for the Abwehr. He is a loyal German.'

'Yet you are talking to him?'

Conrad nodded.

'Well, if you happen to bump into your German friend again, could you ask him about Mr Bedaux? And tell me what he says? There's a good fellow.'

'I can ask him,' said Conrad. Although that would mean explaining that Stevens had spotted Conrad with Theo, which would not please Theo at all. Things were getting complicated.

Payne Best made such good time that they stopped for a quick lunch at a roadside café-restaurant near 's-Hertogenbosch. The atmosphere warmed over food, and the four men were in better spirits as they took to the road again. Stevens sat in the front with Payne Best, and they discussed what to do if the Germans invaded Holland imminently, an eventuality that Payne Best suggested was prudent to anticipate. Stevens jotted down a list of names of people to be evacuated to England. Conrad was a little surprised at their willingness to discuss the people working for them in Holland in front of himself and Klop. But he was also interested to note that Payne Best's fears tallied so closely with Theo's warning of an imminent offensive.

Conrad *had* to get that information to Van quickly. If he couldn't get back to England himself very soon, perhaps he could ask Payne Best for an unofficial way of communicating with London without using the embassy or the Passport Control Office. Payne Best gave the impression of operating with some degree of independence from Major Stevens and the Passport Control Office. Conrad was reluctant to trust him . . . but he might not have any choice.

The clouds were thickening and it looked as if it would soon start to rain. They passed a road sign: nine kilometres to Venlo.

Berlin

Charles Bedaux stood outside the Adlon Hotel and breathed in the crisp clear *Berliner Luft*. Across the Pariser Platz, the weathered bronze chariot atop the Brandenburg Gate gleamed green in the low November sun. Bedaux liked Berlin. It was the most modern city in Europe, with its powerful motor cars, its sleek buildings, its swish department stores, its broad, clean streets and above all its air of bustle, energy and efficiency.

Bedaux was the world expert on efficiency. He had made millions of dollars from the Bedaux System, which revolutionized the productivity of factory workers. He had hundreds of clients all over the world: Ford, General Motors, Standard Oil, ITT and DuPont in the United States; Anglo-Iranian Oil and Imperial Chemical Industries in Britain; Fiat in Italy and Philips and Unilever in Holland. In France his company had been appointed as consultants to the Ministry of Armaments, where he had doubled productivity, ironically by recommending more rest for the munitions workers. Germany, which in many ways was the ideal market for his ideas given the ability of its populace to take orders and its respect for efficiency, had been a difficult nut to crack. Robert Ley, the Nazi head of the Labour Front, viewed Bedaux as competition and had succeeded in keeping his system out of the country.

Bedaux was a consummate businessman. To him upheaval signalled opportunity and there was no greater upheaval than a world war. As an American citizen – he had been born in France, but moved to the United States in 1906 at the age of twenty – he was not wedded to the victory of one side or the other. But he was impressed with Germany's economic power, and determined to ensure that if Germany did come out on top, Bedaux International would be well positioned to benefit. So he needed to find a way to bypass Ley and win the Germans round.

Bedaux was always fizzing with ideas, and he had a good one. A great one. Which was why he had had a number of discreet conversations in Holland over the previous few weeks, and why he had travelled to Berlin.

An enormous supercharged black Mercedes with two little swastika flags fluttering on its front fenders pulled up outside the hotel, disgorging uniformed lackeys on to the pavement. The elegant, trim figure of Joachim von Ribbentrop stepped out of the vehicle, wearing a uniform now war had started. Bedaux thought Ribbentrop was a pompous ass, but he was also Bedaux's best friend in the Nazi hierarchy. Ribbentrop had been a champagne salesman before becoming a Nazi politician and, like all salesmen, he just wanted to be loved. Bedaux was good at giving him the love.

'Great to see you, Joachim,' said Bedaux, pumping the Foreign Minister's hand. Ribbentrop was proud of his English, which was much better than Bedaux's German.

'I'm glad you could make it,' said Ribbentrop. 'How did you get here?'

'Via Brussels and Cologne,' said Bedaux.

'Hop in,' said Ribbentrop. It was no distance to the Chancellery, but Bedaux hadn't been about to turn down a lift from Ribbentrop, and he guessed that Ribbentrop wanted the credit for producing his star American contact.

'I heard about the bomb last night,' Bedaux said. 'I was expecting Herr Hitler to cancel our meeting.'

'Not at all,' said Ribbentrop. 'He is very eager to speak to you. In fact, it is thanks to this meeting that he had to leave the beer hall early. So you could say he has something to be grateful for.'

'I think he will find what I have to say interesting.'

'I am sure he will,' said Ribbentrop.

They drove the short distance down Wilhelmstrasse in two minutes: other vehicles were quick to make way for them. Bedaux had never been inside the new Reich Chancellery building before, which dominated the smaller, older Chancellery next door, abandoned a year earlier. The Mercedes nosed its way into a courtyard and the car doors were swiftly opened. Bedaux and the Foreign Minister climbed some steps and then passed through massive bronze doors to a series of reception rooms and a very long corridor. It was quite a hike to Hitler's office, and their footsteps echoed on the marble floor as they strode past columns, statues, mosaics, tapestries and rigid black-uniformed and white-gloved SS guards. By the time he had reached Hitler's outer office, Bedaux was in awe. Which he realized was exactly the effect the building was supposed to have on a visitor.

They were ushered straight into a massive room, at the far end of which was an oversized desk under a portrait of Prince Otto von Bismarck, the Prussian who had unified Germany.

The Führer himself was walking towards Bedaux, clad not in the brown tunic which he had habitually worn before the outbreak of war, but in a simple field-grey uniform with a swastika on his arm and an iron cross at his chest.

Bedaux stood to attention and thrust out his right arm. When in Rome salute as the Romans do. 'Heil Hitler!'

Hitler acknowledged the American's salute, and smiled. 'Welcome to Berlin, Mr Bedaux. Thank you for coming. I am most anxious to hear what you have to report.'

Ten

Theo sat in the café and ordered his third cup of coffee. At least they still had decent coffee in Holland, compared to the muck that had been served in Germany for the last couple of years. He had the perfect seat, back to the wall with a clear view through the window to the Rapenburg Canal and the gates of the old Leiden University Academy on the other side.

He should spot Conrad approaching the building. More importantly, in the five minutes or so it would take Conrad to find Professor Hogendoorn and be guided back to the café, Theo would be able to check whether Conrad was being followed.

If Conrad showed up. Theo would be patient. Professor Hogendoorn was trustworthy, in his way. He was pro-German and, although he was not actually a member of the Dutch National Socialist Party, pro-Nazi, which was why he was willing to help the Abwehr. Theo would have to be very careful that Hogendoorn never overheard Theo or Conrad's true views on the Party.

It was vital that Theo get to Conrad before he met Schämmel. Conrad hadn't specified the timing of his rendezvous with the fake captain, and Theo just had to hope that the British hadn't betrayed Theo's fellow conspirators already. Ironically, Conrad himself was the most vulnerable to Schellenberg's stratagem. Neither Payne Best nor Stevens would know anything about the real Wehrmacht officers' conspiracy against Hitler, whereas Conrad probably knew as much as anyone in Britain. He knew names, and he knew many of the details of the carefully planned coup of the previous year.

Theo was glad that he had warned Conrad about the leaks in the British Embassy and Passport Control Office. Indeed the Abwehr had just received a report about the arrival of Conrad in Holland via their man in the British Embassy.

But Schellenberg was a wily operator, at least according to Canaris, who should know. Until Theo had the opportunity to warn Conrad that Schämmel was bait, he couldn't be sure that Schellenberg wouldn't tempt something out of him. Theo wondered what the British would do once they knew they were being played by the Gestapo. The obvious thing would be to break off negotiations right away. But intelligence services didn't often do the obvious thing. If Canaris were in charge, he would probably entice Schellenberg to London, and then expose him as a Gestapo spy there. Theo smiled. Schellenberg was dangerous: that would be the perfect way to get rid of him.

It was good to be working with Conrad again. They had had a lot in common when they met at Oxford. Theo came from a long line of soldiers who lived in a rural corner of Prussia where honour and duty to the Fatherland were paramount. But rather than go straight into the army, he had won a Rhodes Scholarship to Oxford. He had loved it there: he was a social success; he charmed men and women alike. With Conrad he had argued late into the night about social injustice, Indian independence and peace. After the crash of 1929 it was clear that the world was broken and Conrad and Theo were determined to fix it, once they had thrashed out exactly how.

After Oxford their paths had diverged. Although they were both disillusioned by the idealism they saw all around them, be it Nazism in Theo's case, or socialism in Conrad's, those long discussions into the night at university gave them a common sense of what was right and what was wrong. Which was vital in a world gone mad.

In less than a week, perhaps General Halder would do what he should have done the previous year, and restore sanity. Then, careful plans had been drawn up, with Theo at the heart of them.

This time Theo hadn't been involved, but from what he could see, there had been much less preparation. That might be because Halder was assuming that those who had been involved before would know what to do from their earlier instructions. Or that in wartime a conspiracy was more obviously treachery.

Or it might just be that Halder didn't really intend to go through with it after all. It was amazing how paralysed even the best generals could be without anyone to give them orders.

Where was Conrad? It was past noon. Students on foot and on bicycles passed back and forth along the Rapenburg, but none of them was his English friend. Perhaps Conrad hadn't got the message. He could easily be meeting Schämmel at that very moment. Perhaps he had received Hogendoorn's message and ignored it. Or perhaps he had been ordered back to London.

There was nothing Theo could do about any of those eventualities but wait. And have some lunch. He asked the waiter for a menu.

Venlo, Holland

Payne Best relinquished the wheel to Conrad, who drove along winding roads through a thick pine forest from the town to their destination: Café Backus, just a few yards from the frontier. The other three had met Schämmel and his colleagues there before, so they knew the place.

There was silence in the car as each man focused on the same thought, the same hope: that what was about to happen that afternoon might herald the end of both Hitler and the war. Yet there was anxiety as well as hope. Would Schämmel be there? Would he finally bring along his general? Would the German officers agree to fly to London for proper discussions? And despite what Payne Best had said about his exploits in the last war at Limburg, the German border was uncomfortably close.

They were a little late; it was three-twenty by the time they rounded a corner and Conrad saw a straight stretch of road to two barriers. The nearer, Dutch barrier was down, but the German barrier was raised. The frontier.

It was quiet. No movement around the two customs houses, and a single German soldier slouched by his barrier. A little girl was playing with a big black dog in front of the customs house.

Café Backus was a substantial white building with a verandah on the first floor, on which stood tables with folded umbrellas. A figure was leaning on the railings, looking out towards them.

'That's Schämmel,' said Payne Best.

The man stood up, waved and pointed into the restaurant.

'I think the general's there!' said Stevens.

'Finally,' said Payne Best.

Conrad pulled up outside the restaurant and reversed around the corner to park in the little car park on the far side of the building from the frontier. The plan was that Conrad, in his guise as Payne Best's driver, would take a seat at another table in the café and listen to the conversation between Schämmel, his general and Payne Best and Stevens.

Conrad switched off the motor. Stevens got out of the car, looking up towards Schämmel.

As he opened the driver's door, Conrad heard the sound of engines in the road, growing swiftly from a hum to a roar, and then the sharp reports of shots being fired.

He reached for the ignition of the Zephyr, but it was too late. Two large vehicles sprouting half a dozen armed men in rough civilian clothes swerved around the corner. One of them screeched to a halt bumper to bumper with the Zephyr. A machine pistol rattled. Conrad pushed open his door and jumped out. He saw one of the men grab Stevens and hold a pistol to his head.

Conrad rushed for the undergrowth beside the car park, but he was knocked to the ground by another German. As Conrad fell, he saw Klop running across the road, firing as he did so, and heard the shattering of a windscreen.

Conrad wriggled to try and break free of the man holding him, but the German stuck a Luger against Conrad's temple. '*Keine Bewegung!*' he growled.

Conrad froze. He stared at the scene unfolding before him. The Germans had hold of both Payne Best and Stevens and were firing at Klop, who was in the open, but dodging from right to left, firing back wildly. The German holding Conrad jerked and let out a curse. He had been hit in the thigh. From the corner of his eye, Conrad saw the man's pistol waver, so he spun and hit him hard across his neck with the side of his hand. The pistol went off harmlessly into the air. The man dropped to the ground, and Conrad ran for the woods.

As Conrad ducked into the trees, he saw Klop crumple in the roadway. Conrad crashed through the thick undergrowth for about ten yards. He realized he was out of sight of the Germans, so he dived under a holly bush and lay flat. Running, he would be a target, like Klop. Hidden, he would be safe as long as the Germans didn't take the time to search the woods. He was gambling they wouldn't; they had almost certainly got Payne Best and Stevens, and from the Germans' point of view the sooner they were back over the border the better.

He heard the two vehicles accelerate off.

He looked up, couldn't see any Germans in the wood, and so, at a crouching run, scurried to the edge of the trees to take a look.

One of the cars was speeding to the shattered Dutch barrier. The other car halted next to Klop's body lying in the road. Two men slung him into the back. Payne Best and Stevens were being frogmarched towards the border with Germans holding machine pistols at their backs. Schämmel accelerated past them in his own vehicle. The big black dog stood in the road barking.

Shouting came from the Dutch customs house, but no sign of armed soldiers yet. Within a few seconds, all the Germans and their captives were under the black-and-white German barrier, which swished downwards.

The often-uttered words of Colonel Rydal ran through Conrad's head. *What a shambles.*

Eleven

Conrad sipped the cup of coffee thoughtfully provided by Mrs Dougherty as he sat and waited outside Sir Robert Vansittart's office. He was tired and hungry.

'You don't happen to have a biscuit, by any chance, Mrs Dougherty?' he asked.

'I'm afraid not, Mr de Lancey,' said the Chief Diplomatic Adviser's secretary, with a look that suggested horror at his temerity and determination to take decisive action if he tried to question the Foreign Office's policy on biscuits. Didn't he know there was a war on?

It was sixteen hours since the Germans had snatched Payne Best and Stevens, sixteen disorienting hours. After being interviewed by Dutch military intelligence, Conrad had been bundled on to an RAF Lysander at The Hague and flown to Hendon Aerodrome, from where he had been driven straight to Whitehall and the doors of the Foreign Office.

The telephone on Mrs Dougherty's desk buzzed and she picked it up. 'Sir Robert will see you now.'

Van looked harassed. Sitting in one of the two chairs in front of his desk was a large man with a florid face and hair brushed back over a wide, shining forehead. His eyes were small and bright blue.

'Lieutenant de Lancey, this is Major McCaigue of the Secret Intelligence Service. Major McCaigue is responsible for counter-espionage. As you can imagine, he is very interested in this affair.'

Conrad saluted the major and took the seat offered by Van.

'Who is responsible for this fiasco, de Lancey?' Van asked.

'I don't know, Sir Robert. It was a mistake to meet Schämmel so close to the border when we were not sure he was genuine.'

'That would be Stevens's mistake?'

'I really couldn't say,' said Conrad.

'And you never met Schämmel?'

'No,' said Conrad. 'Venlo would have been my first meeting.'

'Hmm.' Van tapped his desk with his pen. 'Do you believe Schämmel was an impostor?'

'Once again, I don't know. That seems the most likely explanation to me.'

'Is there a chance he might have been genuine?' asked Major McCaigue. He had a deep rich voice with a trace of Ulster. 'Perhaps von Hertenberg warned his superiors that there was a plot against Hitler, and they arrested Schämmel and our men as a result?'

'I really don't think so,' said Conrad. 'It's not just a question of Theo being my friend. We *know* that Theo was prepared to risk his life last year to get rid of Hitler. Why betray a conspiracy that he is most likely at the heart of?'

'I take your point,' said McCaigue. 'But our two countries are now at war.'

'This is the most almighty disaster,' Van said. 'Stevens knows a lot – too much. He visited most of the Passport Control Offices in Europe before he took up his post in The Hague. After the Gestapo have got hold of him, we can assume that our European intelligence operations are blown.'

'I did get a message from Theo just as Payne Best was about to pick me up to take me to Venlo,' Conrad said. 'He wanted to meet me in Leiden. I have no idea what he was going to tell me. Perhaps he was warning me.'

'Go back to Holland and talk to him,' Van said. 'We need to know how much Stevens and Payne Best have told the Germans. We need to know whether Schämmel was genuine. We need to know whether the coup is going ahead. Did you hear about the Munich beer hall bomb?'

66

Conrad looked blank. 'Haven't had a chance to read the paper in the last day or so.'

'Hitler was speaking at a Party rally in a beer hall in Munich. Ten minutes after he left, a bomb went off. It would have killed him if he had stayed as planned.'

'Who planted it?'

'That is another question for Hertenberg. The Germans are saying it was us. They seem to be pinning the blame on "British secret agents", meaning Payne Best and Stevens, presumably.'

'Was it us?' Conrad asked.

'No,' said McCaigue. 'But was it the German generals? That's the question.'

'I'll ask Theo,' said Conrad. 'I saw him in Leiden the day I arrived in Holland. He didn't know anything about Schämmel at that point, but he did tell me the date of the planned coup. And the offensive.'

'Really?' said Van, leaning forward.

'The fifteenth of November. Theo said that's when the Germans will attack through Holland and Belgium, and that's when the generals will strike against Hitler. Halder, the Chief of Staff, is going to arrest him.'

'That's less than a week away!' said Van.

'Is he certain about the coup?' asked McCaigue.

'Not entirely,' Conrad admitted. 'I mean he was sure that those are the current plans. But he's not confident that the generals will see them through.'

'And he said Holland as well as Belgium?' McCaigue asked.

Conrad realized that was an important point. In the last war, only Belgium had been invaded and Holland had managed to stay neutral throughout. But not this time, it seemed.

'He did,' Conrad confirmed. 'I'm certain of that.'

'Did he give any other details?' McCaigue asked.

'No,' Conrad shook his head. 'Just that it would be like 1914, only worse.'

'He's right about that,' said Van. 'Thank you, de Lancey. You have done a good job. Contact me or Major McCaigue from

Holland directly if you need to, but bear in mind that anything you say might be overheard. Mrs Dougherty will give you the details. Otherwise report to me when you get back.'

'And you had better stay clear of our people in The Hague,' said McCaigue. 'If they were not compromised before, they certainly are now.'

'Stevens or Payne Best may have told the Gestapo all about me,' Conrad said.

'They may have,' said McCaigue. 'So I would be careful, if I were you.'

'Can you get back in touch with Hertenberg?' Van asked.

'I think so,' said Conrad.

'Good,' said Van. 'Speak to Mrs Dougherty about getting back over there as soon as possible. And in the mean time, Major McCaigue will debrief you more thoroughly.'

Twelve

Westminster, London

Sir Henry Alston, baronet, Member of Parliament and merchant banker, strode through St James's Park, with Freddie Copthorne struggling to keep up. Alston liked to walk through London; he frequently covered the distance from his flat in Kensington to Westminster or even the City on foot, and with taxis so hard to find in these days of petrol rationing, he was getting plenty of exercise.

St James's Park, once the prettiest of London parks, had changed over the previous few months. Part of it was the season: the flowers had been slain by autumnal frosts, and wind and rain had stripped the trees of their leaves. But the war had taken its toll too: the lake had been half drained, the railings had been removed from the pathways for the munitions factories, and green spaces were scarred with waterlogged zigzagged trenches, into which people were supposed to dive if there was an air-raid warning. No one did: the ditches were wet and filthy, and besides, not a single German bomb had yet fallen on the city.

It was a grey day, but the park was quite full. At least half the walkers were in uniform. Whereas two months before almost everyone would have been carrying gas masks, now no one was. Alston's eye was caught by a tall dark-haired Wren, elegant in her naval uniform, walking with a shorter, plainer friend. He watched as she chatted animatedly, her teeth flashing as she smiled. They were almost upon her when she looked up, saw him, and for the briefest moment an expression of horror touched her face before she turned away.

As they passed, Alston heard an indistinct whisper from the friend. He felt a familiar surge of anger. You would have thought that by now he would have got used to the effect his face had on people. One side, his left, was almost perfect: high cheekbone, a smooth jaw with the hint of a dimple at the chin, a straight nose, fair hair falling to a mop at his brow. In his youth it was said he looked like Rupert Brooke. But the other side was a twisted mess of white and pink scar tissue, through which, miraculously, a living blue eye stared. The humiliation of the girl's flinch was made worse by that all-too-brief period of his adulthood before his disfigurement when he had become accustomed to surreptitious admiring looks from girls more beautiful than the Wren. Silly woman.

'Have you heard how Chamberlain is going to reply to the King of the Belgians?' Freddie asked, referring to the peace proposal of a couple of days before.

'A big fat raspberry, from what I can tell,' said Alston. 'If he ever gets out of bed.' The Prime Minister had been laid low with gout for a couple of days. 'The Dutch and the Belgians are clever enough to realize that if this war carries on, their countries will be squashed. Why can't we?'

'You don't think we will be squashed, do you?'

'We might be. But that's not the point. The point is that we can divide the world between us. Germany takes the continent of Europe and Britain keeps our empire and the high seas. We leave each other alone.'

'But would Hitler really leave us alone?' Freddie asked.

'Of course he would,' Alston said. 'He as good as told me himself when I saw him with Rib last year.' Alston had met Joachim von Ribbentrop in Berlin when he had travelled to Germany on bank business in the early 1930s, and kept in touch with him when Ribbentrop became German Ambassador to London in 1936 and then Foreign Minister back in Berlin. Ribbentrop had introduced Alston to Hitler the previous spring in an attempt to give the German Chancellor a better idea of the opinion of the British ruling classes beyond the government. Alston had been surprised

70

by the positive attitude Hitler had to the British people, if not to their Prime Minister.

'Chamberlain's a lost cause,' said Freddie. 'Unless the rumours are correct and the German generals do get rid of Hitler. Then he might negotiate something.'

'That will never happen,' said Alston. 'I know Germany. It's inconceivable that a German general would break his oath and overthrow his commander-in-chief in wartime. Somehow we are going to have to make sure we have a government in this country that talks sense.'

'The Jews won't wear it,' said Freddie. 'You know, the financiers. The Rothschilds. The Sieffs. Hore-Belisha. They won't want to stop the war. They need to protect their German cousins.'

Alston smiled at his friend. Tall, thin, with wisps of hair plastered over a bald dome, the second Baron Copthorne looked and sounded like a dim aristocrat. He wasn't entirely dim, but he was inclined to fall for some of the more simplistic notions of his friends. Still, he was loyal, and he was well connected: everyone liked Freddie.

'Don't worry too much about the Jews,' Alston said. 'This idea of a conspiracy of Jewish financiers is overblown. It's true that some of the Jews I know in the City are concerned about what's going on in Germany. But I don't believe they want an unnecessary war and, more to the point, I don't think they have the influence to insist on one.'

'You should know,' said Freddie. But he looked chastened.

'So who is this girl we are going to meet, Freddie?'

'Her name is Constance Scott-Dunton. She's a friend of Marjorie's.' Marjorie was Freddie's 22-year-old niece.

'And are you sure we can't get Marjorie to help us?' Alston had met Marjorie several times and liked her.

'Yes, quite sure. I did ask her, but she said no. The truth is, she was scared. She's a sensible girl most of the time, but she can be a bit of a panicker.'

'And this Constance girl isn't?'

'Not according to Marjorie. She's game for anything, apparently. Marjorie is quite taken with her.'

'Marjorie didn't tell her what we wanted her to do?'

'Oh, no. I thought we would leave that to you, once you've decided you like her.'

'And what is this Russian Tea Rooms place?'

'It's in Harrington Road, opposite South Ken tube station. It's owned by a Russian admiral. Admiral Wolkoff.'

'I think I've passed it. A White Russian, I take it?'

'Oh, very much so. He was naval attaché for the Tsar in the last war, and stayed on in London after the revolution rather than return to Russia to be shot. Marjorie spends quite a lot of time there. She says it's the kind of place a girl can go to unaccompanied quite happily. That's where she met Constance.'

Freddie was flagging as they reached Harrington Road and the Russian Tea Rooms. It was busy. Alston spotted Freddie's niece talking to a girl with black hair whose back was to the door.

Marjorie stood up, waved and kissed her uncle. 'Hello, Uncle Freddie. Hello, Sir Henry.'

She held out her gloved hand to be shaken.

'This is my friend Constance. My uncle, Lord Copthorne, and Sir Henry Alston.'

Constance was striking: pale, with a strong chin and large lively black eyes. They looked straight at Alston as they shook hands, and she smiled. Not a flicker of revulsion.

Alston smiled back.

'Have some tea,' Marjorie said. 'They serve it in samovars. It's really rather exciting. You're not supposed to drink milk with it.'

So they sat down and ordered tea, which came in glasses contained in metal holders with handles.

'Constance is a fan of yours,' said Marjorie. 'She has been dying to meet you.'

'I wasn't aware that I had any fans,' said Alston, bemused.

'I've read all your speeches,' said Constance. 'And Marjorie says you are frightfully clever.'

Alston glanced at his friend's niece, who blushed. 'Shh, Constance, you weren't meant to say that. Constance is very keen on politics,' she explained.

'Oh. What sort of politics?' Alston asked.

'Common-sense politics,' Constance said. 'The war is stupid. The Jews started it. If we leave Hitler alone, he'll leave us alone. We have the greatest empire the world has ever seen, and we should be left to enjoy it.'

'That sounds like common sense to me.' Alston glanced at Freddie, and then back at Constance. 'Are you a member of any political party?'

'No, not really. I was a member of the Nordic League, but they've disbanded that now.' The Nordic League was a hysterical anti-Semitic organization that had blossomed a couple of years before and then wilted with the onset of war. 'That's where I met my husband Patrick. He's away at sea in the navy.'

Alston felt a tinge of regret on hearing that this intriguing girl was married, followed by relief that her husband was probably three thousand miles away in a large metal boat.

'You are not a member of the BUF, then?' The BUF was the British Union of Fascists led by Sir Oswald Mosley. Alston didn't like the British Union of Fascists. Neither, it transpired, did Constance.

'Gosh, no. All that strutting around wearing silly shirts. It's childish, don't you think? And Tom Mosley is a weasel.'

'A weasel?' Sir Oswald Mosley, known to his friends and conquests as 'Tom', was notorious for his ways with women. Usually other people's wives.

'Yes. He mistreated a friend of mine – a friend of ours,' she nodded to Marjorie.

'A weasel,' Marjorie confirmed. 'Look, shall we leave you two to talk? I know you have a scheme you want Constance to join in. Come on, Uncle Freddie. Drink up.'

Freddie did as he was told and left Alston and Constance alone over their tea.

'So what's this scheme, Sir Henry?'

Alston hesitated. He was enjoying the girl's directness. 'It's a little delicate,' he said.

'Oh, I see.' Her eyes widened. 'So you want to veto me first?'

'Vet, I think is the word,' Alston said. 'And yes, I do need to find out a little bit more about you.'

'Fair enough,' said Constance. 'But first I'd like to ask you a question. How did you get those terrible scars? Was it doing something frightfully brave in the war?'

'Sadly, not,' said Alston. He smiled.

'Why are you smiling?'

'Because people are usually too timid to ask me.'

'Are you angry with me?'

'No,' said Alston. 'Not at all. Quite the contrary.'

'Good. Because you haven't told me how it happened.'

'It was a lion,' said Alston.

'No! Really! Where?'

So Alston told Constance all about the business trip to South Africa when he was a young banker, how he had travelled up to Northern Rhodesia with a colleague whose uncle had some mining interests there, and how he and his colleague had gone big-game hunting, wounded a lion and then come face-to-face with it. The colleague had run, Alston had fired and missed, and the lion had knocked him to the ground with a blow to his face, standing over him rather than mauling him further. One of the native trackers had killed the lion with a spear. Apparently Alston had been lucky that it was a lion and not a lioness that had caught him. A lioness would have finished him off right away.

'That's an amazing story!' said Constance, who did look amazed. Then she frowned. 'Was your friend Jewish?'

'Yes,' said Alston. 'How did you know?'

'A banker and a coward. Got to be Jewish, surely?'

Alston checked Constance for a hint of humour but found none. She had a point.

'I loathe the Jews, don't you?' said Constance. 'You must come across heaps of them in banking.'

'Some,' said Alston. 'They're not all bad.'

'But some of them are, aren't they?'

Alston thought of the partner of Bloomfield Weiss in New York who had sold him stock in a radio company in 1928 that had almost brought his merchant bank down. It had taken all of Alston's ingenuity to get it off the bank's books and into his clients' accounts at cost price.

'Yes. Some of them are,' he admitted. Usually he was very careful not to broadcast his mistrust of the Jewish race: he had to work with them every day after all. But there was something about Constance, her directness perhaps, that encouraged him to lower his guard.

'My father was bankrupted by a Jewish stockbroker,' she said. 'Daddy owned a packaging firm in Manchester. He sold it in the twenties and then invested the money in the stock market through a Jewish firm. That and Argentine railway bonds. Nineteen twenty-nine came along and he lost it all.' For once the enthusiasm had left her. 'He killed himself four months later.'

'I'm very sorry,' said Alston. 'So you moved up to London?'

'Yes. My sister, my mother and I. We stayed with my aunt in Dulwich. It's when my life started going wrong. I was fourteen.'

'I hope it didn't keep going wrong?' Alston asked.

'No,' said Constance. 'It's going better now.' She hesitated. 'I, um . . . took steps.'

'I'm glad to hear it,' said Alston, curious as to what those 'steps' were. 'Is that the owner of this place?' He nodded towards a well-dressed man with white whiskers and a pointed beard, sitting over a glass of tea reading a book.

Constance glanced over her shoulder. 'Yes, that's the admiral. He's quite a gentleman.'

Alston looked around the tea rooms. 'What sort of people come here?'

'Right-thinking people,' Constance said. 'Captain Maule Ramsay comes here a lot; you know him, don't you?'

'Yes. He's a fellow Scottish MP,' Alston said. And a fool, he could have added but didn't. Perhaps this wasn't such a good place to meet, after all. Alston was sure that the likes of Ramsay and certainly Mosley would attract the attention of Special Branch. He didn't want to be added to that list.

'So. What would you like me to do?' Constance asked, her eyes glowing with excitement. 'Or do you have some more questions for me?'

Alston smiled. He didn't really know Constance; there were probably more questions he could ask. But he had a good feeling about her. He trusted her. Marjorie had said she was all right, and he knew and trusted Marjorie. She was the right person.

'Just one,' he said, in German. 'Have you ever been to Germany?'

'Oh, yes,' Constance answered, also in German. 'I spent a year in Berlin in 1937 as a governess and to learn the piano. I loved it. I think it's a wonderful country. Modern, exciting, not like fuddy-duddy old England. Have you been?'

Constance's accent was awful, but she seemed fluent and assured, although she had invented the Germanic word *fuddyduddyisch*.

'Many times, working for the bank,' Alston said. Then, switching back to English. 'Yes. I think you'll do very well. But I'd rather not discuss what I want you to do here.'

Constance looked around. 'Oh, I see. We might be overheard. Where shall we go?'

Alston hesitated. 'We could walk up to Hyde Park. It's not too far.'

The glow in Constance's eyes deepened. 'It's quite public, though. And it's much too cold. Marjorie said you lived near here?'

'I do, yes.' Was Constance suggesting what Alston thought she was suggesting? He glanced at her. She was.

'What's the matter? Isn't your place tidy?'

'It's perfectly tidy,' said Alston. He had been married four years, and for the first two and a half he had been faithful. But it was eighteen months since he and Dorothy had had conjugal relations;

he just hadn't been able to bring himself to do it since she had had the baby. Alston had always had a healthy sexual appetite, and that hadn't left him. So there had been a few girls, most of whom he had had to pay. At that moment Alston wanted a woman badly. This woman. 'Why don't I make you a cocktail and we can talk in private?'

Alston grinned as he lay in bed, sweaty, with Constance under his left arm. It was dark outside his flat now. Constance was a tiger in bed; Alston had never come across anyone like her. She had a hunger and a playfulness that had brought out feelings in him that he never knew he had, or that he had always known he had, but were kept deeply buried. It certainly wasn't love. It was more than lust. It was a kind of joyful exuberance.

He felt much younger. And he felt handsome, as if the left half of his face had temporarily taken over the right.

They had gone back to Alston's flat in Ennismore Gardens, a fifteen-minute walk. Dorothy, Alston's young wife, was back in Berwickshire. Since the outbreak of war, they had decided she wouldn't join Alston in London, where he spent most of his time with his parliamentary and banking responsibilities. Besides, it was better for their baby son Robert to be at the castle with all that fresh air.

Alston had mixed them both martinis, and explained his idea to Constance. As Marjorie had guessed, she was game. She was definitely the right girl for the job. Then, well, then they had ended up in bed.

What was it that he liked about her so much? Was it her directness? There seemed a lively intelligence about her, even though she didn't know the difference between 'veto' and 'vet', and, like Freddie, her hatred of the Jews was of the simplistic type. Alston knew that Britain wasn't run by Jewish financiers, nor was it the Jews who had forced Chamberlain to go to war. He thought the War Minister Hore-Belisha should be sacked because he was wrongheaded, not because he was Jewish. Alston prided himself on his ability not to be swayed by the wilder claims of some of his pro-Nazi friends.

And yet, in all his dealings with Jews, Alston had never really trusted them. Constance was right; if there was trouble, there was usually a Jew behind it. Samuel Greenberg had run from the lion in Rhodesia leaving Alston facing up to it. Bloomfield Weiss had damned near fleeced him, and a Jewish stockbroker had driven Constance's own father to death. Maybe Hitler was on to something after all.

He stroked the black curls resting on his chest. 'Why did you ask me about my scars?'

Constance lifted her head. 'Why, shouldn't I have? Was I awfully rude?'

'No. Or at least I didn't think so. It's just that usually people avoid the subject. Or, even worse, they avoid looking at me at all.'

'Silly them,' said Constance. She pushed herself up on to her elbow. And ran her finger down the undamaged side of his face. 'You know, half of you is terrifically handsome.' Then she ran her finger over his scars. 'And the other half is terrifically exciting.'

'You don't mean that,' said Alston.

'I certainly do,' said Constance, in a tone that suggested she was offended at having her candour questioned.

Alston smiled. 'I believe you do.' He kissed her.

'You know what?' said Constance, reaching down towards his loins.

'What?'

'I think I'm going to enjoy working for you.'

Thirteen

St James's, London

After his meeting with Van, Major McCaigue of the Secret Intelligence Service questioned Conrad for an hour in a small room in the depths of the Foreign Office. Conrad told him everything he could remember about his meetings with Payne Best and Stevens and the shoot-out at Venlo. McCaigue took particular interest when Conrad mentioned the list that Stevens had written out of the names of people to be evacuated from Holland in the event of an invasion, which was presumably now in the hands of the Gestapo. Conrad tried to remember the names, but could only recall three or four of them. McCaigue asked for more details about Conrad's meeting with Theo in Leiden, and Conrad gave them.

The intelligence officer was a shrewd listener. His questions, delivered in his pleasant, rich voice with its hint of Irish, were deliberate and thorough and Conrad felt much more confidence in him than he had had in either Payne Best or Stevens.

Conrad dropped into his club for lunch, and to send a telegram to Professor Hogendoorn in Leiden. There he found a note waiting for him from his father inviting him to come to dinner and to stay the night at Kensington Square. Van must have told him about the disaster at Venlo. Conrad took the note into the library and sank into an armchair by the window.

He was lucky to be in a comfortable club in the heart of London when Payne Best, Stevens and Klop were presumably in a Gestapo interrogation cell somewhere in the heart of Germany. Poor bastards. Conrad had spent time in one of those once; he didn't want to do it again.

That is if Klop had made it. He had taken at least two bullets that Conrad had seen.

And now Conrad was going back to Holland. He knew he had to: Van and McCaigue were right to get him to ask Theo questions, to find out what had gone wrong. But there was a chance he might not come back this time.

In which case he shouldn't hide from his father, even though he wanted to avoid a discussion over what he was doing in Holland. So he telephoned Kensington Square and told Williamson he would be staying the night, but he might be a little late for dinner. There was someone else he wanted to see before he went.

Anneliese.

He took the tube north to Golders Green, and it was just getting dark as he walked through the peaceful tree-lined streets of Hampstead Garden Suburb. In some ways it seemed so English: neat, ordered, well kept; even the fallen leaves had been pushed by a tidy breeze into straight lines along the pavement. But in other ways it reminded him of Germany, of the *bürgerlich* suburbs of Berlin like Dahlem. Now Dahlem and Hampstead Garden Suburb were at war.

Anneliese and her parents lived in an upstairs room of a small white pebbledash cottage halfway up a hill. The house was owned by a widow, Mrs Cherry, who had crammed two refugee Jewish families into it. The building was in poor repair and it was clear Mrs Cherry had very little money. What was unclear was whether her motive for stuffing seven people into such a small house was kindness or greed. Anneliese's theory was that it was both.

Anneliese herself wasn't at home, but her parents were. They were both pleased to see Conrad, especially since he had brought along half a pound of sausages. Dr Rosen was racially Jewish, but also a devout atheist. Frau Rosen was a good rosy-cheeked Lutheran. Both of them believed in pork.

'Are you staying for supper, Conrad?' Frau Rosen asked in German. 'I have enough soup for you.' And indeed there was a pot bubbling on the little gas ring by the sink. The room itself had two beds, three armchairs, a small table and a wireless. Two stacks of books were growing ever higher. Although the Rosen family had left Germany without any the year before, one way or another they were steadily accumulating them.

'I promised my father I would be dining with him tonight,' Conrad said. 'I thought I would take Anneliese out for a drink, if that's all right.' He had eaten with the Rosens a couple of times, but he hated to take their scant supply of food, and besides, there was only really room for three at the table.

It was all they could afford. Even with the outbreak of war, Dr Rosen had been unable to find a job as a doctor: the British Medical Association was eager to preserve its profession from the invasion of central European Jewish medics. As far as Conrad could tell, Dr Rosen spent his days at the Golders Green library. Frau Rosen was a cleaner at a variety of houses in Hampstead and Finchley. Only Anneliese had finally been able to pursue her original career as a nurse: she worked at St George's Hospital on Hyde Park Corner.

Conrad heard the door open downstairs, and Anneliese's voice greeting Mrs Cherry. His heart, as always, leaped to hear it.

'Ich bin wieder zu Hause!' she called as she opened the door. Her smile disappeared for an instant when she saw Conrad, and then returned in a different, more guarded form. She was thinner than when he had first met her. The vitality, the quick smile, the ironic laugh had gone. But she was still beautiful to Conrad. Small, with dark curly hair and large green eyes, she reminded him of the woman he had fallen in love with. The woman he believed she could be again.

They had met in Berlin at a dinner party given by Theo soon after Conrad had arrived there the previous summer. Conrad had fallen heavily for her: she was intelligent, witty, courageous, with eyes that hinted at mischief, and he had still been smarting from Veronica running off with the racing driver. Dr Rosen had been locked up in a concentration camp for giving his Jewish blood to an Aryan Nazi road-accident victim. Conrad had helped get him out of the camp and out of Germany. Conrad and Anneliese had spent a blissful few weeks together before she had been snatched away from him by the Gestapo and thrown into Sachsenhausen concentration camp herself. Eventually Captain Foley, the British Passport Control Officer in Berlin, had been able to get her out too, and she had joined her parents in London.

She had been in England for over a year, but things weren't the same between them. Things were, well, difficult. But Conrad wasn't one to give up.

'Oh, Conrad. This is a surprise. I didn't know you were in London,' she said in German.

He bent down to kiss her, and she turned her cheek, in a gesture that could have meant she was offering it to him, or withdrawing it from him.

'I've been abroad,' he said. 'And I'm ... um ... going again. I thought I would drop in and see you before I went.'

'Ah.'

'Can I take you out for a drink?'

Anneliese glanced at her parents, Conrad's allies. She smiled quickly. 'Yes. That would be nice. Shall we go now?'

It was about half a mile to the Royal Oak. As they walked through the pitch-dark streets to Finchley Road – or 'Finchley Strasse', as the bus conductors had taken to calling it following the recent influx of German-speaking inhabitants – Anneliese seemed to warm. She talked about her job at St George's; she had only been there three weeks. Despite all the preparations for a flood of air-raid casualties, the hospital was filled with the victims of traffic accidents as a result of the blackout.

A warm fug of chatter and beer enveloped them as they went through to the saloon bar, and Conrad ordered drinks.

'So where are you going?' Anneliese said, in English this time. Her English had improved dramatically over the last year; although she had a distinct German accent, it was nowhere near as strong as it had been when she had arrived in London the previous

October. It wasn't a good idea to speak German in public places. 'Or I suppose it is a secret?'

Conrad glanced at the stern poster from the Ministry of Information urging patrons 'not to discuss anything that might be of national importance, the consequence of which might be loss of many lives'. True enough, of course. But he had trusted Anneliese before in a much more dangerous place than North London, with more dangerous secrets. He did, however, glance around to make sure there was no one in earshot. The saloon bar was half full, and it wasn't possible for the two middle-aged men closest to them to hear their murmured words above the hubbub of the pub.

'It sounds as if Theo's friends are about to make a move again.'

Anneliese's eyebrows shot up. 'Really! Are you going to see him?'

'I hope so. I don't know. There's been some . . . trouble. I need to find out what he knows about it.'

A look of concern crossed her face. 'You're not going to Germany, are you?'

'No.' Conrad shook his head. 'Don't worry.'

'I am worried,' said Anneliese. 'Be careful, Conrad. Please be careful.' She bit her bottom lip, in a gesture Conrad knew so well.

'I will.' Conrad smiled. Although he couldn't admit it, he was pleased to see her sudden concern for him. And she was perfectly right to be concerned. It was only just over twenty-four hours since he had had a German pistol pressed against his temple.

'Good.' Anneliese smiled quickly. Closed her eyes. Opened them again. 'Conrad?'

'Yes?'

'There is something I must tell you.'

'What is it?' Conrad had a feeling this wasn't going to be good.

'I am planning to go to New York. We are planning to go to New York. The three of us.'

'New York?' Conrad said. 'You can't do that! Can you get the papers?'

'I'm working on it. It's difficult, but I think I can. Father has a cousin over there, and he is prepared to help.'

Conrad could feel disappointment welling up inside him – worse than disappointment: desperation. 'Please stay,' he said.

'We need to make a new life. I mean really new. Somewhere far away. It's ridiculous that my father cannot work here.'

'But once the war really gets going, they will need him, whatever the damned BMA says.'

'Perhaps.' Anneliese looked down at her drink. And then straight at him. Her eyes were dull. 'But I need to go. I need to go somewhere new.'

Conrad reached across the table and took her hand. 'I know I've asked you before. But please marry me.'

Anneliese shook her head. 'I can't. I told you I can't.'

'But why not? I love you. You love me.' Conrad hesitated. 'I think. I know you used to love me.'

Anneliese nodded. She squeezed Conrad's hand. 'I know I did. But I am a different person now. I have been trying to tell you that for the last year, but you won't hear it. Sachsenhausen changed me. I'm sorry, I wish I was the same woman I used to be, but I am not. I'm different.' She let go of his hand. Took a deep breath. 'I need to start again. Somewhere else. Somewhere away from you.'

'I can't accept that,' Conrad said. In Berlin they had made love several times a day. But then Anneliese had spent six weeks in solitary confinement in first Sachsenhausen and then Lichtenburg Castle. It was true: after that she *had* been different. She hadn't let Conrad touch her beyond the occasional gentle kiss. She had joined her parents in London and, with a dull determination, had set herself to survive. She had refused all Conrad's offers of financial help.

Conrad had returned to England from Germany soon after her. He had been patient. He had been understanding. Or at least he had tried to understand, but he hadn't quite managed it. He knew she was hurt, deeply damaged, but he didn't know exactly how, and she seemed unable to tell him.

The night before he had been due to leave for Sandhurst, he had asked her to marry him. She had said no. She hadn't really explained why. He had been disappointed, but he hadn't given up. He had seen her during weekend leave, either in North London or occasionally taking her out to a restaurant or club in the West End. He had even brought her down to Somerset twice to see his own family. They had had some good times; she had smiled, told him she was enjoying herself. They had even kissed. But there was always a barrier. He had been willing to wait, confident that the barrier would eventually melt away and reveal the old Anneliese.

Even now, a year later, he still didn't understand her. All he knew was that she wanted to leave him.

'You have to accept it, Conrad,' Anneliese said. She had switched to German, which soon attracted the attention of the two men at the next table. 'We shouldn't see each other anymore.'

'No, I don't accept it.'

A tear leaked out of the corner of her eye.

She pushed back her chair and rose to her feet. 'Goodbye, Conrad,' she said, bending to kiss his cheek, and then she was gone.

Conrad stared after her. '*Leb wohl*,' Conrad repeated.

She hadn't said '*Auf Wiedersehen*', or 'when we meet again'.

He had lost her.

Fourteen

The Ritz, Paris

Fruity Metcalfe sloped into the lobby of the Ritz and headed straight for the bar. He had had a perfectly bloody day and he needed a drink. Several drinks.

He liked the bar at the Ritz. It was always lively. Although a lot of English soldiers thought that the French officers' uniforms looked a bit effete, they certainly added colour. As did their women. Throw in a few Americans and one or two Englishmen, plus Fruity the Irishman, and you had quite an atmosphere.

'*Un Johnny Walker avec soda, Marcel,*' Fruity said to the barman while taking possession of a free stool. '*Un grand, s'il vous plaît.*'

Fruity sipped his drink with pleasure. A bloody day.

There had been trouble at the mission at Vincennes. Fruity had expected to help the duke draw up his report for the Wombat on their visit to the French lines, but the duke had rebuffed him. Which offended Fruity. Fruity had been a first-rate officer in his time, and it was important to convey accurately what they had seen, especially along the Meuse on the border with Luxembourg and Belgium. Frankly, there was a bloody great hole there that the Germans could stroll through any time they liked, once they had penetrated the forests of the Ardennes. The French troops were mostly reservists: fat, untrained and unfit. The anti-tank defences were pathetic: positioned in the wrong place, in plain view; and in many cases the anti-tank traps and the barbed wire were on top of each other, which meant they could be knocked out simultaneously by well-placed artillery fire. General Huntziger,

Commander of the 2nd Army, oozed complacency. The French 9th Army, just to the west of the 2nd, commanded by the obese Corap, was only a little better.

All this, Fruity and the duke had discussed. And frankly, Fruity wanted to have a part in writing it down. He wanted to be doing a soldier's work in this phoney war.

Instead of being a bloody tourist. A tourist who had to pay for himself. Because the other thing Fruity had learned that day was that no one was going to pay him for what he was doing. The War Office had refused his demand for payment, telling him he was not in France in an official capacity, and the duke had changed the subject when Fruity had raised it. He was so damned mean! Mean about bills, mean about paying his staff. Mean about everything apart from Wallis. One of her Fulco di Verdura brooches would keep Fruity going for the duration.

Not for the first time, the Little Man was taking advantage of Fruity.

He ordered another whisky.

It was not as if Fruity had a private income. His wife did, but a chap needed to pay his own way. He loathed being beholden to Baba. She was loaded. She was the daughter of Lord Curzon, the grandest Indian viceroy, but her real wealth came from a settlement from her mother, an American department-store heiress.

He hated leaving her alone in London. Not just because he missed her – which he did, very much – but also because he had no idea whom she was seeing. He just hoped it wasn't Tom Mosley again. He was sure he didn't know who all his wife's lovers were, but he knew enough of them, and Tom Mosley was the most serious. She had started writing about weekends with Lord Halifax, the Foreign Secretary and another former viceroy. He was about as high-minded as they came, so she ought to be safe with him, although you never knew with Baba.

Fruity needed another whisky. And he needed to take his mind off his woes. He spotted a sociable American he had had a drink with the week before, and called out to him. 'Let me get you one, old man. What will you have?'

At least the duke was paying his bloody hotel bill.

Kensington Square, London

'A glass of sherry, Conrad?'

After all he had been through in the last twenty-four hours, Venlo and then his conversation with Anneliese, Conrad felt like something stronger, but he accepted his father's offer.

Lord Oakford was pleased to see his son. Conrad was relieved that he wasn't in one of his frequent black moods. He poured Conrad a glass from a decanter with his one remaining arm, and then a glass for himself.

'I'm sorry I'm so late for dinner,' Conrad said. 'Thanks for waiting for me. I wanted to see Anneliese.'

'Oh, how is she?' said Oakford.

I don't know how she is, thought Conrad. I don't understand her! Why can't she just agree to marry me? Why does she have to run away to New York? Why won't she see me again? What's wrong with her? Doesn't she know I love her? Doesn't she know I'll do anything for her?

'Oh, you know,' he said.

Oakford looked at him sharply. Conrad stared into his sherry glass.

'I heard about Venlo,' Oakford said.

'I wondered,' said Conrad. He had scanned *The Times* that afternoon in the club. As well as a description of the Munich beer hall bomb, it had reported a confused incident at 'Venloo' involving kidnapped Dutchmen. Clearly his father knew the real story.

'I knew you were going.'

'I thought you might.' Conrad sipped his sherry.

'Why didn't you drop in and see me before you went?'

'It was all fixed up rather quickly,' Conrad said. 'One moment I was at Tidworth, the next I was in Whitehall, and before I knew it I was in an aeroplane bound for Holland.'

'What happened?'

Conrad hesitated and then decided to tell his father everything. For three years in the early 1930s Lord Oakford had been a minister in the National Government. He was a close friend of Van and Lord Halifax, and he had helped Conrad arrange the visit of emissaries from the German conspirators to Britain the year before. He knew secrets.

Oakford listened with interest. 'A shambles,' he said when Conrad had finished.

'My thought exactly,' said Conrad.

'So the Germans have nabbed our agents. Presumably the Gestapo will interrogate them? Will they talk, I wonder?'

'One has to assume they will,' said Conrad. 'Do you know a Major McCaigue? He debriefed me with Van.'

'I've met him once or twice. A good man. Works for the SIS, the Secret Intelligence Service. They're under a lot of pressure at the moment. They have a reputation for being all-seeing, but they didn't spot the Nazi–Soviet pact coming, and this is a very public balls-up. On top of all that, their chief died last week, and they haven't picked a successor yet. Did you contact Theo? Van said you were going to try.'

'Yes,' said Conrad. 'He said he didn't know whether Schämmel was genuine and he was going to check. I never found out his answer.'

'Did you discuss peace terms with him?' Oakford asked. He was trying to make the question sound casual, but Conrad could feel the quickening of his attention.

Conrad pretended not to notice. 'No,' he said.

'Does he think there is still a chance of a coup?'

'They are planning one,' Conrad said. 'To coincide with an offensive in the Low Countries.'

'Interesting. Soon?'

'In the next few days. The fifteenth to be precise. But Theo didn't seem certain either would happen.'

'I've always thought it was a mistake to rely on the generals,' said Oakford.

'I'm going back to Holland to see him tomorrow,' Conrad said. 'Van sent me. He wants me to confirm Schämmel was bait and find out if Payne Best and Stevens have talked.'

'Oh, really?' said Oakford, raising his eyebrows.

Conrad sensed there was something a little odd about his father's reaction, but before he could pursue it, the door opened and a tall girl with dark hair bounded in.

'Millie!' Conrad leaped to his feet. She hugged him. 'I wasn't expecting to see you here! I thought you were down in Somerset.'

'I've come up to find some war work,' Millie said.

'It's lovely to see you.' And it was. Conrad and Millie had always been close. There were four surviving de Lancey children: Conrad, his younger brother Reggie, Charlotte, who was married with a baby, and Millie. Edward, the eldest and Lord Oakford's favourite, had died in a mountaineering accident when he was twenty-two. No one in the family mentioned his name, but Conrad knew they all thought about him. Millie was twenty-three and still unmarried, although Conrad knew she had turned down many advances. The suitors didn't surprise him; in his opinion she would be quite a catch. She was attractive in a gangly kind of way, she was intelligent and she was fun.

'What about the evacuees?' he asked. Millie was helping billet the bewildered families who had arrived from Coventry in September in the homes of an equally bewildered village.

'Most of them are fed up with the country and are going home. I thought I would be more use in London.'

'And Reggie? What's he up to?'

Reggie was twenty-seven, a year younger than Conrad. He was therefore too old to be called up yet, but certainly young enough to volunteer.

'He says that he's wanted on the estate,' Millie said.

'He's quite right,' said Lord Oakford. 'The country is going to need all the food it can grow.'

Reggie had devoted his life to managing Chilton Coombe, the small family estate in Somerset, and irritating the three perfectly capable tenant farmers there. But Lord Oakford was happy to keep at least one of his sons out of harm's way. Conrad didn't have much respect for Reggie.

'Father tells me you have been on another top-secret mission,' Millie said.

'I suppose that's true,' said Conrad. 'Although it didn't go very well.'

Oakford poured his daughter a glass of sherry.

'Cheers!' said Millie, raising her glass to her brother. 'Anything to do with Theo?'

Conrad glanced at his father, who looked sheepish. He must have told his daughter more than he was letting on. Theo had made quite an impression on Millie when he had met her in Berlin the year before; Theo tended to make an impression on women when he met them.

'Theo is in the enemy's secret service, Millie,' Conrad said.

'You're not answering the question, are you, Conrad?'

'No, I'm not,' said Conrad with a grin.

They went in to dinner, the three of them. Tomato soup and pheasant from Chilton Coombe. They talked about the evacuees, and about Conrad's mother and how the village was dealing with a German woman in its midst, which was very well – with the exception of the old bat who ran the village shop, who was causing trouble.

'How's Anneliese?' Millie asked. 'How do people treat her in London?'

'Some people think she's a spy because she's German,' said Conrad. 'Some people think she's a profiteer because she's Jewish. But she says it's miles better than Berlin. Her family seem pleased to be here, although they are all crammed into one room in Hampstead.'

'Can't you help, her, Conrad?'

'Anneliese is very proud,' Conrad said. 'And stubborn.'

'Like your mother,' said Lord Oakford.

'What's wrong, Conrad?' Millie asked.

Conrad hesitated. Typical of Millie to notice there was something wrong, and then to come right out and ask about it. Conrad knew his family liked Anneliese, much more than they had liked his former wife Veronica. With Millie there, he abandoned his earlier reticence.

'I don't know, exactly,' he said. 'She says she doesn't want to see me anymore. No matter how hard I try to help her, she seems to push me away. I don't know whether it's got something to do with what she suffered in the concentration camp, or coming to England, or worrying about her parents. I don't know what it is.'

'But that doesn't make any sense!' Millie said.

'Sometimes these things don't,' said Oakford gravely. 'The mind can work in strange ways after the kind of thing she suffered. I know.'

Conrad and Millie fell silent. Lord Oakford had come out of the Great War a severely damaged man. His life had changed the day at Passchendaele when he had taken and held a German machine-gun position, won his Victoria Cross, lost his arm, and lost his will to fight. Since then, he had done everything he could to stop war. But also since then he had suffered from occasional bouts of black, angry misery. These Conrad and Millie had grown up with. They had come to learn what triggered these moods, but still they didn't really understand them.

'What should I do, Father? About Anneliese?'

It was a long time since Conrad had asked his father's advice on anything. But he had a feeling that Lord Oakford might know the answer.

'Do you love her?'

'Yes,' said Conrad. 'In fact I asked her to marry me. She turned me down.'

Oakford sipped his water. 'Give her space to sort herself out, Conrad. When she wants you, she'll find you. Just make sure you are available.'

Conrad exchanged glances with Millie. That sounded like good advice, although he wasn't sure he could just let Anneliese go. Once she went to New York he might never see her again and he wasn't sure he could bear that. But what choice did he have?

They ate in silence for a moment or two.

'Conrad?' Oakford said.

'Yes?'

'I know I've asked you before now, but I could use your help.'

'With what, Father?' But Conrad knew. He could see Millie tense up. She was right to do so. There was trouble brewing.

'Can you have a word with Theo for me? About peace.'

'You've asked me before. The answer is still no.'

Lord Oakford had asked Conrad to meet Theo in Switzerland the previous spring, before the outbreak of war. Conrad had refused: he was suspicious of his father's desire for peace at any cost, and was concerned that his meddling would just undermine the British government's attempt finally to stand up to Hitler. It was true that in the end he, Conrad, *had* travelled to Holland to talk to Schämmel about peace, but that was at the British government's behest, not his father's. And that little jaunt hadn't turned out very well.

'We need to stop this war before it really gets going,' Lord Oakford said.

'We need to stop Hitler, you mean.'

'They've all got plans, you know. Churchill wants to invade Norway. The French want to invade Russia. Hitler wants to invade Holland and Belgium. It's only a matter of time before the Luftwaffe comes and starts dropping bombs on London. We've got to stop them, Conrad, all of them. And with your links with the Wehrmacht, you can help us.'

'Father, we're fighting a war,' Conrad said. 'And it's a just war. It's not like the first war where your country fought Mother's country. This is a war between good and evil. Hitler is evil, Father. If he wins, Europe will fall into darkness. He has to lose. We have to beat him.'

'But we have no plans to beat him, do we?' said Oakford. 'Our plan is to sit in France and wait for him to attack us. And when he does it will be like the western front all over again. Except this time there will be tens of thousands of air-raid casualties among civilians in Britain.'

'He won't go away until we beat him,' Conrad said.

'Damn it, Conrad!' Oakford hit his palm on the table. 'It takes two to fight a war. We can end this if we want to.'

'Stop it, both of you!' said Millie.

Both men looked at her.

'Stop it! Father, you know what Conrad's views are. And, Conrad, you know how much Father believes in peace. Neither of you is going to change the other's point of view. But Conrad's going off to fight. And Father is right, a bomb might land on this house, or on the House of Lords. Maybe the Germans will invade Somerset. Maybe we won't see each other again. I couldn't bear it if the last time we ever saw each other ended in a fight. So please do shut up.'

Lord Oakford glared at his impertinent daughter. 'Millie!'

The colour in Millie's cheeks rose, but she held his gaze.

'I'll shut up,' said Conrad. 'Millie's right.'

Oakford turned to his pheasant, stabbing it with his fork. 'I wish you would see sense, Conrad,' he muttered.

Conrad let his father have the last word. But, as far as he was concerned, he *had* seen sense. That was the whole point.

Fifteen

Kensington, London, 11 November

Millie and her father walked briskly along Kensington High Street towards the park. Lord Oakford was in good spirits, which pleasantly surprised Millie. An argument with his son about war and peace was just the kind of thing that could set Lord Oakford off on a week-long bad mood. Added to which, it was Armistice Day, which Millie had feared would only add salt to the wound. No one had mentioned the date yet that morning, although the newspapers had been full of the plan to move the two-minutes' silence to the following day, Sunday, in order not to interrupt war production.

She was glad she had put her foot down at dinner. Although the evening had become uncomfortable, it could have been a lot worse. She hadn't realized until she had said it how aware she had been that this might be their last time together: that something might happen to one or other of them. And she didn't just mean Conrad. It was only then that it had truly sunk in that what she was about to do had its own danger, that she might be the one not to come back. For a moment she could feel the fear enveloping her, but she beat it back. Millie de Lancey was a brave woman, at least as brave as her elder brother.

She hated deceiving him, but she had had no choice. She couldn't tell him she had already found her war work, which was why she was in London.

'Where is Conrad off to?' she asked. 'I assumed he was returning to barracks, but he was a bit evasive. Is his battalion going over to France?'

'Heston Airport. He's flying to Holland to see Theo,' Lord Oakford said.

'No!' That made Millie think. 'Do we still go ahead with our plan?'

'Oh, yes,' said Oakford. 'It will be all right.'

'I hope Conrad never finds out. He would be furious.'

'He won't find out,' said Oakford.

Millie had been excited to help her father. She had been brought up by him as a pacifist, as had Conrad and the other de Lancey children. She understood what her father was trying to do, and thought he was right to do it. But she knew Conrad wouldn't approve at all.

'Here we are.'

They were outside a grand white house just to the south of the park, which had been converted into flats. Lord Oakford rang a bell, a maid answered and they followed her up some stairs to the second floor.

'Lord Oakford and Miss de Lancey, sir,' the maid announced as she led them into a drawing room.

Sir Henry Alston rose to greet them.

Millie repressed a shudder as she took his hand. Alston was a fellow director of her father at Gurney Kroheim, her father's merchant bank. She had met him on a number of occasions before – at dinner parties at Kensington Square and he had been to stay the weekend at Chilton Coombe – yet she had never quite become used to his ravaged face.

'Millie, there's someone I want you to meet.' Alston turned to a pale, dark-haired girl of about Millie's own age.

'Lord Oakford, Millie de Lancey, this is Mrs Scott-Dunton.'

'Constance,' said the girl, holding out her hand to Millie. She was smiling broadly. 'I'm so pleased to meet you. This is going to be quite an adventure.'

Bloomsbury, London

It was easy for Anneliese to identify Bloomsbury House; it was the impressive mansion on the southern side of Bloomsbury Square with the queue of Jews outside it. It reminded her a bit of the British Passport Control Office in the Tiergartenstrasse in Berlin. There the Jews were queuing for visas for Britain or Palestine. Here they were queuing for food, distributed by the Jewish Refugee Committee. Just as Anneliese had managed to slip ahead of the queue in Berlin with Conrad to see Captain Foley, the Passport Control Officer, now too she walked right in, feeling just as guilty. But she had an appointment.

Wilfrid Israel had a tiny office in an upper floor of the building. He had thinning blond hair and blue, tired eyes. His suit was immaculately cut and, despite his fair complexion, he exuded the sophistication of a wealthy Berlin Jew. And he was wealthy, or at least he had been. His family had owned N. Israel, one of the most upmarket department stores in Berlin, until he had been forced to relinquish it to Aryan owners.

'Fräulein Rosen! I'm so pleased to meet you at last,' he said in German, smiling. 'And in safety too. Please. Have a seat.'

'Thank you for agreeing to see me,' said Anneliese. 'And in particular, thank you for getting me out of the camp.' The wife of the commandant of Sachsenhausen concentration camp loved to shop at N. Israel, which had given Wilfrid some influence.

'Not at all,' said Wilfrid. 'Mr de Lancey and Captain Foley were quite insistent.'

'I owe you my life,' Anneliese said. 'As I'm sure do many of the people out there.'

Wilfrid gave a tired smile. 'Yes. But there are so many more back in Germany whom I couldn't help.'

'When did you get out yourself?'

'In the spring. Berlin finally became untenable. How do you find London?'

'It's hard,' said Anneliese. 'My father is a doctor, but they won't allow him to take a job. And my mother is a cleaner.'

'At least you have found something,' Wilfrid said, indicating Anneliese's nurse's uniform.

'Yes, I'm working at St George's Hospital. There are good things about London. My family is safe. And when you bump into a bobby in the street he is more likely to give you directions than lock you up.'

'And they know how to queue.'

'And if you tread on their toes, they apologize.'

Wilfrid laughed. 'But they can be difficult to get to know. Even the English Jews.'

'I thought you were English yourself?' Anneliese said.

'Half-English,' Wilfrid said. 'But I miss Berlin. The old Berlin.'

'Before the Nazis came,' said Anneliese.

Wilfrid nodded. Then he checked his watch. 'Anyway, what can I do for you Fräulein Rosen?'

'I wanted to see if you could help me find some work.'

Wilfrid's expression became more businesslike. 'I'm afraid we employ all the people we can already here. And besides, I can see that you have a worthwhile job already. Unlike most of the people out there.'

'No, not working here,' said Anneliese. 'Doing something for the war effort. Against the Nazis.'

Wilfrid raised his eyebrows. 'And how would I be able to help you with that?'

'Perhaps through Captain Foley?' said Anneliese. 'I did help him with some secret work once in Berlin.' She had persuaded her uncle, who worked for an aeroplane manufacturer, to pass plans of a new fighter plane to the British. Conrad had suggested it as a way of encouraging Foley to issue her father a visa for Britain. 'I could do it again. I speak German, obviously. I am willing to take risks. And I need to *do* something, anything, to stop Hitler.'

Wilfrid hesitated, and then smiled. 'All right, I can ask Captain Foley when I next see him. He's stationed abroad at the moment, but we do see each other when he is back in London. I can't think what you would do for him, but he took quite a shine to you in Berlin.'

'Thank you, Herr Israel. I won't take up any more of your time.'

Anneliese had a spring in her step as she made her way back towards Goodge Street tube station and the Northern Line. The idea of trying to do something herself to fight the Nazis had come to her after she had seen Conrad. She had no idea where he was going, but he had said he was planning to see Theo. Which meant he was doing something to actively oppose Hitler. Something more direct than simply joining the army and training in the English countryside.

Anneliese couldn't join the army in an active role, and there was no doubt that being a nurse was helping the war effort, even if at this stage of the war she was dealing with traffic-accident victims rather than air-raid casualties. But now, for the first time since she had arrived in England, she saw a point to life, rather than mere survival.

If only Captain Foley would take her on.

She had suffered a lot in her twenty-eight years. When Hitler had come to power, she had been a medical student at the University of Halle. She and her boyfriend had taken to the streets to protest. They had both been arrested and despatched to concentration camps; she came out after six months, his ashes after two years. Then her father had been locked up for giving his Jewish blood in an emergency transfusion to an Aryan casualty. Desperate to get him out, she had begun an affair with Klaus, a former university friend who had joined the Gestapo. That had not ended well. But somehow, in Berlin, she had always found the resilience to battle on.

In London, things were different. The grey misery of the city, of her family situation, of the loss of the Germany that she loved had borne down heavily on her. She also felt a burden of guilt. It was irrational, but she couldn't make it go away. She felt guilty about her affair with Klaus. Guilty that she and her family had escaped when millions of other Jews were left in Germany to take their chances.

And she felt guilty about Conrad. About betraying him with Klaus. About her own feebleness. About dragging him down with her. She couldn't marry him. He came from a wealthy aristocratic British family. She was, now, a penniless, worthless Jew. Who had deceived him. Who had run away from her country.

She knew he loved her. And she loved him, that was the worst part. That was why she didn't want to drag him down with her. She remembered how in Berlin he had accused her of using her relationship with him to get her father out of jail, in the way she had used Klaus. He had been right.

She had tried to explain all this to him, but he hadn't understood. Sometimes, often, she thought: Why don't I just say yes and marry him? In the old days, she might have done – she would have done. But now? When she had first been locked up in Moringen in 1933, she had coped well mentally. But after Klaus had discovered her affair with Conrad, he had had her arrested. The solitary confinement in Sachsenhausen and then in Lichtenburg Castle had finally broken her spirit.

Conrad couldn't help her now; she was beyond help. He would lead a much better life without her. She could at least give him that; it was all she could give him.

Life was a miserable grind, with no end in sight, which was why she had persuaded her parents to go to New York. America was the country for fresh starts. Yet it was proving extremely hard to get in, and even the process of trying was making her feel guilty. There were so many Jews in Germany and Austria whose need was greater.

But if she could do something for Captain Foley or one of his colleagues in the secret service, maybe there would be some point to her life after all.

Sixteen

Leiden

The bus from Schiphol Airport dropped Conrad by the railway station, and he walked towards the centre of the town, passing canals, barges and a couple of windmills along the way. He was looking forward to seeing Theo, to finding out what the hell had happened at Venlo.

On the bumpy flight over the North Sea, he had mulled over what his father had said to him the night before. The argument over peace or war had been inevitable, but it rattled him, nonetheless. He wished that somehow he could get his father to see his point of view.

Lady Oakford always said that of all her children, Conrad was most like her husband. As a boy he had always been proud of that, because he was proud of his father. There could be no better badge of distinction in the post-war years than a Victoria Cross. But it wasn't just that; there was bravery in Lord Oakford's pacifism, in his willingness to take on a cause that was unpopular with his contemporaries and to pursue it no matter what. Lord Oakford had principles, and so did his son. And in Spain Conrad had discovered that he had bravery, or at least the ability to channel his fear into a spur to defeat the enemy and protect his comrades. When Conrad had voted against the motion that he would fight for King and Country at that infamous debate in 1933, he knew his father was proud of him; he could almost feel the old soldier standing there at his shoulder in the Union.

Then things had gone wrong. Lord Oakford had never really liked Veronica and had disapproved of their marriage. He had certainly disapproved of Conrad's decision to go and fight in Spain, and then to join the British Army. His father had been right about Veronica. He may also have been right about Spain: although Conrad had no doubts about opposing Franco, he had seen the government forces undermined by Soviet commissars. David Griffiths and Harry Reilly had both taken bullets in the back while they were storming Mosquito Hill, bullets from a Popular Army unit with Russian commissars.

But Conrad was damned sure his father was wrong about appeasing Hitler.

Then there was Anneliese. Was his father right or wrong about her? Perhaps she didn't need Conrad after all, at least not for a while. But he hated the idea of abandoning her when she seemed so desperate.

He had no idea what to do.

He turned into the Rapenburg, a canal flanked by old university buildings. It was a Saturday, so the student bicycle count was down on his previous visit, but they still buzzed about him. The sun shone low over the gables, glinting off the still water of the canal and the damp orange leaves on the street running along its edge.

The Academy was easy to spot, a lofty hall that had the appearance of a red-brick religious building from the seventeenth century, guarded by high iron gates. Conrad walked past and then doubled back, checking for watchers. He couldn't see any, but then he wasn't a professional and they probably would be. Somehow he doubted that in its present circumstances the British secret service in The Hague, or what was left of it, would have decided that following Conrad was its chief priority, but perhaps the Gestapo would be on his trail. He had no idea: he would have to rely on Theo.

He walked through the iron gates and stopped at what looked like a porter's lodge. The porter didn't speak English but was expecting him. He led him up some ancient stairs and showed him into a small room with nothing but a table and four chairs in its centre. The porter shut the door behind him.

There was something about the proportions of the room that reminded Conrad of a cell. He was drawn to the table, which was made of old gnarled wood and covered with carvings, initials and dates. He examined them: the oldest he could see was 1641. The walls, too, were almost entirely covered with signatures from floor to ceiling.

Was this some kind of bizarre interrogation room? Was he going to be grilled by the Dutch secret police? Conrad shuddered as he remembered the night he had spent in the basement of the Gestapo headquarters on Prinz-Albrecht-Strasse, with its own sad graffiti. His thoughts turned to Payne Best and Stevens, and Klop if he was still alive.

After five minutes the door opened and a short man with thick dark hair, a full greying moustache, and a waistcoat and watch chain bustled in.

'Mr de Lancey? I am Professor Hogendoorn.' The man gave a sort of high-pitched giggle as he held out his hand. 'Do you speak German, by any chance? My English is not so good.'

'Certainly,' said Conrad in that language.

'Excellent,' said the professor. 'I hope you don't mind waiting here.' The professor giggled again. 'It's known as "The Sweatbox". It's where the students wait before they defend their theses in the room next door. As you can see they carve their initials while they are at it. It seemed a proper place for a spy to wait.' Another giggle. 'More importantly, it's empty and we cannot be overheard.'

'I'm not exactly a spy,' said Conrad, stifling his irritation.

'No, of course not. Herr von Hertenberg said you were an academic from Oxford University, a historian. But I think if anyone here asks you, you should say you are a chemist. Polymers. That's my speciality.'

'I will do that,' said Conrad. 'Now, how do I meet Herr von Hertenberg?'

Professor Hogendoorn ignored the question. 'It's good to meet an Englishman who appreciates modern Germany. But are you English? De Lancey sounds French to me.'

'Huguenot,' said Conrad. 'My ancestors fled France a couple of hundred years ago. One of them fought at Waterloo, but not on the French side.'

'Very wise of them,' said the professor. 'France's democracy is even more decayed than England's. As a scientist, it is clear to me that Germany represents the future. Strength, efficiency, progress. We Dutch should realize that. We are not so different from the Germans. We have the scientific knowledge. We should be their partners, not their enemy. Don't you agree, Herr de Lancey?'

'Absolutely,' said Conrad, wanting to shut him up. 'Herr von Hertenberg?'

'Ah, yes. You should go downstairs, go through the arch into the Botanical Gardens and walk on until you get to the observatory. Turn around and walk back here. If you are not being followed, Herr von Hertenberg will approach you. If you don't see him, it's because Herr von Hertenberg has spotted something, so return here tomorrow morning and we will have a different plan.'

He led Conrad down the stairs to the entrance to the building, and shook his hand. 'I don't know what you are up to, but whatever it is, I wish you luck.'

Slightly disconcerted by his brush with the professor, Conrad strolled through an arch into a courtyard, which had been turned into a formal garden of square plots of tiny hedges, in each of which were plants and labels. Given the time of year, most of the plants were brown and stunted or slumbering underground. Conrad continued on beside a large tropical glasshouse to a canal lined with sycamores. There were half a dozen people nosing around the gardens: a young couple lost in conversation with each other; three women bending down and pointing; a couple of other lone strollers. Conrad couldn't see Theo.

He walked along the canal as far as a grand white building with domes sprouting from its roof: the observatory, no doubt. He stopped, turned around and headed back. Unlike other canals in Leiden, this one wasn't straight, but seemed to bend, with green space on either side. Conrad speculated it was a moat around the old town.

And there was Theo, sitting on a bench, hunched in a coat. Conrad sat down next to him.

'I'm glad to see you,' said Theo. 'I was worried about you when I heard what had happened at Venlo. I knew you hadn't been captured, so at first I thought they must have shot you. You were the chauffeur, presumably?'

'Yes, I was,' said Conrad. 'I slipped away. What about the man who was shot?'

'He died. He was a Dutch officer, apparently.'

'I know. I'm sorry to hear that. What the hell happened, Theo?'

'Schämmel was a plant. The SD were running the operation.'

Conrad remembered that 'SD' stood for Sicherheitsdienst, but he was hazy about the intricacies of the Nazi security hierarchy. 'The Gestapo?'

'More or less. The plan was to use Schämmel as bait to try to uncover any conspirators in Germany who had been talking to the British. As soon as I found out I came back here to try to warn you, but it was too late.'

'I did get your message, but we were just setting off for Venlo,' said Conrad. 'If that's what they were up to, why did they kidnap Payne Best and Stevens?'

'A last-minute change of plan,' said Theo. 'Hitler is convinced that the British organized the beer hall bomb in Munich, and that those two British agents were behind it.'

'They weren't,' said Conrad.

'We know that,' said Theo. 'But it's never a good idea to tell the Führer he is wrong.'

'I can imagine,' said Conrad. 'Do you know whether Payne Best and Stevens have talked?'

'Not yet,' said Theo. 'But they will. The Gestapo have found a list of names on one of them. They passed them on to us: some of them we recognize as Dutch agents in Holland working for the British. But I have a question for you, Conrad.'

'Yes?'

'Did you ever meet Schämmel yourself?'

'No. Thursday at Venlo would have been the first time.'

'Which means he didn't get any information about us from you?'

'No.'

'What about Payne Best and Stevens? Did they know anything about the real conspirators?'

'No. Nothing at all. They asked me, but I refused to tell them.'

'Good. So they don't know anything about me?'

'Damn!' Conrad glanced anxiously at Theo. 'They do. They had me followed in Leiden last time we met. Stevens asked me what I was doing talking to you. He knew who you were, he knew you worked for the Abwehr.'

Theo frowned. 'And what did you tell him?'

'I refused to tell him anything. Apart from to check with Captain Foley.'

'Damn and blast!' said Theo. 'I *knew* you were the weak link.' He looked angry. And worried. 'Do you know if Stevens has spoken to Foley?'

'He won't have had a chance to,' said Conrad. 'All this came out on the way to Venlo.'

'That's something, anyway,' said Theo.

'Sorry,' said Conrad. 'Are you afraid Stevens will tell the Gestapo about you?'

'Eventually, yes. At the moment the Gestapo are trying to get them to confess to planning the Munich beer hall bomb.'

'Poor bastards,' said Conrad.

'They will talk in time.'

They fell silent as the young couple sauntered past. A pair of swans glided along the canal. It reminded Conrad a little of the Cherwell back in Oxford. He wondered about the bend in the waterway. 'Was this a moat once, do you think, Theo?'

'Yes. They call it the Singel. There is one in Amsterdam, you know.'

'You are quite the Dutch expert.'

'It's the place to be, these days, in our business.'

'Your business,' said Conrad. The couple were safely past. 'So if it wasn't the British who planted the bomb, who was it?'

'They've arrested someone at the Swiss border. We are pretty sure he is responsible. What we don't know is who he was working for, if anyone.'

'So it wasn't you chaps? Canaris and Oster?'

'Definitely not. The current favourite theory in the Abwehr is it was a set-up. The Gestapo. It was pretty extraordinary that Hitler just happened to leave ten minutes before the bomb went off. He's calling it Providence. Interesting how he uses the word "Providence" rather than "God", isn't it? It's almost as if even he can't believe that God would be on his side.'

Conrad could feel one of Theo's philosophical digressions coming on, but he wasn't in the mood. 'What about the invasion of Holland and Belgium next week? Is that still going ahead?'

'The weather forecast isn't good. Halder is trying to persuade Hitler to postpone.'

'So there won't be a coup, after all?'

'I don't know,' said Theo. 'This Venlo business has rattled them. I hope they hold their nerve. But that's all it is, just hope.'

Conrad could sense Theo's impatience. The year before, his friend had risked his life to stop Hitler; they both had. It was understandable that he should be frustrated by a lack of courage from the men who were supposed to lead him.

A frustrated spy. A frustrated enemy spy.

'Who is Charles Bedaux, Theo?'

Theo, who had been staring at the swans, turned sharply to Conrad. 'How do you know about Bedaux?'

'Stevens told me. He said that you had been meeting him in Holland. He said he was a shady American businessman who lives in France.'

'He is,' said Theo.

'Does he have anything to do with Schämmel?' Conrad asked.

'Nothing at all,' said Theo.

They sat in silence for a few moments. Conrad's instinct was to wait. Let his friend think.

'You know I'm an Abwehr officer?' Theo said eventually.

'Yes,' said Conrad.

'So most of my job is to try to uncover British secrets and to use them to help Germany win the war?'

'Yes,' said Conrad again. There was something in Theo's voice which told him to shut up and listen.

Theo sucked his lip. 'Sometimes I wonder if that would be a good thing.'

'What would be a good thing?'

'That Germany win the war.'

Conrad nodded. He knew how important that statement was to Theo. Because even when Theo was at his most rebellious, even when he was declaiming socialist theories to his fellow undergraduates, his patriotism was at his core. It was his duty to serve his country, as it had been for all his ancestors.

'If Hitler beats the British and the French, then Germany will rule Europe and there really might be a thousand-year Reich. And that would be a disaster for the human race. For the Germans as well as all the other peoples we will have subjugated.'

'You're right. It would.'

'Someone needs to investigate Charles Bedaux, Conrad.'

'All right,' said Conrad. 'I will tell the secret service when I get back to England.'

'Not your secret service,' said Theo. 'Someone else. You.'

'Me?' Conrad shook his head. 'Don't be ridiculous. I'm an officer in the British Army. A real soldier, not some spy. What's wrong with the secret service? It's not entirely compromised, is it? I thought it was just The Hague?'

'No, it's not that. It's something else. You have to trust me on this.'

'Why?'

'Because if someone doesn't do something pretty soon, you

are going to lose this war.'

'What? How?'

'Check out Bedaux and you will find out.'

'Theo, stop playing games! Tell me what's going on here.'

'No!' Theo's vehemence startled Conrad. 'I'm not playing games. If I tell you all of what I know, then you will have to tell the authorities in Britain and I will be betraying my country. Instead of that I would prefer to point you in the right direction and leave you to discover what you are going to discover.'

Conrad was tempted to ask Theo if that wasn't betraying his country anyway, but he kept quiet. Theo had carefully drawn a line for himself beyond which he would not go. Conrad didn't want him to change his mind and redraw that line.

'It's going to be difficult for me as a serving officer,' said Conrad.

'You'll work out a way,' said Theo. 'I know you.'

Conrad frowned. How would he clear it with Van? How could he persuade Van, or even himself, that the best thing wasn't just to tell Major McCaigue and let the secret service get on with it?

Theo seemed to read his mind. 'You have to trust me on this, Conrad. Investigate Bedaux yourself. Find out what he is up to. And stop him.'

Conrad sat on the bench by the 'Singel' for twenty minutes, while Theo went wherever Theo was going.

Conrad had obtained clear answers to Van's questions. He was booked on a flight back to London at noon the following day. All he had to do was kill time until then. He had left his small suitcase at the station luggage office, postponing the decision about where he stayed the night.

But what about Charles Bedaux?

Conrad and Theo had been through a lot together. Theo had a cool head and sound judgement. If he said Bedaux should be investigated, he should be investigated. In theory this could be some clever Abwehr stratagem to waste the British secret service's time. Perhaps feed them dud information. Mislead them. Yet Theo had insisted that Conrad look into Bedaux himself, and not tell the secret service.

It could be a fiendishly clever bluff or double bluff. Conrad knew enough about Admiral Canaris to know he was capable of all sorts of devious tricks.

But Conrad knew Theo wasn't bluffing him. In fact, Conrad was pretty sure that the Abwehr wouldn't approve of what Theo had just told him.

So he had to trust Theo. Then what?

Conrad stood up and made his way out of the Botanical Gardens, through the Academy's iron gates, and out into the street. He crossed a little bridge over the canal and wandered through a maze of old back alleys and red-brick courtyards.

The more he thought about it, the more sure he became that he had to find out about Charles Bedaux. And he had to do it soon, because once he returned to London, he would be sent back to his battalion. There would be little he could do stuck in Tidworth.

Where to start? Conrad checked his watch. It was just after four o'clock. Conrad had spent several years researching obscure historical subjects in libraries in Oxford, London, Berlin and Copenhagen. He needed a library.

He doubled back to the Rapenburg, and a building he had spotted earlier, on the other side of the canal from the Academy. Sure enough, it was the university library, and fortunately it was open on Saturday, but only until five o'clock.

He found a friendly librarian who spoke German and just had time to locate a couple of Dutch business directories. There was an Internationale Bedaux NV listed at Spuistraat 210 in Amsterdam. The business was marked 'Management Consulting'.

Conrad headed back to the station to catch a train to Amsterdam.

Seventeen

Scheveningen, Holland, 12 November

The breeze skipped in from the North Sea, plucking at Constance and Millie's dresses as they walked along the Promenade. There were a few hardy Dutch couples taking some fresh air on a Sunday afternoon, but not many. The Kurhaus, the grand hotel overlooking the beach and pier where the two women were staying, was almost empty. Scheveningen in November was not a popular place.

The customs officer at the airport had given the women a strange look when they had told him they were going for a few days' holiday by the sea. Scheveningen had seemed a good idea to Lord Oakford and Millie. Millie was familiar with the town – Lady Oakford had fond memories of the place from her own childhood, and the family had spent two summer holidays there when Millie was small. Also, it was only a couple of kilometres from The Hague.

The perfect place to meet Theo.

'This is rather exciting, isn't it?' said Constance, threading her arm through Millie's. 'What's this Theo man like? Describe him to me.'

'He's tall. Dark hair. He has a scar running along his jaw.'

'How did he get that?' asked Constance.

'A duel when he was a student, I think,' said Millie.

'A duel? At Oxford? With pistols?'

'No. At Heidelberg. With a sabre, I should imagine. That kind of German does that sort of thing at university. They think it's terribly smart to have a face cut up like a pineapple. At least Theo has only the one scar.'

'It sounds rather dashing.'

'Perhaps,' said Millie. 'Or stupid.'

'When you say "that kind of German", what do you mean?'

'Oh, you know, a Prussian aristocrat. They don't do that sort of thing quite so much in Hamburg, where my family comes from.'

'Is he frightfully good-looking?'

Millie hesitated. She could feel herself blushing. 'I suppose he is.'

'I thought so!'

'Thought what?' said Millie.

'Thought you were sweet on him. Don't deny it, I can tell. Don't worry, I won't get in the way.'

Millie didn't deny it. She had first met Theo when he had visited their house in Somerset when she was fifteen and Theo had been the impossibly glamorous friend of her elder brother. But then she had seen him again in the woods around the Grunewald in Berlin the year before, while delivering a secret message from the British government to Conrad. He was still glamorous and good-looking, with a roguish charm, but this time she could see from the first glance he gave her that she had made an impression on him.

Then in April her father had asked her to meet him again, in Zurich this time. Conrad had refused to go; he didn't trust his father to negotiate behind the British government's back. Lord Oakford couldn't risk being seen with a young German officer in Switzerland, but Millie could. And did.

She had spent a week there conducting negotiations through Theo on behalf of Lord Oakford. At that stage, Theo and the people whom he represented, meaning Admiral Canaris and his colleagues, wanted peace, as of course did Lord Oakford and Millie. The negotiations hadn't come to anything; Oakford couldn't get Lord Halifax to bend, and Canaris had no real influence over Hitler. But Oakford thought them worthwhile because of the direct channel he had opened with the plotters, if they ever did succeed in getting rid of their Führer.

And Millie had spent a whole week, a wonderful week, with Theo. Much of the time was passed waiting for responses from England. They had taken the train from Zurich up to the Walensee or to Zug, and gone for long walks through Alpine meadows. They had spent a magical day wandering around the old abbey at St Gall, where Theo had told her about Notker the Stammerer, a medieval monk with a vivid imagination and plenty of ribald stories about Charlemagne. Theo was a fascinating man; although he was arrogant, with a tendency to patronize, he did listen to what she had to say. He made her think: about politics, about history, about her family. And most of all about herself.

After that, they had sent frequent letters to each other. Once war had broken out, Theo had come up with an address in Denmark she could use. And in a few minutes, she would see him again, continuing her mission where they had left it six months before.

None of which Conrad knew anything about.

They were approaching the harbour. No longer did they encounter the good burghers of The Hague in their Sunday best suits; now rougher-dressed fishermen and their women in black shawls and white lace caps, each fastened with two prominent buckles, were enjoying their day of rest. The latest craze among the children seemed to be rolling bicycle wheels along the street with sticks.

Since it was a Sunday, the fishing fleet was crammed into port, and the wind made a racket as it strummed the rigging of the sailing vessels. Millie remembered them from her childhood: they had made quite a sight in full sail setting out to sea to scoop up herring.

Whereas most of the cafés on the promenade had been closed for the winter, down by the harbour they were bustling. They found their café, secured the last table, and ordered some coffee in German. Most of the other patrons were local fishermen.

'Where is he?' whispered Constance.

'He'll be here soon,' said Millie.

Constance looked around the café. 'Shall we blend in? Do you think they can tell we are foreign?'

'I think they can,' said Millie. 'But that's all right. Plenty of foreigners come here in the summer.'

'Do they have Jews in Holland?' Constance asked.

'I think there are rather a lot of them,' Millie said.

'That's strange. I haven't seen any,' Constance said.

'How do you know?' asked Millie.

'Oh, I can tell.'

Millie glanced sharply at her companion. 'Don't you like Jews, Constance?'

Constance hesitated with her response. 'I am sure there are many perfectly decent Jews,' she said primly.

'There are,' said Millie. 'In fact, my brother is engaged to one.' She was exaggerating a little, Anneliese wasn't exactly a Jew and she and Conrad were not exactly engaged, but Millie liked Anneliese and she disliked the casual anti-Semitism of so many English people. What she really objected to was the way it seemed to have become more frequent since refugees had begun to arrive from Germany, Czechoslovakia and Austria.

'Your brother is a socialist, isn't he?' Constance said.

'What's that got to do with it?' said Millie.

'Oh, nothing. Nothing at all,' Constance said with a smile. 'Look, I'm sorry, Millie. I am sure there are all sorts of decent socialists too. Really, politics isn't my thing.'

Millie wasn't entirely convinced. If that really was the case, why had Sir Henry Alston chosen her to accompany Millie? It was true that Millie did need *someone* to accompany her to Holland, and that Constance was game for any adventure, yet she seemed terribly innocent and naive. Not a natural person to select for a part in complicated diplomatic negotiations. But she had proven herself a jolly travelling companion so far, and perhaps it was better that Millie be left to deal with the discussions herself.

'Millie!'

Millie looked up to see Theo standing over their table. The sight of him made her heart skip, and she could feel her face flush. She got to her feet. Theo reached for her hand, and in her confusion she thought he was going shake it, rather than hold it to his lips with good old-fashioned German courtesy.

'This is Constance Scott-Dunton,' Millie said.

She saw a flicker of interest in Theo's eyes as he turned to her companion and kissed her hand as well. A preposterous surge of jealousy flashed through Millie's veins. Constance was attractive, there was no doubt about that, but she was also an idiot. There was no chance that Theo, with his intellectual depths, would be interested in her. Besides which, Constance was married. She had prattled on at length about her glamorous husband Peter who was serving on a cruiser somewhere in the Atlantic Ocean.

'Would you like some coffee, Theo?' Millie asked, chastising herself for being so foolish.

'I would love some,' said Theo. They were speaking English: Theo was fluent, of course. 'And I like the look of those cakes over there.'

They talked politely of the women's journey, Millie confessing that she had been sick in the aeroplane, and also that she had been terrified of being shot down by German fighters.

'Isn't it good to be in a neutral country, though?' said Theo. 'Here people aren't afraid of being bombed at any time. Or not yet.'

'Do you think Holland will be brought into the war?' asked Constance.

Theo hesitated.

'You can speak to Constance as to me,' said Millie. 'My father chose her to accompany me. He trusts her.'

As she said it, she wasn't absolutely certain that was true. But she knew that her father trusted Sir Henry Alston, and it was clear that Alston trusted Constance, even if Millie herself wasn't quite sure that was wise.

'Well, Mrs Scott-Dunton, I believe it likely that Holland will be drawn in sooner or later.'

'Ooh. Is your army planning to invade?' asked Constance with a lack of subtlety that appalled Millie.

Theo waited to reply as a waitress delivered some cakes. 'I can't really answer that question. I'm sure you understand.'

'That's a shame,' said Constance.

Theo smiled quickly. 'Well, Millie, I presume you have a message for me from your father?'

Millie reached into her bag and withdrew a plain envelope, which she handed to Theo. He opened it and pulled out a two-page letter. 'Should I read this now?'

Millie nodded, and watched as Theo scanned the note. Millie had read it herself and discussed it in detail with her father. It said that since Britain was at war with Germany, it was very difficult for the British government to negotiate directly with the leaders of a possible replacement regime to Hitler's, should Hitler retire suddenly. But, it went on, Lord Oakford was confident that should a new German government wish to discuss peace terms, then he, personally, would ensure they would have a sympathetic hearing from the British Cabinet, a much more sympathetic hearing than they had received the year before.

'My father asked me to add a couple of things,' Millie said. 'He knows about the talks between Captain Schämmel and British representatives here in Holland, and he says that the Cabinet was prepared to take Schämmel seriously, before they found out he was a fraud. He is a fraud, isn't he?'

'Oh, yes. He's a Gestapo agent.' Theo glanced at Millie. 'You know what happened at Venlo? Your brother was there.'

'I know. I saw Conrad in London a couple of days ago. Apparently he's trying to meet you here.'

'He succeeded,' said Theo. 'I spoke to him yesterday. He doesn't know you are here, does he?'

'Oh, no. And please don't tell him. He would be furious if he found out.'

'I'm sure he would,' said Theo dryly. 'What would you like me to do with this?'

'Can you show it to your friends? I'll wait for a response.'

Theo examined the letter again, nodded, folded it, and put it in his breast pocket. 'I will do as you ask.'

'Thank you,' said Millie, finishing her coffee. 'We'll be here. We're staying at the Kurhaus.'

'I'll walk part of the way back with you,' Theo said.

Millie couldn't help grinning.

Constance noticed. 'Look here. I think I'll just have a root around the harbour for a bit, and then take a stroll through the town. I'll meet you back at the hotel later, Millie.'

'Right oh,' said Millie, thinking that Constance wasn't so stupid after all.

They left the café and Millie took Theo's arm. He led her along the harbour wall past the long line of boats. The wind had picked up and Millie pulled herself close against Theo for protection. There was a strong smell of fish, coming from the boats themselves and the nets neatly stacked on the quay. Three or four hardy seagulls battled against the breeze, searching out scraps of fish that they might have missed from the day before, their cries snatched from their beaks by the wind.

'It's nice to see you again, Millie,' Theo said. 'I've missed you.'

'And me you,' said Millie. 'Thank you for your letters. It's horrid to think we are at war now.'

'Very horrid,' said Theo.

'Are you staying in The Hague?'

'I was last night. But now I will have to fly back to Berlin to discuss this letter. I should be back soon, perhaps the day after tomorrow.'

'That's a shame. I was rather hoping you would be able to stay here while we waited. Like we did in Zurich.'

'I wish I could,' said Theo. They were coming to the end of the wall by the small lighthouse. They looked back along the narrow strip of sand, grey rather than yellow in the gloomy November light. The grandly decorated Kurhaus with its distinctive dome preened itself behind the beach, and a little beyond that, the pier jabbed out into the sea.

'Last time I was here they still had bathing machines,' Millie said. 'Do you remember those?'

'You came here as a girl?'

'For a couple of summers. It was fun. I loved the seaside, and it brought back memories for Mother, who used to come here herself when she was little.'

'Now beaches are for fighting on,' Theo said.

'They are putting up all sorts of gruesome things on ours,' Millie said. 'Oh, I probably shouldn't tell you that. Since you are a spy.'

'I will send a message to Berlin by carrier seagull immediately. I just need to catch one.'

'I think you will find the seagulls here are on our side,' said Millie. 'They have flown in from Suffolk.'

One of the birds a few yards from them squawked, wheeled and was swept back towards the town.

'Sounded Dutch to me,' said Theo.

Millie was tall, but she looked up at Theo. His cheeks were red in the wind, his dark hair flopping over his forehead. She had a strong desire to kiss him. He bent towards her.

And she turned away.

Theo stood back abruptly, stiffening. It was as if a wave of awkwardness had burst over them and the sea wall.

A wave Millie was determined to brush off. She turned back to Theo and reached for his hand. 'I'm sorry,' she said, squeezing it. 'I just think I shouldn't kiss a German spy.'

Theo grinned, taking the opportunity to lighten the mood. 'I suppose it's not very patriotic. But we are allowed to enjoy each other's company, aren't we?'

'Oh, yes,' said Millie. 'We are.' And she left her hand in his.

Amsterdam

Spuistraat 210 turned out to be a stylish modern building called the 'Bungehuis' in the centre of Amsterdam. Bedaux International

118

occupied the second floor. Conrad approached the young woman behind the desk in the reception area and asked her if she spoke English.

'Yes, certainly I do. How can I help you, sir?'

'My name is de Lancey. I work for a merchant bank in London, Gurney Kroheim, you may have heard of us?'

The woman shook her head.

'Ah, well. I am visiting the Netherlands on business. A colleague asked if I would drop by and collect some information on your company. Do you have some brochures, by any chance?'

The woman smiled. 'One moment, sir, take a seat.'

Conrad sat in the waiting area and listened as the receptionist spoke rapid Dutch on the phone to someone. Fortunately there was a pile of brochures on the table in English, Dutch, German and French. Conrad grabbed one and began to scan it. It extolled the 'Bedaux System', which seemed to be a scheme that improved factory productivity. There were photographs of cheerful workers in Holland, France and Britain. There were graphs. And there was a photograph of a short burly man with shiny dark hair brushed back and large jug ears, smiling as he shook the hand of a French company chairman.

Charles Bedaux.

'Mr de Lancey?'

Conrad looked up to see a slim woman of about forty wearing a dark suit.

'My name is Mrs ter Hart. I am the General Manager of this office. Can I help you?' Her English was good; her accent, though slight, sounded to Conrad's acute ear more Eastern European than Dutch.

Conrad rose and shook the woman's hand. 'Ah, yes. I work for Gurney Kroheim in London,' he began, hoping that Bedaux International was not an existing client of his father's bank.

'I know it,' she said.

'Good, good. I was in Amsterdam seeing a couple of the bank's clients, and one of my colleagues asked me to pick up information on Bedaux International.' Conrad held up the brochure. 'This looks very useful. Do you mind if I keep it?'

'Not at all,' said Mrs ter Hart. 'Do you know why your colleague is interested in our firm?'

'Not absolutely sure, no,' said Conrad. 'I think he's interested in the Bedaux System.'

'Yes?'

'Yes.'

Mrs ter Hart was beginning to look suspicious. Keep it vague, Conrad told himself.

'The system is usually implemented in factories not banks,' said Mrs ter Hart. 'It can often double productivity.'

'So I have heard,' said Conrad. 'I think my colleague wants to see whether it can be applied to some of the more repetitive tasks that go on in a bank. He would like to discuss it with Mr Bedaux directly. Where is he? Is he here?'

'That would be a novel application of the system,' said Mrs ter Hart sternly. Then she seemed to consider the proposition. 'Mr Bedaux is always very busy, but he likes novel ideas. He visits Amsterdam fairly frequently, and London occasionally. But he is based in Paris, as I am sure you know.'

'Do you have his address there?'

The Dutchwoman picked up the French brochure and handed it to Conrad. 'It's on the back page.'

'Thank you, Mrs ter Hart,' said Conrad, deciding to make his escape before he put his foot in it.

'Not at all,' said the woman. 'By the way, what is your colleague's name?'

Conrad searched for the name of an employee at Gurney Kroheim, but all he could come up with was a couple of the directors, friends of his father. 'Alston,' he said. 'Henry Alston.'

Mrs ter Hart nodded. She produced a card.

Conrad took it and smiled. 'I'm afraid I have given all mine away this trip. Thank you so much.' He left, clutching the brochures.

He found a café by a canal around the corner from Bedaux's

office. The canal was called 'Singel', just like the one in Leiden. No wonder Theo knew of its existence in Amsterdam if it was so close to the mysterious Bedaux International.

Conrad had three hours until his flight left back to London. He had found out a little about Charles Bedaux. The American ran a very successful international management-consulting business with offices all over Europe. He was based in Paris. And he had big sticking-out ears.

A start, but nothing to indicate why he could possibly be as important to the outcome of the war as Theo implied.

If Conrad went back to London, that was where his enquiries would end. He might be able to find out a little more about Charles Bedaux from friends of friends in business, but to investigate the man properly he needed to go to Paris. And the only time he could do that was right now.

He asked the waiter where the nearest post office was. It was only a few minutes' walk away, just behind the royal palace. It took a while, but eventually his call was put through to Sir Robert Vansittart in London.

Van sounded harassed, but eager to speak to Conrad. 'Any luck?'

Conrad remembered Van's instructions not to be too specific on the telephone in case of listeners. Which, in this case, was very fortunate.

'Yes, I would say so. It turns out our man was a fraud.'

'Are you certain?'

'Quite certain. Our friends haven't had a chance to chat with their hosts much, but it's likely they will eventually. The shopping list was found.'

'I see. What about the beer?'

Conrad smiled at Van's reference to the beer hall bomb. 'No idea who spilled it.' He thought a moment. 'My old friend thinks it was the publican, but that's just speculation.'

'The publican? I think I know to whom you refer. It sounds odd. You are suggesting they spilled it on purpose?'

'That's what my old friend guesses.' Conrad thought he had done a pretty good job of conveying Theo's answers to Van.

'You are flying home today, are you not? Come and see me straight from the airport and you can brief me directly.'

'That might be difficult,' said Conrad. 'The thing is, I need to go to Paris this afternoon.'

'Paris? For what purpose?'

'Something my old friend told me. Difficult to discuss over the telephone. But I can explain everything when I get back to London.'

It was unlikely that concern over Conrad's absence from his unit was high on Van's list of priorities.

It wasn't. 'All right,' Van said. 'How long will you be?'

'Not sure,' said Conrad. 'Two or three days.'

'Be sure to report back here when you return.' With that Van hung up to turn to more important matters of state.

Berlin

There was a spring in Theo's step as he made his way down the Kurfürstendamm. The moon peeked out behind clouds, giving the street a dim, blue, illicit glow. In the blackout, the Ku'damm had lost its bright lights and its glitter, but the pavement was crowded and there was an air of tense excitement, of danger, of pleasure snatched in wartime, which Theo found exhilarating.

He needed cheering up. He had flown in to Tempelhof from Schiphol and delivered Lord Oakford's message directly to Colonel Oster. There he had learned that the offensive on the western front had been postponed, and as a result General Halder had ordered all plans for the coup to be burned. A wave of disappointment had washed over Theo. He had known it all along: the general was a damned coward. All the generals were cowards.

But tonight Theo was going to enjoy himself.

He grinned at the image of the familiar cockatoo, drunk but happy on its sign above the doorway, and descended some steps.

Inside, the Kakadu was doing great business. The trademark barmaids – brunettes alternating with blondes – were having trouble keeping to their pattern behind the bar. Theo winked at Mitzi, one of the Kakadu's *Eintanzers*, wearing a typically absurd dress that laid bare her smooth pale flesh in all kinds of unexpected places. Heinie got him a table, not too far from the floor, and he ordered a bottle of ersatz champagne, a kind of fizzy alcoholic apple juice.

Theo lit a cigarette and examined the crowd. Plenty of uniforms: the grey-green of the Wehrmacht, like his own, the blue of the Luftwaffe and the occasional black of the SS. And there were girls. Lots of beautiful girls, doing their bit to encourage their fighting men.

He could feel her coming. There was a lull in the conversation, men's eyes flicked to follow her, women's eyebrows knitted a millimetre or two. She was tall, she was blonde and she was cool, so cool. She wore bright red lipstick, her high cheekbones were accentuated by clever use of make-up, and she never smiled. Ever.

Hedda didn't need to smile to get what she wanted.

And what she wanted, Theo was pretty sure, was him. At least for that night.

He stood, pulled out a chair for her, poured her a glass of bubbles and lit her cigarette. 'I'm glad you could make it,' he said.

'Günter is away for a couple of days. On exercise. A couple of nights.'

She didn't smile, but there was something in the way she examined him that made him feel taller, stronger, more virile. They had met on the street during an air-raid scare in Berlin in September. They had both ignored the sirens and stared upwards at the searchlights and the flashes of anti-aircraft guns seeking out phantom British bombers. Theo had offered her his umbrella, to protect her from the bombs. She hadn't laughed at this rather feeble joke as he had hoped she would, but she had coolly looked him up and down and then accepted it. Theo knew she was married, but it was only after their third night together that he had learned her husband was a Sturmbannführer in the SS Leibstandarte Adolf Hitler. It made her even more alluring.

'So where have you been, Lieutenant von Hertenberg?'

'You know I couldn't possibly tell you that,' Theo said.

'Is it a secret?'

Theo looked straight into her cool blue eyes. 'Yes.'

'Are you some kind of spy?'

Theo's brain tumbled. Was she joking? How the hell did she know that? He had never talked about any of his work. Perhaps that was how she knew; he wasn't full of the usual soldier's gripes.

He kept his face frozen. 'Are you?'

She held his gaze and then blinked. Once. 'Let's dance.'

Hedda wasn't exactly a great dancer. She didn't have much of a sense of rhythm, but she did know how and when to press her body into her partner's. Theo delighted in the surreptitious glances of the other men on the dance floor as they looked away from their own partners towards his.

He was horny. She was horny. This was going to be a good night. Theo deserved a good night after what he had been going through.

And then suddenly Theo thought of Millie, of her dress wrapping itself around her legs in the wind on the beach at Scheveningen, of her cheek as it turned away from his lips. The music jarred, Hedda's legs knocked into his knee, his hand on her back felt the stickiness of sweat. Was it hers or his?

She sensed something. Hedda could always sense something. She had somehow sensed he was a spy. What the hell was he doing with the wife of a Sturmbannführer in a nightclub full of SS officers? He tried to imagine Millie in the Kakadu and he couldn't.

She stepped back. One long, exquisitely plucked eyebrow arched inquisitively. 'Theo?'

He pulled himself together. He couldn't allow sentiment to spoil his evening. 'I think we need some more champagne, don't you?'

Eighteen

Zossen, Germany, 13 November

It had been a long, hard night with Hedda and Theo was feeling the fatigue. He could barely keep his eyes open as he drove the thirty kilometres south of Berlin to Zossen, which was the wartime command centre for the Wehrmacht. He had passed through the high-wire perimeter, two checkpoints and walked along boards laid over marshland to a large A-framed building, inside which he had taken a lift down to underground concrete corridors. There, in a tiny office, he had found Major Liss.

Major Liss woke him up.

Liss was an officer in the Foreign Armies West Intelligence Directorate. He was an artilleryman from Mecklenburg, so not one of the aristocratic Prussians from whom many of the general-staff officers were drawn, but he was a prize-winning horseman, and in the Wehrmacht that earned you respect. He was also highly intelligent and spoke English, French, Spanish and Italian.

'Thank you for coming out here, Hertenberg. And for all the intelligence you have been providing us with over the last few weeks. As you will see, it has been very valuable.'

'I am very glad to hear that, Herr Major.'

Theo had never met Liss before. He had passed on the information Bedaux had been giving him to Colonel Oster, who then passed it to people at Armies West Intelligence to analyse. People like Major Liss.

'Now, what I am going to tell you, what I am going to show you, is highly confidential,' Liss said. 'Colonel Oster has vouched for you. I have something for you to ask your contact. To ask it properly, and to understand the answer, you need to understand the question.'

'Yes, Herr Major.'

'Come with me.'

Theo followed Liss through the warren. The tunnels were lined with concrete to protect them from Allied bombs, and telephone and electricity cables ran along the ceiling. They came to a large room in the middle of which was a table with a relief map of northern France, Belgium, Luxembourg and Germany.

'We call this "the cowhide",' said Liss. 'As you can see, we have marked the deployment of the French and British Armies, much of it with information given to us by you.'

Theo looked at the map. Liss pointed out the French fortifications on the Maginot Line, then the French 2nd Army along the Meuse around Sedan, then the other French armies lined up along the Belgian border, and finally the British Expeditionary Force at the Channel coast near Calais and Dunkirk.

'You are familiar with Case Yellow?' Liss said.

'Of course,' said Theo. 'It's the plan for an offensive in the west. But I don't know the current details. I assume it involves invading through Belgium and Holland.'

'It does. Last week we played a war game in this room, trying out Case Yellow. I played the part of General Gamelin, the French commander-in-chief.'

'What happened?'

'You see these two armies here?' Liss pointed to two concentrations of units on the German border with Holland, Belgium and Luxembourg. The northern one, Army Group B, was much larger than the southern one, Army Group A.

'Yes.'

'All right. Army Group B thrusts through the flat country of Holland and Belgium, through Brussels and on into Flanders. The idea is to break through around Lille and Amiens and swing south to Paris. Army Group A moves west through the Ardennes forest to the Meuse near Sedan, and pins down the French armies there, protecting Army Group B's flank.'

'I see,' said Theo. 'And you say you fought this battle last week?'

'We did,' said Liss.

'I have to ask the question,' said Theo. 'Who won?'

'Army Group B broke through the Belgian army's forward defences along the Albert Canal, and took Brussels. But then the French 7th Army moved north into Belgium, and met our forces here.' Liss pointed to a gap between the River Dyle and the River Meuse near Namur. 'As you have pointed out, the 7th Army is France's strongest. So this is where the key battle is. Their tanks against our tanks.'

'And we win?'

'Not necessarily. They have as many tanks as we do. And their SOMUA S35 is as powerful as our Panzer Mark III. Coming up behind the 7th Army is the BEF. We get bogged down. We all get bogged down. It's 1914 all over again. Or 1915.'

'Oh,' said Theo.

'Yes. Of course there is some disagreement among the general staff as to what will happen. I think it's fair to say that the Führer is more optimistic than General Halder.'

'And your view?' Theo asked.

'My view is we get bogged down.'

A return to the trench fighting of the last war was every German soldier's nightmare. Probably every French soldier's as well. 'I thought our tanks would avoid that,' said Theo. 'A blitzkrieg, like Poland.'

'The French have more tanks than the Poles, a lot more. And they are better tanks.'

Theo examined the map. The little markers, each one a division, represented thousands of men soon to be propelled headlong at each other in Flanders. 'So what is your request?'

'I told you I played the role of General Gamelin?'

'Yes.'

127

'It's a difficult task,' Liss said. 'The difficulty isn't working out what the French *should* do, but rather what they *will* do.'

'Shouldn't you just assume they pursue the best strategy?' Theo asked.

'No.'

'Why not?'

'Because that's not what the French do.' Liss smiled. 'When we invaded Poland we left only thirty-five divisions of reservists along our western border. The French had seventy-five divisions facing us and three thousand two hundred tanks. We had none. Not one. If the French had ordered an immediate armoured offensive, they would have smashed through the Siegfried Line within a fortnight. We would have lost the war.'

It sounded extraordinary, but Theo believed Liss. He knew the results of a similar war game held in 1938, just before the impending invasion of Czechoslovakia. The Czechs held up the German army long enough for the French armour to roll through the Rhineland. Germany lost the war within months. That was why General Beck and the others had been so desperate to topple Hitler back then.

'So why didn't the French generals just do that in September?'

'It would never have entered their heads. More importantly, it would never enter the heads of the French politicians. Or the British. They have their Maginot Line, and their plans are to sit there and wait for us to attack them. I don't think they realize even now how they could have won the war.'

'All right,' said Theo.

'So what I need to know', said Liss, 'is what the French plan to do if and when we invade Belgium. We can see from their dispositions it's clearly something they are expecting. In particular, what will the 7th Army do? That's what I want you to find out. Then, next time we play this war game I can play Gamelin's role more accurately. Can you do that?'

'I can try,' said Theo.

'Thank you, Hertenberg,' said Liss.

Theo was about to leave, when he paused. 'What about here?' he said, pointing to the French border with Belgium along the Meuse. 'The information I received was that the 2nd Army guarding this section is very weak.'

Liss smiled. 'Yes. Of course the hills and forests of the Ardennes would slow up any armoured assault. But that is something we discussed. The Führer was particularly intrigued.'

Despite himself, Theo couldn't help feeling a surge of pride that the Führer himself was interested in the information he had provided.

As he drove back to Berlin, Theo marvelled at his own inconsistency. On the one hand he prayed for Hitler to be removed. He dreaded a German victory over France and Britain, almost as much as the stalemate that Liss was predicting. On the other, he was helping Liss and the general staff craft a strategy that would smash the Allied armies. Both attitudes made sense. It was his bounden duty as an army officer to do all he could to help his country win a battle. It was also his duty as a good German and patriot to stop an evil madman destroying his country.

But those two conceptions of his duty were contradictory. And Theo wasn't sure how long he could deny that contradiction.

That troubled him. It troubled him deeply.

The Hague

'*Zijn deze plaatsen nog vrij?*'

Millie looked up at two Dutchmen, both about thirty, both good-looking. She and Constance were having a cup of coffee in the Passage, an elegant shopping arcade just opposite the Binnenhof parliamentary citadel.

'We do not speak Dutch. We are English,' she replied in that language.

The shorter of the two men smiled. 'No matter. I can speak English and I can translate for Jan.'

'I'm sorry,' Millie smiled politely. 'We are waiting for someone.

He will be here any moment.'

'I understand,' said the English speaker, his face regretful. 'I apologize for troubling you.' They withdrew and found themselves a seat in the opposite corner of the café.

'Pity,' said Constance. 'They looked rather nice.'

'Better than some of the oafs that have approached us over the last couple of days,' said Millie.

It was hardly surprising that she and Constance had drawn attention. Constance was an attractive woman, and Millie was used to dealing with strange men wanting to start conversations with her. Actually, Constance had proved to be a more amusing travel companion than Millie had expected. She and Millie were very different, but Constance had a general zest for life that was catching. They had spent a couple of days wandering around The Hague, and Constance had been bowled over by the paintings in the Mauritshuis. Millie had the impression that Constance's enthusiasm for the Rembrandts and Vermeers was all the more rapturous because this was the first time she had ever ventured into an art gallery.

They had talked a lot, but Constance's background remained sketchy. She had grown up in Cheshire and then moved to London with her mother to stay with relatives after her father had died, but beyond that Constance had revealed little. She gushed about her handsome husband, a naval officer, but then she also gushed about handsome Dutchmen they bumped into in The Hague.

'So who is this man we are meeting?' asked Millie.

'Otto Langebrück,' said Constance. 'Works for Herr von Ribbentrop, who is an old friend of Henry's.'

'And Foreign Minister, isn't he?' said Millie.

'That's right.'

Millie frowned. 'Should we be negotiating with the enemy's government? I mean, shouldn't that come through official channels?'

'Official channels?' Constance snorted. 'You know what Chamberlain is like. He's too stubborn to negotiate with anyone.

That's why we are here, Millie. That's why Sir Henry and your father sent us.'

'Yes, but Chamberlain is Prime Minister, isn't he? I'm not sure we should be going behind his back.' Millie realized she was beginning to sound like her brother.

'I loathe Chamberlain,' said Constance, her eyes alight. 'He's the one who got us into this stupid war. Have you read *Rogue Male*?'

'I've heard of it. Came out in the summer, didn't it?'

'You should read it. It's brilliant. There's just one problem. The hero at the beginning is trying to shoot a European dictator who is obviously supposed to be Hitler. He should have been trying to shoot Chamberlain. Now *that* would have been worth doing.'

'You are not serious?' Millie said.

'I certainly am,' said Constance. 'I'd do it. Especially if it would stop this war.'

Millie glanced at her companion. She didn't seem exactly fanatical, more matter-of-fact. An odd girl, Constance.

'I think this must be him,' whispered Constance as a well-dressed man of about thirty approached them.

'Mrs Scott-Dunton? Miss de Lancey? Permit me to introduce myself. My name is Otto Langebrück. May I join you?'

'Please do, Mr Langebrück,' said Millie.

The man oozed charm as he took the third chair around the table. His English was very good. 'Herr von Ribbentrop sends his compliments to you and to Sir Henry.'

'Would you like some coffee?'

'Sadly, not. I do not have much time. I believe you have a message for Herr von Ribbentrop?'

'I do,' said Constance. She opened her bag and pulled out an envelope, and handed it to Langebrück, who slid it into his breast pocket without opening it.

'We will be staying here for three days more if there is a reply,' Millie said. 'As I'm sure you know, my father is Lord Oakford. I would be happy to pass on any message to him or Sir Henry Alston.'

'That's all right,' said Constance. 'You'd better speak directly to me. I know Sir Henry a little better than my friend.'

Langebrück glanced at the two women. 'Thank you,' he said. 'I will leave a message at your hotel if I have anything. Where are you staying?'

'At the Kurhaus in Scheveningen.'

'I will be in touch.'

'Sorry about that, Millie,' said Constance with an embarrassed smile when Langebrück was safely out of the café. 'But Henry did give me strict instructions what to say when we hear back from him.'

Millie didn't answer. She now knew why Constance was with her: to act as an envoy for Sir Henry Alston with the Nazi government. Presumably Father knew about this. But the guilt weighed down on her. What would Conrad think if he found out what she and Constance had done? Or Theo, for that matter?

That she should be torn between what her brother and her father expected was nothing new for Millie. But she cared what Theo thought. She cared very much.

Paris

The bar was warm, smoky and crowded. It had been a long train journey from Holland and Conrad was tired. He was also late.

He scanned the tables and saw the man he was looking for wedged in a corner reading a book, an almost empty carafe of red wine next to him. Conrad made his way over to him.

'Hello, Warren. I'm glad I didn't miss you.'

The American looked up and shot to his feet, pumping Conrad's hand. He was shorter than Conrad with floppy hair that hung down over his eyes, and a wide amiable smile that showed off gleaming teeth. 'No chance of that. I can keep myself amused here for hours. We need more wine.' He waved a waiter over.

'It's good to see a friendly face,' said Conrad. And Warren's was a very friendly face. Conrad had met him at Oxford almost ten years before. Warren's ambition had always been to become a novelist, but after a couple of years floundering in Paris, he had secured a job as a junior foreign correspondent for a Chicago newspaper. He had spent the last few years in Berlin and Prague, and had now returned to Paris, covering the war.

'What the hell are you doing here?' Warren asked. 'I thought it was impossible for British officers to get leave in Paris?'

'It may be,' said Conrad. 'I wouldn't know. My unit is still in England.'

'That explains nothing,' said Warren.

Warren's inquisitiveness didn't surprise Conrad; he was a journalist after all.

'I'm here on some semi-official business,' said Conrad.

'Ah,' said Warren. 'I understand.'

Conrad realized that Warren had immediately assumed he was doing something in intelligence. Which he supposed was true, sort of. The good thing about Warren's assumption was that he wouldn't expect further explanation.

'How's Paris?' Conrad asked.

'It's great to be back,' Warren said. 'Although I'm getting a bit sick of this *drôle de guerre*. It would be good to report on some real fighting. Still, it has given me time to work on my novel.'

Conrad noticed that the book Warren was reading was *To Have and Have Not* by Ernest Hemingway, Warren's hero. Rereading it, probably.

'Have you read *Scoop* yet?' Conrad asked. 'It's brilliant.'

Within seconds they had slotted back into the old familiar argument of Hemingway versus Evelyn Waugh. They talked about Paris, about Warren's nascent novel, about the war and whether the Americans would join it. Conrad resisted the temptation to rag Warren for trying to live the cliché of the American writer in Paris. He had attempted to write his own novel while in Berlin, but given up after two chapters, and his occasional journalism for the magazine *Mercury* was nothing compared to Warren's efforts.

They ordered another carafe. The warmth of the bar, Warren's friendliness and the wine relaxed Conrad, so he felt something of a jolt when Warren reminded him of his reason for being there.

'OK, Conrad, what's this semi-official business?' Warren asked. 'And what do I have to do with it? I assume I have something to do with it?'

'You do,' said Conrad. 'If you are willing. I'm trying to find out about someone. An American who lives in Paris.'

'Ah!' said Warren, his eyes lighting up with interest. 'And who might that be?'

'A fellow called Bedaux. Charles Bedaux. A wealthy businessman. You know him?'

'You bet I do,' said Warren.

'Can you tell me about him?'

'Sure. He was born here, but went over to America before the last war, to Michigan, I think. Invented his own time-and-motion system and made a fortune at it. He has companies all over Europe as well as America, although they hate him there. He fancies himself as something of an explorer: he went on a big expedition in the Yukon a few years ago.'

'And he's based in Paris?'

'He moves around all over the place, but he has a company here. I'm pretty sure he has just signed up with the French Ministry of Armaments, telling them how to jazz up their munitions production.'

'That's interesting,' said Conrad. 'You do know a lot about him.'

'Any European journalist would know him. After the wedding.'

'The wedding?'

'The damp-squib wedding of the century. Your Duke of Windsor and Wallis Simpson.'

'I don't understand.'

'They got married at Bedaux's chateau in 1937. Candé, in the Loire. Nobody came. How did you miss that? Where were you?'

'In Spain getting shot at,' said Conrad.

'Oh, yeah,' said Warren. 'I guess you had other things to think about. Anyway, Bedaux loaned the couple his chateau, so, as you can imagine, there were a few newspaper profiles on him at the time.'

Conrad nodded. Like everyone else he had read plenty about the duke when he was Prince of Wales, but Conrad had been fighting in Spain when, as King Edward VIII, he had abdicated the throne. Conrad hadn't given it much consideration, apart from thinking it was careless of his country to lose such a young and energetic monarch in that way.

'Does Bedaux have any connections with Germany?' Conrad asked.

'Sure,' said Warren. 'The Nazis grabbed his company in 1934, but he still has good contacts there. He organized the Duke of Windsor's tour in 1937. Did you know about that?'

Conrad shook his head.

'I covered it from Berlin. It was a big deal in Germany; they loved him. The duke and duchess visited factories and housing projects. Your compatriots weren't so excited, though. There was a half-assed Nazi salute, playing with Göring's train set, shaking hands with Hitler, that kind of thing.'

Conrad winced. 'Ouch. Was Bedaux there?'

'No. But he fixed it all up. Then he fixed a tour for them to America, which fell through when the American unions kicked up a fuss. They despise his time-and-motion system there. Bedaux had a nervous breakdown, I believe, and he's laid low since then.'

'Didn't I read that the duke is in France at the moment?' Conrad asked.

'Yes he is. He and Wally lived here in Paris after the wedding, but they were down in Antibes when war broke out, and skedaddled back to Britain. The British government sent him over here a month ago. He's big buddies with the US Ambassador, William Bullitt, and a lot of the other rich Americans in Paris. In fact he's also buddies with your sister-in-law. At least I assume she's your sister-in-law.'

'Isobel Haldeman?' Isobel was Veronica's younger sister, who had married Marshall Haldeman, an American insurance executive who had moved to Paris a few years before. Conrad hadn't seen her since he had left for Spain.

'That's right.'

'Would she know Bedaux as well?'

'Sure too. All those right-bank Americans know each other. Bedaux's wife is much more American than him. She's an heiress from Kalamazoo. Fern is her name.'

'I can't quite accept that Kalamazoo is a real place,' said Conrad.

'Oh, it is,' said Warren. 'And I wouldn't kid Fern about her home town if I were you. Scary lady, Fern Bedaux.'

'Are the Bedauxs and the Windsors still friends?'

'Don't know. Mrs Haldeman might have a better idea. You should speak to her. Someone else you might want to talk to is Fruity Metcalfe.'

'Fruity?'

'Hey, don't blame me for your dumb British nicknames. Although he's Irish, I think. He was the duke's best man at his wedding and is acting as his royal sidekick now – what do you call it? Aide-de-camp, something like that. Swell guy. Partial to a drink or two. He's staying at the Ritz, and likes to prop up the bar there after a hard day's duking.'

Nineteen

Paris, 14 November

Conrad slept on Warren's sofa. He had a small apartment above Shakespeare and Co., an English language bookshop in the rue de l'Odéon. It was run by an American woman and, according to Warren, it was the centre of American literary life in Paris. Warren loved it.

Warren also had to work, so Conrad left his apartment and, armed with Isobel Haldeman's address, which Warren had dug out for him, found a café in which to while away a couple of hours until he could decently turn up at her house. The sun shone weakly on the quiet street, the coffee was good, and for a moment Conrad was able just to enjoy the fact he was sitting in a café in Paris instead of chasing his men around the mud of Salisbury Plain. An old soldier with a fine white moustache and one leg gave Conrad a gruff nod. He sported the red ribbon of the Légion d'honneur on his lapel, and alternated puffs at a pipe with sips of an early morning *ballon de vin rouge*. He was a reminder of what war could do, what it would do again once it eventually got going.

Which might be as soon as the next day, if Theo was correct about the date of the offensive. Unless Theo was also correct about the generals dumping Hitler. Conrad understood the Prussian military ethos, how difficult it was for them to move against their commander-in-chief and to break the oath that Hitler had made them all take swearing allegiance to him personally. Conrad prayed that they would have the courage to do it.

Because if they didn't, hell would be let loose on the Low Countries and northern France. Again.

That would be a disaster. Conrad was convinced that the Munich peace talks were a colossal error, that the appeasers like his father were wrong, and that the only thing to do was to stand up to Hitler. That was, after all, why he had joined the army. But things were not that simple. Perhaps he should have helped his father negotiate with Theo, if it led to a genuine peace with honour. He knew his father's motives were noble: if your aim was to preserve peace, why start a war? Conrad's argument had always been that you had to show your willingness to stand up to Hitler if you wanted to stop him. If the generals did get rid of him, then Conrad would have been proved right.

But what if they didn't? Conrad wouldn't have stopped Hitler after all. And hundreds of thousands, possibly millions of people would die, soldiers and civilians. Lord Oakford would at least be able to say that he did everything he could have done to prevent the massacre.

It would all become clearer one way or another the next day.

So, where did Bedaux fit into all this? Perhaps he was involved in some way in the coup preparations? Or in thwarting them?

Conrad wasn't sure how the hell to investigate the American. He had no official reason to be in Paris, no means of accessing government records, no credentials with which to approach officials. Despite what Warren thought, he wasn't a spy. What did Theo expect him to do?

He had learned from Warren that Bedaux was working for the French Armaments Ministry. That must mean he was in possession of all kinds of arms-production data, which would no doubt be useful to the German government. But that couldn't be what Theo was driving at. If Warren knew it, the British secret service would know it, as would the French secret service, for that matter. The British already knew that Bedaux was talking to Theo. So Bedaux's role working for the French government could not be the whole story.

At ten o'clock, Conrad left his little café and strolled down to the Seine, crossing it by the Grand Palais. Paris seemed to be less overwhelmed by the war than London. There were uniforms and a few sandbags, but the river made its sedate way beneath the city's beautiful bridges in much the way it had done for the last couple of hundred years.

Conrad found Isobel Haldeman's apartment in a little *place* off the avenue Montaigne. He had always liked his wife's younger sister, although he wasn't sure what she thought of him. Isobel was much less flamboyant than Veronica: small, with a pointed chin, a pretty mouth and kind eyes, she tended to think before she spoke, something that Veronica would never have been caught doing. The fact that Isobel was the first sister to marry, and that she had snared a rich American, had infuriated Veronica. Marshall Haldeman was the son of an insurance magnate from Hartford, Connecticut, who had been placed in charge of the family firm's European operations first in London and then in Paris. Veronica thought him dull in the extreme; Conrad thought him a decent enough chap.

Isobel welcomed Conrad into her enormous apartment warmly, although she was clearly surprised to see him. A maid served them coffee as they sat in the drawing room overlooking the fountain in the middle of the *place*.

'Have you seen Veronica recently?' she asked.

'Not since we were divorced. Over a year ago.'

'Poor you,' said Isobel. 'You always seemed much too nice for my sister. I could have warned you, but by the time I met you, you were smitten.'

'I was,' said Conrad. 'Veronica was someone I could never see clearly. I probably can't now.'

'No one can,' said Isobel. 'Or at least no one male. Did you know she had split up with Alec?'

'No, I didn't,' said Conrad. Alec Linaro was the motor-racing driver whom Veronica had met while Conrad was in Spain. He was married, of course, but that only seemed to encourage her.

'Alec wanted to stay with his wife after all. Veronica was

furious, poor lamb.'

'So what's she doing now?'

'Driving a general around London, I think. Oh, God. I hope it's an old and ugly general.'

Conrad laughed.

'I'm sorry I'm so wicked. I adore Veronica really.'

Conrad stopped himself from agreeing. Veronica was trouble; always had been and always would be. He was much better off without her. He knew that, he just had to remind himself of it at regular intervals.

'And what are you doing in Paris?' Isobel asked.

'Trying to find out about someone,' Conrad said. 'An American. Charles Bedaux.'

'Dreadful man,' said Isobel. 'And an awful wife. Fern. I can't bear her.'

'From Kalamazoo, I understand.'

Isobel laughed. 'I know. Isn't it too wonderful? What do you want to know about him?'

Conrad had realized that if he wanted to get a useful answer, he couldn't just ask an innocent question.

'I'm not sure, precisely. A friend of mine suggested that he might be dangerous in some way. To the Allied cause. Now, I know that Bedaux is working for the French Armaments Ministry, but I think it might be something more than that. Do you have any idea what that might be?'

Isobel looked blank. 'No. But it doesn't surprise me. He's very clever and he has a finger in every pie.'

'Who are his friends?'

'He's the kind of person who has heaps of friends,' Isobel said. 'Marshall would have a better idea of who the important ones are. But Mr Bedaux hasn't been in Paris very much over the last couple of years. He arranged a trip for the Duke of Windsor to the States, and it all fell apart. The American unions hate Bedaux and they made a real stink. Bedaux took it rather badly, I believe. Had a breakdown. I think he went to Germany for a cure. Then he did something glamorous like driving across Africa from Cairo to Cape Town. Or was it the other way? He appeared back in Paris a month or so ago: I saw him at an American Embassy do the week before last at his chateau. He seemed in good spirits, although I didn't talk to him myself.'

'Does he still see the Duke of Windsor?' Conrad asked. 'I understand the duke and duchess got married there.'

'I haven't seen Bedaux with them for years,' Isobel said. 'Not since the duke went to Germany.'

'You see the duke yourself?' Conrad asked.

'From time to time,' said Isobel. 'We have mutual friends among the Americans here.'

'Do you happen to know where Bedaux is living?' Conrad asked. 'Somewhere in Paris, or does he stay at his chateau?'

'No, he has leased Candé to the US Embassy for the war. I'm pretty sure he is staying at the Ritz.' Isobel frowned. 'Why are you so interested in him?'

'A friend wanted to know.'

'And I suppose I can't ask what kind of friend?'

Conrad smiled and shook his head. 'I'm afraid not.'

The frown deepened. Something didn't sound right to her. 'I thought Veronica said you were in the army?'

'I am. I'm on leave.'

'You fought for the Reds in Spain, didn't you, Conrad?'

'I fought for the government, yes.'

'The communists?'

'The socialists. There were communists there. Some of them shot at me; they killed two of my friends. If you are wondering whether the friend I was talking about is a communist, he isn't.'

'But is he British?'

It was a good question, and one Conrad wasn't going to answer. 'Look, I really must be going. I don't want to take up any more of your morning. Lovely to see you, Isobel.'

With that he escaped, leaving behind a very suspicious sister-in-law.

Millie and Constance sat in silence, drinking their tea in the grand ballroom of the Kurhaus. Even on a gloomy Tuesday in November, the brightly painted frieze around the dome that rose high above the ballroom floor hinted at the gaiety of summer dances.

Theo was late. Although Millie knew she should be calm and businesslike, her heart was racing. It had only been forty-eight hours since she had seen him, but it had seemed far too long. Constance had caught Millie's mood, and was nervously silent in sympathy.

There he was! He looked so grave, so handsome as he approached them. Millie smiled broadly, but Theo's expression was frozen as he sat down next to the women. 'I have an answer for you,' is all he said, and handed Millie an envelope.

'What does it say?' Millie asked.

'It gives some idea of what a new German government might expect from the British and French in return for peace.'

'Can I read it?' said Millie. She had hoped to be something more than a mere messenger.

'No,' said Theo. 'I'd rather you didn't. But it doesn't really matter. There's no point now.'

'Why not?' said Millie. Theo was making no attempt to hide his anger.

'Because it's not going to happen. Hitler is not going to be deposed.'

'Have they called it off?'

'Yes,' said Theo. 'We have been ordered to burn all our plans. The generals are too cowardly to take action.' Theo looked directly at Millie. 'We're stuck with him. We are all stuck with him.'

'I'm sorry, Theo,' Millie said. Unthinkingly she reached out her hand over the table. 'I know how hard you have worked for that.'

Theo stared at her hand and made no effort to take it. Embarrassed, Millie withdrew it. 'Theo? What is it?'

'Did you see a man named Otto Langebrück yesterday? At a café in the Passage in The Hague?'

'Y-yes,' Millie stammered.

'Do you know who he is?'

'He works for the Foreign Ministry, doesn't he, Constance?'

'He works for Herr von Ribbentrop,' Constance said.

'He doesn't work for the Foreign Ministry, he works in the Ribbentrop Büro, Ribbentrop's private office.'

'But Ribbentrop is the Foreign Minister, isn't he?' Millie said.

'Yes. And he's a dyed-in-the-wool Nazi. He's one of Hitler's biggest supporters. He's not one of us; he's one of them.'

'From the point of view of those of us who want peace, it makes sense to speak to people in the current German government,' Constance said. 'You said yourself it now seems unlikely Hitler will be overthrown. In that case the British government will have to negotiate with the existing regime.'

'You went behind my back, Millie.'

Looking at the expression of disappointment and anger on Theo's face, Millie felt miserable. 'I'm sorry, Theo, but we had to.'

'You didn't have to. You mean your father told you to.'

Millie felt tears springing to her eyes. She had to control them. She *had* to control them.

'It was Sir Henry Alston's idea,' said Constance. 'Sir Henry got to know Herr von Ribbentrop on bank business in Germany before the war.'

Millie was grateful for Constance's support, but Theo seemed unimpressed.

'I can see why you are upset, Herr von Hertenberg,' said Constance. 'But you must understand that this is too important for considerations of personalities to play a role. We are talking about war or peace here.'

'By "considerations of personality", you mean trust, don't you?' said Theo.

'I trusted my father,' said Millie.

Theo stared at her, his eyes cold. Then he looked up at the high dome above him. A grand piano played a waltz inappropriately in the background.

'Come with me,' Theo said to Millie. 'Not you, Mrs Scott-Dunton, just Millie.'

'Where are we going?'

'Outside.'

'I'll get my coat.'

'No you won't,' said Theo. 'There is something I want to tell you. Come on.'

There was a cold wind outside, and Millie started shivering. Theo led her down some steps on to the beach and she hurried after him as he strode towards the waves crashing on to the beach.

He turned to her. His composure had gone, replaced by a mixture of pain and determination.

'I'm sorry, Theo,' Millie said, the tears streaming hot down her wind-bitten cheeks. 'I'm so sorry.'

'We *have* to trust each other, Millie,' Theo said. 'People like you and me and Conrad are on the same side. The side of reason. The side of peace.'

'I know. But so is my father. And Sir Henry Alston, and Constance. That's why they got in touch with Herr Langebrück. To bring peace.'

Theo turned his back on Millie to stare out at the grey North Sea, flecked by white foam in the stiff breeze. Millie wrapped her arms around her chest. She was cold. But she couldn't abandon Theo.

At last he turned to her. 'All right, Millie. I'm going to tell you something. I hinted at it to your brother when I saw him a few days ago, but I should stop playing games with myself. The British government needs to know.'

'Needs to know what?'

'The Duke of Windsor, your former king, is attached to the French general headquarters and over the last couple of months he has inspected the French lines. He is a surprisingly acute observer. And he has been passing his observations on to someone who has been passing them to me. Vital information about the French deployment and in particular its weak points.'

'Edward is a traitor?' Millie said. 'That doesn't make any sense. He was our king three years ago.'

'I can't be sure if he is doing this intentionally or if he is just indiscreet. But I can assure you he is doing it. And it is very useful information to our intelligence people.'

'That's not right, Theo. Someone is lying to you.'

Theo reached out and grabbed Millie's arms. 'I said we *have* to trust each other, Millie. I am not lying. Your government has to do something about it; they have to stop him. And you must tell your father this – not Alston, your father. Do you understand?'

Millie met Theo's intense stare. There was no doubt he believed what he was saying. She nodded. 'I will tell him,' she said. 'But do you have any evidence? I mean, he might believe me, but will the government believe him? There are all sorts of rumours flying around at the moment, Father says.'

Frustration flashed in Theo's eyes, but then he seemed to see Millie's point. 'Very well. I will try to get you some evidence. I'm not sure what yet, but I will think of something. How long are you staying in Holland?'

'Another three or four days,' Millie said. 'We are waiting for a response from Herr Langebrück.'

'I'll bring you something in the next couple of days.' Theo touched Millie's cheek. 'In the mean time, be careful. Don't trust Langebrück or Ribbentrop. Don't trust anyone.'

'Apart from you?'

'Apart from me.' To Millie's enormous relief, Theo smiled at the irony. 'You should go back inside, you are freezing. I'll see you again soon.'

Millie's emotions were in turmoil as she hurried back across the sand to the warm glow of the Kurhaus. She was ashamed that she had gone behind Theo's back; she was angry with her father for letting Alston open up a dialogue with such Nazis. She was also shocked by what Theo had said about the Duke of Windsor. She had met him once when she was nineteen and he was Prince of Wales. Like most people her age, she had been pleased to see him succeed to the throne in 1936: a young, modern king who understood the twentieth century. The politics of his abdication had baffled her, but she couldn't help admiring a man who had put his love for a woman before everything else, even his throne.

Her father knew the duke quite well. He had railed against his interfering in the Hoare–Laval pact during the Abyssinian crisis in 1935, over which Lord Oakford had resigned his position in Cabinet. But he had been uneasy about turfing a king off his throne. Would he believe her?

She had been right to ask for evidence from Theo. She believed him, she had to believe him, but it was going to be very difficult for Oakford to persuade the government that their former king was a traitor.

But if he was, if the duke really had been passing vital secrets to the Germans, then something had to be done about it.

Constance was hovering anxiously, waiting for her in the lobby. 'Are you all right, Millie?'

'Oh, leave me alone!' Millie snapped.

'What did he say?'

'Sir Henry Alston is a Nazi, isn't he, Constance?'

Constance was taken aback. 'Don't be an ass, of course he isn't. He just wants peace, like your father.'

'He's best friends with Ribbentrop and Ribbentrop is a Nazi. He's trying to sell our country out.'

'Is that what Theo told you?'

Although the lobby was empty, Millie realized she was talking too loudly and lowered her voice. 'Theo thinks the Duke of Windsor is a spy. He has been giving Theo secrets about the French defences.'

'Theo has been talking to the Duke of Windsor?'

'Through some kind of intermediary. He wants me to tell my father.'

Constance frowned. 'I know you like Theo, Millie, but that cannot possibly be true.'

'He's going to bring me proof in the next couple of days. While we wait for your friend Herr Langebrück to come back with his reply, which, by the way, I intend to rip up.'

'You can't do that!' Constance said. 'That was the whole reason we came here.'

'We shouldn't be negotiating with the Nazis behind our government's back,' Millie said. 'Not when we are at war.' What she meant was behind Theo's back. And Conrad's.

'Why don't we leave that to Sir Henry to decide?' said Constance. 'And your father.'

'Because Sir Henry is a Nazi and my father is a fool!' Millie said, the tears stinging her eyes as she did so.

'What are you going to do about the Duke of Windsor?' Constance asked.

'Tell my father, of course, once Theo provides us with some evidence. As soon as we get back to England. I just hope he will listen.'

'I don't think you should do that,' said Constance.

At that instant all Millie's frustration focused on one person, the girl standing in front of her. 'Leave me alone, Constance,' she said. 'Just leave me alone!'

With that she strode off to the lifts and her room. She needed to be by herself to make sense of all she had just heard. She needed to be away from Constance.

Constance returned to her table in the almost empty ballroom and poured herself a cup of tepid tea from the pot. She had some hard thinking to do.

After a few minutes she went up to her own room and placed a telephone call to London.

Twenty

The Ritz, Paris

Conrad lit another cigarette and leafed through the pages of the *Herald Tribune*. He had finished *Le Monde*. He wondered how long he could safely sit in the lobby. The staff of the Ritz didn't seem to mind; people waited for other people in grand hotels all the time.

He glanced up every time the doors opened until finally he saw a face he recognized from the brochures he had picked up in Amsterdam. The photographs had done justice to the boxer's face and the jug ears, but not to the vitality with which Charles Bedaux bounded into the hotel. He spoke to one of the men at reception, requesting the manager.

This was interesting. Nonchalantly, Conrad got to his feet and wandered over to the desk. He asked whether there was a message for him. While the receptionist was looking, the manager appeared. He was perfectly dressed in morning coat, and succeeded in looking both authoritative and deferent at the same time. He clearly knew Bedaux.

Conrad listened to the conversation, which was in French. Bedaux had arranged a private dining room for four people and seemed very concerned about the arrangements. As did the manager. One of the people was 'Madame Bedaux', but Conrad didn't catch the names of the other two. Conrad couldn't hear the whole conversation, he had to respond to the receptionist who hadn't been able to find a message for him, but he did catch a couple of words from the manager: 'eight o'clock'.

Conrad checked his watch. It was half past six. He told the

receptionist he would return later and asked him to keep any messages for him from a Monsieur Madvig. May as well put the old Danish Prime Minister to work again. Then he wandered out into the place Vendôme, and found himself a café on a side street.

At ten to eight he strolled back to the Ritz. He was disconcerted to see Charles Bedaux standing in the lobby, shifting impatiently from foot to foot. Conrad decided he had better not hang around there, and so made his way over to the far side of the square, outside an American bank. But it was dark in the blackout, and from that distance he couldn't make out the occupants of the cars that pulled up at the entrance. He would have to get closer.

He moved over to the shadows outside a jeweller, only a few yards from the entrance to the hotel, confident that no one could see him in the blackout.

At twenty past eight a large Buick rolled up and two faces he recognized emerged. The appearance of the couple seemed to energize the doorman, who ushered them into the hotel. Conrad decided he could risk one more turn though the lobby himself.

Sure enough, as he passed through the blacked-out doors, he saw Bedaux fussing over his dinner guests.

The Duke and Duchess of Windsor.

He span off to the left and found himself in the bar. He ordered a whisky and soda to give himself time to think.

Could *that* be what Theo was getting at? Charles Bedaux's relationship with the Duke of Windsor. Was Bedaux giving Theo secret information about the duke? And if so, what? Something about Wallis Simpson? Surely that scandal had played out.

Conrad remembered Warren mentioning Fruity Metcalfe, the duke's 'sidekick'. Well, here Conrad was, in the bar of the Ritz. Conrad had no idea what Metcalfe looked like; he scanned the room for likely suspects. There was really only one candidate, a tall middle-aged man in a double-breasted suit, propping up the bar, sipping a whisky and looking glum.

Worth a try.

Conrad moved over to him. 'I say,' he said to the man. 'Are you English, by any chance?'

'Irish,' the man replied, looking up.

Conrad perched on a stool next to him. 'I think I just saw the Duke and Duchess of Windsor in the hotel lobby. Is that possible?'

'I'd say it's a racing certainty,' the man replied. 'He's having dinner here tonight.'

'Oh,' said Conrad. 'I didn't realize he was in France.'

'Been here over a month,' said the man, in soft Irish tones. 'As have I. In fact I spent all day with him.'

'Really?' Conrad looked impressed. 'I've never met him, myself. They say he's charming.'

'He is that,' said the man, whom Conrad was now certain was Fruity Metcalfe. 'You could never accuse the duke of lacking charm.'

'Are you dining with him tonight?' asked Conrad. He knew it was a stupid question, because the duke had been wearing a dinner jacket and Fruity wasn't.

'No. I work for him. I'm his equerry.'

'Ah, I see,' said Conrad. 'The name's de Lancey, by the way.'

'Metcalfe,' said Fruity. He was clearly slightly drunk, but seemed happy with the idea of talking to Conrad. The company seemed to be lifting his air of gloom. 'What are you doing in Paris, Mr de Lancey?'

For a moment, Conrad almost panicked. What the hell was he doing in Paris? He couldn't tell Fruity he was trying to find out about Bedaux, and from what he had heard it was difficult for a British officer to get leave in the city. 'Seeing my sister-in-law. She lives here and she needs some help with something.'

'Oh, who's that?' Fruity asked.

'Isobel Haldeman.'

'Oh yes, I know her. Marshall Haldeman's wife. Must be a rum business for you to come all the way here to sort it out.'

'I suppose it is, rather,' said Conrad. 'I shouldn't really have told you her name. Didn't think you would know her.'

'Don't worry,' said Fruity. 'I promise I'll forget all about it.' He took a sip of his drink and looked Conrad up and down. 'Sister-in-law? That makes you Isobel's brother's . . . No, sister's husband.'

Fruity was a bit befuddled, Conrad was glad to see.

'Ex-husband,' said Conrad. 'So does that make Isobel an ex-sister-in-law? Somehow I don't think it does, does it?'

Fruity pondered the question. 'Don't know,' he decided eventually. 'De Lancey, you say? Is your wife Veronica de Lancey?'

'That's her,' said Conrad. 'And she's my ex-wife.'

'Oh, I see. I met her once. Sat next to her at dinner somewhere. Charming woman.'

'You could never accuse Veronica of lacking charm,' Conrad said.

Fruity laughed. 'Can I get you another?' he asked Conrad. Conrad's glass was half full; Fruity's was entirely empty.

'Why not?' said Conrad, finishing his.

'What's it like, being divorced?' Fruity asked.

'I wouldn't recommend it.'

'Was it your idea, or hers? I hope you don't mind me asking, old man, I know you are a stranger, but there are some things it's easier to ask strangers.'

'Hers,' said Conrad. 'I fought it for a year or so, then I gave up.'

'Was Alec Linaro involved in any way?' Fruity asked.

'Yes,' said Conrad. 'I take it he was at that dinner party too?'

Fruity nodded. Conrad felt the anger rise inside him, the humiliation of the cuckold. While he was scrabbling around in the dust and blood of Spain, his wife was openly flirting with other women's husbands in front of total strangers.

'Don't let it get to you, old man,' Fruity said. 'It happens to all of us.'

'Oh?'

'My wife is beautiful. Wealthy. The daughter of an earl. And I have no idea which man she is with at this precise moment. But I would be very surprised if she was alone.'

Conrad raised his eyebrows.

'Are you wondering why I admit that?' Fruity said. 'Why shouldn't I? I mean, she flaunts it. Why should I never mention it, just because no one ever mentions it to me?'

Conrad nodded. 'I know what you mean.'

They stared at their drinks for a moment.

'Do you love her?' Fruity asked.

'I did,' said Conrad.

'Do you now?'

Conrad looked at Fruity sharply. 'No. Maybe. I don't know.'

'I love her,' said Fruity. 'That's the problem. I'll always love her.'

Conrad liked Fruity. He bought him another drink. They changed the subject. They talked about Paris, the phoney war, the army, Fruity's service in India, the Duke of Windsor, the French army, Fruity's trips around northern France.

It was several whiskies later and well past midnight before Conrad left the Ritz and made his way over the Seine to Warren's flat, thinking he now knew why Theo wanted him to track down Bedaux.

His Royal Highness the Duke of Windsor had been passing secrets to the enemy.

And if Theo was right, in only a few hours' time the Germans might be making use of those secrets to attack Belgium and Holland.

Time to go back to London.

Scheveningen

It was about ten o'clock. Millie was in her nightgown having ordered a light supper from room service. She lay with the lights out and her eyes open, listening to the sound of the surf outside and thinking about what Theo had said.

There was a light knock at the door.

'Who is it?'

'It's Constance.'

'Go away!'

'Let me in, Millie! I want to apologize.'

Millie sighed, got out of bed and opened the door a crack. Constance was standing on the landing looking sheepish. 'Can I come in?'

Millie hesitated, and then opened the door wider. Constance sat on the small chair by the desk, and Millie parked herself on the bed.

'I just wanted to say I am sorry, Millie. I've been thinking about it and you are quite right. It's wrong to negotiate with the Nazis when we are at war with them. We should have told your father and Henry that.'

Millie was surprised, but gladdened that Constance seemed to share the doubts that were growing in her own mind after her conversation with Theo.

'It's just so difficult when people you trust ask you to do something,' Constance went on. 'And I do wish someone would do something to stop this dratted war.'

'So do I,' said Millie. 'But I wonder if we shouldn't leave it to our government.'

'Probably,' said Constance. 'I don't think Henry is a Nazi, though.'

'I'm not so sure,' said Millie.

Constance looked as if she was going to argue, but seemed to think the better of it. 'Oh, and I saw Theo earlier this evening.'

'You did?' said Millie. 'Why didn't you send him up to see me?'

'I tried to, but he said he just wanted me to leave you a message. He wants you to meet someone tomorrow morning. Early.'

'Who?'

'He wouldn't tell me,' said Constance. She dropped her eyes. 'I think he doesn't trust me.'

'When? Where?'

'Half past six. In the sand dunes just beyond the beach. Below the watchtower up there. You know. We walked up there yesterday afternoon.'

A mass of low sand dunes covered in scrub stretched along the coast for several miles to the north east of Scheveningen, and

Millie and Constance had explored them the day before. 'Yes, I know where you mean. That's frightfully early, though. It's still dark then.'

'It must be someone quite important,' said Constance. 'I asked if I could come with you, but Theo said no.'

'All right,' said Millie. She looked at her companion. Constance's apology seemed genuine enough, but Millie didn't even begin to understand her. At one moment she seemed to be impossibly naive, but she clearly understood more about international politics than she let on. With Otto Langebrück she had appeared firm and businesslike. And her relationship with Alston was a mystery. She said she was a friend of Alston's niece, but it was odd that Alston trusted her so much.

'Thank you, Constance,' she said. 'Good night.'

After Constance had left her, Millie rang down to the hotel reception to book a wake-up call.

Twenty-One

Scheveningen, 15 November

The phone woke Millie before six, and she was out of the hotel by ten past. It was still dark, although a lighter shade of grey framed the Kurhaus to the east. The breeze was steady rather than strong, and the Dutch flag flapped jauntily from the cupola of the hotel.

The promenade was empty, but one man was walking his dog on the beach down by the pier. Crows and seagulls huddled on the sand. Most of the guesthouses and hotels along the front were dark.

Millie wondered whom Theo wanted her to meet. Her best guess was either someone high up in the conspiracy against Hitler, or someone with evidence against the Duke of Windsor. Millie still found it hard to believe that the duke could possibly be a traitor, but she had to trust Theo. It was odd: she trusted Theo more than her own father.

She wished she could talk to her brother about the pickle she seemed to have got herself into. He would be furious, of course, but then he would be constructive. He would know what to do.

But there was no Conrad, so Millie was left to her own devices. She should have confidence in herself; she could cope.

She lifted her chin as she came to the end of the promenade, where beach met dune. The sand there was soft and had drifted in the wind, but she trudged up to a small footpath that snaked up the dune. The sky was lightening all around now, although sea, sky and dune were still shifting shades of grey and black.

She remembered where she had walked with Constance a couple of days before. There was a Napoleonic watchtower on the highest dune with a view of The Hague to the east and Scheveningen to the south. To get there, one had to climb and descend a couple of times. She assumed that Theo and his companion, whoever he turned out to be, would be waiting for her in one of those hollows.

There was no one around, and although at the top of the dunes she could see for miles, in the hollows she was sheltered from the wind and the sound of the surf.

Scrub encroached: gorse and stunted trees. First one bird and then another announced the dawn from deep within the bushes. The path she was following was not straight, but wound through the humps. She came to a narrow section where it plunged downhill with scrub on either side.

She heard rapid footsteps behind her and the sound of feet sliding on sand.

'Theo?'

She turned.

She saw the knife and opened her mouth to scream.

No one heard.

PART TWO

November 1939

Twenty-Two

Bedaux International
Bungehuis, Spuistraat 210
Amsterdam
16 November 1939

Dear Sir Henry,

It is a few years since we met, but I remember that stimulating discussion over lunch with Baron von Schroeder and Pierre Laval at Banque Worms in Paris.

A mutual friend, with whom you have recently been in contact, suggested I get in touch with you. Gurney Kroheim has a venerable history of banking on the continent of Europe. I hope that some day my own firm will be able to emulate yours with a reputation in management consulting. Both our businesses rely on trade to thrive. This recent war is a disaster for trade.

Your former king the Duke of Windsor is an old friend of mine. You may recall that he and the duchess were married at my chateau. Like ourselves, the duke has a wide understanding of Europe. While there can be no more patriotic Englishman than him, he understands that his country's best interests are not necessarily served by the slaughter of its youth on the battlefields of France.

These matters are sensitive, which is why I am sending this letter by hand. I should like to discuss the European situation and the duke with you face-to-face. I will be in London for a couple days at the end of next week and perhaps we could meet on the 23rd? Please confirm care of Mrs ter Hart at Bedaux International in Amsterdam.

Sincerely yours,
Charles E. Bedaux

Twenty-Three

Kensington, London, 16 November

'What the hell was Millie doing in Holland, Father?'

Conrad's voice was quiet, but full of menace. They were in the library. There had been no invasion of Belgium the day before, no coup against Hitler. But there was other more immediate and far more shocking news. When he had arrived home from Heston Airport half an hour earlier, he was surprised to see his mother up in London from Somerset. One look at her face told him something was dreadfully wrong. It was. Millie had been murdered in Holland.

He hadn't understood for a moment: there was no conceivable reason for Millie to be in the country he had just returned from; it must be some strange mix-up.

But it wasn't. His mother's face told him it wasn't. And although the idea of Millie's death still seemed unreal, a moment's thought gave Conrad a possible reason.

Conrad hugged and comforted his mother, when all the time he just wanted to scream at his father. As soon as he decently could he insisted that he and his father withdraw to the library.

Lord Oakford looked shattered. Thin at the best of times, his face was drawn and wan, the lines that furrowed downwards from the corners of his mouth had become deep ravines. His eyes were dull. The empty arm of his jacket hung limply.

Millie was the second child he had lost; Edward, his eldest son and his heir, had died in a climbing accident on the slopes of Mont Blanc nearly ten years before. For a moment Conrad almost felt sorry for him, but his anger swept that thought away.

'Well, Father?'

Oakford sighed. 'She was there to see Theo,' he mumbled.

'Theo! Why Theo?'

'She . . .' Oakford couldn't get the words out. A tear ran down his cheek.

'I know. It was some hare-brained peace scheme, wasn't it?' Conrad said. 'I refused to go, so you sent Millie along instead.'

Oakford nodded. 'We wanted to open discussions with the plotters. So that if they did succeed in deposing Hitler, we could make peace. Theo was the conduit.'

'How long had you been talking to him?'

'Since the spring. Millie met him in Zurich in April. The conversations came to nothing then, but at least we had a line of communication.'

'You know I saw Theo earlier this week? He didn't say anything to me.'

'We asked him to keep it quiet.'

'So you, Millie and Theo were conspiring against me?'

'We were just trying to bring peace. To stop this war before it kills a million people. It was a noble thing Millie was doing.'

'That's tosh! She was negotiating with the enemy behind her country's back. You made her do it. And now she's dead!'

Oakford hung his head and nodded.

'How was she killed?'

'She was stabbed in some sand dunes in Scheveningen. You remember. We went on holiday there once.'

'Who killed her? Do you know? Was it the Germans? The Gestapo?'

Oakford took a deep breath and raised his eyes to his son. Conrad could tell it took courage for the man, who had become old before his very eyes, to do that, but he was not impressed.

'I don't know. She went with a companion, Constance Scott-Dunton. She's a friend of Henry Alston. I haven't seen Constance yet, I think she is still in Holland talking to the police there.'

'The authorities here have been told, I take it?' Conrad said.

Oakford nodded. 'By our people in The Hague.'

'I bet they weren't happy.'

'No, they weren't,' said Oakford. 'I'm sorry, Conrad.'

'Sorry? Sorry isn't good enough, Father. Sorry is not nearly good enough.'

Conrad couldn't stand the sight of the broken man in front of him. The stupid, stupid old fool! He had brought all this down upon himself, upon Conrad and upon his mother.

He found her in the drawing room looking anxiously at the door. Her face was red, her cheeks stained. He sat down on the sofa next to her and put his arm around her. She let her head fall into his chest and sobbed, her whole body heaving. Conrad patted her hair. First Edward, now Millie.

Eventually, his mother sat up. 'Don't be too hard on him, Conrad.'

'How can I not be hard on him, Mother? It was his fault she went!'

'Yes. But he didn't kill her. Holland is a neutral country. She should have been safe.'

'She was conspiring with someone who wanted to kill the German Chancellor!' Conrad protested. 'That was always going to be dangerous. Father shouldn't have sent her.'

He almost added: 'He should have sent me.' But then he realized he couldn't. Lord Oakford had tried to send Conrad to Switzerland to see Theo earlier that year, but Conrad had refused, and he had refused the previous week when his father had suggested it again. So Millie had gone instead. And Millie was now dead. Because Conrad had said no.

The stupid, stupid old fool.

'I'm sorry, Mother. I can't forgive him. Ever.'

Gestapo Headquarters, Berlin

Walter Schellenberg's chest was swelling as he entered his office. He fingered the unfamiliar shape of the cross around his neck.

He had just been in the Reich Chancellery, marching in with the detachment that had seized the British agents, and had been received in the Führer's study by the Führer himself. Hitler had made a speech about how the British secret service was the best in the world, how Schellenberg and his colleagues had bested them, and how the German secret service was now building up its own traditions. Two thoughts occurred to Schellenberg: that he still believed it a mistake to have seized Payne Best and Stevens, and that Hitler had forgotten Germany's own Abwehr. But he couldn't deny the surge of pride he had felt; they *had* made fools of the famed British secret service.

Medals were handed out all round, Schellenberg and four of the others received an Iron Cross First Class, and the rest Iron Crosses Second Class.

Payne Best and Stevens were locked up somewhere in the Gestapo building next door. Schellenberg hadn't been directly involved in their interrogation: the Gestapo were still pretending to their prisoners that Major Schämmel was a real conspirator. The officers who were interrogating them had been unable to unearth even the remotest connection between the two British agents and Georg Elser, the man who had planted the bomb in the beer cellar in Munich. But Hitler had also ordered Schellenberg to discover the name of all British operatives in Holland, and there had been some success there.

Major Stevens had been carrying a sheet of paper on which various Dutch names had been written: the Abwehr had confirmed that some of these were known agents working for Britain. It seemed likely to Schellenberg that the whole lot were.

Only that morning Stevens had admitted under interrogation that the driver, who had escaped, was a British officer named Conrad de Lancey, who had been spotted in Leiden talking to a Lieutenant von Hertenberg. The British knew him to be an Abwehr officer.

Schellenberg was pleased to see that de Lancey's file was waiting for him on his desk, as he had requested. The Gestapo filing system was its great strength. A vast, meticulously cross-indexed record of the little secrets of thousands of Germans, and, increasingly, foreigners like de Lancey.

Schellenberg picked up the file and leafed through it. Most of the memoranda had been prepared by Kriminalrat Klaus Schalke. Schellenberg remembered him, a big, shambling Gestapo officer who was a favourite of Heydrich's and had been found murdered in the Tiergarten the previous autumn.

The Hon. Conrad de Lancey had been born in Hamburg in 1911. His father, Viscount Oakford, was a former member of the British government and his mother was a daughter of one of the big Hamburg shipping families. De Lancey had gone to university at Oxford and afterwards had fought for the International Brigade in the Spanish Civil War. He had arrived in Berlin in the summer of 1938, where he had quickly aroused Schalke's suspicions. The Gestapo had arrested him with his cousin, Joachim Mühlendorf, who worked for the German Embassy in Moscow and turned out to be spying for the Russians. Mühlendorf had died in custody, but de Lancey had been released. A few weeks later, Schalke had ordered de Lancey's arrest again. De Lancey had been seen with Lieutenant Hertenberg, and at one point Schalke had suspected Hertenberg of hiding him.

Then nothing.

Schellenberg had scarcely known Schalke at all, but his death that September had caused quite a stir. There were rumours that Schalke had been involved in altering Heydrich's ancestry, erasing a Jewish grandparent. Or perhaps adding one. The rumours were vague and brief. No one in the Gestapo wanted to know anything about Heydrich's Jewish roots. The investigation into Schalke's death had been abandoned on the orders of Heydrich himself and the whispers stopped abruptly. There were some subjects you just didn't whisper about.

So who was this Conrad de Lancey? What was Hertenberg up to? And what did it have to do with Heydrich?

De Lancey could be a spy being run by the Abwehr. Or Hertenberg could be a spy being run by the British secret service.

Admiral Canaris might know. Given the involvement of Schalke, Heydrich might know. Asking Heydrich would be stupid. Dropping a casual word to Canaris while riding with him in the Tiergarten might elicit an interesting answer. But then Heydrich would find out that Schellenberg had been asking questions and that might turn out to be stupid too.

Schellenberg needed more information. Following the seizure of the British agents, a number of his officers had been assigned to Holland. One of them should keep a quiet eye on Hertenberg.

Whitehall, London

Still furious with his father and Theo, Conrad left Kensington Square to report to Van at the Foreign Office. His brain was in turmoil as he waited in an ante-room for the Chief Diplomatic Adviser. The reality of Millie's death was pressing in on him, grief piercing through the anger, slowly at first, but more insistently with every minute.

When Mrs Dougherty eventually told him Van was ready to see him, it took a supreme effort of will to focus on his report. He expanded on his cryptic phone call from Amsterdam describing what Theo had told him about Captain Schämmel and the Venlo affair. Then he explained why he had gone to Paris. About Theo and Bedaux. And about the Duke of Windsor.

Van's concern was obvious. Concern tinged with anger, not at Conrad but at the former king. But not as much surprise as Conrad would have expected.

'I need hardly tell you that what you have outlined to me now is highly sensitive,' Van had said. 'Please do not repeat it to anyone. Clearly an allegation that a member of the royal family is a traitor is extremely serious. I can assure you that we will investigate it thoroughly, but until then, it's just a suspicion. Leave it with me. And thank you.'

Conrad stood up to leave. 'By the way, de Lancey,' Van said, his voice uncharacteristically soft. 'I heard about your sister's murder yesterday morning. I am sorry. I met her on a couple of occasions: a lovely girl. Please accept my condolences for you and for your family, especially Lady Oakford.' His voice hardened. 'But tell your father to restrain himself with these independent peace initiatives. They cause all kinds of diplomatic mayhem. And after what happened at Venlo, and what befell your poor sister, it appears they are extremely dangerous.'

'I quite agree, Sir Robert,' said Conrad. 'But my father ceased to listen to me on those matters long ago.'

'We think we know who killed her,' Van said.

Conrad looked at him sharply. 'Who?'

'I received a report from our intelligence services an hour ago, which sheds some light on it, although it also casts doubt on your information about the duke. Apparently her companion Mrs Scott-Dunton followed your sister into the sand dunes and found Millie's body. As she was running for help, she saw someone whom she recognized leaving the dunes.'

'And who was that?' asked Conrad. But as he asked the question, he knew the answer.

'Your friend in the Abwehr,' said Van, his face grave. 'Theo von Hertenberg.'

Twenty-Four

The couple of days following his return from Paris had been extremely painful for Conrad. While the war was still very much 'phoney' for everyone he saw in the street, and for his unit back in Tidworth, it seemed to have already blown his family apart. Millie's death struck Conrad and each of his parents hard in a series of repeating blows interspersed with brief periods of unreal calm. Lord Oakford was suffering from guilt, and so he should be. But then so too was Conrad.

The rational part of his brain knew than he had been correct to ignore his father's requests to contact Theo, that standing up to Hitler was important. But if he had just done what his father had asked, Millie would still be alive. It wasn't as if Lord Oakford had asked him to negotiate with the Nazi government. Theo represented people who were as opposed to the Nazis as Conrad himself.

Conrad didn't know what to make of Van's assertion that Theo was the most likely person to have killed Millie. He couldn't accept it; he didn't want to accept it. The whole point about Theo, what bound him and Conrad so tightly in such difficult circumstances, was that each believed that people were more important than nations or ideologies. Killing his friend's sister would be the repudiation of what they both believed; in a world increasingly full of betrayals, it would be the ultimate betrayal.

But Theo had always been hard to read. There were several different Theos at Oxford: the idealist certainly, the intellectual, but also the womanizer, the drinker, and the arrogant Prussian. More recently there had been Theo the spy.

Theo the spy was especially hard to read. Conrad had no idea why Theo could possibly want to kill Millie, but he knew from first-hand experience the subtle complexities of the German intelligence services where the Gestapo and the Abwehr performed a lethal dance of bluff and counter-bluff and where it was impossible to be sure – to be absolutely sure – on whose side anyone was on.

Including Theo.

All right, Conrad admitted to himself, he didn't *want* to believe Theo had killed his sister: there must be some other explanation, and he must find it. He needed to speak to Constance Scott-Dunton and find out what she knew and how sure she was of her identification.

From his club, Conrad sent a message to her via Sir Henry Alston's office at Gurney Kroheim asking her to meet him as soon as she returned to England. He heard from her the following morning, suggesting that they meet at the Russian Tea Rooms in South Kensington.

He arrived there first, at about half past three. It was a cosy place, with wood panels and a roaring fire. He found a table and ordered some tea. A copy of a magazine named *Truth* lay on the table next to his. He picked it up and leafed through it. There was a particularly unpleasant article about how influential Jews in Britain, including the publisher Victor Gollancz and a bevy of bankers, had pressed Britain to come to the aid of their brethren in Berlin and declare war on Germany. Another criticized Hore-Belisha, the War Minister, for his previous business failures and his support for 'co-religionists'.

Conrad tossed the magazine to one side. Seeing views like this not only written but read by his own countrymen made him profoundly sick. He had seen first hand in Germany how anti-Semitic words could become anti-Semitic actions, and how even a cultured society could succumb to hatred and paranoia. Why couldn't people in England realize that as well as the threat from the continent, there was also the threat from within their own society from poisoners who wrote articles like that?

He looked around the room. The café was half full with respectable people respectably dressed. There was a foreign-looking gentleman with a white beard reading a newspaper in the corner. Then there was a middle-aged man with a beaked nose above a trim moustache drinking tea with a couple of women. Conrad thought he recognized the man: Captain Maule Ramsay, a Scottish Conservative MP noted for his anti-Semitic speeches. What kind of place was this that Mrs Scott-Dunton had brought him to?

'You must be Millie's brother. You look just like her.'

Conrad pulled himself to his feet and took the hand of a dark woman with pale skin and shining eyes.

'I'm Constance. Hello.'

'Hello,' said Conrad. 'Can I get you some—'

But Constance had already indicated to the waitress, whom she seemed to know, that she wanted some tea.

'I'm so sorry about your sister,' Constance said, taking the chair opposite Conrad. 'I didn't know her before we went to Holland together, but we got along famously while we were there. She was a lovely girl. It was dreadful what happened to her.'

'Yes, it was,' said Conrad. But it seemed to him that Constance herself looked more excited than shocked.

'She was very fond of you. She spoke of you a lot,' said Constance.

Conrad was pleased to hear that. 'I was fond of her,' he said. 'When did you get back?'

'Yesterday evening. They flew me back – the Foreign Office, that is. I've had all sorts of interviews with mysterious Dutchmen, and Englishmen for that matter.'

'Thank you for seeing me,' said Conrad.

'Not at all,' said Constance. Her tea arrived in a Russian-style glass.

'Do you mind if I ask you what happened?' Conrad said.

'No, carry on. Everyone else has,' said Constance. 'As your father probably told you, he and Sir Henry Alston sent us over there on a confidential mission.'

'Father did say,' Conrad said. 'You met Lieutenant von Hertenberg?'

'Yes, that's right. Millie said he's a friend of yours from Oxford. A charming man. Or at least he seemed so at the time.'

'Theo is charming,' said Conrad dryly. The man and the two women Conrad had spotted earlier left the tea rooms. One of the women nodded to Constance. 'Do you know, is that Captain Maule Ramsay?' Conrad asked.

'Yes, it is. And that's his wife; they often come here. The other woman is Anna Wolkoff, the daughter of the owner.'

'I see,' said Conrad. 'Sorry, go on.'

'Yes. Well, we spoke to Theo a couple of times, including the day before Millie was killed. We were staying in Scheveningen, by the sea.'

'I know it,' said Conrad. 'We went there on holiday as children.'

'Millie said. Anyway, that night Theo saw me and asked me to tell Millie to meet him early the following morning. He said she had to go alone and I shouldn't come with her. He wanted her to meet someone – he didn't say who.'

Constance sipped her tea.

'So the next morning I got up at the crack of dawn, actually it was before the crack of dawn, to follow Millie. She came out of the hotel and headed off towards the sand dunes. I kept a discreet distance behind her. The sand dunes were quite bumpy, being sand dunes, so I couldn't see her very clearly. Then I heard a short sharp cry. Well, I was worried. I wasn't sure whether to run towards her or away from her – it was still pretty dark. But I thought I had better take a look. And I found her on the ground with . . . with a knife sticking out of her chest.'

Constance looked down at her tea as she said this. Her face was grim. Then she glanced up to check Conrad's reaction. For a moment his mind conjured up an image of Millie lying in the sand, but it was too horrible to think about.

'Did you see anyone?'

'Not straight away. Nor did I hear anything. I ran over to see if she was all right, but . . .' Constance lowered her eyes again. 'She wasn't. She was . . . dead.'

Conrad sighed. Silence lay heavily around them, shrouding thoughts of Millie.

'I'm sorry,' Constance said.

'But then you saw Theo?'

'Yes. When I went looking for help. He was heading towards the tram stop.'

'Did you call out to him?'

'No, of course not! He was quite far away. But more importantly, I thought he had stabbed Millie. I didn't want him to kill me too! So I ran along to one of the hotels on the sea front and got them to ring the police.'

This didn't look good. 'Are you sure it was Theo? You say he was quite far away.'

'Pretty sure. He was tall, wearing the same kind of hat as Theo, and he walked upright like Theo does.'

'But you didn't see his face?'

'Not clearly,' Constance admitted. 'I told the police that. And the men from the Foreign Office.'

'So you are not absolutely sure? It could have been someone else?'

'I suppose it could have been. But it looked like Theo to me.' Constance smiled sympathetically. 'I'm sorry, I know he is a friend of yours. Or was.'

Is, thought Conrad. Is. There *was* some doubt about Theo's identification after all. 'You have no idea whom Theo was bringing with him?'

'No. None.'

'Why didn't Theo want you to come too?'

Constance hesitated. 'I don't know. I thought maybe . . .'

'Maybe what?'

'Your sister was sweet on Theo. Didn't you know that?'

Bloody hell, thought Conrad. 'No. I didn't know that. Are you saying it was some kind of . . . assignation?'

'I don't know,' said Constance. 'It was just a feeling, that's all. A guess. Perhaps Theo really did bring someone else along for Millie to meet.'

'The secret service seem to think that Theo killed her.'

'I know,' said Constance.

'But you can't be certain that you actually saw him, let alone saw him stab her?'

'I'm pretty sure it was him,' Constance said. 'And he is a German spy, isn't he?'

Conrad nodded. 'Well, thanks for telling me,' he said. Then a thought struck him. 'Why did you follow her?'

'Why?' Constance repeated.

'Why?'

'I'm curious. I've always been known for my nosiness. I wanted to know whether Theo really had brought someone to meet Millie, or if they were just, you know, meeting. An assignation. Also I suppose I didn't like being left out.'

'I see,' said Conrad. But he wasn't quite sure that he *did* see.

Mayfair, London

Conrad grabbed the pint of beer and the glass of gin and It and fought his way through the small pub in Mayfair to where Anneliese was sitting in a corner. He had known the place in the past as a quiet pub where they might talk, but there were no quiet pubs in London in wartime, even on a Sunday evening. At least they had been able to find a seat.

Anneliese raised her glass. 'To Millie,' she said.

Conrad smiled. 'Yes. To Millie.' They both drank.

'I needed that.' Anneliese put down her drink. Conrad had introduced her to gin and Italian vermouth soon after she had arrived in London and asked for something English from the bar. Afterwards he had realized it was a favourite of Veronica's, but he hadn't told Anneliese that. She was wearing her nurse's uniform: the pub was full of uniforms of various types, although Conrad was still in his civilian suit.

'I'm glad you rang me,' he said.

'Your mother wrote to me about Millie and I was shocked. I wrote her a note back and then I thought I must see you. I know how fond you were of your sister. I liked her; she always treated me well.'

'Unlike Reggie?' said Conrad.

'Your brother is just ignorant,' said Anneliese. 'Millie wasn't. She was fun.'

'Yes, she was,' said Conrad.

'How do you feel?' Anneliese asked.

Conrad was flummoxed by the simplicity of the question. 'I'll be all right,' he said. 'This is war. People will die.'

'Oh, Conrad, don't be so bloody British! Of course people will die. And it will be horrible for their brothers and sisters.'

'Yes, of course,' Conrad said stiffly. He glanced at Anneliese. His chest was churning with a turmoil of emotions to do with Millie. He hadn't sorted them out; he hadn't expressed them. He hadn't even wept yet. He *had* been angry with his father. With Theo.

Anneliese waited.

Conrad was tempted to change the subject. To make a joke. To avoid at all costs cracking the wall that he was erecting around those thoughts about Millie. To behave how an Englishman should. But Anneliese wasn't like that; his relationship with Anneliese wasn't like that. They had shared a lot in Germany, and she had sought him out then, when she thought he needed support and strength.

It had been so good to hear her voice on the phone. It was good to be with her now, surrounded by a cocoon of noise and uniforms standing around their table.

'I'm sad,' he said, slowly and carefully, concentrating on not allowing his voice to crack. He was speaking quietly and in

German: in the hubbub of the pub none of the servicemen around them would be able to hear. 'I'm very sad. Millie had such a zest for life, such honesty, such enthusiasm. It's wrong that she has gone. And it makes me angry. Very angry. So angry I can hardly think straight.'

'Why are you angry?' Anneliese asked.

Conrad struggled for a moment to maintain his composure. 'I'm angry because it is wrong that a young woman like her should die, even in a war. She's not a soldier. And I'm really angry about how she died.'

'Yes. I don't understand that,' said Anneliese. 'Your mother said she had been killed while on holiday in the Netherlands. That sounded very strange. I remember you saying you were going away. Were you with her?'

'No,' Conrad shook his head. 'I did go to Holland; I just didn't know she was there as well.'

Conrad told Anneliese all about Millie's meeting with Theo, arranged by their father and Sir Henry Alston. He recounted what Constance had told him about how she had found Millie's body in the dunes.

Anneliese listened intently. 'And you knew nothing about any of this?'

'No. Despite the fact that I saw Theo in Leiden the day before he met Millie. And that I spent the night at Kensington Square with Father and Millie just before I left for Holland. She and Constance must have been on the next flight!'

'No wonder you are angry,' said Anneliese.

'It's not just that,' said Conrad. He paused, took a sip of his beer. 'I should have gone instead of her. Father asked me, but I refused, and so he asked Millie instead and she said yes. And that's why she's dead. So I'm angry with myself.'

'You can't blame yourself for that,' Anneliese said. 'You didn't kill her. You didn't send her.'

Conrad shrugged.

'What was she talking to Theo about?'

'I'd better not say,' said Conrad. 'But you can probably guess. My dealings with Theo didn't turn out too well either, although I didn't think then that was Theo's fault. At least I assumed it wasn't. Now I'm not sure what the hell Theo was up to.'

Conrad knew he shouldn't tell Anneliese about Oakford's peace talks, or the shooting at Venlo, which was still being inaccurately reported in the British newspapers. But perhaps he should reassess Theo's profession of lack of knowledge of Major Schämmel's identity. Could he trust his friend after all?

'Damn Theo,' Conrad said, his voice still low.

'For not telling you?'

'For not telling me. And for not protecting Millie for me. You know, this Constance woman says that Millie and Theo had some sort of romance going on? Since last spring when they met in Switzerland. He never told me about *that* either. And also . . .'

'Also what?'

'The secret service seem to think that he killed Millie.'

'No! That can't be right!'

'Constance saw a man walking from the dunes to the tram stop. She thinks it was Theo.'

'Thinks? So she isn't certain?'

'Not one hundred per cent. But close to certain. She seems to have convinced the secret service.'

'And what do you think?'

'I hope it wasn't him.' Conrad shrugged. 'But he's a spy, Anneliese. We can never be sure what he is really doing or why. I want to see him. I really must see him.'

'Can you manage that somehow?' Anneliese asked.

'I don't see how. I do have a way of getting touch with him, but I can't just swan over to Holland again. I have to go back to the battalion on Tuesday.'

Anneliese sipped her gin, thinking. 'What's happened to Millie?' she asked. 'Her body, I mean. Is it still in Holland?'

'The Dutch authorities are keeping hold of her,' Conrad said. 'They have done a post-mortem, of course, but her body is evidence in a murder inquiry. The embassy is supposed to be dealing with it, but they seem useless. It's all rather ghoulish. Mother can't stand it, and it makes it impossible to arrange the funeral.'

'Shouldn't someone go over there to sort it out?' said Anneliese. 'You, for instance?'

'Maybe I should,' said Conrad. He nodded as he thought it through. 'Good idea. I'll talk to Father about it.'

'What about this woman Constance? Who is she?'

'That's a good question. She was Millie's companion in Holland. She is some sort of friend of Sir Henry Alston, who is one of my father's fellow directors at Gurney Kroheim and a Conservative MP. He's definitely pro-German, but then my father is pro-German. Hell, I'm pro-German. But I think Alston might be pro-Nazi, which is a very different thing. You know that as well as anyone.'

'I do,' said Anneliese.

'I have my doubts about Constance.'

'Why?'

'We met at this place called the Russian Tea Rooms. On the surface it looks very respectable, but they had copies of *Truth* there – it's an obnoxious anti-Semitic magazine. A kind of British *Völkischer Beobachter.*'

'I've never seen it,' said Anneliese.

'Good. Don't. Also, I spotted Captain Maule Ramsay; he's a right-wing pro-Nazi MP, much further to the right than Alston. Constance seemed at home there. Her story doesn't stack up very well; for example, she said she got up early in the morning to follow Millie to her rendezvous with Theo, but she didn't really explain *why* she had done that. Or at least not satisfactorily. I'd really like to do some more digging, but I can't. I don't have the time.'

Anneliese sipped her drink. Conrad felt a surge of warmth towards her. Talking to her had lifted some of enormous weight he felt bearing down on him. Only some of it, and only for a moment, but it had felt good to speak to her, and he was grateful that she had made him do it. Naturally he was bloody angry, who wouldn't be?

She seemed different, a little less withdrawn, a little less wrapped up in her own misery, a little more like the old Anneliese.

'Perhaps I could help,' she said, putting her glass down and looking straight at him.

'You? How? You can't go to Holland to see Theo.'

'No. But I could find out more about Constance. She was with Millie when she died. It sounds as if you think she might know what really happened. If I make friends with her, maybe I can discover what that was.'

'But you are half-Jewish. And German. How are you going to do that?'

'I'm half not-Jewish. And I know a lot about Nazis. If you are right about her, she might enjoy having a Nazi German friend.'

Conrad smiled. 'Anneliese, I really appreciate you doing this for me, but don't worry about it.'

'Why not?' said Anneliese. 'I saw Wilfrid Israel last Saturday and asked him if I could do something for Captain Foley. Something secret to help the war. I haven't heard back yet, but I really want to do something useful. And if I can't do something useful for your country, perhaps I can do something useful for you.'

Conrad realized he *was* talking to the old Anneliese. And he liked it.

'All right,' he said. 'It sounds crazy to me, but if you really want to do it, have a go.'

Twenty-Five

Kensington, London, 20 November

'I hope you can persuade them to release her, Conrad,' Lord Oakford said. 'It will be a great comfort to your mother to know that Millie is safely buried in St Peter's churchyard.'

'It will be to all of us,' said Conrad. Although he knew they would all be relieved if he succeeded in bringing Millie back to Somerset, he also knew that the hole she had left in their family would always be there, just as her elder brother's absence had hovered over them for the last ten years. His mother had been near to hysteria, more upset even than she had been after Edward's death. Lady Oakford was usually the calm centre of the family, the stable counterweight to her husband's moods, the source of common sense and sanity. Her raw grief, although it should have been understandable, was a shock for her husband and her son. Any activity was better than nothing.

So Oakford had jumped at Conrad's suggestion that he go and fetch Millie's body, and that morning had spoken directly to the Ambassador in The Hague, whom of course he knew, to arrange it. Conrad had booked a flight to Schiphol in two days' time. Colonel Rydal had reluctantly agreed to a few days' extension of his leave.

They were sitting in Lord Oakford's study in the house in Kensington Square. Although there was a copy of *The Times* by his father's armchair, it was unread. When Conrad had entered the room, his father had been staring out of the window, and when he had turned towards his son, his eyes were glazed, vacant.

Lord Oakford's passivity was worrying in its own way; it seemed fragile, a thin shell that could at any moment be shattered by the rage that Conrad knew must be bubbling underneath. But at least it had allowed Conrad to be civil to him while he was forced to stay at Kensington Square. Conrad was doing his best to control his own temper, which was extremely difficult, given that he still blamed his father for Millie's death. He hadn't forgiven him; he didn't see how he could ever forgive him.

'Can you tell me a bit about the Duke of Windsor?' Conrad asked. 'I missed all the fuss over the abdication, I was in Spain.'

'What do you want to know?'

'Was he forced to abdicate? And if he was, were there reasons beyond his desire to marry Wallis Simpson? His pro-German attitude perhaps?'

'There's no doubt that Mrs Simpson was the main reason. The government, and the dominions, felt he couldn't be king and be married to a divorced woman, which it was clear he had every intention of doing. Many people felt that putting his lover before his country was an appalling failure of duty as king. Winston supported him, but what would you expect from Winston?'

'Was anyone concerned about his friendship with Germany?'

'Yes, they were,' Oakford admitted. 'He had had a number of meetings with senior Nazis, in particular Hess and Ribbentrop. When he became king, he took a more active interest in government policy than his father had. He put pressure on Stanley Baldwin not to react to Hitler's invasion of the Rhineland in 1936. There was a lot of concern about Mrs Simpson and her friendship with various unsavoury Germans in London. Ribbentrop saw her all the time while he was German Ambassador, sent her roses every day. The security service had a sordid file on her.'

'Sordid?'

'Oh, yes. She spent time in China, you know, and there is supposed to be a file somewhere about techniques she learned in brothels while she was there. Something called the "Singapore Grip". Do you know what that is?'

'No,' said Conrad, although he could have a guess. But since he was talking to his father, he decided not to.

'Probably just as well,' said his father. 'They also discovered that while Edward was king, Mrs Simpson was seeing a car salesman named Trundle whom she appeared to be paying.' Oakford sighed. 'It's very painful to watch your sovereign abandon his kingdom for a woman who is sleeping with a car salesman.'

'I can see that,' said Conrad. 'And you? What did you think about the abdication?'

'As you probably remember, I fell out with him over his interference in the Abyssinian affair.' Conrad did remember: in 1935 Mussolini had made a grab for Abyssinia and the British and French governments, with Samuel Hoare as Foreign Secretary had let him get away with it, strongly encouraged by the then Prince of Wales. Lord Oakford didn't disagree with the government's policy, but he had resigned from the Cabinet over what he considered the misleading statements from the government about their negotiations with the French and Italians. Lying, he had called it.

'And I think he was a bloody fool to abdicate. He should have toughed it out. Henry VIII did – you could say that divorce is what kicked off the Church of England. He was also a bloody fool to hobnob with the Nazis, but I'm sure he doesn't actually agree with them. And he has good instincts for peace. Did you read that broadcast he made from Verdun last spring?'

'I read about it,' said Conrad. 'It caused quite a stir, didn't it?' A few months before the outbreak of war, the duke had used the occasion of a visit to the Verdun battlefield to make an impassioned speech for peace, which was broadcast by an American radio station.

'It did,' said Oakford. 'But it made sense to me.' He frowned. 'Why all these questions?'

'After Holland, I went to Paris,' Conrad said. 'And I heard some worrying rumours about the duke.'

'There are always worrying rumours about the duke,' said Lord Oakford. 'People don't like him after he chucked the throne. But he loves his country, I'm sure of that. And he is still a member of the royal family, a former king. It's absurd to think that he would do anything to betray England.'

'Absurd?'

'Absurd,' Oakford repeated. His frown deepened. 'I know what it is! You think because he believes in peace he doesn't love his country. Why can't you understand that it's exactly *because* we love our country that people like him, and me for that matter, believe that we shouldn't be fighting? The war will ruin us. Once it gets going, hundreds of thousands of Englishmen will lose their lives. We might even lose the damn thing. Is that good for Britain? Answer me that!'

The voice was rising; the eyes were glinting. Conrad's father was on the brink of exploding. Conrad wanted to answer, to disagree, to argue, but he knew what that would lead to. For his mother's sake he had stayed on in Kensington Square; for his mother's sake he was still speaking to his father after he had sent Millie to her death in a quixotic lunge for peace.

But then his father did something rather odd. He apologized.

'I'm sorry, Conrad. Millie's death has . . . Well, you know. And then I have just received some news that I should really tell you.'

An apology from his father was rare, and Conrad appreciated it. 'That's all right, Father. What's the news?'

'Are you seeing Theo in Holland?'

'I've contacted him,' said Conrad. He had sent a telegram to the Copenhagen address suggesting that Theo meet him at the University of Leiden. 'I haven't received a reply, and I don't necessarily expect one, but I hope he shows up. There's a lot I want to ask him. He may well know the answers.'

'He may,' said Oakford. His face, already grave, became even graver. 'Van telephoned me half an hour ago. They have more evidence about Millie's death.'

'What?' asked Conrad.

'They have a witness. A walker who saw Theo running out of the dunes with blood on his hands and his shirt. He identified him by the scar on his jaw. I'm sorry, Conrad. There is no doubt now that Theo killed her.'

Conrad refilled his glass from the port decanter and sat in his father's armchair in front of the embers of the coal fire in the drawing room. It was just past midnight: the others had all gone up to bed.

The decanter was almost down to the dregs; Conrad had already helped himself to quite a few glasses. There was something about drinking port that reminded Conrad of Theo, of those long nocturnal conversations at Oxford.

He fixed his eyes on the fireplace, as if an answer would be revealed somewhere in the dying orange glow of the coals, if only he stared long and hard enough.

How could he do it? How could Theo kill Millie?

Had he really killed Millie?

Ever since he had heard about the new witness in Holland, Conrad had been torn between fury and disbelief. Fury that Theo had killed his sister and disbelief that he actually had done so. He tried to cling to the disbelief, but all the time he was afraid he was just hiding from the truth, denying the evidence.

Conrad had known Theo since the age of eighteen. During that time they had shared much: ideas, drink, friendship and, more recently, a sense that the only way to stop global catastrophe was to stop Hitler. They loved and respected their own countries and each other's. They had faced danger together; together they had worked to overthrow the German dictator. It was bad enough for Conrad to learn that Theo had been negotiating with his sister and his father behind his back. To be told that Theo of all people had actually killed Millie was unbearable. Unthinkable.

It *was* unthinkable. Apart from anything else, Theo was not a killer, or not yet. Unlike Conrad, who had killed in Spain and then in Berlin. Chivalry was bred deep into Theo; Conrad could not imagine him stabbing a woman, especially not Conrad's sister.

But the unthinkable had happened.

Why would Theo do it? Conrad couldn't think of a reason, but that didn't mean there wasn't one. In the world of espionage he was beginning to realize that few people if any ever had the whole picture. And the other trait that was bred deep into his friend was loyalty to his country. For the right reason, if there was no other alternative, and if his country demanded it, perhaps Theo could kill, in much the same way his Prussian ancestors had killed, ever since the Seven Years War two hundred years before.

Conrad hoped he would find out something more in Holland, either from the Dutch authorities, or from Theo himself. But deep down he knew he should stop fooling himself, accept the unacceptable.

His friend had killed his sister.

Twenty-Six

Gestapo Headquarters, Berlin, 21 November

Schellenberg examined the short memorandum on his desk, and frowned. When you worked for the Gestapo, there were certain moments where taking the wrong decision, following the wrong path, could be career-threatening. Even life-threatening. Survival came from recognizing those moments; they were not always easy to spot.

Schellenberg's instinct told him this was one of them.

The memorandum came from one of the Gestapo officers detailed to keep an eye on Lieutenant von Hertenberg in Holland. The officer had approached a Dutch professor at the University of Leiden, W. F. Hogendoorn, who was a firm believer in National Socialism and felt that his own country's future would best be served by friendship with Germany. The professor had occasionally been used in the past by Hertenberg as a means of contacting foreigners in Holland. One of these was an Englishman named Conrad de Lancey. Hogendoorn told the Gestapo officer he had his doubts about Mr de Lancey, and by implication about Hertenberg. He wondered whether what they were doing was above board.

It was a good question and Schellenberg didn't know the answer.

The choices facing Schellenberg were the same as before: he could keep the information to himself, he could check with Canaris, or he could inform Heydrich. Schellenberg preferred the first option, but he knew that if he chose not to inform Heydrich now and his decision came to the notice of his superior, he would be in trouble. Possibly terminal trouble. And his instinct was that de Lancey and Hertenberg were likely to cause more difficulties, the kind of difficulties that would get them noticed.

He dug out the de Lancey file from his desk drawer, picked up the telephone and called Heydrich's secretary, telling her he had to see him as soon as possible.

The Gruppenführer was only a few years older than Schellenberg, a tall man with blond thinning hair brushed back over a high forehead. His eyes were small and crafty, and his nose and lips suggested the cruelty of a predator – a hawk perhaps, or even a vulture. Yet there was something feminine about him: his high-pitched voice, his wide hips, his delicate hands. The whole effect was disconcerting, disorienting, a warning. In Schellenberg's opinion, it was sensible to be disconcerted by Heydrich.

Schellenberg remained standing as he passed his chief the memorandum.

Heydrich scanned it quickly, and then waited, his eyes on the paper. Schellenberg knew he was thinking, not reading.

He tossed it to one side, and leaned back in his chair. 'So?' he said.

Heydrich was asking how much Schellenberg knew. This was Schellenberg's chance to tell him he knew very little.

'This is the second time I have come across de Lancey's name,' he said. 'It first came up during the interrogation of Major Stevens a couple of days ago. Stevens claimed that his men in Holland had followed de Lancey, and saw him meet Hertenberg in Leiden. That was probably the seventh of November. I retrieved de Lancey's file and discovered that he and Hertenberg were old friends from Oxford University. In fact they had seen a lot of each other last year, when de Lancey visited Berlin.'

'And what did you do with this knowledge?'

'Much of the file was put together by Kriminalrat Schalke, whom you may remember was murdered in the Tiergarten last year. Having read the file, it seemed to me prudent just to watch Hertenberg and wait to see what he did.'

Heydrich smiled. 'You have good judgement, Walter.'

'I was tempted to continue just to watch and wait, but I thought it was better to inform you.'

'Another good decision. Let me see the file.'

Schellenberg handed it over and Heydrich flipped through it. The Gestapo chief grunted and a small smile crossed his lips. Schellenberg guessed that he was pleased to observe the obvious gaps. Heydrich stood up, walked over to the window, and stared across the Wilhelmstrasse to the new Reich Chancellery. Schellenberg waited.

'Klaus Schalke was a good officer. I'm sorry he died, and I am quite sure that de Lancey had something to do with it. I met him once, next door.' Heydrich meant the Gestapo building around the corner in Prinz-Albrecht-Strasse. There had been nothing in the file about Heydrich interrogating de Lancey, another deliberate omission no doubt. 'I didn't like him. And I have severe doubts about his friend Lieutenant Hertenberg.'

Schellenberg remained silent.

'Get Naujocks to put one of his men on to it. When de Lancey comes to Holland I want him dealt with. And tell Naujocks that it would be most unfortunate if an accident were to befall Hertenberg at the same time.'

Schellenberg knew that when Heydrich used the word 'unfortunate' he meant the opposite. He had no objection to de Lancey's death, but he thought Heydrich was going too far with Hertenberg.

'But Hertenberg is an officer of the Abwehr! Shouldn't we check with Canaris to see whether he knows about the meeting?'

'I am sure that Canaris is being hoodwinked by these two as much as we are. And, as I said, it would be most regrettable if Lieutenant Hertenberg were hurt in the operation. Do I make myself clear?'

'Crystal clear, Herr Gruppenführer! *Heil Hitler!*' Schellenberg clicked his heels and saluted. He understood his orders.

'It's a shame you couldn't get away, Theo.'

'I know, Dieter,' Theo replied. 'I haven't been home since May.' Once again he had had to drop everything and fly to Holland, this time to meet Conrad. He couldn't explain this to Dieter, of course. His aeroplane was leaving Tempelhof that afternoon.

Theo and his younger brother were strolling along Unter den Linden, both in their Wehrmacht uniforms. Although Dieter was only five years Theo's junior, he looked a lot younger than twenty-five. He was an enthusiastic soldier, in fact he was enthusiastic about everything, with a wide grin full of innocent charm, and unruly red hair which even a military haircut could not completely tame.

They had agreed to meet at Café Kranzler on the corner of Friedrichstrasse, but it was too crowded and Dieter said he needed the exercise between two long train journeys: one from Koblenz to Berlin, another to Stettin, and then on to the little town in Pomerania near which their family owned a small manor house and estate. The war was playing havoc with Germany's rail system; the trains never ran on time, with delays of many hours, and there had been two major crashes with hundreds dead. During this *Sitzkrieg* it was safer sitting on the western front than taking a train home.

It was cold, but at least it wasn't raining. Unter den Linden was busy, with sleek modern vehicles fluttering swastikas and men dressed in the smart uniforms of the modern German Reich passing purposefully in front of the grand buildings and statues of the old, glorious Prussia. The biggest statue of all, Frederick the Great, looked down approvingly on it all from his horse further down the avenue.

'Father said we are going hunting tomorrow. The Bismarcks will be there. And the Kleists.'

'Give my regards to Uncle Ewald,' said Theo. 'And the others.'

'So you and Uncle Ewald haven't been discussing things recently?'

Theo knew Dieter was referring to the various plans to remove Hitler. While Dieter had never been involved directly in any of the plotting, it was impossible to be a member of one of those close-knit Prussian families and not know about them. Uncle Ewald – Ewald von Kleist – had been right at the centre of those discussions, and had visited Britain in the summer of 1938 with the help of Theo and Conrad to meet senior British politicians.

'It's been called off,' said Theo. 'I don't think Brauchitsch and Halder ever really had the guts for it.'

'I'm glad to hear that,' said Dieter.

'Are you?' Theo asked sharply.

Dieter walked in silence for a bit. 'Yes, I am. I agree with all of you that Hitler is a madman and the country would be better off without him. He will ruin Germany. But I am a soldier and we are at war. I want us to win, Theo. This isn't the time for a putsch. This is the time for fighting the enemy.'

In some ways Theo admired his brother's loyalty and straightforward patriotism. Dieter was no Nazi; he was a decent man who believed in his country. But it had long been Theo's role in life to explain things to his little brother.

'Look at the linden trees,' said Theo.

'What lindens?' said Dieter.

The tall lindens that gave the street its name had been chopped down in 1934 to facilitate the construction of the S-Bahn. Saplings had replaced them, but it had changed the whole character of the boulevard.

'Precisely. You know the song: "As long as the old trees stay on Unter den Linden, nothing can defeat us. Berlin will stay Berlin." The trees are gone, Dieter.'

'And that's just an old song,' said Dieter. 'I saw what we did in Poland. I know we can do it again in France.'

'What was Poland like?'

'We did well,' said Dieter. 'Mostly the Poles retreated or surrendered, but we were involved in one action. There was a counter-attack near the River Bzura, and we held off a

Polish cavalry brigade for two days. They fought bravely and so did we.'

Theo was curious about what real battle was like. In his role in the Abwehr he had faced danger, but never a visible enemy. Conrad had, and now so had Dieter.

'Did you take many casualties?' he asked.

'Our company lost fifteen men killed and twenty-three wounded.'

'Were you afraid?'

Dieter glanced at his older brother. It wasn't the sort of question one soldier asked another, at least not in the Wehrmacht. 'Yes. I was. But I was also excited. And when we realized on the third day the Polish brigade had given up their attack, I felt so proud. Our unit worked well together: all that training paid off. And, yes, I felt that I was doing what I was born to do, what all those Hertenbergs from Father back through history have done. We fight wars. It's dangerous, sometimes we get killed, but we usually win. I often think you don't understand that, Theo.'

'You are probably right.'

'So I am happy to kill and be killed in battle. Not happy, so much as willing. But the horrific killing I saw had nothing to do with battle.'

'What do you mean?'

'Afterwards we marched past a POW camp guarded by the SS. Except it wasn't really a camp, and the POWs were not really prisoners of war. It was a field outside a village with a couple of hundred Poles inside it, soldiers but also women and children. The SS had set up machine guns around the perimeter of the field. There were about fifty bodies lying in the perimeter where they had been shot – we heard later most of them had been trying to relieve themselves. We took over the camp from the SS; it turned out the prisoners had been given no food or water for days. Our major has filed a report and we'll see what happens. But the whole thing made me feel bad, dirty even. It was as if what those SS men did betrayed the bravery of our own comrades who had died by the River Bzura.'

'That's why Hitler has to go,' said Theo.

Dieter grunted. They passed beneath the Brandenburg Gate and crossed the road into the Tiergarten. A new thoroughfare had been bulldozed through the park, at the end of which was the recently relocated Siegessäule victory statue, which Berliners claimed looked like a giant asparagus. The light was fading.

'So you are on the western front now?' Theo asked.

'Yes. I've been made ADC to General Guderian. Do you know him?'

'I've never met him, but I've read *Achtung Panzer!*' said Theo. 'He's XIX Corps commander in Army Group A, isn't he?' Theo remembered the 'cowhide' relief map at Zossen and his conversation with Major Liss.

'You are well informed.'

'I am,' Theo admitted. 'How did you manage that?'

'I mended his wireless in Poland; all that messing around with electronics when I was a boy finally paid off. Guderian pulled up next to our unit in his command vehicle swearing blue murder. I fixed the set and we got talking about radios. He believes reliable wireless communications are what allow a general to lead panzers from the front and keep the initiative in battle. He seemed to like me and arranged the transfer. Cousin Paul helped – Guderian reports to him.'

'Cousin Paul' was General of Cavalry Paul von Kleist, their mother's cousin, and the commander of Panzer Group Kleist of which XIX Corps was a part. When it came to the Wehrmacht the Hertenbergs were well connected.

'What's Guderian like?'

'Impressive. If you've read his book you'll know he is a great believer in the blitzkrieg. Mobility, concentration, seizing the initiative and keeping it.'

'Army Group A's role is to protect the flank of Army Group B in the Ardennes, as Army Group B drives through Belgium towards the Channel. So no blitzkrieg for General Guderian.'

'That's right,' said Dieter. 'And Guderian doesn't like that. He thinks we should strike in the Ardennes, with him in the

190

vanguard, of course. He's trying to persuade General Manstein, who in turn needs to persuade the general staff and ultimately the Führer.'

'Your chief is absolutely right,' said Theo. 'That section of the line is defended by the French 2nd Army under General Huntziger. They are a bunch of overweight under-trained reservists whose defensive preparations are poor. The French think the Ardennes is impassable to modern tanks; it's the weakest point in the line.'

'How do you know this, Theo? Is this what you are doing for the Abwehr?'

'I know it,' said Theo. 'And so does OKW, although I am not sure yet whether they have drawn the correct conclusions. Your General Guderian has the right idea. The strongest French forces and the BEF are lined up on the Belgian frontier to move north and meet Army Group B in Flanders. Army Group A should make the breakthrough through the Ardennes.'

'I'll tell him,' said Dieter.

'Unofficially.'

Dieter stopped. 'By the way, I know this might sound crazy, but I think that a man is following us. In the brown overcoat on the other side of the road.'

'I know,' said Theo. 'I've seen him.'

'He's not a British spy, is he?'

'Gestapo,' said Theo. 'Almost certainly.'

'So the Gestapo spies on its own spies?'

'It would seem so,' said Theo. 'Don't worry. There is nothing suspicious in me meeting my brother.' Though in truth Theo *was* worried. The Abwehr had many officers and the Gestapo couldn't follow them all. Why Theo? Did it have something to do with Conrad and the capture of the British agents? Or were the Gestapo finally getting to grips with the army officers who opposed Hitler, just when it seemed the Nazis no longer had anything to fear from them?

They were at the edge of the woods in the Tiergarten when Dieter stopped. 'I should head off to the station now. I'm glad I got to see you, even if you can't make it home.'

'Me too,' said Theo. 'Give my love to everyone.' He embraced his brother and turned through the woods towards Abwehr headquarters in the Tirpitzufer.

He had only gone a few yards when an unpleasant thought struck him. Perhaps he would never see Dieter again. Theo had always looked after his little brother. In some ways Dieter's naive patriotism irritated him; Theo felt it was his job to keep Dieter away from danger. Yet for all Theo's worldly experience, Dieter had actually fought for his country and Theo hadn't, at least not yet.

In a few weeks or months, Dieter would be fighting his way through Luxembourg and Belgium, and Theo wouldn't be there to protect him.

Theo could cope with Dieter fighting for his country. He just prayed that his little brother wouldn't die for it.

Twenty-Seven

Police Headquarters, The Hague, 22 November

Conrad was apprehensive about meeting Theo in Holland. Just before leaving England he had received a brief cable from Denmark confirming that Theo would see him in Leiden. At least Theo hadn't ducked it, which Conrad had half expected him to. On the one hand, Conrad knew he had to confront him. On the other, if Theo really had killed Millie, then he would have no compunction in killing Conrad too. Theo his friend would become Theo his killer. Unthinkable. But Conrad knew he had better think it.

It was a risk Conrad just had to take.

But first he wanted to find out what he could from the Dutch authorities. The man from the British Embassy in The Hague was much less friendly to Conrad than he had been when he had rescued Conrad from his Dutch inquisitors after Venlo. Conrad and his family were trouble. But despite his coolness, the official was still polite and efficient, and had arranged an appointment with the Dutch police inspector who was in charge of the murder investigation, and who might have the authority to start the process of releasing Millie's body for repatriation to England.

Police headquarters was a suitably solid-looking building not far from the embassy, in Alexanderplein. Conrad was kept waiting for twenty minutes before he was shown into a small office, which reeked of tobacco smoke. The policeman slumped behind his desk was about fifty, short and flabby, with thick tousled iron-grey hair. He was dressed in a baggy suit. He was smoking a cigarette and two full ashtrays scattered ash like post-eruption volcanic craters amid the jumble of files on his desktop.

Conrad was taken aback. The officials he had come across in Holland so far, while not quite Teutonic, had tended to be clean, smart and efficient.

'Do you speak German?' he asked the policeman in that language.

The man didn't get up, but examined Conrad through narrowed eyes. 'Why would I speak German to an Englishman?' he said in English, with a heavy Dutch accent. 'Take a seat.'

Conrad sat in one of two small wooden chairs. It creaked.

'My name is Conrad de Lancey. I am here to enquire about the murder of my sister, Millicent de Lancey.'

'I know,' said the policeman. 'I suppose you have come to the right place. I am Inspector van Gils, and I am in charge of the investigation.'

'Good,' said Conrad, trying a smile. 'I wonder if you could tell me about her death?'

'Can *you*?' the policeman said, his brown eyes examining Conrad.

'What do you mean?'

'Can you tell me anything about your sister's death? It's a reasonable question,' van Gils said. 'I am *supposed* to be investigating it after all.'

The bitter emphasis on the word 'supposed' was not lost on Conrad. 'No. I'm afraid I can't. I know nothing about it.'

Van Gils's hand darted into the files in front of him and produced a slim one, which he opened. 'Is it true you were in the Netherlands two weeks ago?'

'Yes,' Conrad admitted. He knew his reluctance to answer was obvious to the policeman.

'And did you visit the little town of Venlo, in the east of our country, on the ninth of November? Take a little tour through the woods? Stop at a little café?'

'Yes,' said Conrad. 'But I spoke to your colleagues about that.'

'Not my colleagues. Military intelligence. Believe me, Mr de

Lancey, it is not their job to solve murders. But it is mine. Your country and Germany have your war going on, I understand that, but I do not appreciate your use of my town as a substitute for a battlefield, especially when an innocent tourist gets killed. If she was an innocent tourist?'

Conrad didn't answer.

'Your sister spoke perfect English and perfect German. She had a French name. As do you, of course. So I suspect neither of you was an innocent tourist. Which is, of course, why you won't answer my questions. I understand that. What I don't understand is why I should answer yours.'

'Actually, I don't work for the British secret service,' said Conrad. 'At least not directly.'

'So will you answer my questions?'

The policeman had a half-smile on his face. It was clear to Conrad that this was no Dutch military intelligence stooge. Nor was he a Gestapo or Abwehr agent, and he didn't work for Stevens or the British secret service. He was just a detective trying to do his job, and his job was finding out who killed Millie on his patch.

'All right,' said Conrad. He shrugged. 'Why not?'

The detective's eyes narrowed. 'Are you sure?'

'Yes,' said Conrad. 'I'll answer your questions now. I won't sign a statement, and I won't guarantee that I will testify in a criminal court; somehow I think someone will find a way to stop me, don't you?'

The detective grunted, stubbed out his cigarette in one of the ashtrays, lit another, and as an afterthought offered Conrad one, which Conrad took. He pulled out a torn notebook.

'Very well. Take me through what you did since you arrived in Holland on the seventh of November.'

Conrad answered all the detective's questions. Van Gils's English was good, although Conrad had to pause from time to time to clarify some of his responses. Conrad realized that he was giving away information that was supposed to be secret, but it was information that he was pretty sure both the British and German intelligence services knew already, as did the Dutch probably. He told van Gils about meeting Theo in Leiden, then about travelling to Venlo with Payne Best, Stevens and Klop, about the kidnapping of the British agents, about his return to Holland to see Theo again, and his travel onwards to Paris to check up on one of Theo's agents. Van Gils didn't ask him to be specific about the agent, or about the peace negotiations, and so the issue of plots to overthrow Hitler, real or fake, didn't come up.

The detective asked some questions about Constance Scott-Dunton: who was she, what was her relationship with Millie, why were they travelling together? Conrad told van Gils what he could, including that Constance was a friend of Sir Henry Alston, who was an ally of his father in the quest for peace with Germany.

Then Conrad asked something himself. 'Why all these questions? I thought you had evidence that Millie's killer was Theo von Hertenberg.'

Van Gils snorted. 'It all depends what you call evidence.'

'What do you call evidence?' Conrad asked.

The detective took a pull at his cigarette, examining Conrad. 'You really don't know much about all this, do you?'

'No,' said Conrad.

'Well. Firstly, Mrs Scott-Dunton says she saw Hertenberg heading towards the tram stop from the sand dunes a few minutes after she had discovered Millie's body. She was confident, and seemed to have convinced my military intelligence colleagues, but not me. She might have seen someone who looked a lot like Theo, but she cannot be certain it was him.'

'But then another witness came forward?' said Conrad.

'Yes. A walker says he saw Theo hurrying through the dunes with blood on his hands.'

Conrad's heart sank. 'That sounds convincing. Constance told me Theo had arranged to meet Millie in the dunes that morning.'

'It doesn't sound convincing to me,' said the inspector. 'I haven't interviewed the walker – I wasn't allowed to – I just have a copy of his statement.' Van Gils reached into the file and extracted a sheet of paper. 'A Mr Frank Donkers. He's not a local, he's from Eindhoven. Apparently it was only after he returned home that he heard about the murder and got in touch with us, which explains the delay in coming forward. Or it's one explanation.' Van Gils snorted. 'And that detail about his hands being covered with blood. Really! I think Mr Donkers has been watching too many Shakespeare plays.'

'You said that's one explanation. What might another be?'

'It took them a day or two to manufacture him.'

'"Them"? Who are "them"?'

'I don't know. Our people. Your people. Maybe even the Germans' people.'

'But why would they manufacture evidence?'

'Who knows?' said van Gils. 'Perhaps it was just convenient to blame the German secret service, and then diplomatically forget what happened. I don't know. But I do know that Hertenberg being the murderer does not fit with the one piece of hard evidence we do have.'

'Which is?'

Van Gils puffed at his cigarette, clearly turning over in his mind whether to pass on to Conrad what he knew.

Conrad waited as the detective stubbed out his old cigarette and lit the fifth of the interview.

'The knife in your sister's chest,' he said at last.

'It had fingerprints on it?' Conrad asked.

The inspector shook his head. 'No, it was wiped clean. But an identical knife had been taken the day before from the kitchens of the Hotel Kurhaus, where both your sister and Mrs Scott-Dunton were staying.'

'Really?' said Conrad. 'Is that why you were asking me about Constance?'

'Absolutely. It certainly raises questions about her. Did she have a motive? Did she dislike your sister? Was she jealous of Hertenberg? Constance mentioned that Millie and Hertenberg had some kind of romantic attachment.'

Conrad shrugged. 'I really don't know. I have no reason to think so. Did you question Constance?'

'Oh, yes. She denied all knowledge of the knife, which was hardly surprising.'

'Could someone else have taken the knife from the kitchens?'

'It seems unlikely that a professional spy like Hertenberg would do that. He would have his own knife, one would think.'

'Unless he was trying to put blame on Mrs Scott-Dunton?'

Van Gils shrugged. 'Maybe.'

'You must have seen plenty of suspects lie in the past,' Conrad said. 'Was Constance lying? Perhaps she never saw Theo after all?'

'I certainly have,' said van Gils. 'But actually, she was quite convincing. She is a strange woman, Mrs Scott-Dunton, very strange. She comes across as a naive, innocent English girl. She is very young, only twenty-three, and yet there is something else there, a kind of suppressed excitement. Passion. Most un-English.'

'So you couldn't arrest her?'

Van Gils smiled. 'No. I couldn't even keep her in the country. Remember "my colleagues", as you called them, had informed me they had evidence that Miss de Lancey had been murdered by a German spy. Hertenberg.'

'And you don't believe them?'

'Not one bit. They let her go back to England. The investigation died. Our spies are happy and I suspect yours are too.'

Could it have been Constance? Conrad wondered. There was certainly something distinctly odd about her. But why would she want to kill Millie? That was something Conrad could try to find out back in England, perhaps with Anneliese's help.

'There isn't any chance that they could be right after all? That Theo von Hertenberg murdered her? Did you speak to him?'

'In theory there is a chance. We did ask to see him at the German Embassy. He wouldn't cooperate; he invoked diplomatic immunity, unsurprisingly. He was staying at the Hotel du Vieux Doelen in The Hague that evening, and flew to Berlin the following morning from Schiphol Airport. He has been flying back and forth a lot in the last few weeks. No one whom we spoke to, including the hotel staff on duty, saw him leave his hotel early that morning. Just this mysterious Mr Donkers whom I am not allowed to interview. And of course, if Hertenberg never left the hotel, then it implies he never arranged to meet Millie in the dunes in the first place.'

As Conrad considered the detective's words, a surge of relief flooded through him; he had hated the idea that Theo could have murdered Millie. He much preferred the possibility that Constance had stabbed her. But perhaps that was too much to hope and he was fooling himself.

He would have plenty of questions himself for Theo when they met the following day in Leiden.

'I have a favour to ask,' he said.

'Yes?' The detective's eyes narrowed again.

'Can you arrange for Millie's body to be sent back to England? I assume you have already performed a post-mortem.'

'We have,' said van Gils. 'It shows what one would expect: your sister died from stab wounds to the chest. But I am sorry. Technically the case is still open and the investigation is continuing, although in practice they expect me to do nothing more. But it means we cannot release the body, at least for now.' The policeman sounded genuinely regretful.

'Inspector van Gils. I am sure I have broken lots of rules I don't even know exist to tell you what I have told you. Can you not do the same for me? It sounds as if your superiors would not be unhappy to see evidence related to this particular investigation leave your country.'

'You are right about that.' Van Gils allowed himself a gruff smile. 'I will see what I can do.'

Twenty-Eight

Kensington, London

Alston walked briskly through Kensington Gardens on his way back from a luncheon at the Savoy with Freddie Copthorne, a newspaper proprietor and a general. It was late afternoon, dark, but not yet pitch black, and he could still see his way.

Luncheon had gone well. There was no doubt that Alston was widening his circle of influential admirers, to whom he knew he came across as someone who was sound, reliable yet astute. Not a hothead, but one who would take difficult decisions to do what was best for his country.

He was buoyed by *The Times* leader of that morning, which had floated the idea of a Cabinet shake-up, perhaps involving the War Office, and named him as one of two or three able men with experience of business as well as Parliament capable of providing an injection of vigour into the government.

It was becoming increasingly clear that in war the normal rules of political advancement didn't apply. Alston might only have been in Parliament since 1935, and he was barely forty, but he was indeed a man of energy and vigour, and his country needed him. More importantly, he could see things *clearly* – he always had been able to. For him the issues of the day were unobscured by sentiment or traditional patterns of thought. The world was changing in ways that very few of his colleagues in Parliament understood. Modern Germany pointed to the future; Neville Chamberlain, with his frock coat, winged collar and furled umbrella, tugged Britain back to the past.

When the crisis came – and Alston was sure there was going to be a crisis at some point in the future – Alston wanted to be the one important figures such as the newspaper proprietor and the general turned to. He wasn't at that point quite yet, but he was getting there.

It wasn't just luncheon and *The Times* article that were responsible for lifting Alston's spirits. Constance had said she would drop round to his flat to report on what had happened in Holland. This would be his first opportunity to see her since she had returned to England; Alston had spent the previous few days at his castle in Berwickshire with his wife and son. Alston was worried about Constance: it must have been shocking to discover Millie's dead body like that. And he felt very sorry for poor old Arthur Oakford. Who had killed his daughter? he wondered.

Of course, what he really wanted to do with Constance was fuck her. It was less than two weeks since Alston had taken Constance to his bed, or perhaps it was the other way round. That afternoon had been a revelation. Alston had just told his wife he might not get a chance to return to Berwickshire until Christmas, citing important affairs of state in London. But really he just wanted to see Constance. And fuck her.

But he would have to be gentle with her. She would be upset. He would have to be patient, wait until she had recovered her strength.

As he strode down Ennismore Gardens in the near darkness, he saw what seemed to be the silhouette of a woman on the pavement outside his building.

It was her!

She approached him. As he drew closer, he saw that her face was flushed with excitement, rather than grief.

'You must be cold,' he said, touching her cheek.

She smiled and pecked him on the lips. In the dark street, no one could see. 'I am. Can I come in? Perhaps you could warm me up?'

Alston felt a deep sense of satisfaction as he pulled Constance's naked body close to him. Fucking had been, if anything, wilder than before, as if Constance's experience in Holland had inflamed some primeval passion. Alston, that paragon of culture, intellect and rational thought, had felt like a caveman.

'Could you tell I was pleased to see you?' Constance said, running her hand over his chest.

'Yes.' He squeezed her. 'I was worried in case . . . Well, in case you were distressed about Millie. Are you going to see her brother?'

'I've seen him. In the Russian Tea Rooms, over the weekend.'

'How is he?'

'Rather upset, I'd say.'

'I'm not surprised. Do they know who killed her?'

'They think it was Theo von Hertenberg. The German spy. Millie's friend.'

'But why would he kill her?'

Constance unhooked herself from Alston's arm and sat astride him, pinning him down against the bed.

'He wouldn't.'

'What do you mean?'

'Because he didn't kill her.'

'He didn't kill her? But you just said he did.'

'*They* think he did. But *I* know who really killed her.'

'*You* know?'

'Yes.'

'How?'

'Because it was me.'

'You!' Alston struggled to sit up, but Constance pushed him down on his back and kissed him. At first he struggled, but then he responded.

She came up for air.

'Why? How?' Alston demanded.

'When I telephoned you from Scheveningen you said I should stop Millie telling anyone what Theo had said about the Duke of Windsor. So I stopped her.'

'I didn't say to kill her!'

'No. But it was pretty clear to me that that was the only way

202

to shut her up, and I had to do it quickly, too, before she had a chance to talk to anyone. I don't know what exactly is going on with the Duke of Windsor, but it must be desperately important. Isn't it desperately important?'

'Yes, it is,' Alston admitted. 'So what did you do?'

'I told her that Theo wanted to meet her out on the dunes before dawn. I sneaked into the hotel kitchens and borrowed a knife. Then I got up even earlier than her, and hid in the bushes in the dunes.'

'You stabbed her?'

'Yes. And then I pretended to discover her. I left the knife in her chest, but I wiped the handle clean. To get rid of my fingerprints. And I told the police and the intelligence people that I had seen someone who looked like Theo leaving the dunes. I couldn't sound too certain about it in case it turned out he could prove he was somewhere else, but it was enough to point them in his direction.'

'Good God!' said Alston. He wriggled out of Constance's grasp and sat up, reaching for a cigarette.

'Aren't you pleased with me?' Constance said, smiling.

'No, of course I'm not!' Alston snapped. 'That's murder!'

'No, it's not,' said Constance. 'This is war. People die. In horrible ways.'

'On the battlefield.'

'This is as important as the battlefield. More, probably. Millie's death will have a bigger effect on who wins the war, or how the war ends, than a single soldier on the battlefield. Won't it?'

'Yes, but . . .'

'But what? I did it for you, Henry.'

'I didn't tell you to kill her!'

'No. But I read today's *Times* and I was so proud. You can do it, Henry. You can join the government. And then you can become Prime Minister. Chamberlain is useless. Halifax is a coward. Oakford is a pacifist. Churchill is a warmonger. Mosley has some good ideas, but he's a snake. You can do it, Henry; you can lead this country to a just peace and a glorious future. With no Jews.'

Alston could tell Constance really believed what she was saying. But she had killed a young woman, a woman her own age. Stabbed her in the chest. How had she done that?

Constance seemed to sense his unspoken question. 'There are times when you have to act, to take steps. When doing nothing is the wrong thing to do.'

Alston remembered Constance talking about 'taking steps' before.

'Have you killed anyone before, Constance?'

Constance gave a small smile. 'I couldn't possibly say.'

'Who? Not your father?'

'Of course not my father!' Anger flashed across Constance's face. 'No. Definitely not my father.'

'Who then?'

'I can't say,' said Constance. 'But I did the right thing then, and I've done the right thing now.' She knelt naked next to Alston and stared deep into his eyes. 'Can you forgive me, Henry?' she said. 'You have to forgive me.'

Alston's brain was in turmoil. Millie's murder horrified him, yet what Constance had done and the reason she had done it exhilarated him. She had ignored the petty constraints of petty English morality to act, to be bold. If ever there was a time for boldness it was now.

Her eyes were deep dark pools of intensity.

She put her hand between his legs. 'Forgive me, Henry.'

Twenty-Nine

Leiden, 23 November

Kriminalkommissar Wilhelm Neuser approached the porter's lodge of the old Academy building in Leiden. It was just a few minutes past nine o'clock in the morning. He was a short, barrel-chested young man dressed in a scruffy overcoat, and had donned some clear-lensed spectacles. He spoke to the porter in slow, clear German.

'Dr Fuhrmann of the University of Hamburg to meet Professor Hogendoorn.' He handed the porter a passport bearing his photograph in the name of Dr Heinrich Fuhrmann. After some head-scratching and telephoning on the part of the porter, a man with a thick grey moustache appeared and introduced himself as the professor. He led Neuser up the stairs of the Academy building.

And then up some more stairs. And then up a steep spiral staircase and through a heavy oak door, which the professor unlocked.

They were in the attic of the old building. It was a large space, framed with a network of thick wooden beams; it was clear in the middle, but around the walls was stacked a jumble of ancient academic detritus: boxes, chairs, desks, boards, group photographs, even a couple of sculls. Thin grey light filtered in through narrow windows.

The professor switched on an electric light. 'I plan to take Lieutenant von Hertenberg up here to meet de Lancey,' he said in good German. 'From their point of view it should feel safe; they are out of view and earshot of passers-by. But it is easy for you to hide somewhere and listen.' The professor gave a little laugh.

Neuser scanned the attic. 'This will work very well,' he said.

'I had my suspicions about Lieutenant von Hertenberg,' the professor said. 'And the Englishman he saw last time.'

'You were quite right to warn us,' Neuser said. 'This meeting is unauthorized. I will listen to what they have to say, and if Hertenberg is indeed a traitor, I will tell my superiors back in Germany and he will be dealt with.'

'And my part in this will be kept quiet, I trust?' the professor said.

'Naturally. Although I will make sure that when our two countries become closer, your loyalty to the Party will be remembered.'

Professor Hogendoorn giggled unnecessarily. 'They won't be here for another two hours. With all the comings and goings, no one will be surprised if the porter doesn't remember seeing you leave, and a new man will come on duty at lunchtime. Probably best if you don't go until after that. I'll come up and fetch you about two o'clock.'

Neuser shifted some tea chests around near the entrance to the attic, and created a little nest for himself, from where he should be able to hear any conversation. He had been selected for the task because he spoke English, although his command of that language was not very strong and he was hoping that Hertenberg and de Lancey would speak in German.

He pulled out his weapon and fixed a silencer. He distrusted silencers, they were never really silent and they hampered accuracy. But it was unlikely that even if the students and professors below heard two muffled shots they would identify them as such. And accuracy shouldn't be a problem at a range of two metres.

Neuser turned off the light, made himself comfortable and waited in the gloom.

Conrad strode rapidly from the station at Leiden to the Rapenburg Canal. He hoped the cynical Dutch detective was right about the evidence against Theo being fabricated. But who would do that and why? Conrad knew, because he had seen it, that although Holland was neutral, Dutch military intelligence had contact with their British counterparts. Maybe they were just trying to smooth over a tricky diplomatic incident. Or maybe they knew who really had killed Millie and were trying to cover it up. Why would they do that? Did Van know what had really happened? Did his father?

But Conrad knew he should guard against being complacent. There was still a chance that Van was correct, and that Theo had stabbed Millie, in which case there was also a chance, a good chance, that he might try to kill Conrad too. Conrad would just have to take that risk and keep his wits about him. Second-guessing the spies would never give Conrad the answers he needed; he had to speak to Theo face to face to do that. Only by knowing for sure whether Theo had killed his sister could he begin to make any sense of this damned war and his place in it.

Conrad slowed as he approached the Academy building and strolled past the gates, before turning abruptly and looking behind him. He didn't think he was being followed, but he couldn't really be certain. He hadn't spotted any middle-aged men in raincoats and hats on his tail, but the place was buzzing with students on bicycles and he couldn't keep track of all of them.

Theo would probably have some scheme planned to shake a tail. Perhaps another walk in the Botanical Gardens.

But this time Professor Hogendoorn led Conrad up a spiral staircase within the Academy building itself. 'I thought this would be a good safe place for your conversation,' said the professor as he opened a heavy door at the top of the stairs. 'I'll leave you to it.'

Conrad pushed open the door to reveal Theo waiting for him, standing alone in the middle of a large attic. A thin shaft of sunlight from one of the windows brushed his pale face.

He was unarmed, as far as Conrad could see.

'Hello, Conrad,' Theo said in English.

Conrad ignored the greeting. 'Millie's dead,' he said in German. 'I know,' said Theo. 'And I'm sorry for you.'

Conrad let the words hang there for a moment.

'Did you kill her? Dutch intelligence thinks you killed her.'

'That's ridiculous!' Theo said. 'Why do they think that?'

'Constance Scott-Dunton says she saw someone who looked like you walking away from where she found Millie's body. And then a walker saw you coming out of the dunes wiping blood off your hands.' Even as he said it, Conrad was reminded of van Gils's line about Shakespeare. But he couldn't just choose to agree with van Gils's claim that Theo was innocent. He needed to know.

'That's crazy. You can't believe that, surely? That I would kill Millie?'

'Prove to me you didn't.'

'I didn't leave my hotel until about nine when I went straight to Schiphol to fly back to Germany.'

'So you never asked Millie to meet you in the dunes that morning?'

'Who said I did?'

'Constance.'

'No, I didn't.'

'Can you prove it?'

'Of course I can't prove it, Conrad! You have to take my word for it. There is too much going on now for you not to trust me. We've been through so much together, we can't afford not to trust each other. Besides . . .'

'Besides what?'

'I could never kill Millie. I . . . I liked her. I liked her a lot.'

Conrad studied Theo. His friend. 'All right. But tell me why.'

'Why is she dead? I don't know.'

'Why were you seeing her? Why didn't you tell me you were going to see her? Why did you allow her to be caught up in my father's stupid schemes? Why did you use her? Why didn't you look after her, for God's sake?'

Theo put his finger to his lips, and it was only then that Conrad realized he had raised his voice.

'I owe you an explanation,' said Theo.

'You certainly do.'

Theo pulled out a cigarette from his case and lit it. The tip glowed in the gloom. Then he told Conrad about how he and Millie had met in Switzerland in the spring, and how they had arranged to meet again in Scheveningen, using the same Danish intermediary as Theo had used with Conrad.

'Why didn't you tell me any of this?' Conrad protested. 'You saw me at the same time. Was it the same day?'

'The day after. And I didn't tell you because Millie asked me not to. She said you wouldn't approve of what she and your father were doing. Knowing you, that didn't surprise me.'

'But didn't you consider you were betraying me?'

'I didn't like doing what I was doing, but it wasn't up to me. If the coup had gone ahead, then the new German government would have needed a channel to speak to the British government right away.'

'Was there ever really going to be a coup? And what happened to that offensive you told me about? Germany and Holland should have been at war for a week by now.'

'The offensive was called off. Bad weather. And so was the coup. Cowardice on the part of the generals.'

'I don't believe you,' Conrad said.

'I'm telling you the truth, Conrad,' Theo said, weariness touching his voice. 'You deserve that. Whether you believe me or not is entirely up to you.'

'So what happened to Millie? Who killed her?'

'I don't know.' Theo paused. 'I had seen her that afternoon, in Scheveningen. It had come to my attention that it wasn't only me that she was seeing in Holland. She also met a man called Otto Langebrück.'

'Who is he?'

'He's a crony of Ribbentrop. Used to live in Paris. He's clever and he's a Nazi.'

'Why was she seeing him?'

'She, and her little friend Constance, were negotiating with Ribbentrop as well. Or in other words with Hitler.'

Conrad glared at Theo. He could feel the fury building up within him, and it was all he could do to prevent it from erupting. It wasn't just Theo who was betraying him, it was his father, and for that matter Millie. They were all talking to Hitler's regime. And it was his father's fault. His father, the supposedly sophisticated ex-government minister, had been a fool – an utter, total, complete fool! 'No wonder they didn't want to tell me where they were going!'

'If it makes any difference, I think it was Constance who was responsible for talking to Langebrück. Constance and Sir Henry Alston.'

'But my father knew all about it, didn't he?' Conrad said.

Theo shrugged. 'I don't know. I assume so.'

Conrad's mind was whirling. He wanted to slug Theo. And then he wanted to fly back to England and slug his father too. But this might be his only opportunity to speak to Theo about his sister's death and he wanted to make the most of it.

'Do you think Langebrück might have killed Millie? Or was it the Gestapo?'

'Possibly,' said Theo. 'But I don't know why they would. It could be the British secret service.'

'That's ridiculous!' Conrad protested. 'Why would they do that?'

'I don't know. To stop Lord Oakford's discussions with the enemy?'

Theo was suggesting that his father was a traitor and that his own country would murder his sister. It was outrageous. But possibly true. It would explain why the secret service would manufacture a witness to place Theo in the sand dunes. Conrad was convinced now that van Gils was right to doubt their evidence. But that was about all Conrad was convinced of.

Theo could sense Conrad's distress. 'I repeat, I don't know,' he said. 'I was fond of Millie, very fond of her.' Theo swallowed. 'I'm sorry I let her die; I don't know how it happened. I'd like to know.'

'The Dutch police think Constance killed her,' said Conrad. 'Or at least the man in charge of their investigation thinks so.

Millie was stabbed with a knife taken from the kitchens of their hotel. He thinks Constance was the most likely person to have taken it.'

'Have they arrested her?'

'Oh, no. Dutch military intelligence sent her back to Britain. Remember they claimed *you* killed her, whatever the policeman in charge of the investigation thinks.'

'But why would Constance want to kill Millie?'

'The police inspector has no idea. He suggested that Constance might have been jealous of the relationship between you and Millie.'

'It's not that,' said Theo.

Conrad was about to question Theo's denial, but he kept quiet. Theo seemed distracted, as though he was thinking, weighing something up.

There was silence in the attic. The two men were still standing several feet apart, but for the first time Conrad felt closer to Theo, to his friend. He waited.

Eventually Theo spoke. 'In that letter you wrote to me at the beginning of the war, you reminded me how at Oxford we swore we wouldn't let anyone make us fight each other as they had made our parents fight last time. How we owed our allegiance to the human race, not to our country. How it seemed so simple then.'

Conrad nodded. He remembered. 'Algy.'

Algernon Pemberton was the man who had inhabited Conrad's rooms in 1914 and died at Ypres in 1915. His name was on a wooden plaque on the wall; Conrad and Theo had talked about the doomed undergraduate many times.

'Then it turned out not to be so simple for either of us,' Theo went on. 'You decided to fight for socialism, or at least against Fascism, in Spain. I became involved in trying to rid my country of a madman. You helped me. And now I am fighting for my country and you for yours.'

Conrad wanted to interrupt, to point out that he was fighting as much against Hitler as for Britain, but he kept quiet. He knew what Theo was saying was important to him, and he didn't want to interrupt his flow.

'Well, you would think that as a German officer fighting for my country, I would want my country to win this war. But I'm not sure I do. If Germany smashes France, Hitler's control of power will be total. The only people left who can stand up to Hitler are the generals, and if they achieve a great victory in France, they won't do it. You can see how success in Poland has gone to their heads. If Hitler maintains his control of Germany, that will be disastrous. A thousand years of darkness.

'So, as a good German, as a good German officer, as one of those von Hertenbergs who has served his country for generations, I do not want a successful blitzkrieg in the west. Can you understand that?'

'I can understand that,' said Conrad.

'Good,' said Theo. 'That's why I told Millie something when I saw her in Scheveningen. That's why I told you about Bedaux. Did you look in to him?'

'I went to Paris. I discovered he has been talking to the Duke of Windsor. I discovered the duke has been inspecting the French lines. I guessed that Bedaux has been telling you about it.'

Theo smiled. 'Well done. Did you tell your government?'

'I did,' said Conrad.

'Did they listen?'

'I think so. I'm not sure. The Duke of Windsor is a tricky subject.'

'All right, then. Let me tell you some more. The duke is no fool, it turns out, at least when it comes to military matters. He has identified a significant weakness in the French line, in the Ardennes around Sedan. He has also made clear that the most powerful French forces have been earmarked to push northwards into north-west Belgium when we invade, which we will do, by the way. Now the German general staff knows these weaknesses, they will be able to alter their plans to take advantage of them.'

'Bedaux told you all this?'

'He did. Also . . .' Theo hesitated. Conrad waited. 'Also there are people in the Nazi Party who believe that the Duke of Windsor would make an excellent leader of a British government that was sympathetic to Germany. That he is a man that Germany could do business with.'

'People? What kind of people?'

'Ribbentrop. Hitler.'

'I see. And do you know what the duke thinks about this?'

'That's a good question,' Theo said. 'The truth is we don't. According to Ribbentrop, the duchess would like it and the duke does whatever his wife wants. But Ribbentrop is not nearly as astute a judge of the British as he thinks he is. Do *you* know?'

'No idea,' said Conrad. 'Frankly, it's hard to believe that a man who was king only a couple of years ago would behave in the way you have described.'

'Believe it,' said Theo. 'And tell your government.'

'I will,' said Conrad. He swallowed. The information Theo had just given him would shatter the people who ruled Britain. Van would have to take notice. The government would. So would the present king, George. It seemed so fantastic, could it possibly be true?

Conrad now realized why Theo had taken the time to explain why he was telling him about the duke. To convince him that he was speaking the truth. And Conrad was convinced.

'Good,' said Theo. 'Now you had better be going. You leave first. Don't look for the professor, just go straight down the stairs and out of the building. I will wait and follow you.'

He held out his hand to Conrad.

Squatting behind a tea chest only three metres from the two men, Neuser had heard and understood every word, since they were fortunately speaking in German. He was astounded. He only hoped he could remember it all.

It was absolutely clear that Hertenberg was a traitor. The slight qualm Neuser had felt when first ordered to kill a fellow officer was gone. Hertenberg had to die. They both had to die.

He was glad he had waited to hear so much of the conversation, but now it was time to move. He risked a peek from behind the chest, and saw the Englishman moving towards his German friend, hand outstretched. Neuser ducked back behind the chest and raised his pistol, ready to act.

Just before Theo shook his outstretched hand, Conrad noticed a flicker of movement in the glass of a framed photograph behind his friend. Then it was gone. In the reflection he could see his own legs and the fuzzy silhouette of the tea chests behind him. Something thin and rounded briefly appeared above the tea chest and then it too was gone.

Was that the barrel of a gun?

Possibly. Possibly not.

He would take no chances.

Theo let go of Conrad's hand. Conrad had lost track of what Theo was saying.

'Conrad?'

He had to play for time. Give himself time to think. Toss something to make whoever was behind the tea chest pause and listen.

'Göring,' he said.

'Göring?' said Theo, puzzled.

In similar situations when dealing with Nazis in Berlin the year before, Conrad had alighted upon Göring as the perfect name to intrigue and confuse them. The fat Luftwaffe chief was one of Hitler's oldest allies, but he had his own power base and the SS did not trust him.

'I should have told you before. About Göring.'

'What about Göring?'

Good question, Theo, Conrad thought. 'I've got a message I need to show you. Van gave it to me in London.' Conrad put his hand in his jacket pocket. There was nothing there. 'But we'll need a little more light.'

It was gloomy in the attic.

'That's all right. I'm sure I can read it,' said Theo, holding out his hand for the non-existent message.

Conrad ignored him and turned away back towards the door and the light switch. He was now facing the tea chests. He couldn't see any sign of anyone lurking, but that didn't mean someone wasn't there.

When he reached the door he yelled: 'Down, Theo!' and dived at the tea chests.

There was a cry, and a muffled crack. Conrad found himself on top of the legs of a man holding a pistol with an attached silencer pointing towards Theo. Conrad stretched out and struck the man's elbow as he pulled the trigger for a second time. Both shots seemed to have missed Theo.

The man struggled to his feet and turned to face Conrad, bringing his gun around in a wide arc. He was short, almost completely bald, broad-shouldered and tough. Conrad dived at him again, hitting him full in the chest, and the gun was sent spinning. The man writhed and wriggled and broke free of Conrad's grasp. He scrambled to his feet.

'Freeze!'

It was Theo. He had the gun and he was pointing it at the man. The man froze.

'Kill him, Theo,' said Conrad.

'We don't know who he is,' said Theo. 'Who are you?'

The bald man didn't reply.

'Kill him!' said Conrad. 'Doesn't matter who he is. You know what he heard. Pull the damn trigger!'

The man's eyes were wide. He turned and ran, away from Theo deep into the attic.

'Shoot him, Theo!' Conrad shouted and then set off after the killer. Whether because Theo had doubts who the man was, or was struck by indecision, or just hadn't fired a gun in anger before, there was no shot.

A short flight of wooden steps led up to a small door. The bald man leaped up the stairs, threw open the door and climbed outside on to the roof. Conrad followed him.

The Academy roof had a double gable with a valley in the middle, on to which the door opened. The bald man slid down a couple of feet and then into the bottom of the valley, which consisted of two feet of lead where the two roofs met. He turned, saw Conrad following him, and set off along the valley.

But there was nowhere to go. Beyond the end of roof was air. The building was one of the highest in Leiden, and Conrad could see countryside, windmills and, beyond that, the North Sea.

Conrad slowed, ready for a fight. The bald man stopped and faced him. Conrad was tall, but the other man had muscles and looked like he knew what to do with them.

Theo emerged from the doorway on to the roof and took aim with the pistol. The bald man saw him and launched himself at the roof, clambering up it crabwise, sending slates clattering. This time Theo let off a couple of shots, but he missed. The angle was difficult and the silencer didn't help accuracy.

Conrad set off up the slope of the roof after the bald man. He got into a rhythm and was gaining. At that point, a slip wouldn't be fatal: he would just end up back in the valley.

But the bald man reached the ridge of the roof before Conrad. Gingerly he stood upright and began walking back towards the bell tower.

Conrad hauled himself up on to the ridge. The ridge was narrow, perhaps two inches wide, and it was a long way down on the outer side. Now a slip in that direction *would* be fatal. The Academy building was high, at least sixty feet, and there was nothing to break a fall down to the street below.

Conrad stood upright. He had done some mountain climbing in Switzerland and Scotland with his older brother Edward when he was a boy, so he had a good head for heights, but nevertheless it was difficult not to look down.

He saw there was a small door in the side of the bell tower leading out on to the roof. The man was heading for it, stepping gingerly, arms outstretched for better balance. If the door was unlocked he would be through it and away. Given what the man had overheard, Conrad and Theo would be in big trouble, Theo especially.

Conrad couldn't let him get away.

So he began to run slowly along the ridge. The speed gave him some balance, although he wasn't quite sure how he would eventually slow down. He also wasn't sure what he would do if he caught up with the man – perhaps drag him off to the left down into the valley where Theo had his pistol?

He didn't look down, just kept his eyes looking steadily forward.

The man turned. Saw Conrad jogging towards him. Lengthened his steps into strides, and then he too broke into a run.

And slipped. The wrong way.

With a cry he slid down the roof, rolled twice, and then bounced into the air and fell out of sight. If he made a thud when he hit the ground, Conrad didn't hear it, but he did hear the shouts of passers-by.

Conrad almost lost his own balance as he watched the body fall. He carried on running until he reached the bell tower and grabbed hold of the door handle for support. He twisted it; it was unlocked and opened inside on to a ladder.

He scrambled down it into the attic and then back to the other doorway leading out into the roof valley. He beckoned to Theo.

'Time to go!'

Thirty

The Dorchester Hotel, Park Lane, London

'Cheers, Henry!'

They were at the bar. Freddie Copthorne raised his glass and gulped his beer and Alston sipped his pink gin. It irritated Alston that Freddie insisted on drinking beer in the most inappropriate of places. All right, his family's fortune was based on the stuff, but Freddie's loyalties seemed to stretch to any old brew.

'Do you think we will hear back from Herr Langebrück?' he asked.

'I expect so, somehow or other,' said Alston. 'The important thing is that Rib knows we are ready to talk. It's a shame Constance couldn't have stayed longer in Holland to get a reply.'

'I can't get over what happened to Millie de Lancey,' Copthorne said. 'Poor old Oakford.'

Alston didn't answer. He too couldn't get over what had happened to the de Lancey girl, but for very different reasons. Of course it was a shame that she had had to die, but he had come to realize that Constance was absolutely right: the girl was a war casualty, and when you thought about it, she was a casualty for the enemy. Alston was on the side of peace and sanity. Millie de Lancey had declared herself to be on the side of war.

Alston would have liked to explain all that to his friend, but he couldn't. Freddie wouldn't understand. He didn't have the balls.

Whereas he, Alston, did have balls. He suppressed a smile.

'Sir Henry! Lord Copthorne! It's great to see you!'

The French-tinged American accent was instantly recognizable.

The two men turned to see Charles Bedaux holding out his hand. He looked like a spruced-up boxer, Alston thought. His face was battered, his ears verged on the cauliflower, but his thick dark hair was brushed back with brilliantine and he was wearing a smartly buttoned double-breasted blazer and two-toned brogues. Not exactly the way one would dress in the dining room of a City merchant bank, but Bedaux was certainly not a City merchant banker. Alston smiled and shook the American's hand.

'Do you mind if we go straight in to lunch?' Bedaux said. 'I'm not in the country for long, and I have a lot to do.'

'Of course not,' said Alston. Some might have found Bedaux's direct manner rude, but Alston liked it. The man had energy, and energy was good. It got things done. And it was Bedaux who had asked to see Alston. They knew each other from mutual business acquaintances before the war. There were quite a few British firms who used the Bedaux System in their factories and Gurney Kroheim's money to finance them.

Alston had arranged that the three men should have a discreet table in the corner of the dining room. Freddie ordered lamb chops and Alston and Bedaux both went for the grouse. Alston ordered a bottle of Montrachet '24.

'Friends in Germany tell me you have been in touch with my old friend Otto Langebrück,' said Bedaux.

'You are very well informed,' said Alston.

'Oh, I am,' said Bedaux. 'Always.'

'We passed him a proposition,' Alston went on. 'Through an intermediary in Holland. Unfortunately the intermediary wasn't able to hang around long enough to get a reply.'

'So I understand,' said Bedaux.

'Have you seen Herr Langebrück yourself?'

'I knew him when he was in Paris,' Bedaux said. 'I haven't seen him since war broke out. But I was in Berlin a couple of weeks ago.'

'Oh. Did you meet Herr von Ribbentrop?' Alston remembered Bedaux mentioning in his letter that he knew the German Foreign Minister.

'I did. I also saw the big man himself.' Bedaux beamed. 'The Führer.'

'Good God!' said Freddie, choking on his beer, which he had uncouthly brought with him into the dining room.

'And how is Herr Hitler?' asked Alston with ironic politeness.

'Mighty relieved not to be blown to hell in Munich. I saw him the day after the bomb went off. He seemed to think that God had saved him. Or Providence. Or someone.'

'The devil?' Freddie volunteered.

Bedaux laughed. 'Probably.' His expression became serious. 'Anyway, I became aware of your proposals and your willingness to countenance an end to this stupid war, and I thought it made sense to fill you in on the Führer's thinking. About Britain.'

'Go on,' said Alston.

'He doesn't know your country very well, but he has plenty of respect for it. He admires Britain's traditions and its history, and places Englishmen in the same racial category as Germans. He would like Britain to leave Germany in control of Europe, in return for which Germany would leave Britain in peace to run the rest of the world through her empire.'

'What did I tell you?' said Alston to Copthorne.

'He is also a great admirer of your former King Edward,' Bedaux said. 'He met him when Edward visited Germany in 1937. Hitler feels that if the Duke of Windsor were to become king again, Germany would be able to do business with Britain.'

'I'm not sure that could ever happen,' said Copthorne.

'Couldn't it?' said Bedaux.

Alston met the American's eyes, which didn't flinch. Bedaux seemed unperturbed by Alston's ravaged face.

'Not with the current government,' Alston said. 'But there will never be peace as long as Chamberlain is Prime Minister. Probably not if Halifax was PM either.'

'What about Sir Oswald Mosley? Hitler knows him.'

'Oswald Mosley will never lead Britain,' Alston said. 'The British people are simply not fascists. The uniforms, the parades, the histrionics: they might suit the Germans or the Italians, but the average Englishman would run a mile. No, a government for peace in Britain would be very different. It would be pragmatic, sensible, patriotic in a low-key way, doing what is best for Britain. I also believe that the duke would make a good king for that kind of country. He has charm, much more than George, and a real connection with ordinary people.'

'But what about the government? If not Oswald Mosley for Prime Minister, who?'

'Lloyd George, probably. He is less fiery now he is an old man. He has stature in the country and he would promote peace with Germany in the right circumstances. Of course, he is in his late seventies, so he would need to have men around him to run the government.'

'Men such as yourself?' Bedaux asked. 'I have heard good things about you.'

Alston smiled. 'Possibly.'

Bedaux looked around the restaurant. No one was in earshot. 'Something would need to change for such a government to come to power, wouldn't it?' he said.

'Yes. Chamberlain would have to go.'

'At some point – maybe next week, maybe next month, maybe next year – Germany will launch an offensive against France through Belgium and possibly Holland. It seems to me that there are two possible outcomes.'

Alston was listening closely.

Bedaux leaned forward, his boxer's face animated. 'One. The French and the British stop the Germans like they did in the last war, and there is a long, bloody stalemate. Chamberlain and his friends dig in; the war lasts for years. Not an ideal state of affairs.'

'No.'

'Two. The Germans punch through a weak spot in the French lines. The Allied armies crumble. The French are defeated. The British people realize they must get rid of their prime minister and their king, and make peace with Germany. The Germans make a

221

fair peace with the British and a tough one with the French. The war is over. The killing stops and people like me can go back to peace and prosperity.'

'I see.'

'Now, I was born in France, but even so it seems to me that the second outcome is the better one. Doesn't it to you?'

Alston understood exactly what Bedaux was saying. He glanced at Freddie, who was frowning. But Alston had a question.

'If the second outcome were to actually occur, what would your role be, Monsieur Bedaux?'

'Same as it always is,' said Bedaux with a grin. 'I am just a facilitator. I make things run smoothly, be they factories or peace negotiations. All I would ask is that my friends remember who helped them. I was born in France, I have an American passport, but I am really a citizen of the world.'

Alston was now a politician, but he was also a banker, and he knew how businessmen thought. If the world did indeed turn out as Bedaux had described, then he and his businesses would do very nicely. Very nicely indeed.

'I can ease things, but I can't make things happen,' said Bedaux. 'It's people like you who will make things happen, Sir Henry.' The American dismembered his grouse skilfully. 'By the way, my Amsterdam office had a visitor recently, a colleague of yours from Gurney Kroheim.'

'I wasn't aware that Bedaux International was one of our clients,' said Alston.

'No. Neither was I. But this man said that you had been enquiring about me and my company. Apparently you personally were interested in using the Bedaux System in bank processes.'

Alston frowned. 'That's very strange. I mean, I am sure your system would be very useful, Bedaux, but I know I didn't ask a colleague to look into it. Did your office get the man's name?'

'Yes. De Lancey. Do you know him?'

Alston's frown deepened. 'Yes, I do know him. And he doesn't work for Gurney Kroheim.'

'Then what was he doing claiming he was?' said Bedaux.
'That is a good question.'

As promised, Bedaux left the lunch early, before the pudding, leaving Alston and Copthorne with their spotted dick and custard.

Alston was excited. Bedaux's vision matched closely his own. And it was clear that Hitler would go with it, even if the current British government wouldn't. 'What do you think of that, Freddie?' he said.

But Freddie Copthorne looked unhappy. 'I don't like that man, Henry. I don't like that man at all.'

Thirty-One

Heston Airport, Middlesex

It was dusk in Middlesex as Conrad's aeroplane landed. It had been touch and go getting out of Holland. He had plunged down the stairs and out of the Academy building and hopped on a tram to the railway station, from where he had taken a taxi to the airport. Schiphol wasn't far from Leiden, but he had had a couple of hours to wait before the aeroplane on which he had booked a seat was due to take off, two hours of anxiety lest he was accosted by a Dutch policeman or airline official and asked to 'come this way, sir'.

But the Dutch authorities weren't quick enough, and it was with a sigh of relief that Conrad looked down over the coastline of Holland retreating behind him.

Professor Hogendoorn would have quite a lot of explaining to do. Fortunately, he must have preferred to prevaricate rather than point the police towards Conrad. It was clear that the professor had betrayed Theo. It was just a shame that Holland was not yet at war with Germany; then Hogendoorn's actions would be classified as treason. Or would they? Was betraying one German to another really treachery against Hogendoorn's country? Working out who was on whose side was becoming increasingly complicated in this damned phoney war.

As Conrad descended the steps to the tarmac at Heston, he was surprised to see a burly figure he recognized: Major McCaigue. The major held out his hand.

'Welcome back, de Lancey. After your journey, I thought you might like a lift back to London.'

'I would indeed,' said Conrad. 'As a matter of fact, I have quite a bit to tell you.'

McCaigue's car crept through the unlit Middlesex suburbs. Fog mixed with darkness to create a dangerous murk. McCaigue, who was unaccompanied, had to split his concentration between Conrad's story and the road ahead.

Conrad told him everything. What Inspector van Gils had said about Millie's murder; his doubts about the evidence against Theo; how Millie had met Otto Langebrück; what Charles Bedaux had told the Germans about the weak spots in the French lines; the identity of Bedaux's source within the British Expeditionary Force and what the Nazi leadership thought of the Duke of Windsor. Finally he told McCaigue about the presumed Gestapo agent who had tried to kill both him and Theo.

'You do seem to bring trouble with you whenever you visit Holland, don't you, de Lancey?'

'I used to like the country,' said Conrad. 'Now I'm not so sure. For a neutral nation it seems awfully dangerous.'

'I would stay away from there for a bit if I were you,' said McCaigue. 'Is your friend Theo telling the truth?'

'About not killing Millie or about the Duke of Windsor?'

'About both.'

'I am sure he didn't kill Millie. He convinced me that he had no reason to – quite the opposite. And the detective convinced me that the evidence against Theo was doubtful.'

'I see,' said McCaigue.

'Was the testimony of that witness against Theo fabricated?' Conrad asked. 'Was Constance Scott-Dunton lying?'

McCaigue didn't answer the question. 'What about the Duke of Windsor? Hertenberg is betraying his country telling you all that. That's a big step for a German officer.'

Conrad decided not to try to pin McCaigue down on the witnesses. Either McCaigue knew they were false or he didn't. If he did, he wouldn't admit to it to Conrad. If he didn't, he might try to find out what was going on. That was the best Conrad could hope for.

'He did warn me about the date of the offensive,' Conrad said. 'I know it didn't happen, but I am sure the date was genuine. It was cancelled because of bad weather. The weather was bad, wasn't it?'

'It was,' McCaigue conceded. 'And the Dutch received a similar warning from Berlin. But there was no coup.'

'Nevertheless, I do believe Theo is telling the truth about the duke,' Conrad said. 'That he has been passing on secrets to the Germans. I know how Theo thinks. In his view, a decisive German victory in France would be a disaster for his country. Theo genuinely believes Hitler is evil and must be removed at all costs. I saw the lengths he went to last year to try to make that happen. He's telling the truth.'

'Hmm.'

'You sound as if you would rather he was lying,' Conrad said.

'What he has told you is very inconvenient, to put it mildly,' said McCaigue. 'A lot of people are not going to like it.'

'But you are going to tell them?'

'Oh, certainly. And despite the determination of some people to thrust their heads in the sand, it is much better to know uncomfortable truths than to not know them. Or even worse, pretend they don't exist.'

They drove on in silence, as McCaigue mulled over what he had heard. 'De Lancey, there is something you should know,' he said eventually.

'What's that?'

'Your loyalties are doubted in some quarters.'

'What do you mean?'

'Some people think you are a communist. We have looked at your file: the Labour Club at Oxford; fighting for the socialists in Spain.'

Conrad snorted. 'That's ridiculous. The communists shot two of my best friends in Spain. In the back. And anyway the Nazis and communists are at opposite ends of the spectrum, aren't they?'

'One would have thought so,' said McCaigue. 'But then in August they teamed up to carve up Poland.' He grinned. 'As far as I am concerned you have just carried out a difficult mission in dangerous circumstances. I just thought I had better warn you.'

'You will be able to convince them that I'm telling the truth, won't you?'

'I'll try.'

McCaigue slammed on the brakes as the back of an Austin 7 suddenly emerged out of the gloom in front of them.

'Major McCaigue?'

'Yes?'

'Do you believe me?'

'Oh, yes,' said McCaigue, turning to face Conrad. 'I believe you.'

Abwehr Headquarters, Berlin

It was after ten by the time Theo arrived at Abwehr headquarters, but he was relieved to find Admiral Canaris and Colonel Oster still at work, having dined together there. He knew how vital it was to report back to them before the Gestapo realized that their man had been killed in Leiden. Unlike Conrad, he hadn't already had a reservation on a flight from Schiphol, but he did manage to get a train to Brussels, and from there fly on to Berlin.

'What's wrong, Hertenberg?' Canaris asked the instant he came into the room. 'Not another Venlo, I hope?'

'Not quite. But I have just been shot at, probably by a Gestapo officer. In Leiden.'

'And where is this Gestapo officer now?' asked Canaris.

'He's dead, Admiral.'

Theo noticed his direct boss, Colonel Oster, stiffen at this news, but Canaris seemed to take it calmly. Theo could see his brain begin to work through the possibilities.

'Explain.'

So Theo explained. He didn't divulge quite everything; he certainly didn't admit to telling Conrad about the Duke of Windsor or about Charles Bedaux. But he did say that they had met and that Conrad was trying to find out more about his sister's death in the sand dunes at Scheveningen, and that the British secret service seemed to have decided that Theo had killed her. Why, he wasn't sure.

'We know how much Heydrich dislikes de Lancey,' Canaris said after Theo had finished. 'And frankly I am not surprised that he took the opportunity to get him killed. But I am most unhappy that one of my officers was a target too.'

'It's outrageous!' said Oster. 'We can't possibly have the Gestapo taking it upon themselves to murder our men. You should speak to Himmler. To the general staff. To Hitler! It cannot be permitted.'

'No, it cannot, Hans,' said Canaris. 'But no doubt Heydrich would say that Hertenberg was an innocent victim caught in the crossfire. Are you sure the man who tried to kill you was alone?'

'Yes,' said Theo. 'Although I suspect my contact at the university tipped off the Gestapo that we were meeting.'

'If he was alone and he's dead, the Gestapo won't know what happened. They might well assume that Conrad killed him single-handedly.'

'We can't just turn a blind eye!' said Oster.

'Oh, I think we can, Hans,' said Canaris. 'I think that would be better all round. It's time for one of my early-morning rides with Sturmbannführer Schellenberg.' He picked up the phone.

Kensington, London

McCaigue deposited Conrad at his parents' house in Kensington Square. Conrad's mother greeted him in the hallway. She seemed calmer than he had seen her since Millie's death, and pleased to see him in one piece.

'Will the Dutch authorities release Millie's body?' she asked at once.

'I hope so,' said Conrad. 'Technically they are not allowed to because of the murder investigation, but I met the policeman in charge, and he seemed sympathetic. I am sure he will do his best. I am not sure that will be enough, but there is nothing more I could do.'

'Thank you, Conrad. I know it's silly, but it will be a great relief to know that she is back in Somerset where she belongs.'

Conrad took his mother by the arms and kissed her forehead. 'It's not silly, Mama. It's not silly at all.'

'Did the policeman know who killed her?'

'No,' said Conrad. He knew his father hadn't mentioned the British secret service's suspicion of Theo, and Conrad had decided not to pass on van Gils's theory about Constance. It would distress his mother and he wanted to speak to his father about Constance first. 'The Dutch intelligence people are saying it was the Germans, but they don't really know. Where's Father?'

'He's dining at the club tonight. Reggie's up in town from Chilton Coombe. He'll be back for dinner. And Charlotte is staying as well for a few days. She has brought Mattie.'

'I'm glad to hear that. I haven't seen them since Millie died.' Charlotte would be good for his mother, as would her son Matthew, on whom Lady Oakford doted. And it would be good for Conrad to see his brother and sister too, the living ones. He hoped he would have the patience to tolerate the crass comments that he knew Reggie would let drop. It was his father who would be the really difficult one to talk to. Conrad wasn't sure he could ever forgive him for what he had done. But he would have to at least pretend to, for his mother's sake.

And he knew his father; Millie's death would be eating him up. Despite his anger with him, Conrad couldn't help feeling a sliver of sympathy.

'There's someone else here to see you,' his mother said. 'Anneliese. She came about an hour ago. We had a lovely talk. It was so nice to be able to speak to someone about my daughter in German.'

Conrad smiled. 'She liked Millie.'

'She's in the drawing room,' said Lady Oakford. 'I think she has things she wants to tell you. I'll leave you alone.'

Conrad went into the drawing room where Anneliese was curled up on a sofa by the window. It was a shock to see her, in his own house, looking so delectable. She was wearing a skirt and green blouse Conrad recognized from their days in Berlin; it brought back all those days, and nights, spent together. She smiled brightly when she saw him, a warm, amused smile at once familiar and yet unseen during the past year.

'Any luck?' she asked.

'I hope so,' said Conrad. 'We'll see. At least I know now that Theo didn't kill Millie.'

'I'm so glad to hear that,' she said. 'As must you be.'

Conrad moved towards the drinks tray. 'I really need a drink. Do you want one?'

'Why not? A gin and It, please.'

Conrad poured her one, and himself a whisky and soda. He wanted to sit on the sofa next to Anneliese, but decided she might prefer some distance, and so took an armchair.

'I've been busy too,' said Anneliese. 'I've visited the Russian Tea Rooms. Twice.'

'Did you meet Constance Scott-Dunton?'

'I did the second time. The first time I went was Tuesday. I spoke to a girl called Marjorie Copthorne. I told her I was a German, that I was living here with my family, and that I was stuck in this country because of the war. I made out I was a committed Nazi and I had heard that the Tea Rooms had English people who were sympathetic to modern Germany. So I had come there to meet some of them. Marjorie had all sorts of questions about Germany, which of course I could answer.'

'Did she believe you?'

'She did. But then a Russian woman sat with us. Her name was Anna Wolkoff; she is the daughter of the owner. She asked me right away if I was Jewish; she claimed I looked Jewish. She said that she had become an expert in Russia at identifying Jews.'

Anneliese didn't look particularly Jewish to Conrad, but then he had never set himself up as an expert on racial matters.

'What did you say?'

'I said my father was an atheist who was racially Jewish, but my mother was Christian and so was I. I told them I hated my father for running away from our country, and I wanted to return to Germany, but my parents insisted I work in London to pay for their keep. I was planning to return anyway, if the German authorities would let me back in, when the war broke out.'

Conrad raised his eyebrows. Like all good lies, the story had an element of truth to it, but knowing Anneliese, she must have found it painful to publicly denounce her father, for whom she had done so much.

'I know,' said Anneliese, noticing Conrad's reaction. 'I didn't like it. But I almost convinced Anna and I definitely convinced Marjorie. So I decided to have another go. I returned to the Tea Rooms last night, and this time I met Constance Scott-Dunton.'

'What did you think of her?'

'You are right, she is queer. I mean, she is lively and friendly, but she has such intense dark eyes, they unsettle me. She seemed to like my stories of modern Berlin. Then Anna Wolkoff arrived again, with a good-looking American man named Kent, I think. She was clearly still suspicious of me.'

'I assume Constance didn't tell you about her trip to Holland?' Conrad asked. Even Anneliese couldn't get that out of a stranger on first meeting.

'No. But I did talk to her about Henry Alston and Captain Maule Ramsay. I had read back copies of the newspapers in the Golders Green Library with my father to learn something about their backgrounds. It turns out that Marjorie is the niece of a good friend of Alston, and that she introduced Constance to him. Constance seems to think that Alston is a great man. It was almost as if she was in love with him, although he has a terribly damaged face, doesn't he?'

'He does,' said Conrad. 'Attacked by a lion in Africa, I believe. He's clever; my father has always had a great deal of respect for him. They are both directors of Gurney Kroheim.'

'From what Constance says, Alston is a strong supporter of Germany. As is the other one, Captain Maule Ramsay, although he is much more blatant about it. I said how pleased I was to hear that some British politicians had sensible views.' Anneliese shuddered. 'I think she likes me.'

'The policeman I met in The Hague thinks she might have murdered Millie.'

'Really?' Anneliese eyes opened wide. 'Does he have proof?'

'Some. Not enough. The knife that was used to stab Millie was taken from the kitchen of the hotel she and Constance were staying in. Also, it appears Constance lied to Millie about Theo wanting to meet her in the sand dunes. And the policeman thinks she lied to him about seeing Theo leaving the scene of the murder.'

'Sounds pretty clear evidence to me,' said Anneliese. 'Why didn't he arrest her?'

'He was told to send her back to England. Dutch intelligence are convinced Theo killed her. Or at least that's what they say.'

'Did the policeman have any idea why she would want to kill Millie?'

'No. And that's the key question. Perhaps you can find out?'

'Perhaps I can.' Anneliese frowned. 'It's strange to see Nazis again. Oh, I know they might not strictly speaking be Nazis, but it reminded me of the attitude of so many Germans. It's odd how a hatred of the Jews seems to nourish people like that. It's almost as if they thrive on it; they feed off hatred to sustain their political views, give them some shape.'

'I'm sorry you had to pretend to think like them,' said Conrad.

'That's all right,' said Anneliese. 'I mean, it is a vile way to think, or even to pretend to think, but it feels good to be able to do something to stop those people. It's better standing up to them, even claiming to be one of them, than denying that they exist or that they matter.'

'You don't have to see them again if you can't face it,' said Conrad.

'You want to find out what happened to Millie and you think Constance knows?'

'That's right,' said Conrad.

'Well, in that case I will get her to tell me. It might take a while, but she will trust me eventually.'

'Thank you,' said Conrad, smiling. 'Here – take some money. You might need it if you are hanging around there trying to make friends.' He pulled a couple of notes out of his wallet.

Anneliese hesitated but she took the money. She didn't have any, Conrad was right that she would need some, and there was no point in pretending otherwise.

'And thank you for whatever you said to my mother,' Conrad said. 'She was in a bad way. You have cheered her up.'

'I like her,' said Anneliese. 'And I do feel so sorry for her.' She got to her feet. 'Now, I must be going back to Hampstead.' She said it firmly, as if she didn't want to be contradicted.

Conrad was tempted to contradict her. He would much rather take Anneliese to the cinema and have supper with her somewhere than face his own family. She seemed different this evening, different than she had seemed for months, really since she had arrived in England. But perhaps his father was right. Conrad didn't want to risk breaking her new-found confidence. He should back off, and wait for her to come to him when she was ready.

So he let her go.

Thirty-Two

Admiral Canaris rode in the Tiergarten almost every morning, sometimes alone, sometimes with his fellow Abwehr officers, and sometimes, like that morning, with SS Sturmbannführer Walter Schellenberg.

The two men knew each other well. Like Heydrich, they lived in the wooded Schlachtensee suburb of Berlin, and they had met socially through the Gestapo chief. As effective head of the new foreign-intelligence branch of the Gestapo, Schellenberg was a rival. Although at that point much smaller than the Abwehr, Canaris knew Schellenberg's nascent organization was bound to grow rapidly given the ambitions of his bosses Heydrich and Himmler. But rather than make an enemy of his rival, Canaris treated the younger, junior officer as a friend, something Schellenberg appreciated.

The Tiergarten had originally been preserved as a hunting forest, and in parts of its wooded heart, in the cold foggy murk of a November dawn, it still felt like one. Except one stumbled across occasional statues of dead composers rather than the odd hind or stag. Here one could think, away from the hubbub of Berlin traffic or War Ministry gossip. Here one could talk.

'Walter, one of my top agents had an unpleasant experience in Holland yesterday morning.'

'Really?'

'Yes. He's an Englishman. Actually he is half-German. Conrad de Lancey. Do you know of him?'

'I've seen his file,' said Schellenberg. 'There wasn't much in it.'

Canaris laughed. 'No, I suspect there wasn't. There was some unpleasant business with de Lancey last year involving documents relating to your chief's ancestry. I didn't believe any of it, of course, and I am not going to discuss specifics.'

'Please don't.' The last thing Schellenberg wanted to be told was that Reinhard Heydrich was part Jewish.

'We had some difficulties with de Lancey last year, of which Reinhard is well aware, and we dropped him. But when war broke out one of our officers reactivated him. If we manage him correctly, he could become a valuable source of information for us.'

'I see.'

'And now we come to the unpleasant experience. Our officer, Lieutenant Hertenberg, met de Lancey in Leiden yesterday. Afterwards, de Lancey was attacked by a man with a gun. De Lancey is a resourceful fellow and managed to overcome his attacker and kill him. Chased him off the roof of a university building, I believe. Our embassy in The Hague has been informed by the Dutch police that the man's identification suggests he was a Dr Heinrich Fuhrmann from the University of Hamburg. They are saying it was suicide: he jumped. Needless to say there is no such man on the university faculty.'

'I see,' said Schellenberg quietly. 'Could this Dr Fuhrmann be a British agent?'

'Possibly,' said Canaris. 'Although it had occurred to us that he might have been working for you. No need to answer that, Walter. It would be perfectly understandable if given de Lancey's activities last year you had assumed he was an enemy agent.'

'And you are telling me de Lancey is one of yours?'

'Yes. He is a bit of a loose cannon, but he is our loose cannon. And please reassure Reinhard that he hasn't divulged any of the information he uncovered, or claims to have uncovered, about Reinhard's family history last year. Which is a good thing, because I am sure he made it all up anyway.'

'I understand,' said Schellenberg. 'I'll pass that on.' And he would, faithfully. He suspected that the sly admiral had outfoxed

Heydrich on this one. Leave de Lancey alone and no nasty rumours about Jewish ancestors would emerge. That should work. And, frankly, that was fine with Schellenberg. He still had his hands full with Payne Best, Stevens, and the man who had planted the Munich beer hall bomb, Georg Elser, who was giving every indication of being the demented loner he claimed.

They emerged from the dark woods into an open green space, shrouded in grey curtains of fog.

'Come on, Walter!' called Canaris as he urged his horse into a canter. Schellenberg followed him into the bank of mist.

Mayfair, London

'Why are we here, Freddie?'

Here was Erskine's, a club on a side street in Mayfair. Freddie Copthorne was a member, but Alston had hardly ever been there. It was a bit young, a bit chaotic for him. And now Freddie had asked to meet him there for a drink.

Alston's doubts about Freddie were increasing. He liked the man, everybody liked Freddie, and as a result his contacts among those British nobility who were suspicious of war were excellent, especially the younger ones such as Lord Brocket and Lord Tavistock. But Alston's reputation was quietly rising in both Houses of Parliament. He didn't really need Freddie anymore.

They were in the club's tiny library – it wasn't the sort of club where one went to read – and they were alone with a pink gin and a glass of beer.

'I want to talk to you, Henry, and I wanted neutral territory on which to do it.'

'This is hardly neutral territory. I'd say you were playing at home.'

Freddie ignored him. 'Ever since we met that man Bedaux, I've been thinking.'

'Yes?' Alston refrained from warning Freddie against doing anything so dangerous.

'I have concerns about what he was suggesting. About what we are doing.'

'Concerns about stopping a world war?'

'No. But concerns about how we do it.'

'We've been through this before, Freddie. It's perfectly clear. If the present government won't make peace then we need a new government. The logic is inescapable.'

'Yes. But do we need a new king?'

'We need a government that Hitler will talk to. That may mean a new king.'

'But should we really be talking to Hitler's people now? Should we be talking to someone as shady as Charles Bedaux?'

'Yes, Freddie, we should.' Alston fought to control his impatience. 'Because that's the only way we will get peace.'

'I've thought about it long and hard, Henry, and I think it's treason.'

'Don't be ridiculous.'

'My loyalty is to my king, who is George VI, and to my country, which is at war with Germany.'

'But you have to look more deeply than that, Freddie,' Henry said. 'Nothing is straightforward—'

Copthorne held up his hand. 'Yes, it is. That's my point. It is straightforward. I've been bamboozled by your ingenious arguments, Henry, and I've lost track of what is really important, which is beating the Hun. And serving my king.'

Alston didn't like the look in Freddie's eye; he had never seen such determination in his friend before. Alston's instinct was it was dangerous. Time to drop him.

He leaned back in his armchair. 'All right, Freddie. I understand. Perhaps we should leave you out of these discussions. You and I can meet socially, of course – I'd like to continue to do that – but I will ensure that you remain in the dark about what I am doing.'

'No, Henry, it's not that simple,' Freddie said.

Alston smiled. 'I thought you just said you liked things simple.'

Freddie took no notice of the dig. 'You see, if I am right and what we have been discussing is treason, it should stop.'

'Stop?'

'Yes. I'm not suggesting that we should stop agitating for peace. But we shouldn't negotiate with the German government behind our own government's back. And we shouldn't even mention the Duke of Windsor becoming king.'

Alston held Freddie's gaze. He was deadly serious. But Alston was not going to be threatened by Freddie Copthorne. 'No. I'm sorry, Freddie, but no. I will not abandon this country's best hopes for peace because of your illogical scruples.'

'If you don't, Henry, then I shall be duty-bound to inform the authorities what we have been doing. What *you* have been doing.'

'Is that a threat?'

'I don't know. I'm trying to tell you I'm not playing games. I will *not* be party to treason. And if I see treason I will stop it. I know right from wrong, and I know my duty.'

Lord Copthorne was sitting ramrod straight in his chair, his gaze unflinching. Alston could see he had chosen the role of stubborn Englishman and he was going to stick with it.

Alston knew that in his own way, Freddie was incorruptible. He had his principles and he kept to them. Until that moment his principle had been to support an alliance between Britain and Germany. But now he had dredged up what was for him a more important principle.

'Whom will you inform?'

'Winston.'

'Winston! But he's the worst of the warmongers. He'll make a meal of this and scupper any chance of us bringing in a more sensible government.'

'Exactly. That's why I would talk to him.'

That wasn't so stupid. Other more obvious people that Freddie might have chosen to speak to could have been persuaded to keep quiet by Alston or his friends. But not Winston Churchill. After years out of office, he had been brought into Cabinet as First

Lord of the Admiralty at the beginning of the war. He was by no means the most senior member of the government, but he was the noisiest and the most energetic. And the one least likely to be swayed by Alston.

'Well?' said Freddie.

'Well what?'

'Are you going to agree not to negotiate secretly with the German government? Will you rule out bringing in the Duke of Windsor as king?'

'No, I bloody well won't, Freddie. Don't be such a damned idiot. This is much bigger than your scruples. This is history we are talking about.'

'I know,' said Freddie. 'And that is why I shall speak to Winston tomorrow unless you give me the assurance I ask for.'

'Bugger off, Freddie,' Alston said, slamming his glass on the table. Usually good at controlling his temper, he was furious. He stormed out of the little library, grabbed his coat from the cloakroom and headed out into the night. Unusually, he had driven to Mayfair: he had dropped Constance off at her aunt's house in Dulwich before meeting Freddie.

He sat behind the wheel and seethed. He couldn't possibly abandon his whole strategy to please Freddie's scruples. Alston told Freddie and everyone else that he wanted peace, but what he really wanted was an alliance with Germany. Germany represented the future: a modern, ordered, effective society whose citizens believed in their country and in its destiny. Britain too could be such a country, but only if radical changes were made to the British government, probably including the monarch. Ideally, Alston himself would have an important role in the new government. And this government would work with Nazi Germany, not against them. That meant talking to them. That meant the Duke of Windsor becoming king. It probably meant Lloyd George becoming Prime Minister. It meant speaking to people like Charles Bedaux, Otto Langebrück and Rib. Eventually even to Hitler. Freddie just didn't understand that.

But Freddie wasn't bluffing. He would go to see Churchill the following morning, and once he had done that it would all be over. Britain would be stuck in the war until it was finished, probably until the Germans invaded. And what was so damned patriotic about that?

Alston regretted not playing for time. He could have told Freddie he would think about it, given himself a week to work out what to do. Perhaps he should go back into the club and have another word.

There was a little light on the blacked-out London street from half a moon, enough to see a man step out of the club and walk along the lane thirty yards ahead of Alston's car. Although Alston couldn't see his face, he could recognize Freddie Copthorne's thin frame and slightly stooped posture.

Now was his chance to jump out of the car and demand from Freddie a week to think about his 'proposal'.

Or. Or he could do what Constance had done, what she would no doubt do at that very moment if she were the one sitting behind the wheel. Seize the initiative.

This was a war. The course of history was at stake. People were dying all over Europe for causes they believed were just.

Sir Henry Alston switched on the engine of his car and put his foot down hard on the accelerator, changing up into second gear ten yards before he hit Lord Copthorne from behind and sent him flying through the air into an unlit street lamp.

Thirty-Three

Kensington, London, 25 November

The family, or what was left of it, were at breakfast, and they were all well behaved. Charlotte's presence was calming. She was two years younger than Conrad, married to a banker who had just joined the navy. She had brought her nine-month-old son Mattie with her, although he was asleep at that moment upstairs in the old nursery. Reggie seemed to have run out of idiotic opinions, at least temporarily, and Conrad resisted asking him why he wasn't in uniform.

Conrad and his father were stiff and polite to each other. Conrad had repeated to him what he had told the rest of the family, that he was hopeful that the Dutch would release Millie's body soon, but he couldn't guarantee it, and that they didn't know who had killed her. Conrad hadn't yet had the opportunity to ask Oakford more about Constance, but he would wait until they could speak privately. Then he would be on his way back to Tidworth and soldiering.

In the middle of a general discussion about arrangements for Millie's funeral, assuming they eventually got her body back, his father's valet Williamson appeared with a letter addressed to Conrad. Conrad opened it. It was handwritten on Foreign Office notepaper and dated the day before. What he read shocked him.

Dear Mr de Lancey,

Major McCaigue has passed on to me the information you gave him this afternoon about your trip to Holland, and in particular the rumours you heard concerning the Duke of Windsor.

I urge you to return to your battalion forthwith and require you to desist from making any more enquiries on this subject. The matter is in hand.

Yours sincerely,
Robert Vansittart

No doubt Van was a busy man, but Conrad was offended by the abrupt tone. It was at least clear; Conrad was being told to shut up and look the other way. Which was all very well, but he had put his life at risk at Venlo for Van, and again in Leiden, although admittedly that was not at Van's request. It was to serve his country, though.

McCaigue had clearly passed on what Conrad had told him, but, as the intelligence officer had expected, the reaction had been less than enthusiastic. When Van had said 'The matter is in hand', did that mean he was burying it? The tone of the note suggested he was.

'What's the matter, dear?' enquired his mother anxiously. 'Has someone else died?'

'Oh, no,' said Conrad. 'It's not that.'

'Is it about Millie?' Reggie asked.

'It's from Van, isn't it?' said Oakford.

Conrad glanced at his father and in an instant he could tell he knew what was in the letter.

'Come into my study,' Oakford said. 'Would you excuse us?'

Conrad followed his father in silence up the stairs to the small room that served as Lord Oakford's study. 'Shut the door.'

Conrad shut the door.

'Can I see it?'

Conrad handed the note to him. Oakford scanned it. 'Well, that's pretty clear, isn't it?'

'Theo told me that the Duke of Windsor is effectively spying for the Germans. That the Nazis want him to be king again. That's what I told McCaigue and that's what McCaigue told Van. Are they burying it?'

242

'Van says here that they are going to look into it,' said Oakford. 'It's a sensitive issue; I'm not surprised they don't want you blundering around. And I doubt that they view Theo as a reliable source. Neither do I. He killed Millie, didn't he?'

'I don't believe he did, Father,' said Conrad. 'And they are burying it. They don't like what they are hearing and so they are ignoring it.' He shook his head. 'I would have thought better of Van.'

'We had a visitor here a couple of days ago,' said Lord Oakford. 'A Captain Hobson-Hedges of the SIS. He asked me lots of questions about you. About your political beliefs. I told him honestly about your socialism, and your pacifism, but I said that you had never been a communist, as far as I was aware. They asked about poor Joachim, how close you were and whether we knew he was a Soviet spy. I told him you were cousins and you had been close, but I had no idea he was a spy. Was he?'

'Probably,' said Conrad. 'At least according to the German secret service. Theo said so.'

'You never told me that.'

'I only found out after the Gestapo killed him. He was on leave from the German Embassy in Moscow, and he approached Theo last year just as I arrived in Berlin. Theo thinks that the reason he contacted him was to try to find out about the conspiracy against Hitler for the Russians. The Gestapo arrested him and he died in custody.' Joachim had been a couple of years older than his cousin Conrad, and had introduced him to socialist ideas when he had stayed with the de Lanceys for a few months while Conrad was still at school. Conrad had liked his company. And listened to his political opinions.

Conrad remembered McCaigue's warning about suspicions about him.

'They think I'm a Russian spy?'

'They suspect that.'

'Who are "they"?' asked Conrad. 'Apart from being idiots.'

'You never know who "they" are,' said Lord Oakford. 'The SIS. MI5. Special Branch. The important thing is they have almost persuaded Van. He telephoned me last night. I insisted you were no Russian spy, but I'm sure that is why he has warned you off.'

'That's ridiculous!' said Conrad. 'You know I'm not a spy, don't you, Father? As far as I am concerned Stalin is almost as bad as Hitler. I told you how those Popular Army soldiers shot David and Harry in Spain. I've seen how Russian commissars corrupted the Republicans.'

'I know,' said Lord Oakford.

'And even if I was a Russian spy, why would I make things up about the Duke of Windsor?'

Oakford shrugged.

'What do you think I should do?' Conrad asked his father.

'Do as Van tells you,' Oakford said. 'And be grateful they haven't arrested you.'

'I almost wish they had,' said Conrad. 'Then I would be able to defend myself.'

'This is wartime,' said Oakford. 'I wouldn't count on your chances of a fair trial.'

'All right,' said Conrad. 'But there is one other thing I learned in Holland that I should tell you.' He explained van Gils's doubts about Theo's guilt, and what he had said about Constance and the knife that had killed Millie.

'Who knows about Theo?' Oakford said. 'But you can forget about Constance. She is a young Englishwoman and a friend of a friend of mine. What would she have had against Millie? And you have seen how Holland is crawling with spies. My bet is that Millie was killed either by the Abwehr or the Gestapo. It's the alternative that scares me most.'

'What's that?'

'That it was the British,' said Oakford.

Conrad remembered Theo's speculation. 'To put off unofficial peace talks?'

Oakford nodded. 'I don't *think* anyone in the British government would do that, but we can't rule it out.'

Conrad closed his eyes. The idea of his own country killing his sister was too much to contemplate. He sighed. 'You can't trust spies, can you?'

Lord Oakford shook his head.

'Well, I had better head back to my battalion,' Conrad said. 'Do what Sir Robert wants.'

He stood up. 'Good luck,' said Lord Oakford. 'And – although it's difficult in war – be careful.'

Thus spoke the man who had won a Victoria Cross and lost an arm in 1917 at Passchendaele while taking a German machine-gun post and turning the weapon on the enemy. He had not been careful then.

But it was the horror of that day that had turned Lord Oakford against war, and made him pledge that his own son would not have to repeat the experience.

'Thank you,' said Conrad. But he didn't tell his father he was damned if he was going to be careful either.

Conrad headed to Waterloo for a train that was supposed to leave at 4.06 p.m. He had scribbled a quick note to Anneliese telling her he was going back to his battalion that day and asking her to keep him informed of anything she discovered about Constance. He warned her not to be too explicit in her letters and to assume his post would be read – with more attention than usual, he suspected.

At Waterloo Station he bumped into a face that was becoming too familiar. Major McCaigue.

'What are you doing here?' said Conrad. 'Checking I actually get on the train?'

'We need to have a little chat,' said McCaigue.

'It had better be quick then,' said Conrad. 'My train leaves in five minutes.'

'Then you will have to get the next one. Come with me.'

Conrad wanted to tell him to sod off. For one thing he had no idea when the next train would be and how long it would take to make its way to Wiltshire. But he couldn't just ignore McCaigue. He was curious what the spy had to say.

245

McCaigue led Conrad north towards the river, down a narrow alley between two warehouses. They emerged with a view of the Thames and the Houses of Parliament on the other side. The river was busy with boats, and a line of barrage balloons bobbed overhead. The long slender barrels of ack-ack guns could be seen along the banks, pointing skywards.

McCaigue leaned on some wooden railings overlooking the water. 'I have two messages for you, an official one and an unofficial one. And it's vital you remember which is which.'

'All right,' said Conrad, despite himself. It was strange how, for such a shady character, McCaigue's rich warm voice, with its hint of Ulster, conveyed trustworthiness.

'This is the official message I am required to give you,' McCaigue said. 'My employers have come to the conclusion that you are probably a spy for the Soviet Union. As a result they question the reliability of the information you provided me two days ago regarding the Duke of Windsor. We will attempt to verify it, but we remain sceptical. We suspect that it is a plot by Germany's ally Russia to undermine the royal family.'

'From what I can tell the royal family seems perfectly capable of undermining itself, or certainly the Duke of Windsor is. And I'm not a Soviet spy, Major McCaigue,' said Conrad. 'It's absurd to think that I am. Do they believe Theo is a Russian spy as well?'

'It's a possibility they entertain,' said McCaigue. 'Both of you were socialists at Oxford. It would explain Hertenberg's opposition to the Nazi regime. You both met your cousin Joachim Mühlendorf in Berlin last year.'

'And what about Millie? Was she a Russian spy as well?'

'It can't be ruled out,' said McCaigue.

'Bollocks!' said Conrad.

'She was your sister,' said McCaigue. 'And you fought in Spain on the side of the communists. We have other evidence.'

'What other evidence?'

'I'm not at liberty to say.'

'So I am found guilty without even knowing the evidence against me?'

'That's my point, de Lancey. You haven't been found guilty. In fact it has been decided to let you go. Provided you stay with your unit and don't come back to London asking foolish questions.'

'Are you threatening me?'

'Yes,' said McCaigue. He turned to look at Conrad, his blue eyes steady. 'That was the official bit. I trust you understood it?'

Conrad didn't answer. Just stared across the river to the Houses of Parliament, that historic symbol of liberty, where politicians through the ages had conspired to bury awkward information.

'Now the unofficial bit,' McCaigue said. 'Speaking personally, I'm not convinced that you are a Soviet spy.'

'Well, that's awfully big of you,' said Conrad.

'There is some debate within the service about the loyalties of the Duke of Windsor. We have uncovered evidence over the last few years that has brought those loyalties into question, and more has come to light since the outbreak of war. Actually "come to light" isn't strictly accurate, since such evidence is kept firmly in the dark, but you know what I mean. Not enough to prove anything conclusively, and with the duke, we need conclusive proof before we can even begin asking him questions. So if you do happen to stumble across something, let me know, won't you?'

'On the off chance I'm not a Russian spy?'

McCaigue's small eyes twinkled. 'On the off chance.'

'You did tell the British general staff that the Germans know about the weaknesses in the French line at Sedan?' Conrad said.

'I did,' said McCaigue.

'That's good.' That seemed to be what most concerned Theo, and if the Allies plugged that gap, then Conrad's efforts would have been worthwhile.

'Keep in touch,' said McCaigue, handing Conrad a card.

Conrad snorted and turned on his heel back to the station. He had missed his train and couldn't catch another until six o'clock. He didn't get to barracks until eleven.

It was tempting just to forget all that had happened over the previous fortnight and concentrate on practising how to kill Germans.

But his sister had died and he didn't know why. And his former sovereign was telling the enemy how to defeat the country they both shared.

Those two facts he could not forget.

PART THREE

May 1940

Thirty-Four

Extracts from Lieutenant Dieter von Hertenberg's Diary

2 May 1940

I nearly died this afternoon.

We have spent a week planning the exercise, and by and large it went very well. We used a stretch of the Moselle which is supposed to look a lot like the Meuse near Sedan, our objective in the first week of the offensive. It's a fast-flowing river, especially now with the snow melting so late this year, and there are steep banks on the western side. The exercise started at 1000 with artillery bombardment, air assaults from Stukas, and infantry crossing the river in dinghies. They established a bridgehead and then the engineers set up a pontoon bridge. It was quite a sight to see them constructing it in such difficult circumstances. Of course it will be infinitely worse under enemy fire, but our engineers are brave men who know what they are doing.

Once the bridge was constructed the first of our Panzers rolled across.

Just as the exercise was coming to the end, I drove out on to the middle of the bridge with General Guderian. I was having a cigarette and watching the infantry's dinghies make their way back to the eastern shore, when I heard a shout, and a splash. A man had fallen in. The current was swift and he was quickly swept down towards the bridge. He clearly couldn't swim.

I can swim. Without thinking very hard I dropped my belt, kicked off my boots and jumped off the bridge to intercept him.

The cold was extraordinary. I've swum in what I thought were cold lakes before, but nothing like this. The breath seemed to leave my body instantly, and I was numb. I forced myself to focus on the soldier, who was only metres away. His arms were flailing and he was going under.

I just managed to reach him, and tried to get him to keep still while I kept his head above water. I was already thirty metres downstream from the pontoon, but his colleagues were paddling furiously with the current after us.

The man wouldn't stop struggling. I don't think he knew what he was doing, but he pushed me underwater so that he could try to keep his own head high. I went down, and fought for air. The bastard was going to drown me!

I took in one gulp of freezing water, forced my head up for air, and then he pushed me down again. I tried to keep my mouth shut, but there was water in my lungs and I knew I couldn't hold out any longer. Then arms grabbed my shoulders and dragged me upwards. A moment later I was in the dinghy, choking.

Afterwards, the infantryman thanked me. But he was embarrassed. We both knew he had nearly killed me.

The exercise was a success according to the general, and I think he is right. We are ready now. After the exercises in the Eifel Mountains, we know we can organize ourselves to cross the Ardennes forests and hills, and we can bridge the Meuse at Sedan when we get there. Morale is high; we have faith in Guderian's leadership, and in our own tactics. Keep moving. Keep the enemy off balance. Concentrate our armour. Those are his mottos and I think they will work.

The trouble is, we will be sitting ducks. Both when we are in long columns of vehicles on mountain roads, and when we try to cross the rivers. Will speed and boldness really protect us? I think they will. I have to trust they will.

It all depends on whether the French army we will be facing really will be as weak as the High Command seems to think it will be. I know Theo is behind our intelligence on that, and if there is one person I trust on that kind of thing, it is Theo. Now we are at war, politics are behind us. I am willing to fight for the Fatherland and die for it if necessary, just like my ancestors before me. It's good Theo finally seems to feel the same way, and is doing his bit to help us. It's just a shame he can't be out here at the front fighting with us.

3 May

Got in big trouble this morning. A group of us decided to take a couple of dinghies out on the river and paddle about. We hadn't had the chance yesterday. After my ducking I thought it was important to overcome any fear and get back on the water, a bit like falling off a bicycle.

It was a peaceful, misty morning, and everything was quiet compared to the din of the exercise yesterday. The Moselle really is a beautiful river, at least on this stretch. But when we returned to shore, the chief was waiting for us. He was furious, and went into one of his highest gears of temper tantrums, which is pretty high. 'Joyriding on the river is strictly forbidden!' I think he overreacted, especially with me.

That bothered me afterwards, but Gustav said the chief was only angry with me because he had been so shaken by nearly losing me yesterday.

I wonder if that is true. I hope it is.

There is nothing I wouldn't do for General Guderian.

Thirty-Five

Liverpool Street Station, London, 4 May 1940

Conrad lit yet another cigarette and watched the steam-smeared iron, steel and blackened brick jolt and judder past the train window. The train was just outside Liverpool Street Station and had been for a quarter of an hour. The journey from Ipswich had taken two hours longer than it should, with an hour spent stationary in Chelmsford, and Conrad had stood all the way.

If the soldiers of the British Army had been trained in one skill during the long phoney war, it was patience. But even with so much practice, Conrad found it hard to maintain his. He couldn't wait to get to London. He hadn't been to the capital since November – indeed he had scarcely been away on leave. A couple of days down to Somerset for Millie's funeral in December, another three days at Christmas. Then nothing.

Part of the reason was that the battalion had been despatched to Galloway in January, shivering on a frozen hillside in one of the coldest winters on record.

The other reason was that Conrad's CO, Colonel Rydal, had been told by 'the powers that be' not to let his lieutenant take leave in London. The colonel never spoke to Conrad about this directly, and Conrad didn't ask him. Until, one afternoon at the beginning of April, when the colonel summoned Conrad to join him on a recce to plan an exercise for the following week.

They drove up into the hills and then Colonel Rydal consulted his map and set off at a rapid pace up a slope beside a burn, swollen with spring meltwater. There was sunshine, and the snow had almost disappeared from the hills. After half an hour's strenuous climb, they reached the top of a crag, with a dramatic view to the north of moors and lochs and to the south of a patchwork of fields glistening in the spring sunlight, dotted with barrel-shaped sheep on the brink of giving birth, and the white-belted local cows.

The colonel sat down and pulled out his pipe. Conrad lit a cigarette, and began to examine his map for likely rallying points for the exercise.

'Sod the exercise, Conrad. I already know what we are going to do.'

Conrad smiled. 'Very good, sir.'

'You are a damned good officer, Conrad.'

'Thank you, sir.'

'If I ask you something will you give me an honest answer?'

Conrad mulled over the colonel's question before replying. One of the things he liked about his unit was the trust between the officers. And the men, for that matter. They were all very different – some of them didn't even like each other – but they trusted one another. And they all trusted Colonel Rydal. He led by example.

'I won't give you a dishonest answer,' said Conrad. 'I might say I can't answer the question. Depends what it is, obviously.'

Rydal frowned. 'I suppose that will have to do.' He puffed at his pipe. 'Conrad, are you a Soviet spy?'

'No, sir,' said Conrad firmly. But he appreciated the directness of the question.

'Thought not,' said Rydal. 'But there are some people who think you are. You clearly got yourself into some hot water when you were away on Sir Robert Vansittart's business last autumn.'

'I did. I discovered some things that some people with power would rather I hadn't.'

'I gathered something like that might be going on. Look here, it's not right you've been stuck up here without any leave for so many months. If you give me your word not to cause trouble and ask difficult questions, I'll grant you some leave. Will you give me your word?'

'I'm afraid I can't do that, sir.'

'Why the devil not?'

Conrad explained. If Rydal trusted him, then he should trust Rydal. He told him about Millie's murder and about Theo's allegations that the Duke of Windsor had been indirectly providing information about the French deployment to the Germans.

Colonel Rydal listened, his frown deepening as Conrad's story progressed. 'Is this true, de Lancey?'

'Absolutely true, sir.'

Rydal examined his lieutenant closely. 'Well, I can see why they want to keep you stuck up here.'

'So can I, sir.'

'Leave it with me, de Lancey.'

Two days later Rydal told Conrad he could have seven days' leave the following week, during which time he could ask all the questions he damn well wanted, but he should ask them as unobtrusively as possible.

But then Germany invaded Norway. All leave was cancelled, and the battalion loaded up on to their lorries and spent several days driving erratically around the north-east of England and Scotland. The general staff couldn't seem to decide whether a motorized battalion was an asset or a liability in the Norwegian mountains. In the end half the battalion embarked on a ship at Newcastle without their vehicles, and steamed out into the North Sea. They were given maps of the countryside around the small town of Namsos. But they never made it. Within sight of the coast of Norway, the ship was given orders to turn around and steam back to England.

After a further week loitering in the Northumberland countryside, they were sent down to Suffolk to protect East Anglia from a German invasion, and Conrad was finally granted a weekend's leave.

During his time in Scotland Anneliese had sent him perhaps half a dozen letters. They spoke obliquely about 'their friends in Kensington'; although Anneliese didn't mention the Russian Tea

Rooms by name, she did mention Constance. It was clear that she was becoming friendly with the woman, but it didn't sound as if she had learned much of interest. Conrad was very pleased to see her trying so hard to help him, especially dealing with such hateful people, although reading between the lines it was clear that Anneliese enjoyed the cloak-and-dagger aspect of her endeavour. He replied with carefully constructed letters, encouraging her, telling her he was thinking about her but not scaring her off with too much sentiment.

The truth was he *was* thinking about her. It would be odd if stuck in a frozen hut in Scotland with a group of fellow soldiers he hadn't thought about the woman he had fallen in love with in Berlin: so spirited, so sensual, so enchanting. He wondered whether the month or so they had spent entwined with each other back then was all that there ever would be. In his more disheartened moments, when it was particularly dark and cold, and the boredom was reaching extremes, he feared that might be the case.

Was it just the old Anneliese he had been in love with? Had the Nazis changed her permanently with their callous brutality, their concentration camps, their murders? They had trampled on her soul, injured it perhaps beyond repair. He knew he could still love her. But could she love him? And if she couldn't, shouldn't he just let her go?

Then, just a few days after the invasion of Norway, he had received an excited letter from her saying she had learned some gossip from their Kensington friends that she simply must tell him in person. That was three weeks ago, and it was only now that he had managed to arrange to see her: she had promised to meet him at Liverpool Street Station that afternoon. Conrad hoped she would still be there, despite the lateness of his train. Knowing Anneliese, she wouldn't give up unless she had to, but then a shift at the hospital might force her.

He was eager to hear what she had to say. Millie's death was still unresolved. Stuck away in darkest, coldest Scotland without hope of leave, there had been nothing Conrad could do about that, but he could think about it. He was sure that Theo wasn't responsible, but he had no idea who was, and time did nothing to reduce his need to know. *Something* was going on, probably something involving Sir Henry Alston, Charles Bedaux and the Duke of Windsor. Conrad could hope that Major McCaigue had made some progress in finding out what, but even if he had, he probably wouldn't tell Conrad. Conrad's feelings towards his father were mixed: on the one hand he blamed him for letting Millie go to Holland on such a hare-brained scheme, on the other he felt desperately sorry for him for the loss of his daughter. And Conrad himself wasn't free of blame. If he had only done what his father had asked and talked to Theo about peace, Millie would still be alive.

But Conrad's father couldn't help him find out about Millie's death either. His only hope was Anneliese.

Conrad almost missed her in the crowd of men in uniform enthusiastic for their weekend leave, barging their way towards the station exits. She saw him first, and jumped up and down, waving to attract his attention. She was wearing her nurse's uniform, and she was smiling as Conrad kissed her cheek.

'Thanks for waiting,' he said. 'I'm sorry the train is so late.'

'That's all right,' said Anneliese. 'It's hardly your fault. There is a café around the corner. Shall we go there? I have something I want to talk to you about.'

Anneliese led Conrad between the piles of sandbags at the station entrance, across Bishopsgate to Artillery Lane, and there they found a small café with a spare table. As they walked Anneliese chattered about her shift at the hospital, what her parents had been up to and a picture she had been to see with her mother: *The Lambeth Walk.*

'Thanks for your letters,' said Conrad as they finally sat down. 'You've been busy.'

'I have. They are such dreadful people, Conrad! Truly awful.'

'I'm sure,' said Conrad, amused by Anneliese's improving grasp of English idiom. 'So you don't like Constance?'

'I can't stand her. But she loves me. I'm her pet German. As we thought, the Russian Tea Rooms is full of anti-Semites. They have formed some secret society, called "The Right Club". Anna Wolkoff is the secretary, and the president is a Conservative MP, Captain Maule Ramsay.'

'I spotted him when I met Constance there.'

'Horrible man. Hates the Jews and doesn't know the first thing about them! The others all love him.'

'So who are the members of this "Right Club"?'

'Not me. I did try, and Constance pushed for me to be let in, but they wouldn't have me. I am pretty sure Anna Wolkoff doesn't trust me.' Anneliese sipped her tea. 'There are lots of women. Most of the men have gone off to war, and it's tricky for them, poor darlings. They hate the Jews and love the Nazis, but they are true patriots and want to fight for their country. There is a loyal band of regulars: Maule Ramsay, his wife, Constance, her friend Marjorie Copthorne, a pretty woman called Joan Miller – a model, I think. Then there is Anna Wolkoff and a suave friend of hers called Tyler Kent. He's American, does something at their embassy in London, and seems to have been posted to Moscow before that. He speaks Russian.'

'Not Alston?'

'No. Constance says she tries to get him to come, but he refuses. He's afraid of being seen there. I don't blame him.'

'So Constance is still in touch with Alston?'

Anneliese smiled. 'Oh, very much so. In fact she is his mistress!'

'Really?' Conrad was surprised, although the idea that a Tory MP might have a little mistress to keep him entertained while he was in London and his wife was in the constituency shouldn't have shocked him.

'She's desperately proud of it. She thinks the world of him. She thinks he's going to be Prime Minister.'

'He's only been an MP a few years, hasn't he?' Conrad said.

'Since 1935. But she is certain he will be. Soon. And what's more interesting, he's just as certain.'

'That is interesting. How?'

'He has a plan. I'm sure Constance knows what it is, but she won't tell me.'

'Is it a coup? Is he in touch with Oswald Mosley?'

'Oh, no. He hates Mosley and therefore so does Constance.'

'Has she mentioned the Duke of Windsor at all?' Conrad asked.

'Not in that context. We have spoken about him. She likes him, but I think that's because he is good-looking and charming and she likes the romance of him giving up the throne for the woman he loved.'

'Nothing about him and Alston?'

Anneliese shook her head. 'No. But I'm sure there is *something* going on.'

'That's just what I've been thinking.' What he wasn't sure of was how he could find out what. 'Any luck with Millie's murder?'

'Not directly. But I did learn something a couple of weeks ago that just might be connected. That's why I wrote to you.'

'Yes. Sorry I couldn't come right away. They wouldn't let me.'

'Were you in Norway?'

'Almost,' said Conrad. 'So what did you learn?'

'I was talking to Marjorie, and Constance was there. For some reason we were discussing her Uncle Freddie. He was a close friend of Alston. He was killed in November last year, run over by a car in the blackout. Whoever did it didn't stop. Anyway, Marjorie said that her aunt, Freddie's wife, is convinced that it was Henry Alston who ran him down! They were having a drink together at Freddie's club, and Alston left a couple of minutes before Freddie.'

'Why would he want to kill Lord Copthorne?'

'That's what I asked. Apparently Lord Copthorne was worried about what Alston was up to, although it's not clear what precisely that was.'

'Did the police investigate?'

'For a day. Then it all went quiet. Lady Copthorne thinks they are covering something up. Specifically that they are protecting Henry Alston.'

'Good God!'

'Constance was looking daggers at Marjorie as she said this. Marjorie said that her aunt was paranoid, and no one could possibly want to kill her sweet Uncle Freddie on purpose, especially his best friend. Then Constance said something rather interesting. Or at least I thought it was interesting.'

'Which was?'

'That Marjorie's Aunt Polly – Lady Copthorne – was completely bats. Marjorie seemed a little put out by this and pointed out that Constance had never met her aunt. Constance said everyone knew it, and was furious with Marjorie.'

'So you think Constance jumped in to shut Marjorie up?'

'Yes. Because she knew she was right. Alston *did* run down Lord Copthorne.'

Conrad smiled. 'Yes, that is interesting. But I suppose it is conceivable that Constance was defending Alston because she is dotty about him.'

'It's conceivable,' said Anneliese. 'But it seemed to me at the time that it was more than that. That she wanted Marjorie to shut up because her aunt was on to something.'

'Could Lord Copthorne's death have had something to do with why Millie was killed?'

Anneliese shrugged. 'Maybe. It might all be just a coincidence. But it's worth checking, don't you think?'

'I do,' said Conrad. 'I most certainly do.'

'Did you know Lord Copthorne? Do you know anyone who knew him? Or his wife?'

'I didn't,' said Conrad. 'My father certainly did; in fact, I remember at Christmas he mentioned Freddie Copthorne had died. He might know Polly Copthorne. I can certainly ask him. I'm not sure he will give me a straight answer.'

'How are you getting on with your father?'

'I haven't seen him since Christmas. We write to each other every now and then, but we don't really *say* anything. I don't know what to say. I mean, I still blame him for sending Millie to Holland,

261

but he didn't mean her to die, obviously. In fact, he asked me to go and I refused. And although I still profoundly disagree with him, I do understand that his motives for trying to stop the war are noble. He's a noble man.'

'And you haven't told him any of this? In your letters?'

'No,' Conrad admitted.

Anneliese shook her head. 'You English!'

'I do write to my mother,' Conrad said. 'I tell her about how I feel.'

'Except about your father,' Anneliese said.

Conrad shrugged. Then a thought struck him. 'Come to think of it, there is someone who definitely knows Polly Copthorne.'

'Who is that?'

'Veronica.'

'Veronica! As in "Mrs de Lancey" Veronica?'

'I think they are the same age – Polly is a lot younger than her husband. They came out together.'

'Came out?'

'Met the king. When they were eighteen. They were debutantes.' Conrad saw Anneliese's expression and laughed. 'Don't look so disapproving.'

'Why not? Your ex-wife sounds like an awful woman. You told me all about her. You have such dreadful taste in women, Conrad.'

'Veronica's not so bad,' said Conrad. 'At least not now we are divorced. Are you jealous?'

'Don't be absurd,' said Anneliese. But she looked guilty.

Conrad realized that she *was* jealous. 'How are you feeling these days?' he asked. 'You seem, I don't know, better.'

'I feel a bit better. My New York plan fell through; usual story, we couldn't get the right papers. My father still hasn't got a job. But I am doing something useful at the hospital. And maybe time does heal after all. I never heard back from Wilfrid Israel or Captain Foley about working for the British government, but doing this for you has definitely helped.'

'I think it's important,' said Conrad.

They sat in silence for a few moments. Conrad didn't want Anneliese to go, and he sensed she didn't want to leave. 'By the way, I don't have dreadful choice in women,' he said. 'I chose you.'

'My point precisely. That was a waste of time.'

'Don't be silly, Anneliese. The weeks I spent with you in Berlin were the best in my life.'

A warm smile crept across Anneliese's lips and she lowered her eyes.

The café was small and the tables were crammed together. Anneliese and Conrad were squeezed close to each other so that their knees were almost touching.

Conrad leaned over and kissed her.

For a moment she stiffened and he thought she was going to push him away, but then she relaxed.

'Conrad, I'm shocked,' she said as they broke apart. 'An English gentleman like you in a public place like this!'

'This is wartime,' Conrad said. 'People do this kind of thing all the time.'

'You're telling me. When I go to the hospital in the middle of the night the streets are teeming with prostitutes. It's worse than Berlin before the Nazis! You English have become sex-obsessed.'

'Sorry,' said Conrad with mock sincerity. He took out a scrap of paper and scribbled something on it. 'I'm having dinner with my father this evening, but I'm not staying at Kensington Square tonight. Mama is in Somerset and I can't face Father alone all weekend. This is my hotel. It's in Bloomsbury.'

Anneliese took the piece of paper.

'Are you going to the hospital now?' Conrad asked.

Anneliese nodded.

'What time do you finish?'

'It's not too bad tonight. I'll probably get away about two.'

'Come and see me then. We can discuss politics. Art. Music. Like we used to.'

'I remember what we used to do.'

Conrad shrugged and smiled.

'At your hotel?'

'Yes.'

'At two in the morning! They won't let me in.'

'Of course they will. A respectable nurse like you.'

Anneliese glanced at the piece of paper and then at Conrad. 'You have spent far too long up in Scotland with no female company.'

'That's definitely true.'

Anneliese folded the paper and put it in her bag. 'No, I won't come and see you in your hotel, Conrad. But I will write and tell you how I get on with Constance, and we can talk again next time you get leave. Now I must go to work.'

Conrad watched her go. Oh, well. It had been worth a try.

Pall Mall, London

It was several months since Conrad had last seen his father, and Lord Oakford was looking well, certainly much better than he had in the immediate aftermath of Millie's death. Since Conrad wasn't staying at Kensington Square, they were dining at his father's club. In the bar they had discussed the shambles of Conrad's unit's manoeuvres around Britain and the North Sea during the Norwegian campaign. Oakford seemed despondent about Norway and the conduct of the war in general.

Conrad was surprised how well they were getting on; perhaps he should have stayed at Kensington Square after all.

They went through to a corner of the crowded dining room, and as their soup came, Conrad broached the subject of Lord Copthorne.

'Yes, it was a tragedy,' said Oakford. 'Hundreds of people have died on the roads in the blackout. Things should get better with these longer days, thank God.'

'Did you know him well?'

'Not very well, no,' said Oakford. 'Only through Henry Alston – they were good friends. Nice enough chap, but his political views were a bit simplistic, I thought. I went to his funeral. Very sad.'

'Do you know his wife, Polly?'

'No. Met her for the first time at the funeral. She's quite a bit younger than him. Far too young to be a widow; but with the war there will be many more like her. Why do you ask?'

'I understand that she thinks Alston might have run him down.'

Oakford spluttered into his soup. 'Now that is absolutely ridiculous! Who told you that?'

'Apparently her husband and Alston had some kind of disagreement.'

'That doesn't mean Henry ran him down.' Oakford laughed; the idea seemed genuinely absurd to him. 'As I said, poor Freddie's political views were a bit simplistic for my taste, and probably for Henry's as well. He had that ignorant anti-Semitism that so irritates me. I don't have to tell *you* about that. If they did have a bust-up it might have been over Freddie's extremism.'

'Veronica and I are seeing Polly Copthorne tomorrow,' Conrad said. 'Veronica is an old friend of hers.' Conrad had just telephoned Veronica, and although he hadn't told her why he wanted to see Polly, she had agreed to introduce him. She had sounded enthusiastic, in fact.

'To ask her if Alston killed Freddie?' Oakford said.

'To ask her why she thinks he might have done.'

'Waste of time,' said Oakford. 'Complete waste of time. And I didn't realize you still saw Veronica.'

'I don't,' said Conrad simply.

Conrad was pretty sure that his father didn't know anything useful about Lord Copthorne's death, and so he let it drop. 'Can you imagine Henry Alston as Prime Minister one day?'

Oakford thought. 'Yes, perhaps one day. Maybe after the war. As you know I have a high regard for him: he's brilliant.'

'But not sooner?'

'He has only been an MP for five years. If Chamberlain falls, which is becoming more of a possibility every day now Norway is such a disaster, then I wouldn't be surprised if Alston found himself in the Cabinet.'

'And you?' asked Conrad. It hadn't occurred to him before that his father might return to government.

'I would serve if asked,' said Oakford. 'It would depend who was PM. It would be a good opportunity to make my views about peace known.'

'Does Henry Alston know the Duke of Windsor?' Conrad asked.

'Hold on a moment, Conrad,' said Oakford, frowning. 'Are you trying to create some conspiracy here? I thought Van warned you off all that.'

'He did, it's true,' Conrad admitted.

'Then why do you ask me these things?'

'I wonder if in some way they are connected to Millie's death.'

'That's outrageous!' said Lord Oakford, his eyes alight. 'Don't pull Millie into your paranoid fantasies. Yes, Alston and I both met the Duke of Windsor when he came to London in February. And yes, we did talk about ways of bringing this war to an end. Which is a perfectly honourable goal. And I resent your implication that it isn't!'

Conrad wanted so badly to argue with his father. But he knew he wouldn't get anywhere, and nor would he get any useful information from him. If Anneliese was correct and there was something fishy about Lord Copthorne's death and about Henry Alston's political ambitions, his father would deny all knowledge of it.

So he bit his tongue. 'Sorry, Father,' he said. 'How are Charlotte and Matthew?'

Bloomsbury, London

Conrad was awakened by a gentle knocking at his door. He turned on the bedside light and checked his watch. Half past two.

It took him a moment to realize who it was.

He smiled as he hopped out of bed and padded over to the door in his pyjamas. He opened it.

There was Anneliese, in her nurse's uniform, her fist raised to knock again.

'Hello,' he said, grinning.

'Shut up,' she said. She pushed him into the room and shut the door behind them. She reached up and kissed him, her tongue darting around his mouth. He felt her hands on his chest under his pyjamas. She pushed him back towards the bed, and then, with a sudden movement, ripped open his pyjama jacket, causing buttons to scatter across the room.

She pushed him back on to the bed and tugged at the cord holding up his trousers. He was already hard as she pulled them down.

'Anneliese—'

'Shh . . .'

She strode across him still in her uniform and kissed him again. He clumsily began to unbutton her dress.

She stood back from the bed, and slipped it off. In a couple of moments more she was naked.

She was beautiful. So beautiful. He wanted her more than he had ever wanted her before.

She lowered herself on to him and began to move, slowly for a few seconds and then with an increasing urgency. He responded, until with a final upwards thrust he pushed her high off the bed.

'Hello,' she said a moment later, and kissed his nose.

Thirty-Six

Bloomsbury, London, 5 May

Veronica picked Conrad up from his hotel in a Rolls-Royce. She was wearing the uniform of the First Aid Nursing Yeomanry, the FANYs. Conrad hadn't seen her for over a year. Tall and slim, her red hair stuffed under her cap, she looked good in her khaki uniform.

Anneliese had slipped out of Conrad's hotel room at dawn, leaving him a little groggy but in better spirits than he had been for a long time.

'What is this, Veronica?'

'It's my Aunt Peggy's. She donated it to the war effort. I drive a sweet old general around London in it.'

'Very nice,' said Conrad. 'And why the uniform on a Sunday?'

'People will ask fewer questions. Hop in the back and pull your hat down over your face. You look far too young for me to be driving you around in this.'

It was next to impossible to get petrol these days, unless you knew how. Obviously, Veronica knew how. Conrad wasn't going to complain; being driven in Veronica's aunt's Rolls along empty roads to the Copthornes' house in Buckinghamshire was infinitely preferable to struggling with the wartime train timetable again. He didn't have much time before he had to return to his unit, and Polly Copthorne was his best chance to find out what had happened to Millie.

As they drove, Veronica chattered on about her life during the war. How she loved driving old generals but she was looking for something more exciting. How Linaro was a beast. What their mutual friends from their brief marriage were doing – people Conrad could scarcely remember and certainly didn't care about. They had always been Veronica's friends really. He responded briefly to her own enquiries about his life.

'How's that little Jewess you found in Germany?' she asked brightly.

'"That little Jewess" is finding life difficult,' Conrad said, Veronica's casual condescension puncturing his good mood. 'It turns out it isn't much fun being half-Jewish in Nazi Germany. Or being in solitary confinement in a concentration camp. Even here her father can't find a job despite being a qualified doctor.'

Veronica was silent in the front seat. 'Sorry, Conrad,' she said eventually. 'The war hasn't really touched us properly yet, has it? One forgets about the people who have already had to suffer Hitler for years.'

Conrad felt slightly guilty; he should feel grateful that Veronica had dropped everything to chauffeur him up to see her old friend. He was grateful.

They drove on in silence for several minutes until they approached the village in the Chilterns where the Copthornes lived. Their house could be seen from a distance. It was a dull nineteenth-century pile, but it overlooked a pretty valley of woods, hedges and lush green pasture. The Copthornes had come by their title recently, through trade, like the Oakfords: merchant banking in the Oakfords' case, brewing in the case of the Copthornes. Not like Veronica's family, whose father, the twelfth Baron Blakeborough, stomped over the same fields as his ancestors had for hundreds of years. There was a difference: you couldn't be brought up in the English aristocracy without being aware of it, and knowing that everyone else was aware of it too.

'I came here after Freddie's funeral,' Veronica said. 'And I used to join Polly here for house parties when Freddie was wooing her – that was when his father was still alive. Polly was dotty about him then. In fact, I really think she was always dotty about him.'

Conrad thought he could detect a hint of wistfulness in Veronica's description of a happy marriage.

'My father said Freddie's politics were extreme,' Conrad said.

'Not exactly extreme,' said Veronica. 'A lot of people used to think like he did. It's just others have changed their minds and he didn't.'

'Like you?' Conrad well remembered Veronica's excitement at the new, modern, well-ordered Germany.

'Yes, like me. I used to tease you about being a Red. Well, you were right about Germany, I will grant you that. I knew things were wrong when the Nazis invaded Czechoslovakia last year. Then they invaded Poland and we went to war with them. And look what they have done to people like your poor German friend. You were right all along: Hitler is a beast, and we have to stop him. I'm trying to do my bit, however pathetic that might be. But I envy you being a man, Conrad. You can actually go and fight.'

'But that's not what Freddie thought?'

'We'll have to ask Polly.'

Polly Copthorne answered the large front door herself, threw her arms around Veronica and burst into tears. Conrad stepped back.

After a few seconds, Polly stood back. 'I'm sorry, Mr de Lancey. I'm still quite emotional since Freddie died. And Veronica is such an old friend. I am surprised myself how pleased I am to see her.'

Conrad recognized Polly from a couple of the dances he had attended when he was in pursuit of Veronica. She was a small woman with a delicate round face, not much in the way of chin, but dark, clever eyes. Her face looked younger and more innocent than Veronica's, but two straight lines had been scoured downwards from her eyes towards the edges of her lips. It was a face that was being changed by grief.

'I remember you,' said Polly, and held her hand for Conrad to shake. She led them into a drawing room, which was surprisingly prettily furnished given the bland austerity of the house's façade. Polly asked a maid for tea and then talked about her worry of what to do with the house. She would like it to be a convalescent home or a hospital for wounded soldiers. The problem was there were just not that many of them.

'That may change soon,' said Conrad.

Polly glanced at him. 'Norway?'

'That. And France. The Germans will attack France some time, I am sure of it.'

'So tell me Mr de Lancey—'

'Conrad.'

'Conrad. Veronica says you want to talk to me about poor Freddie's death?'

'I do,' said Conrad. 'But let me tell you first about my sister, Millie, who also died last November.' Veronica had suggested that this would be the best way to win Polly's trust, and it worked. Conrad was vague about which Germans exactly Millie had met in Holland, but he did speak about Henry Alston and Marjorie Copthorne's friend Constance.

'I'm so sorry to hear all that,' Polly said with the sympathy of someone with a fresh understanding of grief. 'So you think this Constance might have killed your sister?'

Conrad shrugged. 'That's what the Dutch police think. And Constance and Henry Alston are lovers.'

'Lovers? I didn't know Henry had a mistress! I wouldn't have thought he was the type.'

'I'm sure he kept her very quiet.'

Polly put down her tea cup and stared hard at Conrad, assessing him. Conrad waited. People usually trusted him because he usually told the truth, and he was certainly telling the truth now.

'My husband and Henry Alston knew each other for several years,' she said eventually. 'Ever since Henry became an MP. They were very good friends, especially in the last year or so. They shared the same views on the war: they both wanted to stop it at any cost. I met Henry a few times, but he gave me the creeps. It wasn't his scars; there was just something about him. And Freddie and I disagreed about the war. I think if we are fighting the Germans we should jolly well beat them, and that Hitler is an awful monster.'

'There's something to be said for that,' said Conrad.

'I know Freddie and Henry used to see your father sometimes. Freddie had a lot of time for him, and for Henry. Said they were both brilliant men and just what the country needed. Freddie, love him though I did, poor darling, wasn't brilliant, and he knew it.

'Then, just before he died, Freddie became worried about something. Dreadfully worried. I don't know what it was, but I know it had something to do with Henry Alston, some sort of scheme he had which upset Freddie. He almost told me but then he changed his mind. I tried to push him on it, but he said I was better off not knowing. That worried me in itself.'

'Have you any idea what this scheme was?'

'No, none, except that it troubled him deeply.'

'My father says that perhaps Freddie was too extreme for Alston and that is why they fell out?'

Polly Copthorne laughed. 'It was always Henry who had the ideas and Freddie who followed. Freddie never told me what those ideas were, he thought I would disapprove, but they excited him. Until they didn't. And then he was run over.'

'You think Alston might have run him down deliberately?'

'Yes. I do. He was meeting Henry that night at Erskine's. Henry left a few minutes before him. Freddie was run over in the lane before he got to St James's. Why would anyone be driving fast enough to kill someone in a dead-end side street in the dark unless they wanted to do just that? Kill them.'

'Did you tell the police?'

'Oh, yes. They were very interested. They had questioned Henry once, and were going to question him again. Then it all went quiet. I asked the policeman who had interviewed me why, and he said they had evidence a driver unknown to Freddie had knocked him down and just drove off. The policeman wouldn't say what that evidence was. He didn't look happy about it; he looked sorry for me.'

'You suspect a cover-up?'

'I am jolly certain that Henry Alston killed my husband.'

Conrad nodded. 'Thank you, Polly. Did you ever hear Freddie speak of my sister? Or Constance Scott-Dunton?'

'No. I do know that Freddie was going to ask his niece Marjorie to help him with something, but I don't know what came of that. Constance Scott-Dunton, presumably.' She smiled at Conrad. 'I am sorry about your poor sister. If there is anything I can do to help you prove Sir Henry Alston was involved in her death, or Freddie's, I will.'

'I liked your friend Polly,' Conrad said as Veronica drove him back to London.

'Do you think she's right, or do you think she's imagining things?' Veronica asked.

'I rather think she's on to something,' said Conrad. 'What about you?'

'The thing people don't realize about Polly is that she's really quite clever. And perceptive. She may well be on to something.'

Veronica turned to look behind at Conrad. Then the car wobbled and she looked ahead on the empty road. 'I am sorry about Millie, Conrad. That's dreadful for you.'

'Thanks.'

'Look. We'll be back in London in no time. Do you want to drop into the Ritz for a cocktail on the way back to the station?'

Conrad was tempted. No matter what she did, Conrad was always tempted by Veronica. 'I'm sorry, I had better get to the station as early as possible. The trains never run when they should.'

'I don't know,' said Veronica. 'What does a girl need to do to get a drink these days?'

Thirty-Seven

Zossen

'So, Hertenberg. Can you see the changes?'

Lieutenant Colonel Liss, as he now was, was grinning as he glanced at Theo. They were standing over the cowhide: the relief map of northern France and the Low Countries.

Theo examined the German deployment. There were still three army groups: C by France's eastern border with Germany, A just to the east of the Ardennes and Luxembourg, and B further north on the Belgian and Dutch borders.

'You have switched some divisions from Army Group B to Army Group A,' said Theo.

'You have a good memory. I remember you suggesting it. Army Group A will now make the main thrust through the Ardennes to Sedan, and Army Group B will push through central Belgium to engage the Allies in Flanders.'

'I suspect it wasn't me who changed your mind.'

'No. It was General Manstein and General Guderian. And the Führer. The crash at Mechelen helped.'

'Really? I thought that was disastrous.' In January an aeroplane transporting a staff officer carrying plans for Case Yellow from Munster to Cologne had somehow got lost and crashed in Belgium, near the town of Mechelen. The documents had been captured: they detailed the original Case Yellow invasion plan of Holland and Belgium, with the main thrust being carried out by Army Group B to the north. Theo knew that the plans had swiftly found their way to the French and British general headquarters.

'The Führer was of the view that we had to change Case Yellow, now that the enemy knew the original plan. So, given the weaknesses you had highlighted around Sedan, we have.'

'And when you play the war game, do we win now?' Theo asked.

'That depends,' said Colonel Liss. 'And that's why you are here.' He pointed to the French 7th Army, deployed around Lille on the western Belgian border. 'If the French send their most powerful troops north into Flanders according to their Plan D, then Guderian breaks through here.' He pointed to the Meuse at Sedan. 'And there is no one to stop him. But, if the French 7th Army moves immediately eastwards to reinforce the front near Sedan, things get bogged down.'

Theo's brother Dieter would be with Guderian's armoured corps at Sedan.

'Won't the French assume that we have changed our plans, now we know they have them?'

Liss grinned. 'According to your colleagues, they seem to believe that the Mechelen crash was staged by us as a bluff. I can see why: it's extraordinary that any pilot could get so lost as to stray over the Rhine into the wrong country, however bad the weather, but there you are. So, as far as we are aware, the French are still using Plan D. I would like you to confirm that.'

'I haven't heard of any changes of plan,' Theo said. 'But my sources have gone quiet.' The Duke of Windsor had finished his inspection of the French lines and, according to Bedaux, was spending the occasional day twiddling his thumbs at the British Mission to French general headquarters at Vincennes. Bedaux himself was cannoning around all over the place. As far as Theo knew he was in Spain trying to secure steel supplies for France, and he had plans to go on to Morocco to look for coal.

'We don't have much time, do we? The operation is scheduled for the tenth of May.' That was in five days' time.

'That's correct,' said Liss. 'And the forecast is good.'

A miserable winter, one of the worst on record, had been followed by a lush, sunny spring. Delay was unlikely this time.

'I will try to get hold of my sources and see if I can find out anything new. It might be difficult in the time.' Especially since Theo had lots of other agents to deal with in Holland, giving him last-minute indications of Dutch preparations for invasion. The flat Dutch countryside and straight roads were perfect for an invading army, but there was a risk they would pull their fingers out of the dykes and flood the whole country.

Looking at the new version of Case Yellow, Holland was just a sideshow. The battle would be decided in the hills and forests of the Ardennes, and then the French countryside behind them.

'Do what you can,' said Liss.

Liverpool Street Station, London

Conrad arrived at Liverpool Street Station early for his train back to his battalion in Suffolk. Which was lucky, because as he was deciding whether to get a cup of tea or read a book, Major McCaigue materialized.

'You again,' said Conrad. 'Don't you take Sundays off?'

'I do usually,' said McCaigue. 'And I have today. Officially. Do you remember I had an official and an unofficial message for you last time we met?'

'I do.'

'Well, I'd like to have a word with you unofficially. About what you have discovered this weekend, if anything.'

'Why should I tell you?' Conrad said.

'We are getting more and more concerned about the Duke of Windsor,' said McCaigue. 'But he is still protected. I need all the evidence I can lay my hands on to change that.'

'I have discovered very little about the duke this weekend,' said Conrad. 'But I did find out quite a lot about Sir Henry Alston.' What the hell. There was a chance that telling McCaigue what he knew would throw a spanner in the works of whatever plan Alston was hatching.

'Sir Henry Alston?'

'Do you know him?'

'I know of him. Conservative MP. Possibly pro-German. Either less extreme or perhaps more clever than Maule Ramsay and Oswald Mosley. The man who sent your sister and Constance Scott-Dunton to Holland.'

'That's him. I *think* that he might have had Constance kill my sister. And that he might have run down Lord Copthorne about the same time last November.'

'Those are grave allegations. Do you have proof?'

Conrad told McCaigue about his visit to Lady Copthorne. He didn't mention Anneliese. 'But you probably know all this already. Lady Copthorne said that the police were very keen to drop the investigation. Orders from on high. Friends of yours, no doubt.'

'Acquaintances, possibly,' said McCaigue. 'I work for the counter-intelligence section of the Secret Intelligence Service. That means I worry about foreign spies abroad. If someone like Sir Henry Alston needed watching, it would be Special Branch of Scotland Yard, or MI5, who would do it. I wouldn't find out about it, unless someone like you told me.'

'It's my pleasure,' said Conrad.

The irony was not lost on McCaigue, but he ignored it. 'It's appreciated,' he said. 'Keep me informed, will you? And if you do need help, telephone. You have my card.'

As Conrad took the train back to Suffolk, he was unsure whether he had done the right thing in trusting McCaigue. And a question nagged. How had McCaigue found out that he was in London? On one level it was easy to assume that the secret service was all-knowing. On the other, someone must have told them. It couldn't have been Colonel Rydal. And it was unlikely to be any of the people he had seen over the weekend: Anneliese, Veronica, Polly Copthorne. No, it was more probably someone in the battalion. The adjutant, perhaps: someone junior to Colonel Rydal whom the secret service had instructed to keep tabs on him.

An unpleasant thought.

Eight men sat around the table in the private dining room of the Dorchester. Sir Henry Alston was at one end, Lord Oakford at the other. Between them were a General, an Admiral, a Newspaper Magnate, a Civil Servant, a Politician, and an Industrialist. Alston, although he was responsible for bringing everyone together, was the youngest man there. The dinner had been excellent; somehow the Dorch had managed to keep its kitchens well supplied despite the eight months of war.

Alston lit a cigar. 'There's no hope for Norway, is there?'

The General shook his head. 'The Hun is running rings around us. We have evacuated Namsos. We're making a stand at Narvik, but our fellows have no chance. The whole thing is a muddle; the politicians have let us down again. Winston doesn't have a clue what he is doing. I blame him entirely.'

'It's Neville who will take the blame,' said the Politician, who was also a junior minister.

'Is he in danger?' asked Alston.

'I rather think he might be,' said the Politician. 'I'm sure he doesn't think so – we have a large majority after all. But he's getting complacent, and the House doesn't like that.'

'The country will want someone to take responsibility,' said the Newspaper Proprietor. 'Neville is the obvious candidate. He can't get away with dropping Winston and carrying on regardless.'

'Then who will become PM?' asked the Industrialist.

'Halifax?' The General phrased it more as a question than an answer.

'Edward commands a lot of respect,' said the Politician. 'But he sits in the House of Lords. The country needs a leader from the Commons. Someone who can deal with Parliament directly.'

'Even at a time like this?' asked the General.

'Especially at a time like this,' said Lord Oakford. The table turned to him, anxious for his opinion. They knew how close he was to Lord Halifax. 'Edward is an old friend of mine and I admire him immensely. He is a good man to have at your side in a crisis. I'm sorry to say it, but I don't believe he has the courage to step forward and lead the country now. You need a certain kind of man to take decisions which will be of such historical importance. He knows nothing about military strategy, as he will freely admit. He'll say it's because he is in the Lords, but the truth is he isn't up to it, and he knows it.'

'So who would become PM?' asked the Admiral.

'Not Winston, surely?' said the General.

'He's popular in the country,' said the Newspaper Proprietor.

'But he's the one who is principally responsible for the balls-up in Norway!' protested the General.

'What we need most of all is peace with Germany,' said the Industrialist. 'Churchill is the last man to achieve that.'

There were murmurs of 'hear hear' and 'absolutely' around the table.

'The whole country is bored with the war,' said the Newspaper Proprietor, who prided himself, with some justification, on knowing what his readers thought. 'And once we start losing it, they will want it stopped.'

'So, if not Churchill, who?' asked the Industrialist.

'Lloyd George,' said Alston. 'He's well known in the country. He wants peace. He's not tarnished with this war so far. And he won the last one.'

'He's an old man,' said the Industrialist. 'He must be eighty. He would need help.'

'He's seventy-seven,' said Lord Oakford. 'And he would have help. Henry and I would support him. And I suspect that there are some members of Cabinet who would serve in a government for peace?' Oakford glanced at the Politician.

'There are,' said the Politician. '*I* would serve under him. And there are quite a few others.'

'It would be difficult to make peace behind the Frogs' backs,' said the General.

'Wait until the Germans attack them,' said the Admiral.

'They'll give up in no time. France is much weaker than it was in 1914. No backbone.'

'Shame Edward VIII isn't still on the throne,' said the General. 'He would be the one to lead an honourable peace. I never understood why he had to abdicate just because his wife was divorced.'

'Neither did I,' said Alston, quietly.

'I spoke to him when he was in London in February,' said the Newspaper Proprietor. 'With Henry and Arthur. Suggested he do a tour around the country campaigning for peace. He seemed keen, but I haven't heard anything since he went back to France.'

'It's difficult for him,' said Alston. 'He can't be seen to be usurping his brother. But if he was asked to step into the breach when his country really needed him, I'm sure he would.'

'Absolutely,' said the Newspaper Proprietor.

There was silence around the room. Alston sensed that the table had edged too close to treason. He knew they all wanted peace with honour, and they needed a way to achieve it that would fit with their idea of patriotism and duty to their country. It was Alston's plan to give it to them.

'Well, let's hope we turn things around in Norway,' he said. 'And it's the Germans who sue for peace.'

'I'll drink to that,' said the General. But he knew that wouldn't happen. They all knew it wouldn't happen.

The Tiergartenstrasse, Berlin

Theo lay on his back and stared up at the ceiling of his bedroom. Next to him, Hedda slept, snoring gently, her fair hair spread out on the pillow. Her husband's unit had been sent to Trier, ready to join Guderian and Dieter and a few hundred thousand other German soldiers on their drive through Luxembourg.

Theo had been distracted at dinner at Horcher's with Hedda. Hedda had noticed – she really didn't like being ignored. They had left early, and back at his apartment, Hedda had put everything into turning his attention towards her. The resulting sex had blown his mind.

But now his mind was recovering, and turning back to what Colonel Liss had said. Back in November, Theo had taken the decision to warn Conrad of the weakness in the French line. The enormity of what he had done had impressed him, even tormented him, in the following months. He told himself he wasn't a traitor to his country, but sometimes he thought he was just fooling himself. How would he feel when German soldiers, including his own brother, ran into stiff opposition at Sedan because of his efforts? Especially his brother. The last time Theo had seen him at the family's manor house in Pomerania, Dieter's enthusiasm for General Guderian and the forthcoming battle in the Ardennes had known no bounds. Theo could hardly bear to look at him.

What Theo hadn't considered was that Conrad's message would fail to get through. He was confident that Conrad would have passed it on, but he now realized that his assumption that the British generals would act on it was optimistic. Conrad himself had pointed out how badly humiliated the British had been by believing in Major Schämmel before Venlo. Why should they believe Conrad now?

Because the weakness in the French lines should have been just as obvious to them as it had been to the Duke of Windsor. Perhaps they were confident that armoured divisions really couldn't make their way through the woods and forests of the Ardennes.

If that's what they thought, Theo knew they were wrong. The Wehrmacht had practised in the woods of the Eifel Mountains. They knew it could be done.

Dreadful though it was to him as an officer of the Wehrmacht, Theo still believed that a swift victory over France would be a disaster. Hitler would be firmly entrenched. Europe would become a National Socialist continent for years, decades, maybe even centuries to come.

He could not allow that. Even though he was risking his comrades' lives, including that of his own brother, he somehow had to get a message to Conrad to tell the British what was about to happen. Conrad might be a lowly lieutenant, but Theo admired his resourcefulness.

Besides. It was the only thing he could think of.

Thirty-Eight

It was late. Conrad decided to take a stroll around the football field of the prep school in which he was billeted before turning in. He needed fresh air after the all-too-familiar boiled-cabbage-and-bleach smell. After returning to England from Spain, he had spent a grim six months as a teacher at another school about fifteen miles away. He thought he recognized this school as one a team he had been coaching had played at football. It had rained hard and his school's side had lost 4–1.

The battalion was a mobile reserve, ready to rush to the site of a landing should the Germans decide to invade East Anglia, an eventuality which seemed to Conrad unlikely, but not impossible. The Royal Navy was the first British line of defence, supported by the RAF. It would be extremely difficult for German invaders to get through to the beaches all the way from northern Germany, out of range of air support.

It was a dark night. Although the moon was almost full, it was shrouded by thick cloud. Conrad thought again about how he could try to return to London to ask more questions. As far as he was aware, the CO had heard nothing yet about his last visit. Would this weekend be too soon to try his luck?

It was infuriating that he was stuck here in the wilds of Suffolk when he had been making such good progress in London. It looked highly likely Alston had killed Freddie Copthorne. And if Alston was willing to kill his own friend, then it was quite possible that he had arranged for Millie's death through Constance. Then there was the question of Bedaux and the Duke of Windsor. Was there a link between them and Alston? And if there was a link, what were they planning? His father had admitted that he and Alston had had lunch with the duke in February.

He wished he could discuss all this with his father. Lord Oakford knew Alston well, and he had access to everyone in power in London. He could ask questions and get answers. If Alston had indeed arranged for Millie's death, then Conrad should be able to rely on his father to help him. But Oakford and Alston were not just colleagues, they were friends, and Polly Copthorne hadn't given Conrad absolute proof that Alston had killed her husband – certainly nothing that would persuade Lord Oakford that Conrad's accusations weren't fantasies.

If only his father trusted him! Conrad was certain that Lord Oakford would never do anything to betray his country or his son, but who knew what he might say to Alston in the mistaken belief that his fellow director was harmless? Lord Oakford was a fine man in so many ways, he was the man Conrad admired most in the world, yet he couldn't trust him. It was so frustrating.

He would just have to rely on Anneliese and McCaigue. Anneliese was doing well; what McCaigue was up to, he had no idea.

'Sir! Mr de Lancey, sir!'

He turned to see a lance corporal running towards him.

'Yes, corporal?'

'Message from Lieutenant Dodds, sir. Three Home Guard have wandered into a minefield. They need sappers to get them out.'

Conrad swore under his breath.

The minefield was only ten minutes from the school on a stretch of boggy pasture half a mile in from the sea. The minefield was clearly marked, although in the dark it was impossible to make out the writing on the wooden signs. Dodds was there with the Home Guard platoon commander and he had alerted the engineers who were on their way. Even in the gloom, Conrad could see three figures in the field about a hundred yards away waving towards them. One of them was shouting for help. He sounded more like a child than a man.

'How did they get in there?' said Conrad to the Home Guard officer, who was a middle-aged man with the rank of captain. 'I thought you people were supposed to know the local terrain. That was the whole point.'

'They come from a village ten miles away,' said the captain meekly. 'They have never patrolled here before.'

'Well, can't they just keep still and wait?' Conrad said. 'The sappers will be here in twenty minutes.'

'That's Cobbold shouting,' said the Home Guard officer. 'He's only seventeen. He's just joined up.'

Conrad stood up and roared. 'Private Cobbold! Stay calm and wait for the sappers! They won't be long.'

Private Cobbold shut up.

'I could go through the minefield and lead them out, sir,' said Dodds. 'It's quite muddy. You can see their footprints in the field. If I tread in them exactly, I shouldn't blow up a mine.'

'Don't be silly, Dodds. Just wait for the sappers.'

'He was shouting about running for it earlier,' said Dodds.

'Why would he do that?' said Conrad. 'If he's that scared he will just stay put.'

'Message from the sappers, sir.' It was Lance Corporal Fowler. 'Their vehicle has broken down.'

'They are engineers, aren't they?' said Conrad impatiently. 'Can't they fix it?'

'Fan belt has snapped.'

'All right, you men out there!' Conrad shouted. 'There's been a delay with the sappers. Hold tight, we'll sort it out!'

He turned to send his own vehicle to head back to pick up the sappers. Just then there was a cry from the field. Conrad turned to see a figure sprinting towards them. 'What the hell?' said Conrad. 'Stop!' he yelled. 'Private Cobbold, I said—'

There was a loud explosion and Private Cobbold was sent flying into the air, landing hard on his shoulder.

Then there was silence. The watching soldiers held their breath, straining to hear sounds of life. Then it came, a long low moan.

'Are you all right, Cobbold?' the Home Guard officer shouted.

His request was met by another moan.

'I'm going to get him,' said Dodds.

'Wait for the sappers. It's his own bloody fault he's in there. There is no reason he should get you killed too.'

The moan rose to a scream. And then another.

Conrad turned to Corporal Fowler to give him orders to drive off and pick up the sappers.

When he turned back, Dodds was in the minefield. He had a torch and he was sweeping the ground in front of him, stepping gingerly from footprint to footprint.

'Mr Dodds! Come back here at once!' Conrad shouted, but Dodds ignored him.

The screams continued.

Conrad held his breath as he watched Dodds pick his way through the field. At any moment he expected to hear another explosion and to see Dodds turned into a rag doll flying through the air. But perhaps Dodds's theory would hold true. Perhaps by sticking to the footprints he would dodge any mines.

Conrad liked Dodds, and he was turning into a very good officer. This would be a very stupid way to lose him.

He reached the point at which the Home Guards' path into the minefield was closest to Cobbold's moaning body. But there was still ten yards distance between the two men, ten yards of virgin minefield. Dodds hesitated. For a moment Conrad thought he would chance his luck by stepping on to untrodden grass, but then he eased himself on to the ground, and began to crawl. It was hard to see in the dark, but standard operating procedure when forced to traverse a minefield was to crawl on your stomach, using a bayonet to probe ahead for mines, and that was what Conrad assumed Dodds was doing.

It was still dangerous, though, and Private Cobbold was still yelling.

Those last ten yards seemed to take an age. Then the moon appeared from behind the clouds, and a few seconds later Dodds's tall frame was silhouetted against the grey horizon above the sea in the distance. Conrad could hear the officer talking soothingly to the fallen man, whose screams decreased to whimpers. A barn owl shrieked.

Dodds bent down, slung Private Cobbold over his shoulders and stepped back the way he had come. The screams intensified: Dodds had given no consideration to Cobbold's wounds – he couldn't afford to.

Carefully, slowly, Dodds picked his way to the edge of the minefield where four men and a stretcher were waiting for him.

He ambled over to Conrad and stood to attention. He was breathing heavily and his tunic was covered with blood.

Conrad felt the fury explode within him. 'Mr Dodds! I gave you a clear order not to go in there! Are you trying to get yourself killed?'

'Yes, sir! I thought we had discussed this before, sir!'

'You're an idiot, Mr Dodds.'

'Yes, sir! No doubt at all about that, sir!'

Conrad stared at the tall, blood-spattered, nineteen-year-old officer with the rosy cheeks, standing to attention in front of him. A wave of relief rushed through him, extinguishing the anger and replacing it with a sort of giddy euphoria. He felt his lips twitch into a grin. Dodds smiled too. Very soon they were both bent over laughing, as the Home Guard captain looked on bemused.

It was a long night. The sappers eventually arrived and cleared a path to the two men still stuck in the field. The boy survived, but only just. He had lost a lot of blood and the surgeon said he would lose his leg below the knee.

When Conrad and Dodds eventually arrived back at the prep school for breakfast, there was an envelope waiting for Conrad, addressed in his father's writing.

Conrad tore it open. It contained an unopened telegram with a covering note from his father saying it had arrived at Kensington Square and he had forwarded it immediately.

Good for him, thought Conrad.

The cable was from a Hubert Berger of a bank in Liechtenstein. 'MEET ME IN HOLLAND 11 MAY AT 6 PM MADVIG'.

Given the invasion of Denmark in April, Copenhagen was no longer operational as a letterbox, and so Theo had used a neutral Liechtensteiner to pass on his message. According to the code they were using, 11 May at 6 p.m. actually meant 8 May at 3 p.m., which was the following day.

It must be urgent. Probably something about an imminent invasion of Holland and Belgium, Conrad guessed. But how the hell could he get there in a day?

He could try to persuade Colonel Rydal to give him leave, but since he had only been back at the battalion for less than forty-eight hours, that was a long shot. If the colonel did agree, then Conrad might be able to book a seat on an aeroplane to Holland: it would be tight but it was possible he could get to the airport in time. But would they stop him getting on the aeroplane at passport control?

Probably. Given how Major McCaigue had somehow known about his trip to London the previous weekend, it seemed quite likely that someone would stop him.

He could try to get authorization from McCaigue or from Van. But that would take hours, or even a day. And even then the chances were he wouldn't get it.

Was there anyone he knew who could or would just up sticks and get on an aeroplane to Holland? Someone he could trust and so could Theo?

Anneliese? No. Insurmountable border-control difficulties. His father? Definitely not. His brother Reggie? Worse. Veronica?

Veronica.

He found a telephone and gave Veronica's number to the operator. Amazingly, she was already awake. Must be the war and the driving job.

'Darling! How lovely to hear from you!'

'Veronica, can you do me a tiny favour? It would involve

288

dropping everything and getting on an aeroplane right away. The ticket's about eleven pounds. I'll pay.'

'Oh, is it something cloak-and-dagger?'

'As a matter of fact it is.'

'How divine! Tell me.'

Ten minutes later Conrad composed a telegram back to Herr Hubert Berger in Liechtenstein: 'SORRY CANT MAKE TRIP STOP WIFE WILL COME INSTEAD STOP DE LANCEY'.

Thirty-Nine

Constance found the pub easily enough, just off Lavender Hill in Clapham. She ignored the hubbub coming from the public bar, and pushed open the frosted glass door of the saloon bar, which was empty, with the exception of a big man perched on a stool, accompanied by a half-empty pint of beer.

He grinned when he saw her. 'Hello, Connie, my love! Good to see you!'

'Nice to see you too, Joe,' said Constance. Normally she hated people calling her Connie, but it somehow seemed all right coming from Joe Sullivan.

'What will it be?' asked Joe.

'A glass of sherry, please.'

'Ada!' Joe yelled through towards the public bar. 'A sherry for the lady.'

They sat down at a table. Joe Sullivan was a big man with a broad chest, a thrusting jaw and two distinct bumps on his nose. He was probably about thirty: old enough not to be called up yet. Constance had met him at a Nordic League rally and, despite his tough appearance, she found him remarkably easy to talk to. They shared an enthusiasm for the literature of the movement, and had become experts on the various theories of Jewish, Freemason and communist conspiracies. Constance knew that Joe had done some bodyguard work for the Nordic League and the British Union of Fascists. He could be firm. The truth was he liked a fight. And he believed in the cause. So, the right man to come to.

Within a couple of minutes they became involved in an intense discussion of a pamphlet they had both read: *The Rulers of Russia* by an Irish priest, which demonstrated that fifty-six of the fifty-nine members of the Central Committee of the Communist Party in Russia were Jews.

'Why can't people see what's right in front of their faces?' said Joe. 'This war is being run by the Jews for the Jews.'

'You're right there,' said Constance. She glanced at the bar. Empty. They were alone. The time had come. 'Joe? Could I ask you a favour?'

'Course you can, Connie. What is it?'

'Have you ever killed someone?'

Joe froze, his blue eyes coolly examining her. For a dreadful moment Constance thought she had made a mistake, but it was too late. She ploughed on.

'Would you kill someone for me?'

Still no response from Joe.

'I'd pay you.'

'Who is he?' said Joe. 'A lover? Or is it a she? Your husband's mistress?'

'Nothing like that,' said Constance. 'There's something going on. Something I can't tell you about at the moment, but it will change the government and end the war. In a good way, a way you would approve of. But only if we can get rid of this man. His name is Conrad de Lancey.'

'Is he Jewish?'

'No,' said Constance. Then she had an inspiration. 'But his father works for a Jewish merchant bank.' Henry had told her that Gurney Kroheim's roots were actually Quaker, but there was no need for Joe to know that.

'How much?'

'Five hundred pounds. I have two hundred and fifty with me to give you now, and two hundred and fifty afterwards.'

'And I'm supposed to take it on trust that this will help stop the war?'

'Yes,' said Constance. '

Joe smiled. 'Who would have thought it? A nice well-brought-up lady like you?'

Constance stared at him. 'I'm deadly serious, Joe. This *has* to be done.'

Joe laughed. 'I know you are. All right. I'll help you. Do you have the money with you?'

'Yes,' said Constance, reaching into her bag.

'Not here,' said Joe. 'Somewhere more private. And you'll need to tell me something about this Lancey bloke. Come back to my place and we can talk some more about it.'

He was smiling. Constance knew what he wanted.

'Where's Ivy?' Ivy was Joe's pretty wife.

'At work. Peter Robinson in Oxford Circus. Works all hours, my missus. Won't be back till late.'

For an instant, Constance felt guilty about betraying Henry. It was possible that Joe would still do the deed if she didn't sleep with him. But if she *did* sleep with him his help was guaranteed.

And that would keep Henry safe and his plans intact.

She finished her sherry and smiled at the big man. 'Yes. Let's go back to your place.'

Leiden

Theo lit his third cigarette as he dawdled over his coffee in the little café in the Diefsteeg, a Dutch newspaper open on the table. Just as they were parting, after the Gestapo agent had slipped off the roof of the Academy building, Theo had suggested the café to Conrad as a future rendezvous. Although the British agent had spotted them there before, the Gestapo hadn't, and it was somewhere they both knew.

Theo was enjoying his coffee. Almost reason enough to come to Holland, a neutral country which still served decent coffee. Not for long, though. Maybe he should have another cup while he could.

Theo was not happy that Conrad wasn't going to meet him himself. He wondered who 'his wife' was. It could be someone from the British secret service, in which case Theo wasn't sure yet what he would do. The British were blown in Holland, and approaching one of them with his message would be foolish. Yet perhaps he should risk his own safety, given the importance of what he had to say.

Or perhaps Conrad meant his real wife, or ex-wife, Veronica. Theo had never met her. She belonged to the five-year period between 1933 and 1938 when Conrad and Theo hadn't seen each other.

Just then the door opened and a tall Englishwoman entered the café. She was striking: red hair, pale skin, high cheekbones, long legs, wearing an expensive tweed suit. Theo was sure the woman was British: she had that air of cool arrogance of the English upper classes. She scanned the small café. There were only three customers: two old men drinking beer in companionable silence, and Theo.

For a moment Theo caught her eye. The Englishwoman raised a carefully plucked eyebrow. Theo smiled vaguely and turned back to his newspaper. Out of his peripheral vision he could see the woman hesitate, clearly deciding whether to approach him. Then she ordered a cup of tea in English, and sat at one of the other tables, lighting her cigarette. Theo was confident she wasn't a professional; she had no tradecraft at all. She must be Veronica de Lancey.

The four customers sat together in silence for half an hour; then the two old men left and a couple of male students dropped by for a cup of coffee and a slice of cake.

Eventually, at four o'clock, Veronica gave up, paid her bill and went out on to the narrow lane.

Theo followed her rapidly. He glanced up and down the alley: it was empty. She turned and saw him.

'Theo?'

'Yes,' Theo replied in English. 'Who are you?'

'Veronica. Conrad's wife.' She looked angry. 'Why did you let me wait for so long looking like a chump?'

'I wanted to be sure we weren't being watched.'

Veronica looked up and down the lane. 'Well, are we?'

'I don't think so,' said Theo. 'This will only take a moment. If I tell you something, can you remember it without writing it down? It's extremely important that you repeat it to Conrad as soon as you get back to England.'

'I can do that,' said Veronica.

'Right, then. Listen carefully. The German offensive will start on the tenth of May. That's Friday. We will invade Holland, Luxembourg and Belgium. And the main thrust will be through the Ardennes at Sedan. Have you got that?'

Veronica repeated it accurately.

'Good,' said Theo. 'Now we should part. I'll go back up to the Breestraat, and you go down there.' He pointed down the lane towards the Pieterskerk.

'Goodbye, Theo,' said Veronica with a smile. 'Perhaps we'll meet again after this stupid war.'

'That might be a while,' said Theo as he turned on his heel. He had a lot still to do before dawn on Friday.

House of Commons, Westminster

Alston was sitting on the government benches a couple of rows behind and a little to the right of the Prime Minister, Neville Chamberlain. The House was packed, and although they were well into the second day of the debate on Norway, no one was bored. The tension was growing. History was being made in front of them. But it was not clear to Alston which way history was going.

The Prime Minister was holed below the waterline and was sinking. He had opened the debate the day before with a lacklustre performance. Criticisms had mounted during the day, culminating in a powerful speech in the evening by Leo Amery, who had wheeled out the famous quotation of Oliver Cromwell when dispatching the Rump Parliament: 'You have sat too long here for any good you have been doing. Depart, I say, and let us have done with you. In the name of God, go!'

Brilliant. Quite brilliant.

Chamberlain had shipped more water the following morning. Herbert Morrison for the Labour Party had indicated that his party would regard the motion as a vote of censure, thus raising the stakes. Chamberlain had mishandled this challenge by saying that he hoped he could rely on his friends to support him. This was an error: he was swiftly losing friends, and his only hope of staying afloat was to receive support from the Parliament as a whole, not just his cronies. Lloyd George responded with a sharp, powerful speech, demanding that the Prime Minister give an example to the country of sacrifice in wartime by sacrificing his own seals of leadership. There was no doubt the old man still had his wits about him.

Chamberlain was sinking fast.

But there was a problem. Somehow, Churchill was wriggling free of blame for the Norwegian fiasco. Speaker after speaker was blaming Chamberlain and exonerating Churchill. The most remarkable was Admiral of the Fleet Sir Roger Keys, Member for North Portsmouth, who, dressed in full uniform with six rows of medals and thick gold braid on his sleeves, extolled his admiration for Churchill and his desire for bold leadership.

When Chamberlain sank, Arthur Oakford was still firmly of the view that his friend Lord Halifax would duck the opportunity to become Prime Minister. Apparently, Halifax's stomach was giving him severe trouble at the mere thought of it. But Alston was becoming increasingly worried that if that were the case, Churchill might emerge as his successor.

The First Lord of the Admiralty rose at ten o'clock that evening. Churchill was in an impossible position, somehow having to declare loyal support for Chamberlain while still laying the blame for the Norwegian disaster on the Prime Minister rather than himself. But he did it. Churchill was going to fight the war and win it, and he brought the House with him.

When it came time for the division, Alston knew what he had to do. He was one of forty-one Conservative MPs to vote against his party. In the end, the government won the debate, but with a majority of only eighty-one. Given that the Conservatives had a nominal majority of over two hundred, it was a disaster.

As Alston went to bed that night, it seemed certain that what he had been praying for for months was finally about to happen: Chamberlain was on his way out. Yet suddenly, inexplicably, it looked likely that he would be replaced as Prime Minister by the biggest warmonger of them all.

Winston Churchill.

Forty

Mayfair, London, 9 May

Veronica went straight from Heston Airport to the small flat in Dunraven Street she shared with a friend, and telephoned Conrad on the Suffolk number he had given her. It took a long time for the captain she spoke to to get hold of him, but eventually she heard his voice.

'I'm back,' she said.

'Did you see Theo?' Conrad asked.

'I did.'

'What did he say?'

Veronica passed on Theo's message verbatim.

'But the tenth is tomorrow!' Conrad said.

'I know. Can you get hold of a general or something?'

There was a pause on the line. 'You'll have to do it, Veronica. Have you ever met Van?'

'You mean Sir Robert Vansittart? Once, at your parents' house in Kensington Square. I'm not sure he would remember me.'

'Remind him, Veronica. I know you can do that. Go immediately to the Foreign Office and demand to see him. Say you have a message from Holland about the invasion. Be persistent. You know how to be persistent, don't you?'

'Of course I do, darling. I'll make him listen to me, I promise.'

'Once you have spoken to Van, ring Major McCaigue on this telephone number and tell him exactly what Theo told you.' Conrad read out the number. If Van didn't believe Veronica, it was likely that McCaigue would.

'Do you think we are too late?' said Veronica.

'I don't know,' said Conrad. 'But we have to try. Oh, and Veronica?'

'Yes?'

'Well done.'

Veronica hung up, and ran downstairs. She found a taxi in Park Lane. 'Whitehall, please.'

Kensington, London

After the excitement of the previous two days, Alston felt deflated as he made his way back to his flat in Ennismore Gardens. Arthur Oakford had just confirmed what he had feared; Halifax had turned down the premiership. Didn't have the stomach for it, quite literally. Which meant Churchill. There seemed to be a consensus in the House that the next government should include the Labour Party, and the Labour leaders preferred Churchill to Chamberlain. Despite the disaster in Norway, the House of Commons was suddenly well disposed towards the warmonger-in-chief. Churchill was going to become Prime Minister the next day. This was not how it was supposed to be.

He was surprised when he opened the door to his flat to see a light was on. It was past eleven o'clock. It couldn't possibly be Dorothy down from Scotland to surprise him, could it?

'Hello?'

'Henry!' He smiled as Constance rushed in from the sitting room, flung her arms around her neck and kissed him.

'What are you doing here?' he asked her.

'I told my mother I was staying with a friend in town. I wanted to be with you tonight.' She broke away from him. 'What's wrong? Did Halifax become Prime Minister after all?'

'No,' said Alston. 'It's worse than that. It's going to be Churchill.'

'But Churchill's responsible for the mess we're in!'

'I know. But suddenly everyone loves him.'

'So no Lloyd George?'

'No,' said Alston, pouring himself a Scotch with barely a splash of soda. He sat down on the sofa and Constance snuggled up close to him.

'That's awful. Will Churchill make you a minister?'

'I doubt it very much,' said Alston. 'He knows my views on the war. I suppose he might ask me to join the government, to create a "broad church", but I would have to refuse. I couldn't possibly serve under him.'

'Oh, my poor darling,' said Constance. 'That's so unfair!'

'I know,' said Alston. It was nice to be able to briefly drop his guard with Constance.

'Maybe it's not so bad,' said Constance.

'How can it not be?' said Alston.

'You said Churchill was a fool. Maybe he will lose the war and then they'll dump him too.'

Perhaps Constance had a point. In a way, the biggest risk to Alston's vision of a modern pro-German government was not Churchill, but a coalition of tired old moderates who would be able to negotiate a peace with Germany that left Britain alone to continue its path to decline and decay. That was not what Alston wanted.

Alston wanted a strong government, with himself at the heart of it, with Lloyd George as Prime Minister and the Duke of Windsor as king. A government that was an ally of Germany, that had the strength of purpose to rule the world in partnership with Hitler, that would lead Britain to greatness once again.

'Maybe the Germans will finally attack France tomorrow and knock the Frogs out of the war with one of their blitzkriegs. With Chamberlain gone and Halifax out of the picture, there will be only you left to save us all from the warmongers!'

'Maybe they will,' said Alston. He smiled and stroked Constance's hair. Her unquestioning support helped. And although she seemed naive and ignorant of politics, in fact she had good instincts.

Alston banished all thoughts of giving up. Next time, when Churchill slipped up, he had to be ready to move. Constance was right: that time might not be very far away.

'By the way, you don't have to worry about Conrad de Lancey anymore,' Constance said. 'I saw Joe Sullivan today and gave him the money. He'll make sure de Lancey won't be asking any more difficult questions about Lord Copthorne or me or the Duke of Windsor. We just need to alert Joe when de Lancey is back in London.'

'Sullivan agreed to do it just like that?'

'Yes. It wasn't just for the money. I explained that de Lancey was against the cause.'

'It's more than that,' said Alston. 'I have heard de Lancey has been asking a lot of awkward questions, and unless we do something very soon he will find some very awkward answers. He's getting very close.'

'Well, Joe will put a stop to that.'

'Good,' said Alston.

Alston sipped his whisky and smiled. Only a few months ago, the idea of killing de Lancey would have shocked him. But now he knew that it was the right and necessary thing to do if de Lancey were not to blow the whole thing open. In moments of national crisis, like now, he had to have the moral strength to do what was necessary. Anything less was weakness and, unlike Lord Halifax, Alston was not weak. Herr Hitler and Signor Mussolini had not achieved what they had by being weak. Constance had taught him that. Which was remarkable for such a young woman.

'You have been an enormous help to me, Constance. But someone like you shouldn't be involved in this kind of thing.'

'I love helping you, silly!' She smiled at him. Then the smile disappeared. 'Besides, I told you I had once killed someone. Before Millie.'

'I remember you saying you had "taken steps".' Alston had been curious at the time what those steps were. He was even more curious now.

'It was my uncle.'

'The one you went to live with?'

'That's right. After Daddy killed himself, my mother, my sister and I went down to Dulwich to stay with him and my aunt – my aunt is my mother's sister. After the factory closed we had no money and they did. I knew there was something wrong with Uncle Cedric, but I didn't know what. On the surface, he seemed very correct and proper, kind even, but he was cruel to my aunt and my mother. He had my aunt under his thumb and he soon had my mother in the same position.

'Then one night he came into our bedroom. My younger sister Lucy was asleep. He tried to kiss me. So I whacked him. For the next three months there was war between us, he did all he could to turn my mother and my aunt against me. It was horrible, but I refused to give up.'

Constance sighed. 'But he knew how to really hurt me. One morning I came back to our bedroom and found him with Lucy. She was naked. She was only thirteen! When he saw me, he smiled.'

'How old were you?'

'I was fifteen. The next morning he fell under the eight-thirty-nine train to London Bridge. A witness said she thought he was pushed. I told the police he had wanted to kill himself. I was late to school that morning, but no one noticed.'

'My God,' said Alston.

'And the thing of it is,' said Constance, 'life was better for me and for my sister, and for my mother and my aunt. Much better.' She kissed his scarred cheek. He loved the way she seemed to favour that side of his face with her tenderness.

'I've never told anyone that before. I didn't think anyone would understand. But you understand, don't you, Henry? Now.'

'Yes,' said Alston, stroking her hair. 'I understand.'

'It's either de Lancey or us, Henry. You can't become Prime Minister if you are in jail for murder, now can you? Come to bed. And tomorrow, who knows? Perhaps the war will be lost and you will have your chance again.'

PART FOUR

May 1940

Forty-One

Extracts from Lieutenant Dieter von Hertenberg's Diary

10 May

*It's started! We crossed the River Sûre on the Luxembourg
border at 0530 this morning with the tanks of 1ˢᵗ Panzer
Division. I am in the armoured command car with General
Guderian; I go everywhere he goes. The roads are narrow and
winding with steep wooded valleys. The weather is gorgeous;
the sky is blue and clear. Tanks stretch out for kilometres – we
are sitting ducks for French aircraft, but fortunately we haven't
seen any. The Luxembourg border guards were overwhelmed
by detachments of our infantry and we drove straight through.*

*Our orders are to push through the Ardennes forest to
Luxembourg and Belgium until we reach Sedan. Then we
establish a bridgehead over the River Meuse.*

11 May

*Delayed by minefields and demolition of bridges on the
Belgian border with Luxembourg. Brief fighting with
French cavalry and Belgian Chasseurs Ardennais around
Neufchâteau. Reached the Semois River at Bouillon. It's
not very wide, but the banks form a good defensive line for
the French and Belgians. The French are digging in at the
town of Bouillon.*

I think we have created the largest traffic jam in Europe; apparently the columns of vehicles stretch back all the way across Luxembourg to Germany. Still seen only a couple of French reconnaissance aircraft, which is lucky because we are trapped on these narrow forest roads.

12 May

Whitsun. The French have blown the bridge over the Semois, but it is fordable in places. The French have retreated from Bouillon. Our engineers constructed a new bridge and 1ˢᵗ Panzer crossed into the town.

We have suffered enemy bombing for the first time. We set up Corps HQ in the Hôtel Panorama in Bouillon, which does indeed have a wonderful view of the Semois valley. Guderian was standing by a fireplace in the parlour. Hunting trophies lined the walls, including a particularly large wild boar's head. Suddenly some British bombs landed nearby, one of which hit an ammunition supply column. There was a series of massive explosions: glass shattered, and the trophies flew off the wall. The giant boar missed Guderian by only a few centimetres. He was badly shaken.

But I am impressed with the general. He is a hard task-master and drives around the forward units manically. We get very little sleep. But his doctrine of leading from the front works. We have a wireless, a map table and ciphers in the command vehicle – much better than sitting twenty kilometres to the rear with a row of telephones, which is what all the other generals do. He keeps the tanks moving, which keeps the enemy off balance.

He has just flown off in a Storch to have discussions with Cousin Paul in the rear. Expected back later this evening.

Later . . . Guderian returned and had some pretty nasty things to say about General Kleist. I decided not to remind *him that he was being rude about my relative! Our orders are to cross the Meuse tomorrow afternoon. Kleist has heard from Berlin that the French 7th Army with all its armour is moving north into Flanders rather than east to meet us. This is very good news, and just what Theo predicted.*

A lot to do to get the orders out for tomorrow's attack. And although we have crossed the Moselle on exercise, the Meuse will be much more difficult when properly defended. I think I will be seeing real action tomorrow.

13 May

Exhausted. I have scarcely slept at all for the last seventy-two hours. Or is it ninety-six? It's been a long and dangerous day, but we have a toehold across the Meuse!

The morning was spent frantically trying to produce orders for the assault. I had the idea of using the same orders in our files from the war game on the Moselle we did a couple of weeks ago. Simply added six hours to everything, so the start time of 1000 became 1600.

The French have abandoned the larger part of Sedan which lies on the east bank of the Meuse. The river itself is wide and fast-flowing, and on the west bank are steep green hills with trees, pillboxes, stone towers and gun emplacements. It is like a mountain spitting fire! I thought there was no chance of us ever getting across.

Then our Stukas came, wave after wave of them. They dive down out of the sky, sirens screaming, and drop bombs on the French positions. They kept it up all afternoon. The noise is indescribable, even on our side of the river. It must be hell under it, and it seems to have kept most of the French artillery and machine guns quiet.

At 1600 our infantry paddled across the river in dinghies. They took casualties but have established a couple of bridgeheads on the far bank. Once the orders were issued, Guderian drove back and forth between 1st Panzer and 2nd Panzer. Then we boarded a dinghy to cross the river, under fire of course. When we got to the other side, the smart-arse commander of the 1st Rifle Regiment said, 'Joyriding is forbidden on the Meuse.' To be fair to Guderian, he laughed.

At nightfall we returned here to Corps HQ. The engineers are building a pontoon over the river for the tanks to cross tomorrow.

I am so tired. I must get some sleep!

14 May

Fierce battle around Sedan. The bridge has been built and tanks have crossed over. Intelligence suggests that French armour are massing for a counter-attack. Some of the French have turned and run, but some are still fighting, and they have superb positions on the heights looking down on the river. Now we are seeing a lot of French and British aeroplanes. It's touch and go.

At noon General von Rundstedt, Commander of Army Group A, arrived to take a look. Guderian took him, and me, out on to the centre of our new bridge in the middle of an air raid. The British bombers are not very accurate, but they are aiming at the bridge! Rundstedt tried to take it as calmly as Guderian, but you could see he was rattled. There were bodies in the river, but I didn't jump in after them this time. These fellows weren't struggling, they were face down in the water and covered with dark patches of blood.

The noise is extraordinary: artillery gunfire, the rattle of machine guns, the thuds and splashes of bombs, the screams of the Stukas, and the constant rumble of tanks on the move. And yet the sun shines.

15 May

French tanks arrived. Air attacks continue. We are hard pressed.

16 May

We are out in open country! We drove 65 kilometres today. Sedan is secure, as is our beachhead over the Meuse. Without warning, the French gave up their counter-attacks and turned tail. We have no orders for what to do in this situation, so Guderian decided to push west. We reached Montcornet, where we took hundreds of prisoners who had no idea we were anywhere near them.

It's a wonderful feeling, like a long-distance runner pulling ahead of his competitors in a sprint for the finish line. Like the runner, though, I fear we will become exhausted. Guderian's philosophy is not to bother about our flanks, but to stay moving and keep the enemy off balance. That seems to be working so far, but I can't help worrying that when the French finally bring up serious reinforcements our flanks will be in trouble.

You can see why they call him Schneller Heinz.

17 May

Looks like I have lost a commander! General Kleist flew in first thing this morning, and without even saying 'good morning', let alone 'well done', he gave Guderian a public bollocking for disobeying his orders. Apparently we should have halted at the Meuse. Guderian calmly asked to be relieved of his command. This took Kleist aback for a moment, but then he told him to hand over to one of his divisional generals and stalked off. I think he recognized me, but didn't show it. I always used to admire Cousin Paul, but I think his behaviour is outrageous. What is the point of sacking your best general at the moment of a stunning victory?

So we are hanging around at Montcornet until General List arrives with orders from Rundstedt to sort things out.

18 May

Guderian has been reinstated. Technically we have to keep our HQ at Montcornet, but we are permitted 'reconnaissance in force', which means we are off again!

2nd Panzer reached Saint-Quentin this afternoon. The whole of northern France is opening up before us.

Forty-Two

Extract from Lieutenant Dieter von Hertenberg's Diary

19 May

> Crossed the old Somme battlefield. War has changed in the
> last twenty years, thank God.
>
> Close shave this afternoon. Our command vehicle was in
> a wood, virtually alone save for a battery of AA guns, when
> we heard French tanks close by. If they had found us, they
> would have captured us. Fortunately they moved off.

Regent's Park, London, 19 May

It was a glorious day in the park. After a brutal winter, flowers were
shooting up in the few beds that had remained undisturbed by
war preparations. Even the ack-ack guns and the bobbing barrage
balloons seemed to be celebrating spring. The iron railings had all
been removed, turning the city park into something more akin to
a lush rural meadow. There were few people about, just some old
codgers snoozing in deckchairs and a group of small boys sailing
their boats on the lake, untroubled by German submarines.

The weather matched Alston's mood, if not that of his
compatriots. The news from France was bleak, and getting bleaker
by the day. The Germans had cut through the French like a knife
through Camembert. The English press were trying to find ways of
coming to terms with what was turning into a humiliating defeat.

Those in the know – the MPs, the society hostesses, the generals, the gossips of club and dining room – already feared a disaster was in the making. This was worse than 1914. Some thought the French and British generals might be able to pull a Marne victory out of the hat. Realists thought that unlikely.

People laid the blame in two places: the French and Churchill.

Only the day after Churchill had taken over as PM, many Tory backbenchers wondered what they had done. At just the time when the country needed a cool rational brain, they had plumped for a leader who seemed to be struck by bizarre ideas at random, and who wrapped himself in sentimental bombast.

The party had made a mistake and they knew it. Constance was right. Between them, the French and Churchill were losing the war. Peace was the only rational alternative. But this time Alston would make sure he was in control of how that peace was achieved.

He spotted the plump Swede sauntering towards him. They 'bumped into each other' at the prearranged spot at the stone pillars by the rose garden where a splendid wrought-iron gate used to stand before it was melted down.

'Ah, Lindfors, fancy seeing you here!' said Alston loudly, holding out his hand and smiling. Karsten Lindfors was a Swedish banker whom Alston had met a number of times before the war in London and Berlin. Alston did not know him well enough to trust him, but in March Lindfors had approached Alston with a message from Joachim von Ribbentrop, who it appeared did trust him. Since then they had met twice. Lindfors was a much better intermediary than Constance and Millie de Lancey had been. Alston knew exactly where the Swedish banker's loyalties lay. The opportunities for profitable trade finance, given all the raw materials and ordnance that were flowing from Sweden to Germany, would be extraordinary. A neutral banker's dream.

After a few words of greeting, Alston turned to join Lindfors on his stroll, as if they were acquaintances who had met by chance, and had decided to walk together and chat for a few minutes.

'I have a message for Joachim,' Alston said. 'Churchill is

vulnerable; it won't take much of a prod to topple him. It's likely that this will happen within the next two weeks, especially if the news from France gets worse.'

'And then what?'

'Then we need a new regime. We have plans. But it's vital that Herr Hitler refuses to deal with the existing British government and insists on a new regime of leaders who are sympathetic to Germany. That will give the ditherers enough of an excuse to give way to us.'

'Who are the ditherers?'

'Churchill. Chamberlain. Halifax.'

'And who will be in this new regime?'

'Lloyd George. Myself. Sam Hoare. Rab Butler. Other sympathetic souls. And be sure to tell Ribbentrop that we will invite back a king whom he can deal with.'

'The Duke of Windsor?'

'King Edward. Or Edward the Eighth Part Two as Shakespeare would call him.'

The Swede smiled quickly. 'How confident are you that you can achieve this?'

'Very confident. As long as the German government refuses to deal with Halifax and Churchill. It's all planned.'

'I'll tell Joachim.' He shook Alston's hand again. 'Somehow I suspect we will be seeing each other again very soon.'

Alston nodded, and turned back towards the rose garden.

Mayfair, London

'All right, can you see anyone?' hissed Constance.

'No. The coast is clear,' Anneliese replied. They were on Grosvenor Street. There were no clouds and some moonlight, just enough for them to see what they were doing. They were following Anna Wolkoff's detailed instructions. Keep on the dark side of the street. Look out for doorways in the shadows where policemen liked to lurk.

They passed a bus stop. Always a good spot.

In a practised movement, Constance whipped the poster out of the shopping bag she was carrying, and unfurled it. The back was already covered with glue, and both women pressed it down over the timetable.

Printed on it was a little ditty written by Captain Maule Ramsay beginning:

Land of Dope and Jewry
Land that once was free
All the Jew boys praise thee
Whilst they plunder thee.

But this time perhaps they had had a little too much to drink. The coast wasn't clear after all.

'Oi! What are you two doing?'

'Run!' shouted Constance, and they ran. Both women were fast and had avoided heels for just such an eventuality. Anneliese turned to see a helmeted silhouette after them. A bulky silhouette. The policeman blew his whistle.

They shot across Regent Street and into the warren of alleys that was Soho.

A quick left and a quick right and they thought that they had lost him.

'Here! Let's go in here!'

Constance pulled Anneliese down some stairs, past a doorman, into what was clearly a nightclub. As they penetrated the heavy blackout drapes over the entrance they were hit by a fug of smoke, alcohol and piano music in a dim blue light. The tables had shiny black tops, the chairs were red wicker and fake plaster columns propped up the walls, or were propped up by them. The lighting changed to red.

'This brings back memories of Berlin,' said Anneliese.

'I need a drink!' said Constance. 'Have you got any money?'

Anneliese had. She had kept some of the cash Conrad had given her in November for just such an eventuality.

314

The manager found them a table in the back, and at Constance's suggestion they ordered black velvets. Immediately, two men in army uniform approached them, bearing lopsided smiles of charm and alcohol, but Constance told them the women were waiting for someone.

She laughed as she raised her glass to Anneliese. 'Cheers!'

'*Prost!*' said Anneliese. Then '*Heil Hitler!*' in a whisper.

Constance giggled. '*Heil Alston!*' she said.

'That's a good one,' said Anneliese.

They were already both tipsy. They had been taken out to dinner at La Coquille by Captain Maule Ramsay, Tyler Kent and a diplomat from the Italian Embassy. Anna Wolkoff and Joan Miller, the model, had been there as well. Much alcohol had been consumed and Tyler Kent and the Italian diplomat, who was a count, were at their most charming. It was clear that Anna Wolkoff was acting as some sort of intermediary between Jock Maule Ramsay and the American Embassy employee.

'Did I see Tyler give Jock something?' Anneliese said.

'You did,' Constance said. 'And it's very secret. I persuaded him to keep a copy for Henry.'

'A copy of what?'

Constance looked around the room. No one was listening to them, but two men dressed in dinner jackets were staring. 'Tyler works as a cipher clerk in the American Embassy. He has been deciphering correspondence between Churchill and President Roosevelt. It shows Roosevelt is sympathetic to the British.'

'Isn't that obvious?' asked Anneliese.

'No, it isn't at all.' Constance turned to two more men approaching them. 'Go away!' she snarled before they had even got to the table. They went away.

'Apparently the American public don't want to go to war with Germany.'

'Very sensible,' said Anneliese.

'Precisely. And Roosevelt must be seen to be keeping his distance.'

'Which he isn't, according to Tyler.'

'Quite right. So Henry's plan is to pass the correspondence on to an isolationist US senator he knows. The senator will publicize the messages, and Roosevelt will be forced to disown them. It should stop America from coming in to the war.'

'Wonderful!' said Anneliese, trying to make herself believe that the news was indeed wonderful, and succeeding. She had developed a technique when she was with Constance of persuading herself that she was in fact a loyal Nazi stuck in a foreign country. She had known enough of them in Berlin, and she tried to react to whatever she saw and heard in that role, blanking out all thoughts of the true implications until later.

Constance's eyes were shining. She was excited, she was drunk, and she was enjoying being with Anneliese.

She wanted to talk.

'You did something similar for Henry when you were in Holland last year, didn't you?' Anneliese said. 'Something hush-hush?'

Constance frowned. For a moment, Anneliese thought she had gone too far, and raised Constance's suspicions. Then the Englishwoman smiled and leaned forward. 'I was talking to some representatives of the German government for Henry. It was all a bit of a disaster.'

'Really? What went wrong?'

'I can't say. But I had to . . . take action.'

'Take action? What do you mean?'

'I had to kill someone.'

'No!' Anneliese raised her hand to her mouth. She suppressed the excitement she felt and smothered it in feigned shock. But only mild shock, not enough to put Constance off.

'You look surprised,' said Constance.

'I am,' said Anneliese. 'Who was it?'

'I can't say. But wouldn't you kill someone for the Fatherland? If it absolutely had to be done?'

'I never have,' said Anneliese. Then she seemed to give it consideration. 'But if the circumstances demanded it, I would.'

She sat up straight. 'I would be proud to.'

Constance smiled. 'I knew you would understand. But don't tell a soul.'

'I won't. Are you still in discussions with the German government?'

'I'm not. But Henry is.'

'Will there be peace?' Anneliese said. 'Surrender?'

'Peace. It will look like a draw but it will be victory for Germany. Henry has it all worked out.'

'A revolution? A coup?'

'No!' said Constance. 'This is England. This will all be done in a very British way. No goose-stepping. No Roman salutes. In fact the public will hardly realize what has happened until it has happened. That is the beauty of his plan.'

'Tell me,' said Anneliese.

Forty-Three

Extract from Lieutenant Dieter von Hertenberg's Diary

20 May

> Orders allow us to move as far as Amiens, so we have taken
> Amiens. It's a beautiful city and a fine cathedral. Captured
> some English prisoners. The roads are full of French refugees.
> 2nd Panzer claimed they were out of fuel, but Guderian didn't
> believe them. His theory is that's just an excuse commanders
> use when they are tired.
>
> Two of our own aircraft attacked us this afternoon. We
> shot them down and the crew drifted to the ground under
> parachutes. Guderian was there to meet them and gave them
> a severe bollocking. Then a bottle of champagne.
>
> Abbeville taken this evening. The Channel is only 20
> kilometres away!

Suffolk, 20 May

Conrad read the cable that was waiting for him in the mess. 'YOU
MUST MEET ME IN LONDON AS SOON AS POSSIBLE VERY URGENT
ANNELIESE'.

That was at least clear.

The battalion was keeping itself busy. The disasters on the
Continent had injected a dose of urgency into their preparations.
Intelligence analysis suggested that the Germans were considering

an immediate assault on England, before France fell. If that were true, then such an invasion would have to come from the north German ports, since the Germans would not have had time to prepare the Dutch harbours they had captured to launch an armada. And if an invasion fleet left from Hamburg or Bremen, it would almost certainly alight in East Anglia.

Personally, Conrad didn't believe the intelligence reports. In fact, from what he had learned of intelligence over the last few months, there was more bluff and double bluff going on than straightforward acquisition of genuine secrets. If he were in charge, he would junk the whole lot and rely on common sense. Common sense told him that the Germans would be as preoccupied with the invasion of France as the Allies were, and would be very unlikely to have taken the time to plan an assault on Britain right away.

So Conrad was wasting his time in Suffolk and had been desperate to get back to London. But since the German blitzkrieg, all weekend leave had been cancelled, and Colonel Rydal had been unwilling to make an exception for him.

Conrad would just have to try harder. He went to see the CO.

Colonel Rydal was at his desk. Conrad handed him the cable, on the basis that honesty was most likely to earn him Rydal's trust.

'Who is Anneliese?' Rydal asked. 'Your girl?'

'Yes, sir. But I met her in Germany last year. And she is helping me with my investigation of the Duke of Windsor. If she wants to see me that urgently, she has discovered something important.'

'I take it you want leave to see her right away?'

'Yes, sir.'

The colonel raised his eyebrows. 'And what if she wants to tell you she is pregnant?'

That stopped Conrad; the thought genuinely hadn't occurred to him, but it was one of the classic reasons for requests for leave from his own men. 'It's not that, sir,' he said. 'If it were, Anneliese would wait to tell me. Besides which the timing is wrong.'

Rydal grunted. 'I have received another order from the War Office not to grant you more leave.'

319

'Did they say why?'

'No. But they were firm about it.'

'Doesn't that rather suggest that there is something to learn in London?' Conrad said. 'I'm not a Soviet spy, sir. The very idea is ridiculous.'

'I know it is,' said Rydal.

Conrad could tell the colonel wanted to believe him. He just needed some help. 'When I went to Holland last November I was told that the Germans had received information from the Duke of Windsor that the French lines were at their weakest at Sedan. I passed that information on to the British authorities, who seem to have ignored it. They didn't like the idea of the duke being a German spy. Now I quite understand that – I don't like it either. But you know where the German army broke through last week?'

'Sedan.' Rydal frowned. 'And you think that your friend Anneliese has more information about the duke?'

'She may well have. She has been investigating an MP who has been involved with the duke, or friends of the duke. An MP who is pro-Nazi. Sir Henry Alston.'

'Is Alston pro-Nazi?'

'Oh, yes, sir.'

'Do you have proof?'

'Absolutely not. That's why I have to see Anneliese.'

Rydal stood up and turned towards the window. Conrad waited. Rydal's shoulders stiffened. He had made a decision. He turned back to Conrad. 'I can't give you leave. But I can send you to see someone at the War Office. A different department. As you know, I have been having a long-running argument with the WO about our Bedfords being armoured. Here's the man's name and the department.' Rydal scribbled a name.

'Do I have an appointment?'

'No. And don't make one. Just claim I told you you had one. It will sound like a typical army balls-up.'

Conrad smiled. 'Thank you, sir.'

'Very good. Leave an address where we can get you at short notice. Between us, there is a good chance that we may be ordered to France in the next few days as reinforcements. If that happens, I want you back with the battalion right away.'

Pall Mall, London

Alston sipped his whisky and listened to the secret-service officer. They were meeting in Alston's club, having decided a long time before that it was more discreet to meet openly. There was nothing suspicious about a Conservative MP having a quiet conversation with a senior member of SIS, whereas a clandestine meeting would be more remarkable.

'De Lancey is coming to London tomorrow,' the officer said.

'But damn it, McCaigue! I thought you had arranged for him to be confined to barracks.'

Major McCaigue shrugged. 'His CO seems to have sent him here on an errand. There's not much one can do about that, at least not right away.' He raised his eyebrows. 'But isn't this good news? I thought you had arranged a welcome for him, next time he came to town.'

'I suppose so,' said Alston.

'We've discussed this,' said McCaigue. 'I can't help you with that kind of thing, at least not directly. I can't be seen to be conspiring with you, even by my colleagues.'

McCaigue was Alston's man inside the secret service. He had provided Alston with sound advice for several months now, part of which was that if the secret service was to be seen conspiring to launch a coup, any new government's legitimacy would be questioned. So McCaigue had been very careful.

'I understand,' said Alston, embarrassed by his own squeamishness. 'I'll deal with de Lancey.' All he needed to do was to tell Constance, and she would get Sullivan to take care of it. 'We intend to make a move in the next week or so. Churchill is becoming more vulnerable by the day.'

'Good,' said McCaigue.

'How do you think your colleagues will take it?'

'It's hard to say. Provided you can avoid it seeming like a coup, then I think they will go along with it. You know, "peace with honour". And most of us are still more worried by the Soviets than the Nazis. I know I am. I don't trust that Nazi–Soviet pact. Stalin just wanted half of Poland, and that was his way to take it. You wait until he wants the other half and see what happens then.'

Alston knew that McCaigue's main motivation wasn't his loyalty to Alston or even the Duke of Windsor, but a deep conviction that the Bolshevik revolution of 1917 had just been the start of a long-term grab for power by the working classes. He loathed and feared Russia, or, to be more precise, the idea that had become embodied in the Soviet Union. McCaigue was fighting for civilization against communism. In that battle, it made much more sense to have the Nazis with you rather than against you.

Alston could go along with that idea.

'Have you heard about the arrests this morning?' McCaigue asked.

'What arrests?'

'An American diplomat called Tyler Kent and a Russian woman, Anna Wolkoff.'

'No, I hadn't heard about them,' said Alston.

'Do you know them?' McCaigue asked.

'Isn't Anna Wolkoff the manager of the Russian Tea Rooms?'

'You don't go there, do you?' McCaigue asked with a hint of disapproval.

'Just once or twice, but that's all. It didn't seem very discreet.'

'It certainly isn't that. And don't go again. There will be more arrests.'

'Ah.' Alston sipped his whisky. 'There is a friend of mine, Mrs Scott-Dunton – you probably remember she was in Holland last November. You helped tidy up after her then.' Alston knew it was McCaigue who, on his own initiative, had arranged for suspicion for Millie de Lancey's murder to fall on a German spy rather than

Constance. 'I'm afraid she spends quite a lot of time at the Tea Rooms, and she knows Mr Kent. She has been very helpful to me in various important ways over the last few months. It would be disastrous if she were arrested. It might undermine the whole plan.'

'Oh dear,' said McCaigue. 'She hasn't exactly been careful, has she?'

Alston didn't like his tone. 'I'm serious, McCaigue. It would be bad for all of us.'

McCaigue smiled quickly. 'Don't worry, Sir Henry. I'll see what I can do to protect her.'

'On the other hand, what about Mosley?' said Alston. 'It might be convenient if he was arrested. The last thing we want is him taking advantage of the government in disarray to launch his own coup.'

McCaigue grinned. 'It would be convenient, wouldn't it?'

Forty-Four

Extract from Lieutenant Dieter von Hertenberg's Diary

21 May

Saw the English Channel this morning! Blue sea in brilliant sunshine. There was haze to the north so we couldn't see the white cliffs of Dover, but we are probably too far away here anyway. It's remarkable that only eleven days ago we were crossing the border into Luxembourg. That's 350 km! But I am so tired. We are all tired, including the tanks. But it turns out that 2nd Panzer hadn't run out of fuel after all.

The Allied armies are cut in two. Now – do we head north or south? The British Expeditionary Force is to the north, Paris to the south. Waiting for orders.

I am immensely proud of what we have achieved. I wonder what Theo would think. From what I can tell, the intelligence he gathered helped the High Command come up with the plan we have just followed with such success. We are taking part in possibly the most glorious victory in our country's history. As a German officer, how can Theo not be proud of his part in that?

The French and the British must realize they have lost. Maybe now there will be peace. That must be a good thing.

As Conrad waited outside the entrance to the hospital, he was reminded of those times nearly two years before when he had stood outside St Hedwig's in the Jewish quarter of Berlin, waiting for Anneliese. The uniform was different, but it was the same woman whose face lit up when she saw him. The same smile.

She kissed him quickly, and led him over the road to the park. 'I was worried you wouldn't be able to come.'

'I have a very understanding CO, thank God. I'm here on official business: talking to the War Office about equipment.'

'How long until you have to return?'

'A week is the maximum. Unless the battalion is sent to France, in which case I will have to rejoin them immediately. What have you got to tell me?'

'Let's wait till we are in the park.'

They walked rapidly and in silence across Rotten Row. Only when they were a good distance from Knightsbridge did Anneliese talk.

'Oh, Conrad. She did it! Constance killed your sister.'

'I thought so,' said Conrad, anger surging through his body. 'How did you get her to admit it?'

'She was showing off. About the secret mission she had been sent on to Holland by Alston.'

'Did she say why?'

'Not really. She said the trip had been a disaster and she had been forced to kill someone. She didn't say who, but it can only have been your sister, can't it?'

'It must have been,' said Conrad. 'It's hardly conclusive proof. I'm not even sure it would count as evidence.'

'I'm sorry,' said Anneliese. 'It was the nearest to a confession I could get.'

'Oh, no,' said Conrad. 'You did well. Very well. At least now I know for certain.'

'There's more,' said Anneliese. 'Constance told me Alston's plans for a new government.'

'Which are?'

'He thinks Churchill is unpopular and going to fall very soon. Halifax doesn't have the guts to become Prime Minister.'

'So who replaces Churchill?'

'Lloyd George. Backed up by Alston and . . .'

'And who?'

'Your father.'

'No!'

Anneliese reached out and squeezed Conrad's hand. The anger he had felt on hearing confirmation that Constance had killed his sister mixed with shock. Betrayal. Fear.

'Are they going to make peace with Hitler?' Conrad said.

'More than that. They are going to put in place a regime that will become firm allies with Germany. They are going to bring the Duke of Windsor over from France to demand peace. They will force King George to abdicate and make the duke king again.'

'The British people will never put up with that.'

'There's a newspaper campaign planned. Alston has friends in every part of the ruling class, according to Constance. It will seem like common sense, like a great escape from defeat. Or at least that's the idea.'

'It will never work.'

'I've seen it work. So have you. In Germany. Hitler was voted into power by the people, remember? This will be different, because you British are different, but that's why it will work. According to Constance and Alston.' Anneliese looked up at Conrad. 'Don't be too quick to dismiss these things as impossible. That's what we did in my country.'

Conrad stopped. They were in the middle of a large green meadow, bordered by trenches that had been dug a couple of years before as protection from air raids. No one had ever used them.

'What the hell is my father doing with Alston?' Conrad said. 'I can't for a moment imagine he is a willing participant. Alston

326

must have pulled the wool over his eyes somehow. Father is much too naive.'

'Constance said that Lord Oakford is going to France to tell the Duke of Windsor to come back to Britain and reclaim his crown. Apparently he and Alston discussed it with the duke when he was here in February.'

'Don't be ridiculous!' Conrad said. 'I can just about believe that he might help Alston make peace with the Germans. But we already have a king and he's called George, not Edward the bloody Eighth. If my father is trying to get the duke to come back that's treason, pure and simple. And whatever else my father is, however stupid he is, he's not a traitor!'

'I can only say what Constance told me,' said Anneliese.

'I'll talk to him now,' said Conrad. 'Tell him he shouldn't be such a fool.' Conrad turned on his heel and walked back towards the Knightsbridge underground station.

'No, Conrad!' said Anneliese. 'No. Listen to me.' She tugged on his sleeve, urging him to stop.

Conrad turned to her. 'Anneliese. I have to sort this out! Maybe Constance is making it up. Or she is confused.'

'Conrad. Listen to me. Your father *is* involved. We don't know how and we don't know why, but Constance would have no reason to lie to me. She doesn't know that I know him or you. But we have to assume that your father knows what he is doing. Which means that you can't tell him that we know it too.'

'Why not?'

'Because he will stop you from doing anything about it. Your father is an idealist. If he thinks he is doing the right thing, he won't let you get in his way. You know that, you've told me yourself about the arguments you've had with him.'

'How could he stop me?'

Anneliese shrugged. 'I don't know. What I do know is that you think you are safe in nice cosy Britain and you are not. All those horrible things that happen over the English Channel are coming here soon. Very soon.'

'My father wouldn't hurt me.'

'This kind of thing tears families apart in my country. It will in yours too.'

They were a few yards away from a bench and Conrad headed towards it. He sat down and leaned forward, his head in his hands. He felt Anneliese's palm on his back.

'I just can't believe Father would betray his country like that,' he said. 'I know peace is important to him, but this is treason. He's betraying everything he believes in. Everything I believe in. Everything!'

'He probably doesn't think it is,' said Anneliese. 'That's the whole problem. He probably thinks he's doing what's right for his country. Alston and Constance think that too.'

'When you told me just now you had proof that Constance had killed Millie, I thought I could finally go to Father and convince him that Alston was evil, that he was a traitor, that not only had he killed Millie but he was conspiring to lose the war and overthrow our king. I thought Father would listen to me, help me. I thought he was a good man and he would prove it to me. But now? Now I don't know what to think.'

Conrad blinked. He could feel tears springing to his eyes. He could see Anneliese had noticed, and he fought to control himself.

Anneliese reached for his hand and squeezed it. 'I'm sorry, Conrad.'

Conrad sat up and took a deep breath. 'All right. So what do we do?'

'We tell someone,' said Anneliese.

'Tell someone that my father's a traitor?'

'Yes,' said Anneliese.

Conrad turned to her. Her familiar green eyes were looking into his. No irony, this time. No humour. Concern. Love even. Sincerity.

'I can't do it,' he said.

'You have to do it,' Anneliese said. 'This is bigger than you and me. You know that.'

What about Mama? Conrad thought. What about Millie and Charlotte and Reggie?

For a second he had forgotten Millie was dead. And Edward was dead. His family had been torn apart. More than that, it was as if a mortar bomb had landed right in the middle of it and exploded.

'Do you know why I didn't want to marry you when I came to London?' Anneliese said.

'No,' said Conrad.

'Because I didn't want to drag you down with me. I felt worthless. I felt that what had happened in Germany had destroyed me. The only reason for me existing was to help my parents, and even they didn't have much of a future. I felt that if I once was worthy of you, I wasn't anymore. I loved you and I was absolutely certain that you would have a better life without me.'

'But that doesn't make any sense!' Conrad said.

'It made sense to me. It was as if I was carrying the evil of the Nazis inside me somehow, that it had infected me like some plague and that I had brought it with me to England. I didn't want to infect you.'

Conrad reached out his hand and stroked Anneliese's hair.

'Can you understand that?' she said. Her eyes were steady, her jaw firm.

Conrad thought of all Anneliese had suffered. Of her stoic misery in London. Of the confidence that he had always felt that she loved him really, and the frustration that she wouldn't allow him to love her.

'I think so.'

'But going to the Russian Tea Rooms, pretending to be some kind of Nazi myself, has made me feel better. I am worth something; I am doing something worthwhile. The world is on the edge of a thousand years of darkness. Don't you feel it? If France surrenders, if Alston and your father create their puppet government, the Nazis will control Europe. They will control Britain. They will destroy the Jewish people. They will destroy civilization. There will be a new Dark Ages.'

Conrad nodded. She was right.

'Doing what little I can to prevent that has given my life meaning again. You must do what you can too. Even if it means betraying your father.'

Conrad looked at Anneliese. She knew how important his father was to him; her own father meant everything to her. She knew him; she understood him.

She was right.

He stood up. 'Let's go,' he said.

'Where?'

'We need to tell someone. Someone who can actually do something about it.'

'Who?'

'Sir Robert Vansittart.'

It turned out that that was much easier said than done. It was only a fifteen-minute walk across Green Park and St James's Park to the Foreign Office, but once there it transpired that the Chief Diplomatic Adviser was busy. Conrad scribbled a note for the commissionaire to give to Mrs Dougherty, saying that he had information of national importance, and then he and Anneliese waited in the grand entrance hall of the Foreign Office.

And waited.

Eventually, two hours later, Conrad heard a familiar deep Ulster voice behind him. 'Lieutenant de Lancey, would you be good enough to come with me?'

It was Major McCaigue. Conrad introduced Anneliese and they followed McCaigue up to a small windowless office on the third floor that he must have borrowed.

'Sir Robert asked me to see you at short notice,' McCaigue said. 'He thought I would be best able to deal with what you had to say.'

With relief that someone in authority was willing to listen to him, Conrad explained everything that Anneliese had told him.

Major McCaigue listened carefully.

Forty-Five

An hour later Conrad and Anneliese emerged on to Whitehall.

'What now?' said Anneliese.

'I suppose we leave it to McCaigue.'

'Do you trust him?'

'I think so. But I'm not sure I trust those around him. The government. The "authorities".'

'What do you mean?'

'Van won't see me. The "powers that be" seem to think I'm a Russian spy. The War Office is trying to get me confined to barracks.'

'Major McCaigue seemed confident he could stop Alston,' said Anneliese. 'Captain Foley did a good job in Berlin.'

'That's true,' said Conrad. For a mild-mannered bureaucrat, Captain Foley had indeed been effective, springing Anneliese from a concentration camp and spiriting her and her family over to England, as well as hundreds, possibly thousands like her. 'But somehow I think McCaigue is up against more serious opposition.'

'Where are you going now?'

'The hotel in Bloomsbury. I won't stay at Kensington Square. I think you are right about Father; I don't trust myself with him. And I have to ring up Veronica.'

'Veronica?' Anneliese sounded disapproving.

'She wrote to me that Polly Copthorne had rustled up a man called Parsons with important information about her husband's death, and I should get in touch when I was next in London.'

'Can I come with you?'

'To see Veronica?'

'No,' said Anneliese, slipping her hand in his. 'Just to your hotel.'

'Yes,' said Conrad, grinning. 'I rather hoped you would.'

Mayfair, London

It was still light as Conrad walked up the small street in Mayfair where Veronica lived. Anneliese was unhappy that he was seeing her that evening, but Veronica had insisted on meeting the mysterious Mr Parsons with him. Anneliese had decided to head off to the Russian Tea Rooms to see if she could squeeze something more out of Constance. But she had at least agreed to see him at the Bloomsbury hotel later. Conrad suspected that she just wanted to be sure where he spent the night.

Which was ridiculous. After the afternoon he and Anneliese had spent together, Veronica wasn't a danger. Conrad was glad to be doing something rather than leaving everything to McCaigue. He wasn't sure what to make of what Anneliese had told him. Should he really ignore his father? Was there nothing he could do or should do? McCaigue had urged him to go back to his unit, but Conrad would find that very difficult.

Perhaps he would learn something from this man Parsons.

He was taken aback for a moment to see his own name, 'De Lancey', on one of the four bells by the front door of the building. He pushed it, and a few moments later Mrs de Lancey appeared, wearing a stunning green dress.

'You do look dashing in your uniform, Conrad,' she said.

Conrad was about to compliment his ex-wife on how she looked, but decided not to. 'Where are we meeting this fellow?'

'We're not seeing him until eleven. He said he wanted to wait until it was dark.'

'So what am I doing here now, Veronica?'

'I thought we needed a drink beforehand. We can't go to a rendezvous unfortified, can we, darling?'

'Do we really?'

'Don't look so disapproving, darling. I was clever finding this chap, wasn't I? You might show some appreciation.'

'Yes, you were,' Conrad said. 'Of course I can buy you a drink. Where do you suggest?'

They went to the Café de Paris near Leicester Square, which was crowded. Veronica said it was always crowded. They ordered cocktails; Conrad was disconcerted by Veronica's choice of a gin and It, which had now become Anneliese's drink in his mind. That was his fault for introducing his wife's favourite drink to his girlfriend.

Veronica seemed to sense Conrad's tension, and was friendly and well behaved. Conrad even found himself relaxing a little. He was careful not to discuss what Anneliese had told him about Alston and his father. Reluctantly, he danced with Veronica. Twice. He enjoyed it.

Then it was time to go. It was completely dark when they emerged on to Piccadilly.

'Where are we meeting him?' Conrad asked.

'Not far. A street near Shepherd Market.'

'That's an interesting choice,' said Conrad.

'Apparently Mr Parsons thinks that no one will notice people meeting each other around there.'

'That's certainly true,' said Conrad. Shepherd Market had been a haven for whores for centuries. And in wartime, it was bustling. Or perhaps rustling was a better word. Women stood around alone or in pairs, whispering to the servicemen who prowled the streets.

The corner Veronica was looking for was a few yards from Shepherd Market itself, and a little quieter. They stopped. It was exactly eleven o'clock. Veronica lit a cigarette.

'This is all rather interesting, isn't it?' Veronica said, watching a French girl discussing her skills with a fat middle-aged man.

'I don't know,' said Conrad.

'Aren't you tempted? Some of these girls look rather pretty.'

'They look cold and they look desperate,' said Conrad.

'If you want to slip away afterwards, I won't object,' said Veronica, a hint of amusement in her voice. 'I might even come along and watch.'

'I know what you are doing,' said Conrad.

'And what's that, darling? I would have thought bringing your wife along would make the whole thing more, I don't know, respectable?'

'Ex-wife,' muttered Conrad, trying to maintain his grumpiness. But it was oddly pleasurable being teased by Veronica.

Three men sauntered past, talking loudly. They had American accents, but were probably Canadians.

'Do you know what this Parsons looks like?'

'I told you I haven't a clue about him, apart from that you simply must meet him. You are sweet on this German girl, aren't you? Anneliese.'

'Yes,' said Conrad. 'Yes, I am.'

A man appeared at the top of the narrow street. A big man.

'That's a shame,' said Veronica, quietly.

Conrad glanced at her keenly. She looked away from him as if embarrassed.

The man was now having difficulty keeping on the pavement. Drunk. Very drunk. And easy game for the local traders.

Not Parsons.

Veronica's eyes widened. 'Conrad!' she yelled as she pushed him sharply off the pavement.

Conrad saw a blade moving rapidly towards his side. He went with Veronica's shove and twisted. The blade ripped his tunic.

Conrad took two steps back. In the gloom he could make out the drunk, holding a thin, pointed knife, legs apart, balanced perfectly. Not drunk. He was big and he was dangerous.

Veronica screamed. The man ignored her, and Conrad backed towards the wall, hands open, eyes on the blade.

The man feinted to the right and then plunged again towards Conrad's left side. Conrad was quick and skipped to his right, turned and somehow grabbed the man's wrist.

The man tripped Conrad, but Conrad didn't let go and they both fell on the street, the man on top. Conrad stared into his eyes, black in the darkness. His nose was broken, a boxer no doubt, or at least someone who had been in a few fights in his time. The man was pushing the knife downwards towards Conrad's neck. Conrad was strong, but the man was stronger. Conrad stared at the blade as the man pressed it down to his chin; below his chin.

Then the man let out a cry, and his face contorted in pain. The downward pressure reduced a little, so Conrad could resist it. The man was trying to concentrate on the knife and Conrad's throat but was finding it very difficult ignoring whatever was causing him such agony.

Conrad jerked suddenly to one side so that the knife struck the pavement, then he butted the man hard in the nose.

The man cried out and dropped the knife.

Conrad's fingers knocked it away.

He saw Veronica grab it.

Both men got to their feet. Veronica held the knife in front of her.

'Throw it to me!' shouted Conrad as the man charged Veronica.

She did as he had asked her and he caught the spinning knife by the handle. The man had pushed Veronica into the wall, and pulled back a fist to strike her, when Conrad plunged the blade into his back. He slumped to the ground.

With difficulty Conrad withdrew the blade and stabbed him again.

The man lay face down on the pavement. Still breathing, from what Conrad could see. Dark liquid oozed out from under his body on to the cobbles.

Conrad stood up straight, panting. 'Did you grab his balls?' he asked Veronica.

'Did you kill him?'

'Not quite, unfortunately,' said Conrad. Two men who had heard the scuffle were making their way cautiously towards them down the alley. 'Time to go. Let's split up: you run that way!'

'Shouldn't we wait for the police?' said Veronica. 'If you *have* killed him, it was self-defence.'

'No!' said Conrad, grabbing Veronica by the arm and propelling her up the street. 'We run. Now!'

Veronica hesitated and set off.

Once Conrad was sure she was moving, he slipped down an alleyway, brushing off a relatively sober corporal who tried to grab him. He emerged from the other end of the alleyway as he heard the first police whistle and slowed to a stagger, just another one of the many men looking for a little fun in the middle of a war.

Conrad took a long route back to Veronica's flat. He rang the bell, and her flatmate answered, a very thin blonde woman who introduced herself as Betty. She looked shocked.

Conrad walked up the four flights of stairs to find Veronica on the sofa of their tiny sitting room, still wearing her green dress.

'We don't have a drop to drink in the house,' she said.

'I could use a stiff one myself,' said Conrad. 'But you should stay here. Betty can look after you.'

'Hold me, Conrad.'

Conrad hesitated, but then sat down next to Veronica and held her. Her smell was familiar, yet she was shaking in a most unfamiliar way.

'What if you killed that man?' she said when they broke apart.

'I've killed a few men,' said Conrad. 'He was trying to kill me.'

'Why?'

'I don't know,' said Conrad. 'But I can guess. Are you sure that wasn't Parsons?'

'I don't know if it was bloody Parsons!' said Veronica. Then: 'Sorry. Sorry, Conrad. I'll ask Polly about him tomorrow.'

'Find out who he is, how well she knows him.'

'Yes. Yes, I'll do that.'

'Now I have to go.'

'Please stay, Conrad.'

'No. I have to go.'

Conrad smiled encouragingly at a still-stunned Betty, and left.

Anneliese was waiting for him back at the Bloomsbury hotel. Conrad wondered briefly how she had managed to get up to his room. Hotel-keepers really were lowering their standards in time of war, although she was still wearing her nurse's uniform, which might have helped.

'Where were you?' she said as soon as he entered his room. And then, when she saw his expression. 'What happened?'

Conrad told her about the attack. Anneliese had her own news from the Russian Tea Rooms. Tyler Kent and Anna Wolkoff had been arrested the previous morning. Constance hadn't been there; in fact none of the regulars were there. Anneliese herself had left quickly and returned to the hotel.

'I'm glad you waited for me,' said Conrad.

'I'm scared,' said Anneliese.

'Come here.' Conrad pulled her close to him and held her tight. He kissed her forehead and then her lips.

Forty-Six

Extract from Lieutenant Dieter von Hertenberg's Diary

22 May

Ordered to head north. Advanced on Boulogne. Heavy fighting.

Hampstead Garden Suburb, London, 22 May

Anneliese got up at five-thirty to get an early bus back to her home in Hampstead Garden Suburb. She was frightened for Conrad, and a little concerned for herself. She was worried about the war, about Alston's plan, and about what would happen to her own family if he succeeded. It was hard to imagine British anti-Semitism at the level of what was occurring in Germany. Yet in the 1920s Germany had been the most accommodating country in Europe for Jews. Things had changed there; they could change here.

But despite her worries, her fears, she felt *alive*. She could face this. Especially if she had Conrad she could face this.

It was a lovely morning. The birds were singing and a paper boy gave her a cheery greeting. She walked down the road to her little white cottage, thinking how similar this seemed to the tidy suburbs of Berlin. She passed an empty police car and two bicycles leaning against a hedge. The police in this country were just not as threatening as those in Germany, let alone the Gestapo. Despite what she had said to Conrad she couldn't imagine a British Gestapo.

She noticed a group of four policemen ahead of her walking down the pavement looking at the houses. Perhaps one of the neighbours had had a burglary.

They stopped outside her house. Went through the gap in the hedge where the iron gate used to be. Rapped on the door.

It was only then that Anneliese realized what was happening. She halted. One of the policemen glanced up the street and saw her.

She turned and ran. There was a shout as they followed.

But this wasn't Soho in the dark. This was an empty suburb in broad daylight. She darted to the left into a small wood, hoping to find somewhere to hide. But one of the policemen was young and very fast.

She reached the wood, but the trees were thinned and there were no bushes. She heard footsteps and panting closing in on her, and then hands on her shoulders knocking her to the ground.

She looked up to see a tall bobby several years younger than her getting to his feet. 'Madam, you are under arrest,' he said politely.

Bloomsbury, London

Conrad couldn't get back to sleep after Anneliese had left. The fact that it hadn't bothered him that he had stabbed his attacker twice the night before bothered him. The first thrust was understandable, unavoidable. The man was about to hit Veronica. But the second? With the second he had been trying to kill. Like it or not, he was a killer now. So much for all that pacifism. In 1940, if you turned the other cheek, your enemy would blast your head off from close range.

That's just the way it was.

Had the attacker survived? It was possible; Conrad had no way of knowing. But he thought it highly unlikely that the man would finger Conrad as the person who had stabbed him. Unless he was some kind of officially sanctioned killer.

Which also seemed unlikely. Far more probable was that the man had been working for Alston. Alston had killed Freddie

Copthorne and Millie. Why not Conrad? But had he had help? Help from 'the authorities', 'the powers that be', 'the high-ups'?

Who were these people? Right-wing aristocrats like Freddie Copthorne? Confused pacifists like his father? The army? The police? The secret service?

Van?

Van was an old school friend of Lord Oakford. From what Conrad knew of him, he was famous for his anti-appeasement, anti-German foreign policy. But could he have been got at in some way?

And then there was the secret service. Naturally, Conrad knew next to nothing about them. In November his father had let slip that the head of the SIS had died and they were looking for a successor. Who was he? It couldn't be McCaigue, could it?

Conrad had met four members of the SIS: Foley in Berlin, Payne Best and Stevens in Holland, and McCaigue in London. Foley was impressive. Payne Best and Stevens unimpressive. McCaigue seemed trustworthy, but could Conrad really be sure even of him?

And even if Alston had had no help, he was still dangerous. He could find himself another killer to go after Conrad. McCaigue had suggested Conrad return to his unit. Ironically, that would be the safest place to lie low. Conrad could leave it to McCaigue to wrap up Alston and his friends. But that was a tall order. Perhaps McCaigue could manage it, or perhaps the major himself would be the next victim: arrested, sidelined or even murdered. And if that happened, there would be no one to stop Alston.

Apart from Conrad. But what could he do? See his father for a start. Anneliese was right that he shouldn't try to confront him with his treachery. But if Conrad approached him with the right degree of innocence, he might discover when Lord Oakford was leaving for France. Maybe McCaigue had already arrested him? Dreadful thought though that was, it was the best outcome to hope for.

Then he should go to see McCaigue. Tell him what had happened the night before and see if there was anything more constructive Conrad could do to help. Perhaps he should see Polly

Copthorne himself, or telephone her, to find out more about the mysterious Parsons. And he should also drop in at the War Office to discuss armoured Bedford lorries, for Colonel Rydal's sake as much as his own.

Conrad arrived at his family's house in Kensington Square just before nine.

Williamson answered the door, with surprise and pleasure. 'We weren't expecting you, sir.'

'Leave is becoming more and more unpredictable, Williamson. Is Father in?'

'No, sir. He left for Paris this morning.'

'Did he really?' said Conrad. 'What is he doing there?'

'Government business of some kind, I believe. It all came up rather suddenly.'

'Do you happen to know where he is staying?'

'Presumably the Meurice, sir. If he gets a room. It's where we usually stay. He promised to let me know.'

So Lord Oakford had left his valet behind and Williamson had missed out on a trip to Paris. Given what the newspapers were saying about the situation in France, he probably didn't mind this time.

'Is my mother here?'

'No, her ladyship is at Chilton Coombe. Will you be staying?'

'I don't know, Williamson. But I'll come in for now.'

Conrad thought he had done a reasonable job of registering only mild surprise in front of Williamson, but he was troubled. His father was already on his way to fetch the Duke of Windsor.

And what was Conrad going to do about that?

He went out into the garden at the back of the house. It was looking lovely; the wisteria was just popping out, as was the climbing rose on the back wall.

His father had to be stopped. And Conrad couldn't trust anyone else to stop him.

If McCaigue could wrap up the plot in London, arresting Alston and whoever else was necessary, all well and good. Conrad

341

couldn't do much more about that. But he could stop his father. If he could get to Paris.

He went back into his father's study and telephoned Thomas Cook's. There were no seats on any commercial flights to Paris and the agent seemed to think he was a bit of a fool for thinking there might be. He would need official help, of the kind his father had no doubt had.

Who could get him a seat on an aeroplane? That day, preferably.

Van?

No.

McCaigue?

Possibly. Probably not. In fact McCaigue would be much more likely to forbid him from going to France.

Who then?

Conrad had an idea. He dialled a number in Suffolk, and asked to be put through to Colonel Rydal.

'Rydal.'

'Lieutenant de Lancey here.'

'Ah, Mr de Lancey. Are you having any success?'

'I'm making progress. But I need to get to France urgently. And I thought you might be able to help me.'

'How could I do that?'

'I don't know. Send me as an advance party. Liaison officer. Or something.'

'I will be in trouble enough for sending you to London as it is.'

'It's vital I get to Paris.'

'Mr de Lancey, you told me it was vital you get to London.'

'And it was!' Conrad realized he was going to have to tell Rydal the truth. Or at least most of the truth. 'Look, sir. An envoy has been sent to France to invite the Duke of Windsor to return to England and lead a new regime to make peace with Hitler. I know that envoy and I can stop him. But only if I fly to Paris today.'

'Good God,' said Colonel Rydal. 'You are not exaggerating, are you?'

'No, sir. These are desperate times.'

'You are damn right there.' There was silence for a few seconds. 'I might have an idea. Give me your number and I'll ring you back in half an hour.'

Conrad gave him the telephone number of the house in Kensington Square and waited, staring at the phone. As he sat there, his whole being focused on how to get to France. How to stop his father.

Half an hour passed. Thirty-five minutes. Then the phone rang.

'De Lancey,' Conrad answered.

'This is Rydal.' The name was familiar, the voice less so. 'I'm with the Air Ministry. I understand you have been speaking to my brother.'

'I have,' said Conrad.

'All right. Go straight to Hendon Aerodrome, taking only a light bag and your passport. When you get there ask for Squadron Leader Ebsworth and tell him who you are. He will put you on an aeroplane to Paris – there is a spare seat but it's leaving at eleven-thirty so you will have to be quick. On no account tell anyone at all why you are going. If they ask, just say you are not at liberty to answer. That usually works.'

'Thank you, sir.'

'When you get to Paris, you're on your own. And you will have to make your own way back.'

'I understand. Thank you so much, sir.'

'Thank my brother. He told me what you were doing, he had to, to get me to agree to help you.'

'Of course.'

'Good luck, de Lancey.'

It was just before ten. Conrad didn't have much time to get to Hendon. No time to tell McCaigue, who would probably only try to stop him anyway, and certainly no time to go to the War Office. He would tell Williamson he was going back to his battalion. But he dialled Mrs Cherry's telephone in Hampstead Garden Suburb.

The English voice at the other end was colder than usual.

The German voice that replaced it a minute later was distraught. Anneliese's mother.

'Ach, Conrad,' she said. 'The police came and arrested Anneliese this morning. We don't know why.'

Conrad felt cold. This was all too familiar. London was becoming Berlin.

There was nothing he could do for Anneliese, certainly not in the few minutes he had before he went to Hendon Aerodrome. This news just made it more important that he go to Paris. He gave Frau Rosen Major McCaigue's telephone number, and told her to make sure Anneliese asked to speak to him. McCaigue should be able to get her out; Conrad was glad that he had introduced her to the intelligence officer the day before. With any luck she might not even spend one night behind bars.

At first Conrad assumed he knew why Anneliese had been arrested – because of her association with the Russian Tea Rooms. But then he wondered whether it had anything to do with the attempt on his own life the night before. Perhaps Alston and Constance had discovered that she was on to them.

Either way, the best thing Conrad could do was foil Alston. He ran upstairs, changed into a suit, packed a couple of shirts into a small bag and set out for the High Street in the hope of finding a taxi.

Forty-Seven

Hendon Aerodrome, Middlesex

Squadron Leader Ebsworth watched the de Havilland Flamingo transport plane bearing its collection of VIPs and hangers-on heave itself off the runway at RAF Hendon into the skies, bound for Le Bourget. This was the second flight to Paris so far that morning. There was a lot of toing and froing between Hendon and France these days. The Prime Minister himself was due to return from Paris that afternoon after a two-day trip to see his French opposite number.

The panic was palpable. It was in the faces of the politicians and the staff officers. It was in the papers carried in the briefcases that they clutched so tightly. At times they seemed to Ebsworth like hens in a chicken run running back and forth with nowhere to hide from the fox outside, who was rapidly digging his hole underneath the wire.

'Message from the ministry, sir.'

'Thank you, corporal.' Ebsworth took the piece of paper and examined it. It was from Rydal at the Air Ministry: Please tell Lieutenant de Lancey to cancel his mission and travel to Southampton docks immediately to join up with his unit.

Too late. Ebsworth scribbled out a quick reply informing Rydal de Lancey was already in the air. He wondered briefly what the lieutenant's mission was, and why he was in mufti, not uniform. It was a secret of course, but then wasn't everyone's business these days?

Just another chicken.

Alston strolled through the park, trying to maintain his nonchalance. He had telephoned Constance earlier that morning; she hadn't heard back from Joe Sullivan, but she was sure that Sullivan would have successfully dealt with de Lancey.

Arthur Oakford was on his way to France. He had dined with his old friend Edward Halifax the evening before, and Halifax had intimated that he was ready to press Churchill on making overtures to Hitler for peace, probably via the Italians. Oakford was confident the issue would split the Cabinet, leaving it vulnerable to the shove which the Duke of Windsor's arrival in the country would provide.

Not long now.

But long enough for the British Expeditionary Force in France to be destroyed.

Alston was approaching the rose garden and once again saw the Swedish banker. He realized that that was probably a mistake. For them to bump into each other several times in the same park was possible, for it to be in the same place in the same park was too much of a coincidence.

They spent the obligatory minute smiling, shaking hands and moving off together.

'I have an important message for Joachim,' Alston began.

It only took three minutes for Alston to convey what he wanted to convey, and then, after agreeing a different spot to meet in the park next time, the two men split up.

Alston walked briskly south to Pall Mall and his club, where Major McCaigue was waiting for him. Armed with a sherry each, they found a corner of the library.

'Your man was Joe Sullivan, wasn't he?' said McCaigue.

Alston nodded imperceptibly.

'Sullivan was found stabbed in Mayfair last night. He died before they could get him to hospital.'

'That's unfortunate,' said Alston. Damned unfortunate! 'Any news of de Lancey?'

'Yes. We have been following him. He is currently on his way to Paris on a flight from Hendon.'

'How the devil did he manage that?'

'Special orders from the Air Ministry. There can only be one reason why he has gone to Paris.'

'To catch up with his father and try to stop him,' said Alston. 'Is there anything you can do about it?'

'I can't do anything obvious,' said McCaigue. 'But I can get someone on to him.'

'Good. Do that. I wish Sullivan had done what he was paid to do. De Lancey should be dead.'

'Quite so,' said McCaigue.

Three hours later, Alston poured Constance a cup of tea at his flat. She was uncharacteristically quiet; Sullivan's death had shaken her.

'De Lancey has to be stopped,' said Constance. 'Before he gets to his father.'

'I know,' said Alston.

'Can't your friend in the secret service do something?'

'He says he can keep an eye on him, but if he were to use his contacts to get de Lancey killed it would raise questions. At the moment his colleagues think de Lancey is a Russian spy and they aren't listening to him. If they become suspicious of McCaigue it might blow the whole plan.'

On balance, Alston believed McCaigue's caution was justified. It had been useful to have a man on the inside in the SIS and his support had been valuable. Pinning Millie de Lancey's death on the German spy Hertenberg. Calling the police off their investigation into Freddie's street accident. Keeping de Lancey out of the way. And numerous useful titbits of information that had come the SIS's way and that McCaigue had passed on to Alston.

Alston owed McCaigue. When he became a leading member of a sensible pro-German government he would be happy to make good that debt.

But he couldn't make McCaigue kill de Lancey.

347

'Do you know anyone else who would do it?' he asked Constance. 'Any other ex-Nordic League thugs?'

'Not really,' said Constance. 'Joe was always the best bet. I don't know how we can get hold of someone, tell them to drop everything and get over to Paris immediately. You must have contacts in Paris?'

'Yes. Bankers. Businessmen. The odd politician. No one who could organize what we want done.' Except Charles Bedaux; that was just the kind of thing he might well be able to deal with. But Alston knew Bedaux had left Paris on a mission for the French government in Spain and North Africa, and was now in Madrid. 'It would take a while to set up. A few days at least. And we don't have a few days.'

Alston was finding the tension difficult to control. On the one hand success seemed so close. On the other, Conrad de Lancey seemed about to ruin everything. At least he was able to share his frustration with Constance, to let his habitual mask of impassive confidence slip for a few moments.

They sat in silence, Constance sipping her tea with a look of intense determination. 'I'll do it,' she said. 'Get me to France and I'll stop de Lancey.'

Madrid

Theo and Otto Langebrück waited in the opulent lobby of the Ritz Madrid. Langebrück had turned out to be a much more congenial travel companion than Theo had imagined. He was a Rhinelander, about Theo's age, widely read, and a Francophile – much more intelligent than his boss, Ribbentrop. This last was a good and a bad thing. Mostly a bad thing.

Theo had never been to Spain before. Like Holland until very recently, Spain was a neutral country, but there the similarities ended. Holland had enjoyed over a century of peace and prosperity. Spain, and Madrid in particular, had been torn apart by years of civil war. Half-destroyed buildings were everywhere, and the people still had a haunted look about them, even in the spring sunshine. Theo wondered whether Berlin would ever look like that; he couldn't imagine it would.

Conrad had been involved in fighting around Madrid, Theo knew, although he had never got to grips with the intricacies of the civil war and who had fought whom where. The whole city was humbling; a reminder of what war, real war not the *Sitzkrieg*, could do.

'Theo! How good to see you!' Theo stood up to greet the familiar, ebullient person of Charles Bedaux. He introduced Langebrück. 'Can we find somewhere more discreet to talk?' Bedaux asked.

'I know a place,' said Theo, who led Bedaux to a quiet café he had reconnoitred earlier, over the Paseo del Prado in a side street a hundred metres from the hotel. It was a while since he had seen the Franco-American, who had been spending time in Spain securing steel supplies for French armaments factories, and in Morocco finding coal for the Spanish steel mills.

The three men sat in a rear corner of the café and ordered wine. 'I was pleased to see that your general staff took notice of my friend's observations on the state of the French lines,' said Bedaux.

Theo smiled. 'They did. With extraordinary results.'

'It looks as if my time here will prove to be a waste,' said Bedaux.

'I hope so,' said Theo. 'But I am sure that if France is defeated your talents will still be of use to my country.'

'As you know, I am always willing to make things work better,' said Bedaux. 'It's what I do.'

'After France comes England,' said Langebrück. 'And that is what Hertenberg and I have come to speak to you about.' Since Langebrück had never met Bedaux, Theo's role was to introduce him. And to listen to what was said and report back to Canaris.

'Very good,' said Bedaux, lighting a cigar.

'You know my boss, Herr von Ribbentrop, I believe?'

'Very well.'

'I understand that you have discussed the Duke of Windsor with him before?'

'I have indeed. In fact I met with him and Herr Hitler to discuss the duke in November in Berlin.'

'Well, following our successes in France, both the Führer and Herr Ribbentrop think the time is right for a change in the government in Britain. They know that there is a significant element of the British people, especially those in the higher reaches of society, who believe that the time has come for peace. Further, they believe that the Duke of Windsor would provide these people with the leadership they need to give their cause legitimacy. If he were king again, Germany could work with Britain as an ally rather than an enemy.'

'That was the point I made to Herr Hitler in November,' said Bedaux.

'What we are not sure of, is how the duke himself would react to such a suggestion. You know him well. What's your opinion?'

Bedaux puffed at his cigar. 'That's a good question. I have discussed it with him in the past, indirectly. The duke is well disposed towards Germany and Herr Hitler, but he loves his country and would not dream of doing anything that seemed to be betraying it. Which means that the impetus to do what you are suggesting must come from the British and not from Germany.'

'Could you persuade him?' asked Langebrück.

'I could suggest it, but no more than that,' said Bedaux. 'Do you know Sir Henry Alston? He's a British politician.'

'Herr Ribbentrop knows him well,' said Langebrück. 'We have been communicating with him through intermediaries.'

'I believe that Sir Henry's intentions are that the duke should be invited to return to England.'

'Like William of Orange in the seventeenth century?' said Theo. 'Invited by Parliament to become king?'

'Something like that,' said Bedaux. 'I heard from Alston yesterday that they are sending an important figure in the House of Lords to Paris to talk to him.'

'Do you know who that is?' said Theo.

'Lord Oakford. A former Cabinet minister.'

Theo couldn't believe what he was hearing. Conrad's father? He knew the old soldier was a pacifist, but surely he couldn't have thrown his lot in with Alston.

'You look surprised, Theo,' said Bedaux. 'Do you know Lord Oakford?'

'Yes. I think I met him several years ago,' said Theo, doing his best to recover his composure. Bedaux was sharp; he noticed everything.

'I'm glad to hear that,' said Langebrück to Bedaux. 'I understand what you say about the invitation coming from the English. But is there anything we can do to make his decision easier? Money perhaps? Anything else he wants that we can promise him?'

Bedaux considered a moment, savouring his cigar. 'The duke is always concerned about money,' he said. 'His wife has expensive tastes, and the duke no longer has a kingdom to rely on.'

Langebrück nodded. 'Anything else?'

'He is always worried about Wallis. Her safety. Her material comfort. And particularly her status. For example, I believe that what most upsets him about his treatment by his brother is King George's refusal to allow Wallis to be called Her Royal Highness.' Bedaux grinned. 'As a good American citizen, I cannot understand it, but I never underestimate it.' He nodded. 'Yes. Money and Wallis. Those are the keys to the duke.'

Forty-Eight

Paris

Paris was oddly quiet, as though it were an early Sunday morning rather than a Wednesday afternoon. There were few cars in the streets, and of those many were stuffed full of people and their worldly goods, refugees from the north. Several bore the red-and-white number plates of Belgium. People walked fast, faces taut, hurrying from place to place, making arrangements, gathering possessions, preparing to flee. The sun was shining, but in the cafés few if any of the patrons were sitting back watching the world go by, as was their habit. They leaned forward over their cups of coffee, puffed at cigarettes, frowned, conversed earnestly. A good number of the city's population had left already, and the rest were thinking about it.

But when Conrad walked through the doors of the Hôtel Meurice on the rue de Rivoli, it was like entering another world of hushed, unhurried calm. Conrad had stayed there a couple of times with his parents when he was growing up. It was grand, in a restrained way, without the opulence or the *joie de vivre* of the Ritz.

Conrad strode up to the reception desk. 'Good afternoon,' he said in English. 'I'd like to see Lord Oakford, please.' They liked to speak to their English guests in their own language at the Meurice.

'I am afraid that Lord Oakford left the hotel an hour or so ago, sir. Is he expecting you?'

'No, he isn't. But I heard he was in Paris and I thought I would drop by. Will he be here for dinner, do you know?'

'And who are you, may I ask?'

'I'm his nephew,' said Conrad. This seemed less likely to scare his father than admitting that he was his son. Puzzle him, perhaps. Lord Oakford had two nephews: Stefan in Hamburg currently serving in the Wehrmacht, and Tom who was seventeen and living in Shropshire.

'Ah, I see.' The clerk checked a book. 'No, he doesn't have a reservation for dinner here this evening, but he is staying with us tonight. Shall I tell him you were looking for him?'

'No, don't do that,' said Conrad with a smile. 'I'd like to surprise him. I'll try him later.'

It sounded as if Lord Oakford had gone straight to the Meurice, taken a room and headed out again. Presumably to see the duke. But where?

If the duke worked normal hours, then he would be at the British Mission at French general headquarters at Vincennes, a few miles to the east of Paris. Or he could be at home. It seemed unlikely that Oakford would try to approach the duke at the British Mission – much too public. Better to see him at home. Conrad had taken a note of the address when he was in Paris the previous November: 24 boulevard Suchet, out by the bois de Boulogne.

He decided to head out there. If he was lucky, he would find his father waiting for the duke. If he was unlucky he would be too late and Lord Oakford would already have spoken to him. No time to lose then.

The Métro was working well, and boulevard Suchet turned out to be a long road stretching along the edge of the bois de Boulogne from the Porte d'Auteuil Métro station. It was nearly a mile to number 24. Conrad strolled past, checking for signs of his father lurking in a vehicle or on the street, but he couldn't see any. The house itself looked quiet.

Conrad hesitated. Should he wait for his father to show up? He might get a chance to intercept him before he reached the front door. But what if the duke wasn't at home? Or was out for the whole day and evening? What if his father met him somewhere in the middle of town? Conrad would have wasted valuable time.

Somehow he needed to find out the duke's movements.

So he climbed the steps to the imposing front door and rang the bell.

A very tall, very English-looking butler answered the door.

'I wish to speak to my uncle, Lord Oakford,' said Conrad in English.

'Lord Oakford is not here, sir,' said butler. 'He called this morning to see His Royal Highness, but I informed him that His Royal Highness is not in residence at the moment, and so he left.'

'Pity,' said Conrad. 'Where is the duke, might I enquire?'

The butler raised his eyebrows. 'I am not at liberty to say, sir.'

The man did not look bribable, but Conrad was desperate. He reached into his pocket for his wallet.

The butler glared down his nose at Conrad, turned and shut the door in his face, leaving Conrad on the street feeling like a heel.

Where to now?

It was possible that the butler would have been more forthcoming to Lord Oakford, a peer of the realm and a former Cabinet minister. In which case, his father would know where the duke was, and would be heading there now. So Conrad had to find out the whereabouts of the duke, and quickly.

Fruity Metcalfe! Of course there was a good chance he might be with his master, but there was also a chance he might not, and it was the only chance Conrad had. So he retraced his steps to the Métro and headed for the Ritz.

It was the cocktail hour by the time Conrad got there, and the bar was crowded. Conrad was relieved to see Fruity propping up the bar, a drink in front of him. Conrad squeezed next to him, and then pretended to recognize the Irishman. 'Major Metcalfe? De Lancey. We met here in November.'

Fruity frowned, and then smiled broadly. 'Oh, I remember you! What are you doing back in Paris? Or can't you say?'

Conrad remembered how his evasion last time had been misread as involvement in sensitive work of some kind, and was pleased that Fruity had remembered that too. He didn't answer, but smiled vaguely. 'Can I get you a drink?'

'By all means,' said Fruity.

Conrad ordered them both whiskies. 'How are you?'

'Bloody furious,' said Fruity.

'Oh really? Why?'

Fruity stared into his glass and shook his head in an attempt at discretion.

'Are you still working for the Duke of Windsor?' Conrad prompted.

'I was yesterday. I really couldn't tell you whether I am today.'

Conrad winced sympathetically. 'Did you get the heave-ho?'

Fruity hesitated, but he was desperate to talk. 'Worse than that. The man has cut and run.'

'What do you mean?'

'I dropped him off at his house last night. Rang him this morning for instructions and the butler said he had left first thing! Taken both cars and headed down to Biarritz to be with Wallis! He never told me. He must have had it all planned last night, but not a dickie bird.'

'Why wouldn't he tell you?'

'I don't know,' said Fruity. 'Perhaps he felt guilty about not taking me. Or perhaps he was worried about what I might say. He might be a royal bloody highness, but he's also a serving officer, and he has just left his post. It's cowardice, that's what it is! Bloody cowardice.'

Fruity took a gulp of his whisky. 'Sorry, I shouldn't be saying this, but he really has dropped me in it. How am I supposed to get out of here? The Germans will be looking in any moment now.'

'That is a bit awkward,' Conrad said.

'Awkward! It's bloody disastrous.'

'Do you really think the Germans will take Paris?'

'Bound too. At least the French have replaced that fool Gamelin with Weygand, but it's far too late now. I could have told them what would happen. In fact we did tell them, HRH and me.'

'What do you mean?'

'We've spent the last few months liaising with the French. We saw their pitiful attempts to defend the Meuse. Reserve divisions with no training and badly sited defences. We pointed out the weaknesses; I helped HRH write the report.'

'Will you take the train down to Biarritz to join him?' Conrad asked.

'You haven't been here very long, have you? Not a hope in hell of getting a seat on any train heading south. You need a car. And no chance of getting one of those, either. None for hire. You might be able to buy one, but it would cost a fortune.' He shook his head. 'No. I'm on my own. I will have to work out my own way back to Blighty.'

'Best of luck,' said Conrad. 'I say, you haven't seen my father around have you. Lord Oakford?'

Fruity shook his head. 'Sorry, old chap. Another one?' Fruity pointed to Conrad's drink, now almost empty.

'No thanks,' said Conrad. 'I must be off.' He hesitated. 'The duke didn't happen to mention any of what you saw at the Meuse to Charles Bedaux, did he? I remember he was having dinner with Bedaux here in November.'

'Probably, in passing,' Fruity said. He frowned. 'I say, you don't think Bedaux has been talking to the Germans, do you? He is a mysterious cove. And he has been to Germany a couple of times.'

'And to Holland,' said Conrad.

'Good Lord,' said Fruity. He was looking troubled. 'How do you know about Bedaux?'

'Must dash,' said Conrad, keen to avoid that particular question.

He extricated himself from Fruity and emerged into the place Vendôme, from where he walked swiftly back to the rue de Rivoli and the Hôtel Meurice. There he discovered that his father, or 'uncle' as Conrad referred to him, had just checked out of his room, without staying the night. He was with Hyram Leavold, an American banker whom Conrad knew was a friend of his father, and a young woman whom the hotel clerk did not recognize.

They had loaded Lord Oakford's luggage into an American car, a Packard. Lord Oakford and the young woman had driven off, leaving the American banker to hail a taxi.

Conrad left the hotel and stopped at a nearby café for a beer and to gather his thoughts. Which was difficult, since at the next table an exquisitely dressed young woman of about twenty was arguing with an older man. It was unclear whether the man was her lover or her father, but whoever he was, he was intending to leave Paris without her, and she was not happy. Probably a lover, Conrad decided, who was saving the passenger seat in his car for his wife. The woman stormed off; the man caught Conrad's eye and shrugged.

Lord Oakford had stayed one step ahead of Conrad. He had discovered that the duke had left for Biarritz and then found himself an American with a car who was willing to lend it to him.

Biarritz was a long way away, close to the Spanish border in the south-west corner of France. It would take the duke, and Oakford, a couple of days to get there. More if the roads were jammed. It was unlikely that Oakford would have discovered where the duke was spending the night en route, in which case he would probably drive straight to Biarritz and approach the duke there.

So Conrad had to get to Biarritz. Fruity had been adamant that trains were not an option, and neither was hiring a car. Conrad didn't have enough money to buy one. He needed to borrow one. And who the hell would lend him one in current circumstances, with the Germans poised to enter Paris any day?

Conrad needed his own generous American. Or a woman married to a generous American. His sister-in-law, for example.

Forty-Nine

Holloway Prison, London

Anneliese sat in her cell deep in the heart of Holloway Prison and waited. Waited for British justice to take its course.

It had taken an immense effort of will, but she was calm, and she was determined to stay calm.

She had been all right at first, in the police car with the British bobbies whom she admired so much. They weren't friendly, far from it, but they were polite and they hadn't hit her.

It wasn't far to Holloway Prison, but once the police car had turned off the sunny, civilized English street and stopped in front of the prison's forbidding battlements, something snapped. She started to scream and to yell in German, and she couldn't stop. All rational thought was overwhelmed in a flood of terror and hopelessness. Holloway wasn't exactly like those other places she had been, Moringen or Sachsenhausen or Lichtenburg, but it was an old evil prison, built like a medieval castle, with warders who looked at her with contempt. A German spy.

At the entrance, two large stone dragons perched on top of stone plinths, fangs bared. One of them clutched a great key in its long talons. It terrified her.

They threw her into a holding cell and she lay there sobbing for perhaps half an hour. But somehow, with a great effort of will, she pulled herself together. She had done nothing wrong. They had no doubt arrested her because of her presence at the Russian Tea Rooms. She could explain all that. She would ask to see Major McCaigue; he would release her and she would be home for supper.

Then she was processed: fingerprinted, strip-searched, weighed, given a medical examination and a delousing bath and placed in a proper cell. It was a small room with a table, chair, narrow bed and one fragmented window a foot above her head. The walls were whitewashed and the floors stone. The cell was filthy, the sheets stained and grey with grime, but they gave her cocoa in a mug without a handle embossed with the letters 'GR' and a crown. They hadn't given her cocoa at Sachsenhausen.

She could survive this.

She was calm at her initial interview with two detectives. She had indeed been arrested for her attendance at the Tea Rooms and her friendship with members of the Right Club. It turned out Joan Miller, the model, was working for the authorities. Anneliese was impressed: Joan had been convincing. Anneliese calmly stated that she too had been trying to uncover subversive activities and that Major McCaigue of the secret service would back her up. The detectives didn't seem to believe her, but they did write it all down. And took her back to her cell.

There was a jangling of keys outside, the metal door opened and a warder appeared. 'Rosen? Follow me.'

Anneliese followed the warder along corridors lined with cell doors, down two flights of stairs and into the interview room. Waiting for her were the two detectives and a large man with a bald head and florid complexion. Major McCaigue.

Anneliese felt giddy with relief and smiled at the major. He nodded and indicated the chair. The warder stood behind Anneliese.

'Thank you for coming,' Anneliese said.

Major McCaigue ignored her. 'Miss Rosen, I've come to urge you to cooperate with the police in this investigation.' His voice, which had seemed rich and friendly when he had spoken to Conrad and her in the Foreign Office, was now grave, with a hint of menace.

'Of course,' said Anneliese, struggling to control a surge of panic. This wasn't going as she had expected.

'What we want to know is whether you are working for the Russians or the Germans.'

Anneliese frowned. 'Neither. I'm working for you.' She glanced at the older detective, but there was no reassurance there. 'I told you everything I had discovered at the Tea Rooms. About Henry Alston and Lord Oakford and the Duke of Windsor. You were going to investigate it.'

'And I have,' said McCaigue. 'And there is not a shred of truth to any of it, as you well know.'

'Of course it's true!' said Anneliese. 'And you must stop it.'

'We have suspected for a long time that your boyfriend Lieutenant de Lancey is a Soviet spy. He has been trying to undermine the morale of the British people by denigrating the royal family. And you have been helping him.'

Anneliese listened, shocked.

'My colleagues here will ask you about de Lancey. Whom he works for, what his plans are, what else he intends to do, whether you had help from the Right Club. And you will answer.'

'I will answer any questions you ask me truthfully,' Anneliese said, glancing at the detectives. Keep calm. Don't shout at him. 'And you are mistaken about Conrad. I am sure that the plot he has uncovered – we have uncovered – is a real one. Sir Henry Alston and his friends want to replace the current government with one that will make peace with Germany. More than that, become Germany's ally.'

'You have been arrested under Defence Regulation 18B,' McCaigue said. 'This allows for the internment without trial of persons who are members of organizations under foreign control or who sympathize with the system of government of enemy powers. That means you will be incarcerated for the duration of the war. That's the best you can hope for. But if we find evidence that you have been spying, then you will be tried for espionage, found guilty and hanged.'

McCaigue leaned forward. 'Luckily for you, the choice as to which will apply is yours. Cooperate and you go to jail. Refuse to tell us everything you know and you go to the gallows.'

Anneliese held McCaigue's stare. That 'Regulation 18B' sounded a lot like the 'Protective Custody' dodge that the Gestapo had employed to lock her and her father up in a concentration camp and throw away the key. Cold fingers of panic reached out towards her, clutching at her and threatening to pull her into a deep dark abyss of hopelessness and despair. For a moment she felt she couldn't go through all this again.

She could. She would. She would do everything she could to persuade the detectives that McCaigue was wrong about Conrad, that there was indeed a plot to end the war involving Alston and others. If she failed, then she would hang, and so be it.

'I will tell you everything I know,' she said. 'You need not worry about that.'

'Good,' said McCaigue. 'I'll leave you to it.'

The detectives followed him out of the door, promising to return soon to continue the interview.

Anneliese watched them go. She wondered what had happened to Conrad. Could he somehow throw off McCaigue's suspicion and get her freed? Or had they arrested him too? Not for the first time, she felt alone and afraid. But she had survived before; she would survive again.

Paris

It only took Conrad twenty minutes to walk to the Haldemans' apartment in the eighth arrondissement. Isobel was having supper with her husband.

'Conrad? It's lovely to see you but we weren't expecting you.'

'No, I'm sure you weren't. I'm dreadfully sorry for barging in like this.'

Isobel rose to the occasion immediately. 'Have you eaten? Do join us. Marie was just leaving, but I'm sure she can rustle up something before she goes. An omelette perhaps?'

'That would be wonderful,' said Conrad. 'Thank you.'

'You remember Conrad de Lancey, Marsh? Veronica's husband.' She smiled at Conrad. '*Former* husband. The one that got away. Veronica is furious.'

Conrad was impressed by Isobel's ability to make him feel at home so quickly. Marshall Haldeman less so. The American was in his late thirties, with an oversized square jaw. A catch himself, as Veronica had admitted to Conrad in better times.

'Take a seat, de Lancey,' he said as Isobel darted into the kitchen. 'What brings you to Paris? I thought Isobel said you were in the army.'

'I'm on leave,' said Conrad.

'Huh,' said Marshall with the clear implication that he didn't believe a word of it.

'That's rot, Conrad, and you know it,' said Isobel, returning from the kitchen.

'I admit it's a special kind of leave,' said Conrad. He knew he would have to tell Isobel everything, and hope firstly that she would believe him, secondly that she would want to help him and thirdly that she would be able to persuade her husband. He didn't look a pushover, but Conrad well knew it was foolish to underestimate a Blakeborough girl's ability to push men.

'I'm after my father. I have to get hold of him before he catches up with the Duke of Windsor.'

'But the duke is in Paris,' said Isobel. 'We saw him only last week. He had dropped Wallis off in Biarritz and returned to duty.'

'Not anymore, he isn't,' said Conrad. 'He left for Biarritz again first thing this morning. My father arrived from London today to look for him, and I am looking for my father.'

'What's all the urgency about?' asked Haldeman, who did at least look interested, if sceptical.

Conrad told them. About Henry Alston and Lord Oakford's plans to topple Churchill and replace him with a government that would make peace with Germany. His hosts listened closely. As he spoke, Conrad was aware that Haldeman was a neutral, and an influential neutral at that, and that Conrad had no idea of his views on the war.

'I see,' said Isobel when Conrad had finished. 'So what do you want from us?'

'He wants our car,' said Haldeman. He put down his fork and looked straight at Conrad. 'Don't you?'

The maid brought in Conrad's omelette. 'That's right,' said Conrad. 'I'll bring it back when I have found my father.'

'Unless this is a German city by then,' said Haldeman.

'Then I'll find you wherever you are,' said Conrad. As he did so, he realized that without their car, they wouldn't be going anywhere.

'We are planning to stay on in Paris,' said Isobel. 'America is neutral, and Marshall's business is here.'

Conrad was tempted to point out that they wouldn't need their car in that case, but decided not to. His plan was not going to work.

'I see,' he said. 'Can you spare it?' He had to try.

'I'm sorry, de Lancey. The answer has to be no,' said Haldeman.

Isobel didn't look as if she was going to argue with her husband. 'But you are welcome to stay here tonight if you wish.'

'I understand,' said Conrad. 'And thank you for your offer. But I think I should continue my search elsewhere. You don't happen to know anyone else who might be willing to part with a car? Or who is leaving anyway and has room for an extra body?'

'No,' said Haldeman simply.

The American wasn't being unfriendly, just straight. The chances of Conrad getting hold of transportation were nil.

The bell rang. The maid had just left and so Isobel answered it. From the hallway, Conrad heard the familiar shriek of his ex-wife. 'Darling!'

'You'll never guess who's here,' said Isobel, leading Veronica into the dining room. 'It's your husband. What a surprise.' The irony was heavy.

'Oh, how lovely!' said Veronica. 'I knew Conrad was in Paris, but it's dreadfully lucky to find him here.'

'Hello, Veronica,' said Conrad coldly.

'Here comes trouble,' said Marshall in a gruff voice, but he couldn't repress a smile. Veronica had got to him.

'Veronica, what are you doing here?' asked Conrad.

'Don't sound so cross, darling. I've come here to help.'

'How did you know I was in Paris?'

'Williamson told me.'

'But I didn't tell Williamson.'

'You don't have to tell servants things for them to know them, Conrad. Williamson sees things. He hears things.'

'And then he tells you?'

Veronica's smile had a hint of triumph.

'I was just leaving,' said Conrad.

'Oh, don't go,' said Veronica.

'He came to borrow our car,' said Haldeman.

'Aren't you going to lend it to him?' said Veronica.

'No,' said Isobel. 'We need it. There's a good chance that this city will be German soon.'

'Why does he want it?'

'He says he's got to catch up with his father before he sees the Duke of Windsor in Biarritz,' said Haldeman. Conrad was glad that he had at least been paying attention.

'Well, then you definitely must let him have it,' said Veronica.

'It all sounds a bit fishy to me,' said Haldeman.

'Of course it's fishy,' said Veronica. 'The whole thing stinks. Poor Freddie Copthorne was run down by some horrible MP. You've met Freddie, haven't you, Isobel? Then someone tried to murder Conrad last night. There is definitely something fishy going on and Conrad is the man to sort it out!'

'I think they thought I was the fishy one,' said Conrad, impressed with Veronica's loyalty.

'He did come asking some rum questions about the Duke of Windsor last time he was here in November,' said Isobel. 'You remember I told you.'

'He claims that his father is planning to get the duke to return to England and persuade the British to sue for peace,' said Haldeman.

'Well, then you must definitely help Conrad stop him!' said Veronica. 'Look. Conrad might be a stubborn brute, but he's definitely not fishy. This is your chance to help the war effort, Bel. Do something that really will make a difference.'

Isobel frowned at her sister. But she was listening.

'Look. I'll go with him. And I'll make sure I bring the car back to Paris afterwards. I'm a professional driver now. And Alec taught me some racing-driver tips if we need to go fast.'

'What if the city is German by the time you get back?'

'We will only be gone for a few days. And I'll sneak back in somehow. I promise. On Magic's grave.'

Isobel smiled. 'Magic doesn't have a grave. In fact I dread to think where Magic ended up.'

'Who is Magic?' asked Marshall.

'Magic was Veronica's first pony,' said Isobel. 'He lived to be twenty-six.'

'There you are then!' said Veronica, although it wasn't clear to any of them what her pony's longevity had to do with Conrad's need for a car.

'What do you think, Marsh?' said Isobel.

Conrad was stunned. It looked as if he might, he just might, get his hands on their car.

Marshall was smiling. 'I'm impressed by your powers of persuasion, Veronica, but the answer is still no.'

'You love peace, liberty and democracy, don't you, Marshall?' said Veronica. 'You have to, a nice American like you.'

'I guess I do,' said Marshall, still smiling.

'Well, when the beastly Germans have been goose-stepping around the Paris streets for a year or so, and you are doing your neutral business here, you will like looking back to today and thinking: I did my bit for peace, liberty and democracy. I know you, Marshall. You will like that, I promise.'

Conrad could see that Veronica had got to him. So could Isobel. And so could Marshall himself.

'OK,' he said, shaking his head but smiling at the same time. 'But you make sure you bring it back here by the end of next week.'

'Hurrah!' said Veronica and turned to Conrad triumphantly.

'Thank you, Haldeman,' said Conrad.

'When do we leave? Right away?'

'I don't know,' said Conrad. 'I do want to catch my father up, but the roads will be tricky in the dark. Even with a professional driver in the car.' He realized that he was now committed to a long drive across France with his ex-wife, but there was nothing he could do about that, and she had done a good job.

'If I were you I would get some sleep now and leave early tomorrow morning,' said Marshall. 'You'll make better progress that way.'

'But first can someone get me a drink?' said Veronica. 'I do find aeroplanes too thirst-making.'

Fifty

Extract from Lieutenant Dieter von Hertenberg's Diary

23 May

Still fighting in Boulogne. Ironically, we were held up by the medieval walls of the city. We needed an 88-mm anti-aircraft gun to breach them near the cathedral, but we broke through eventually. The British are putting up stiff resistance. Calais surrounded.

Paris, 23 May

Veronica and Conrad left at five the next morning in the Haldemans' smart red Cadillac, loaded with food, wine and spare cans of petrol. The Paris streets were quiet, as were the suburbs, but once they got outside the city and on to the main Paris–Chartres road, they ran into a column of slow-moving traffic, comprising every kind of motor vehicle: tiny Simcas piled high with possessions, roadsters, family saloons, bakers' vans, ice-cream trucks, lorries of all shapes and sizes. These were the Parisians, but interspersed with them were the farmers and peasants fleeing from the north, with their horse-drawn wagons bearing mattresses, birdcages, grandmothers and small children, and their cows ambling along beside them.

Many of the Parisians hooted and waved at the fleeing peasants to let them by. Veronica, who had insisted on driving, copied their technique, and added her own invective in appalling schoolgirl French – although she had never actually been to school, being taught at home by a German governess.

Every now and then a French aeroplane would fly overhead causing many of the refugees to dive for the ditches at the side of the road. This gave Veronica a chance to force her way ahead in the temporarily empty road.

Conrad didn't like the attitude of the fleeing Parisians in their cars towards their less fortunate compatriots, and was tempted to insist that Veronica show a bit more consideration. But they had to catch his father up. He was comforted by the thought that Lord Oakford would have been similarly delayed.

Veronica had been talking almost non-stop since they had left the Haldemans. She was clearly excited with their 'mission', as she called it, and pleased with herself for wangling the car from her sister. She occasionally asked Conrad for his opinion, and he answered with a monosyllable.

Eventually, she had had enough. They had come to a complete halt. A quarter of a mile further up a hill they could see a baker's van was blocking the road, either broken down or run out of petrol. No matter how hard the line of cars hooted, and they hooted hard and long, the van would not move. 'Why so glum, Conrad?

'I've been thinking.'

'About your father?'

'No. About you.'

'About how clever I was to get the car?'

'Not exactly. About how you got to Paris at such short notice.'

'Imperial Airways from Heston. Fearfully expensive.'

Conrad raised his eyebrows. 'You see, I know that's not true, Veronica. I tried to get a flight here yesterday and there wasn't a seat. Thomas Cook laughed at me.'

'Ah, but you're not me. You know I have ways of getting what I want.'

'Why did you suddenly decide to come and help me?'

'I thought you might need me. I was right, wasn't I?'

'And the other night. Why didn't Parsons turn up? And how did the big man who tried to kill me know I was going to be there? Does Parsons even exist?'

Veronica turned to him. 'Conrad, do you think I am lying to you?'

'Veronica, I know you are. We were married for three years. I know you are lying to me. I just don't know why.'

Veronica opened her mouth and shut it. The gaiety left her. She stared ahead and hit her horn hard. The driver in front hit his in response. Nothing moved.

'Who sent you, Veronica?'

'Major McCaigue.'

'McCaigue!'

'You remember you told me to see him when I came back from Holland after meeting Theo?'

'Yes.'

'I told him about the attack the Germans were planning. And then he said he wanted me to keep an eye on you. He seemed to know a lot about you already and quite a bit about me. I think he had been talking to Alec.'

'Linaro?'

'Yes. Linaro. McCaigue said that he thought you were spying for the Soviet Union. He said you had a misguided idea about the Duke of Windsor returning to England to reclaim the throne. He asked me to watch you for him.'

'And you did it?'

Veronica swallowed. She was speaking quietly. 'Yes. I thought it was my duty. And to tell you the truth, I was quite excited by the idea. Frankly, I could believe that you might be a Russian spy. You've always been a bit of a leftie, and you did leave me to go to Spain.'

'You encouraged me to go!' protested Conrad. 'You were going to come too. It was going to be a wonderful lark; you were going to drive an ambulance or something. And then you never came. You stayed in England with Linaro and I got shot at in Spain for a year.'

'Yes, all right, darling,' said Veronica. 'But it wasn't as though McCaigue asked me to do you any harm.'

'What about that fellow who tried to knife me?'

'Yes,' said Veronica. 'I wondered about him. But McCaigue told me there really was a man called Parsons. He was delayed, but when he arrived in Shepherd Market, he found someone had been stabbed. So he scarpered.'

'So it wasn't Polly Copthorne who put you on to Parsons?'

'No,' said Veronica. 'McCaigue said Parsons would have something very interesting to say to you that night. And I didn't believe that big chap who tried to stab you was him; McCaigue assured me he wasn't. I have no idea who he was.'

'McCaigue sent you over here?'

'Yes. At short notice. I flew in an RAF plane from Hendon. I saw Churchill land in it.'

Conrad's brain was racing. He could believe that Veronica might be persuaded to keep tabs on him by someone purporting to be from the secret service. But what worried him most was McCaigue.

'Are you a Russian spy, Conrad?'

'Of course I'm not a bloody Russian spy!' Conrad answered.

It sounded as if not only was McCaigue trying to keep tabs on him, which would have been disappointing but understandable, but he was trying to get Conrad killed. Which meant he was on Alston's side. He was the 'power that be' who had placed doubts in Van's mind about him, who had spread the idea he was a Soviet spy, who had tried to keep him confined to his unit. And who had tried to get him killed.

And Conrad had trusted him! Told him everything he had learned about Alston and the Duke of Windsor and Freddie Copthorne's death. He had brought Anneliese along to speak to him. Christ! Was that why Anneliese had been arrested?

Conrad hated the thought of Anneliese in a cell, a British cell, after all she had suffered in Berlin. And McCaigue had put her there!

'Then all this stuff about the Duke of Windsor is true?' Veronica asked.

'Henry Alston is planning to use the duke to precipitate a change of government,' Conrad said. 'Churchill will go, Lloyd George will become Prime Minister, Alston and my father will be in the government, Edward will become king again and we will make peace with Germany. Britain will become a Nazi satellite.'

'No! So isn't McCaigue really in the secret service? You told me to go and see him.'

'He is,' said Conrad. 'But I shouldn't have trusted him.'

'Oh,' said Veronica. She glanced at Conrad. 'I'm sorry, Conrad.'

Up ahead, a group of men had manhandled the van off the road and into a ditch, ignoring the remonstrances of its driver. A few minutes later the traffic began to move.

'I can understand why you came over to Paris to find me,' said Conrad. 'But why did you persuade Isobel to give us her car?'

'Major McCaigue told me to prevent you from getting to your father. He didn't tell me why, he just said it was a question of utmost importance to the war effort. But actually I was worried about that man attacking us too. I wondered whether there was something in what you said. I mean, I know you, Conrad. You are about the most honest person I've met. So I thought I would help you get the car and keep a close eye on you to see what happened.'

Conrad stared out of the window over the flat green farmland, empty and peaceful compared to the clogged road on which they were stuck.

'Conrad? What now?'

Strangely, Conrad didn't feel anger towards Veronica. She had done what she thought was her duty. She had been pro-German, even pro-Nazi in her time, but now her country was at war, she was doing what she thought was the right thing. Wasn't she?

'I'll give you the choice, Veronica,' Conrad said. 'If you believe that Hitler is evil, that Nazism is wrong and that Britain should fight it to the bitter end, then stay in the car and help me. If you think it would be wiser for our country to make peace with the

Germans, if you think Hitler isn't so bad really, then get out and go back to Paris. It's your choice.'

He watched Veronica as she drove. To his amazement, a tear ran down her cheek. Veronica never cried.

She sniffed. 'You were right all along, Conrad,' she said. 'You and people like Anneliese. And Winston Churchill. We were all so blind, people like me and Diana Mosley, and Unity Mitford and Freddie Copthorne and my father. We thought that Hitler was a little over-excitable and didn't do things the British way, but he gave Germany just the kind of leadership it needed, and he was stopping Europe from becoming communist. And the uniforms were just divine.

'The Nazis are horrid, beastly people, and I feel horrid and beastly for not realizing that before. So yes, I want to help you. I want to stop Sir Henry Alston. And I want to stop your father.'

Conrad looked at his former wife. She meant what she said.

'Good,' he said. 'Now, let's find him.'

They drove on, slowly, oh so slowly, rarely getting above walking pace. The verges were littered with broken-down cars, or vehicles that had simply run out of petrol. They passed one elderly and impeccably dressed couple eating a picnic lunch out of the boot of their Rolls-Royce. What was much more distressing were the old people, sitting or lying on the grass, exhausted. Conrad hoped their families hadn't just left them there, but it appeared that they had.

There was a ripple of excitement in the column of traffic as a detachment of French tanks came barrelling along, heading for Paris. One way or another, everyone managed to get off the road to let them by, including the cows.

They had planned to stop in Chartres for a late lunch, but the city was crowded to overflowing. After an hour of battling through medieval streets, they emerged on the far side. Conrad examined the Michelin map that Marshall had provided them with. 'Let's get off the main road,' he said. 'I know these lanes are narrow and don't go in a straight line, but they must be quicker than this.'

And they were. Not much quicker, but Conrad and Veronica were zigzagging their way south towards Tours, like a dinghy tacking against a stiff breeze. They stopped for half an hour for a pleasant picnic next to a small stream.

Conrad took over the wheel of the Cadillac. Afternoon turned to evening. 'Shall we stop in Tours, or carry on?' said Veronica.

'I'm not sure,' said Conrad. 'I wonder where Father is staying.'

'He can't have gone much faster than us. But of course we don't know what route he has taken.'

'I bet there aren't any hotel rooms free in Tours,' said Conrad.

'Do we sleep in the car, then?' said Veronica.

Conrad looked again at the map. A hamlet caught his eye: Blancou. He had stayed at the Abbaye de Blancou once with his parents when he was a boy. It was the family home of a French banker whom his father knew well. It was a fair bit south of Tours, but not too distant from the main road.

If his father couldn't find anywhere to stay en route, then he may well have decided to try his luck there. Worth a shot. Even if Lord Oakford wasn't there, Conrad and Veronica might be able to beg a room. Conrad resigned himself to sleeping with his wife that night.

Conrad explained his idea to Veronica, who agreed they should give it a try. The problem was that the broad River Loire, with its limited number of bridges, created bottlenecks.

It was nearly midnight when they crossed. They decided to sleep in the car in a wood for a few hours and get up at dawn to continue their journey.

Veronica curled up on the back seat under a travel blanket. Should Conrad trust his ex-wife? Frankly, he didn't have much choice. Slumping in the front of the car, Conrad listened to her gentle breathing, a familiar sound from a much simpler time.

Northern Spain

Theo examined the woman sitting opposite him in the second-class carriage through one slightly open eye. She was very attractive, dark – Theo usually preferred blondes – slim, but with a full bust

373

under her black dress. Mid twenties, he would guess. A small girl was asleep on her lap. A widow, no doubt; there were plenty of young widows in Spain.

It was dark in the carriage, but he was pretty sure he saw her open one eye and study him.

Theo shut his own eye and told himself not to be so stupid. What would she want with a Yugoslav businessman named Petar Šalić who was travelling to France in search of his own wife?

The train journey from Madrid had been interminable. He was involved in a slow-motion pursuit of Otto Langebrück, who was travelling in a similar train under the name of Georges Braun, a Frenchman from Mulhouse in Alsace. Both Otto and Theo had brought false identities with them to Spain in case they were needed to travel to France. Otto spoke fluent French and could mimic a convincing Alsatian accent. Theo's cover was much less secure. Theo's French was not nearly good enough to pass as a native of any description, so he had used a Yugoslav passport. But he spoke no Serbo-Croat; he was sunk if by chance he came across a French official who did.

He was nervous about entering France in wartime. It was rare for German officers in the Abwehr, or any other agency for that matter, to operate on enemy territory. That's what neutral countries and neutral agents were for. But France was in chaos, and Ribbentrop had decided that it was imperative that someone approach the Duke of Windsor immediately. Otto Langebrück was the man he had in mind. Theo had tried to insist that he travel with Otto, since at least he had training in espionage, but their covers were not compatible, and it was felt, rightly, that Otto would arouse less suspicion if he travelled alone. What clinched it was the news that the Duke of Windsor had left Paris for Biarritz, only a few kilometres over the Spanish border with France.

Theo's bosses in the Abwehr were unhappy at the idea of the Duke of Windsor being persuaded to return to England, so Theo had been dispatched two hours after Otto, with instructions to dissuade him from talking to the duke. The hope was that if Otto and Theo could get to Biarritz before the duke, then Theo might be able to tell Otto he had been sent to warn him that the duke was travelling to his house at Antibes instead. If the Spanish trains had followed their timetables, that might have been possible, but it was becoming clear that Spanish trains never followed their timetables.

In which case Theo would have to think of another way of stopping Otto Langebrück.

Which would be a pity. Theo was growing to like the Rhinelander.

Fifty-One

Extract from Lieutenant Dieter von Hertenberg's Diary

24 May

*Direct order from the Supreme Command. Halt. 'Dunkirk to
be left to the Luftwaffe. Should the capture of Calais prove
difficult, this too should be left to the Luftwaffe.' The order
comes from Hitler himself and there is no explanation. When
I handed the order to Guderian he couldn't believe it. He
wants to argue, but since there is no explanation, there is no
logic to argue against. It makes no sense! The British Army
are trapped and demoralized; we could capture the whole
lot of them if only the Führer would let us.*

I have seen Guderian's Achtung Panzer! *doctrine in
action over the last couple of weeks. Keep moving, keep the
enemy off balance. Well, the British are well and truly off
balance, and now we are staying put and giving them time
to regroup and reorganize!*

*At least it means some rest for some of us, although there
is still fighting in Boulogne.*

The Loire Valley, 24 May

The first bird woke Conrad. It was still dark, with just a glimmer
of grey peeking through the trees to the east. He stretched and
nudged Veronica, curled up on the back seat of the Cadillac. It
was cold.

They shared some bread, cheese and Evian water for breakfast and were soon on their way. They made reasonable speed along the main road south of Tours. There were plenty of cars pulled over on to the verges for the night, and as dawn came, more and more of them started back on the road. But Conrad and Veronica were definitely making better progress than they had the day before.

'Maybe we should keep going,' said Veronica, who was driving. 'Perhaps we could make Biarritz by tonight after all.'

'Let's check Blancou first,' said Conrad. 'It's not too far out of our way.'

So they turned off the main road, but it took them half an hour of tiny country lanes before they came to a sign to the hamlet.

They turned left and descended into a wooded valley. Ahead of them, they could see the house, which was actually a small stone medieval abbey, clad in thick green ivy. A number of semi-ruined buildings lined one side of a dark fast-flowing stream. An ancient footbridge crossed the water to a lush green meadow dotted with a dozen or so cows. It was difficult to believe that this particular corner of France was at war.

'It's beautiful,' said Veronica. 'You came here as a boy?'

'Just once when I was about twelve,' said Conrad. 'There are supposed to be wild boar in those woods. Father's banker friend used to hunt them. Very exciting.'

'Someone's there,' said Veronica. 'And they are awake. There's smoke coming out of that chimney.'

It was just after six. Early. Conrad's hopes rose. If Lord Oakford was staying there, he would no doubt want an early start.

The road plunged down the side of the valley and they lost sight of the house. Five minutes later they came to a pair of ancient stone gateposts with no gate, and drove along a track past a lodge, which seemed to be inhabited. They turned a corner and there was the abbey. A large American car was parked in front of it, and in an open courtyard off to one side, by an open door, stood a table covered with a white tablecloth, around which three people were having breakfast.

They turned to stare at the approaching car. There was an old lady in a high-necked black dress and a shawl, whom Conrad didn't recognize. There was his father. And there was Constance.

Conrad remembered that the concierge at the Meurice had mentioned a woman was present with the American picking up his father. That must be her.

'What do we do?' asked Veronica.

'Just park the car and follow me,' said Conrad.

Veronica pulled up next to the Packard, and they both got out. Conrad approached the table with a smile. In the quiet courtyard so early in the morning, the birdsong was extraordinary, like a welcoming overture. 'Good morning, Father. Constance.'

'What the devil are you doing here?' Lord Oakford barked.

Conrad approached the old lady. 'Madame de Salignac, I presume,' he said in French. 'We met many years ago, when I came to stay with you as a boy. I'm Conrad de Lancey, Lord Oakford's son. And this is my wife, Veronica.' For once, Conrad was not eager to disown Veronica as his ex-wife.

'Delighted to see you again,' said the lady, who was very old, very wrinkled, but had clear blue eyes. 'Forgive me if I don't get up.' She indicated a walking stick. 'But please join us. Cécile!'

A woman, just as old as her mistress but quite a bit fatter, shuffled out of the house, breathing heavily. 'Please fetch these people some coffee.'

Lord Oakford glared at his son, his manners just getting the better of his desire to shout at him. 'I thought you were in England,' he said, in French.

Conrad continued the introductions, this time in English. 'Veronica, this is Constance Scott-Dunton. Mrs Scott-Dunton murdered my sister last November.'

Constance, who had been playing along with the polite charade and had held her hand out towards Veronica, froze at this.

'Don't be absurd!' snapped Oakford.

'Excuse me for speaking English, Madame,' said Conrad in French to his hostess. 'But my wife doesn't speak French.'

The old lady looked at Conrad sharply; her bright eyes seemed to be staring right into his soul. Conrad held her gaze. She nodded slightly.

'That is absolute rot!' said Oakford. 'Your German friend Theo von Hertenberg killed Millie. You know that, you are just unwilling to accept it!'

Conrad sat down at the table, as did Veronica. 'That's not what Constance says,' said Conrad.

Constance glared at Conrad. 'I don't what you mean.'

'You told Anneliese Rosen that you had been to Holland on an errand for your lover, Sir Henry Alston. And you told her that you had killed someone there. That someone was my sister, Millie.'

'Your Anneliese?' said Oakford.

'She's certainly not my Anneliese,' said Veronica.

'You also told Anneliese about Alston's plan to form a new government to discuss peace with the Germans. And that my father was on his way to France to fetch the Duke of Windsor.'

The maid arrived with some coffee. She could sense the tension around the table. Everyone was silent as she poured two cups for Conrad and Veronica.

'Apparently, Constance was a little drunk at the time. She and Anneliese had been sticking up anti-Jewish posters in Mayfair.'

Oakford glanced at his young companion, who sat silent and grim-faced, two pink circles of colour emerging on her pale cheeks. Anger rather than shame, Conrad thought.

'Anneliese was exaggerating,' said Oakford. 'It's true that Henry and I are trying to bring about a sensible settlement with Germany and I am on my way to discuss how the duke can help. But the rest is the result of Anneliese's overwrought imagination. Or yours.'

Everyone around the table was looking at Conrad.

'Don't go, Father,' Conrad said quietly. 'I know you hate war. I know you have always wanted peace with honour, and I know that's what you think you are seeking now. But that's not what this is. This is peace with *dis*honour. Alston effectively wants Britain to surrender to Germany. He wants Britain to become a vassal state, a neo-Nazi protectorate. I know that's not what you want. But that's what you are helping him to do.'

'How do you know what Henry wants?' said Lord Oakford. 'Don't you see that the sooner we negotiate peace with Hitler, the less we will have to give up? We are losing this war. Let's call it off before we have lost it.'

'Is there nothing you wouldn't do for peace, Father? Is no price too high?'

'One life is priceless,' said Oakford. 'Fifteen million people died in the last war. That's fifteen million times priceless. So no, Conrad, no price is too high.'

Conrad understood his father. The war hero with the Victoria Cross and the missing arm had devoted his life to preventing another war. He believed in peace at any cost. In Henry Alston he saw the means that justified that end. He was blind, wilfully blind, to Alston's motives for bringing peace. He didn't care as long as an armistice was declared.

'You know Constance did kill Millie, Father?' said Conrad, trying another tack.

'I'm not listening to you any more,' said Oakford. 'In fact, Constance and I are leaving now.' He got to his feet. 'Thank you for your hospitality, Madame de Salignac,' he said in French. 'I am afraid we must leave. I apologize for the suddenness of our departure.'

'I won't let you go,' said Conrad, also standing.

'One moment,' said the old lady, in French. 'I have something inside for you.'

She climbed to her feet, took her stick and hobbled inside. Her four guests waited.

Conrad knew he could never persuade his father to abandon his mission. He hated seeing Constance, Millie's murderer, at his father's side. He would have to stop him somehow.

The old lady reappeared. 'Here, you might need this,' she said in English. She had put her stick to one side and was limping out into the courtyard. In her hands was a shotgun. She handed it to

Conrad. 'I was ten in 1870 when the Prussians arrived in Paris. I saw how they behaved then. Two of my three sons died in the war of 1914. I hate the Boche, Lord Oakford. The French people will never surrender to them again, and neither should the British.'

Her blue eyes were blazing with anger. 'You should listen to your son, Lord Oakford.'

Conrad took the shotgun, and slowly pointed it at his father.

'What are you going to do with that, Conrad?' said Oakford. 'Shoot me?'

'I will if I have to,' said Conrad. Would he? He didn't know.

'I think you might,' said Lord Oakford. 'But I don't care. I told you once about that afternoon at Passchendaele when I took that machine-gun post, didn't I? How, after I turned the German machine gun on those young German boys and mowed them down, I walked unarmed towards their line. How I expected them to shoot me – I wanted them to shoot me. I was sick with myself for killing so many. I vowed then that I would never kill another man, that peace was more important than my life.'

Conrad remembered that story well.

'Come on, Constance,' said Oakford. He began to move towards the Packard.

'You can't let him go, Conrad,' said Veronica. 'You must pull the trigger!'

Conrad knew she was right. If Conrad was prepared to sacrifice his own life for what he believed was right, and he knew he was, then he should be willing to sacrifice his father.

Whatever he decided, he knew he would have to live with it for the rest of his life.

He couldn't do it. Logic might tell him to pull the trigger, but he couldn't do it.

His father had his back to him and had almost reached the car. Conrad took several rapid paces towards him. Lord Oakford's shoulders stiffened as he sensed Conrad's approach, but he didn't turn round. Conrad raised the shotgun and brought the stock down hard on his father's skull.

There was sickening crack, and Lord Oakford crumpled to the ground.

'Take this,' said Conrad, handing the shotgun to Veronica.

He bent down over his father. He had had no idea how hard to hit him. Lord Oakford was fit, wiry and not yet sixty. Conrad's intention had been to knock him out, without doing him permanent damage, but he feared he had hit him too hard. It was impossible to judge the weight of a blow like that.

Oakford was lying face down on flagstones, blood seeping from a cut on the back of his head. His eyes were shut and he was motionless. Conrad couldn't tell whether he was breathing. He put his fingers on his father's neck hoping to find a pulse.

He heard movement behind him, and turned to see Constance lunge at Veronica, who was staring at Conrad and Oakford, holding the shotgun loosely in front of her. Veronica was a bigger woman than Constance, but was taken by surprise. Constance grabbed the barrel of the shotgun with both hands and yanked. Veronica let go.

Constance skipped backwards a few paces and turned the gun on Veronica. 'Keep still, or I'll blow your head off!'

Fifty-Two

The Loire Valley, 24 May

Veronica kept still.

'Get back!' Constance ordered.

Veronica hesitated and then retreated. It was clear that Constance had never fired a shotgun before. She was holding the gun awkwardly in front of her. But it was pointed directly at Veronica, Constance's finger was on the trigger and Conrad could see that the safety was off. All she had to do was squeeze and Veronica would be dead.

'Further back,' said Constance. Veronica took two steps back. She was now standing next to Conrad and a few paces away from Constance.

'Is he all right?' Constance asked Conrad.

'I don't know,' said Conrad.

'Well, check!'

Conrad bent over his father again and searched for the artery in his neck. At first he felt nothing. He forced himself to take it slow. He moved his fingers and felt something. A pulse! 'He's alive,' he said. 'But he's out cold.'

'All right,' said Constance. She was clearly thinking through what she would do next. Conrad tried to guess her next move. Shoot him; that was the obvious answer. It was a double-barrelled shotgun, presumably with a cartridge in each barrel. So she could afford to loose off one at him and keep the other to cover Veronica and Madame de Salignac.

In which case, maybe Conrad should rush her first, in the

hope that somehow she missed him. The odds didn't look good, but the odds of doing nothing looked worse.

Then his father groaned. His eyes flicked open.

'Leave him!' said Constance.

Get her talking, thought Conrad. Distract her. Play for time.

'You did kill Millie, didn't you, Constance?' Conrad was hoping for an admission that his father might hear.

'Yes,' said Constance. 'I had to. I liked your sister, she had good intentions, but in the end she was going to blow the whistle on the whole plan. Your friend Theo told her that the Duke of Windsor had been passing secrets to the Germans. That he was a traitor. At that stage I didn't know the details of what Henry was planning, but I knew I had to shut her up. There was only one way of doing that.'

'And Freddie Copthorne? Was he the same?'

'Yes. He lost his nerve. Henry had to do something. At least your father knows his duty.'

'What do you mean?'

Oakford groaned again, and moved on the ground.

'You heard him,' said Constance. 'He was willing to die for the cause of peace with Germany. Lloyd George is a very old man. It won't be long before he steps aside for Henry, and then Britain will have a truly great Prime Minister. Don't you see that with Germany as our ally and not our enemy, there will be nothing to stop Britain becoming great again? The French are pathetic; all the Americans are concerned about is money. Only we know how to rule. And the Germans.'

Oakford pulled himself to a sitting position and rubbed his skull. Then he looked at his one hand. There was blood on it. The hair on the back of his head was matted red.

'Help your father into the back of the car,' said Constance.

Conrad lifted his father to his feet, but Oakford's knees buckled. So Conrad lifted him bodily and carried him to the Packard. He opened the rear door and eased his father into the back seat.

'Did you hear that?' Conrad whispered. 'She did murder Millie in Holland. And once I have got you into this car, she will shoot me. Don't you care?'

'Don't talk to him!' Constance said.

Oakford groaned again. He was sitting on the car seat with his legs dangling down to the ground. He was trying to say something.

'Yes, Father?' If Conrad was going to die he may as well die hearing what his father wanted to say.

'I do care,' he whispered. 'If she killed Millie, I . . . I cannot forgive her. There's a pistol in my coat pocket. Use it.'

Conrad glanced at his father's suit jacket. There was indeed a heavy weight on one side; Conrad wondered how he had missed it.

'I said, don't talk to him!' Constance shouted.

'All right,' said Conrad. And he put his hand around his father, slipping it into the side pocket of his jacket, out of sight of Constance. His fingers closed around a small gun.

It was a revolver. No safety to worry about then. He extricated the gun from the pocket and cocked the hammer, all out sight of Constance. He kept his back to Constance and straightened up. His father, still groggy, looked at him with unfocused eyes and nodded.

Conrad spun around, crouched and fired. He hit Constance in the shoulder just as she pressed the trigger. There was a double bang, the shotgun's drowning out the crack of the revolver. He heard his father yell from the car behind him, and Constance screamed, dropping the shotgun and grabbing her shoulder.

'Leave it!' Conrad shouted.

Constance whimpered in pain. Already blood was spreading over her white dress.

Behind him, Lord Oakford groaned.

'Are you hit, Father?'

'Just my leg.'

Veronica darted forward and grabbed the shotgun. She took a few paces back from Constance.

Constance's eyes blazed. 'You're too late!' she said. 'You won't be able to stop Henry.'

'*Donnez-le-moi*,' said Madame de Salignac to Veronica, hobbling towards her.

Veronica looked at the shotgun in her hands and passed it to the old woman.

Madame de Salignac took the gun, pointed it at Constance's chest and pulled the trigger. They were only five yards apart. Constance's whimpers stopped as she fell backwards, her chest a bloody mess. She was dead before she hit the ground.

'Someone should have done that a long time ago,' said Madame de Salignac.

Conrad stared at the body of the woman who had killed his sister. He didn't feel any thrill of revenge, or even any pity, just wonder that a nice English girl could have such a poisoned soul.

Another scream. This time it was Veronica. She was looking at Lord Oakford, who was slumped on to the back seat of the Packard, blood pumping out of his leg.

'Father!'

Conrad leaned into the car, and lifted his father out, laying him on to the ground. It wasn't 'just his leg'. His left thigh was peppered with shot, and his trousers were already soaked in red. Blood was streaming out on to the ground beneath him.

Conrad remembered when his comrade Lofty Bennett had been shot in the leg at Brunete. The medics had tied a tourniquet above the wound to try to stanch the flow of blood. It had worked, sort of. Lofty survived the loss of blood, but died of gangrene a week later.

Conrad needed a strip of cloth, fast. He flung off his jacket and unbuttoned his shirt, tearing it off as his fingers fumbled on the buttons.

'Pass me that knife!' he shouted to Veronica, pointing to the breakfast table. She grabbed it and gave it to him. He cut his father's trouser leg above the wound and pulled it down, revealing a pulsing mass of blood-soaked flesh. He wrapped his shirt around the leg above the wound and pulled tight. Within seconds the flow seemed to slow, but not stop completely. He tried to adjust the shirt, but then the blood started streaming again.

Oakford had already lost a lot.

His father's eyes were open as he watched his son. He seemed to be conscious, but not in pain.

Veronica offered Conrad a towel from the kitchen.

'Well done,' said Conrad. 'Push that down on the wound.'

'Conrad?' his father whispered.

'Yes?'

'You know we never agreed on much, did we?'

Conrad couldn't help grinning as he kept the pressure on the tourniquet. 'No, Father, we didn't.'

'Your mother always says you are just like me.' He was struggling to get the words out. 'I've always done what I believed to be right. You have always done the same. My time is over now. So you do what you think you have to do.'

Conrad looked at his father sharply. What was his father saying? He wasn't admitting that Conrad was right and he was wrong, that wasn't Lord Oakford's way. But he was giving him permission to stop Alston. His blessing.

'All right, Father. But let's talk about it later.' Conrad didn't want his father's blessing at that precise moment. He just wanted him to live.

But Lord Oakford's eyelids were closing. He made an effort to speak. 'Conrad,' he whispered.

Conrad bent down.

'*Sag deiner Mutter, dass ich sie liebe.*' Tell your mother I love her.

'Don't give up now, Father!'

But Arthur Oakford closed his eyes.

Guillaume, Cécile's aged husband, had emerged from the keeper's lodge by the gate to see what the fuss was about. Madame de Salignac sent him off at once to the village to fetch the doctor. But by the time he returned with the man, Lord Oakford was dead.

'I think we need to call the police, Madame,' said the doctor, surveying Constance and Lord Oakford, whom he had confirmed were both dead.

'Let's wait until my guests have left,' said Madame de Salignac. The doctor, a squat man of about sixty, raised his eyebrows.

'That woman shot the gentleman,' said the old lady.

'And who shot her?'

'I did,' said Madame de Salignac. 'In self-defence.'

'And your guests? Are they not witnesses?'

'I am sure they did not see anything, doctor.'

'But, Madame . . .'

'We have known each other a long time, doctor. You must trust me on this. For France, and for her ally.'

Conrad and Veronica were back on the road within half an hour, Conrad wearing one of his own clean shirts, and a suit belonging to the late Monsieur de Salignac, which was too short and too wide for him. His own was ruined with his father's blood. They were heading back towards the main road.

'I'm sorry, Conrad,' said Veronica, who was driving.

Conrad closed his eyes, trying to sort out in his head what had just happened. 'Do you think it was the head injury? Or the shotgun wound?'

'The shotgun wound,' said Veronica. 'Without a doubt.'

'How can you know?' said Conrad. 'How will I ever know that it wasn't me who killed him?'

'He was talking coherently, and he lost a massive amount of blood.'

'I can't be sure.'

'Conrad, listen to me,' Veronica said. 'You have two choices. You can fall apart. Blame yourself. Blame your father. Or you can assume that Constance killed him. You can remember your father's last words and do what you have to do.'

Conrad was listening.

'Your father was right, this is a beastly war, and he was one of its casualties. But it's a beastly war we have to win. So let's win it.'

Conrad closed his eyes. Took a deep breath. Veronica had a point. He needed to focus.

'All right.'

'So, Lord Oakford, pull yourself together.'

'Lord Oakford?' Conrad was confused.

'Like it or not, you are the third Viscount Oakford now.'

'I don't like it,' Conrad muttered.

'No,' said Veronica. 'It's absolutely beastly. Look! We are coming up to the junction. Do we turn right for Paris, or do we turn left for Biarritz?'

'I need to get back to London to do what I can to stop Alston,' Conrad said. 'But we also need to prevent the duke from returning to Britain. Now my father is . . .' He hesitated. '. . . is gone, Alston might send someone else. Or he might persuade the duke over the telephone.'

'I'll go to Biarritz,' said Veronica.

'But how can you stop him?'

'I'll think of a way.' Veronica smiled. 'I can always think of a way.'

Conrad examined the map and, after judging that the chance of him getting a seat on an aeroplane in the current chaos were nil, decided that a boat from Bordeaux was his best bet. So when they hit the main road, they turned left.

Pall Mall, London

It was a pleasant stroll across St James's Park to Alston's club. Britain, or at least the British ruling classes, were panicking, and Alston was relishing it. The news from France was bad; no one believed anything would come of the British and French counter-attacks which were supposed to nip off the neck of the advancing German panzer divisions. According to the Newspaper Proprietor, it would be only a matter of days before the panic seeped down to the general populace. There were rumours that the General was about to get the sack: dismaying for him, no doubt, but it would leave him angry and free to help the cause. Alston had heard from Constance two days before in Paris that she had caught up with Arthur Oakford, but that the duke had left for Biarritz. They would follow him there in a borrowed car. No sign of de Lancey yet. Alston needed to arrange for an aeroplane to fetch the duke from Biarritz back to England.

The timing should be just about perfect. In a few days the pressure on Churchill would become intolerable, and the duke's sudden appearance in Britain demanding peace would break him. Alston and his colleagues would be ready.

But Oswald Mosley would not. He and Maule Ramsay had been arrested the day before under the new Regulation 18B, leaving Alston and his friends a clear shot at power.

Alston greeted the porter at the lodge. His guest was waiting for him in the library, and there was also a message for him. The message was from Lindfors. *Both your requests have been accepted. Good luck.*

Alston smiled. That meant Hitler had agreed to give the BEF some breathing space to allow peace negotiations, and that he would refuse to do business with a government including Churchill.

He climbed the stairs to the club library, where the Civil Servant was waiting for him with the latest information on the War Cabinet meetings.

Not long now.

Fifty-Three

Extract from Lieutenant Dieter von Hertenberg's Diary

25 May

> Boulogne captured. 10th Panzer fighting in Calais. Asked
> British to surrender, but they refused: 'The answer is no, as it
> is the British Army's duty to fight, just as it is the German's.'
> Fair enough. Perhaps I am getting overconfident, but I don't
> give them more than a couple of days.
> Still forbidden to advance on Dunkirk.

Biarritz, 25 May

Theo identified a choice of two cafés opposite the Hôtel du Palais,
Biarritz's grandest hotel, where the British royal family always
stayed on their visits to the resort. He had had little difficulty with
the French officials at Hendaye on the Spanish frontier – there
were very few travellers entering the country, and a mass of unruly
people of all nationalities trying to leave it. They hadn't searched
his luggage, so the pistol he had stowed in the false bottom of
his suitcase had remained undetected. Biarritz was only twenty
kilometres north of the frontier. It was much easier to get a seat
on a train heading north than south.

Once in Biarritz, Theo had solved the problem of whether the
duke had arrived by asking English tourists leaving the hotel.
He had, in fact, joined his wife the night before. What English

tourists were doing in Biarritz in the middle of a war, Theo had no idea, but they were there in some numbers, and willing to chat to a friendly young Yugoslav.

So Theo was too late to divert Otto Langebrück with his story that the duke and duchess were actually on their way to Antibes. But it was possible that Otto had not yet had a chance to speak to the duke himself. Theo's plan was to find a seat at a café and watch out for him.

And there he was! Sitting at a table outside one of the two cafés himself, checking the entrance to the hotel. Theo strolled past. Otto spotted him, smiled and stood up. The amateur! Theo caught his eye for a second and then looked away. It was unlikely that he or Otto were under surveillance, but not impossible, and Theo wasn't about to abandon his most basic tradecraft, even though it was clear Otto had never been taught it.

But Otto was quick enough to realize what Theo was doing – out of his peripheral vision Theo could see him looking down at his coffee. Theo walked slowly past and strolled along the beachfront road. The hotel was a grand building of red and white plonked on a little headland between the town's two beaches. Theo walked the length of the southernmost beach towards the cliffs at the end. He found a path down to the sand, checking behind him to make sure that Otto was following. He was, at a discreet distance, but not really discreet enough if he were under professional surveillance. Oh, well. There was nothing Theo could do about that.

It was still too early in the year to swim, but there were a number of holidaymakers strolling along the beach, although none at the far end by the cliffs. The tide was almost in, and Theo felt out of place dodging the waves in his businessman's suit and shoes. He reached the point where the cliffs jutted out towards the sea, and clambered on to the rocks. He was looking for a cave or a small crevice in the cliff face that would put him out of sight of the people on the beach, and he found one. It stretched only a few metres in, but that was enough. He climbed in, sat on a rock and waited. The Atlantic waves lapped the shore just a few metres in front of him. In an hour or so, the sea would be in the cave.

A minute later, Otto joined him. He grinned and shook Theo's hand. 'I'm sorry I showed I recognized you back there,' he said. 'That was foolish.'

'Never mind,' said Theo.

'What are you doing here? Is something wrong?'

'Have you had a chance to speak to the duke yet?'

'Not yet. I was just writing a note for him asking him to meet me.' Otto pulled a sheet of paper out of his jacket pocket.

Theo examined the young diplomat. He had found out quite a bit about him in the few days they had spent together. Like Theo, he had trained as a lawyer. He had spent some time in France and a little in England. Although he wasn't from one of the close-knit Junkers landed families like Theo's, Theo could imagine being a friend of his at university. Otto wasn't Gestapo, and although he may well be a member of the Nazi Party, he didn't strike Theo as a fanatical supporter at all. During the plans for the coup in 1938, Theo had had to approach a number of men in important positions to sound out support. He had been surprised how even long-term Party members had listened to him favourably.

Otto was worth a try.

'I don't think you should approach the duke,' Theo said.

'Why not?' said Otto. 'Surely if he became king again and presided over peace talks with Germany, it would be good for us.'

'It would be good for Hitler,' Theo said.

'Of course it would,' Otto agreed. Then he frowned. 'Are you suggesting what I think you are suggesting?'

'What's good for Hitler is not necessarily good for Germany,' Theo said. 'Or Europe.'

'But we would win the war, Theo! That's certainly good for Germany.'

'Is it?' said Theo.

Otto stared at Theo. He nodded slowly to himself. 'Yes, Theo, it is. And to suggest otherwise is treachery against the Fatherland.'

'I don't believe it is,' said Theo.

'Well, I do,' said Otto. 'I don't agree with everything Hitler does or says, but he has made Germany a great country again, and as a German I am proud of that.'

With a heavy heart, Theo realized he had misjudged Otto Langebrück.

'Look, Theo, I like you,' Otto went on. 'I'm not a member of the Gestapo, and I won't tell them what you have just said to me. But I *will* go and speak to the Duke of Windsor and persuade him to return to England. There will be thirty million francs held for him in Switzerland and we will promise that him becoming king and Wallis queen will be a precondition of peace talks no matter what the British government says. With those assurances and Lord Oakford's invitation, he will return to England. And you won't stop him.'

Otto turned to leave the cave.

Theo had retrieved his pistol from the false bottom of his suitcase, which he had left at the station. Now he pulled it out of his jacket. 'Otto?'

Otto turned. His expression changed when he saw the gun. His eyes opened wide in fear. 'Theo? No, Theo.'

Up until that point in his life, Theo had never killed anyone, although he had seen Conrad do it a couple of times. He believed killing people was wrong and should be avoided at all costs. And if he was going to kill someone, he would much rather it was a Gestapo officer than someone like Otto.

But the time had come. He pulled the trigger. Twice.

The bullets hit Otto Langebrück in the chest and he crumpled to the ground. The noise was deafening in the cave, but Theo hoped it would be muffled by the surf outside before it reached the ears of the walkers on the beach. He searched Otto's neck for a pulse to confirm he was dead, and then dragged him into a dark corner of the small cave and shoved him into a crevice. The body didn't fit completely, and he might well be spotted by a tourist closely examining the inside of the cave. But Theo hoped that wouldn't happen for a few hours, or at least until after high tide.

Shaking, and feeling slightly sick, he left the cave, clambered along the rock to the sand, and headed back up to the beach road and the café.

There he ordered a cup of coffee and waited for Lord Oakford. He hoped to God he wouldn't have to do again what he had just done. But he feared he would.

Veronica made good time on the drive from Bordeaux to Biarritz. She and Conrad had arrived in Bordeaux late the night before, but had somehow found a room in a *pension*. They had slept in the same bed; there was no choice. Early that morning they had driven up to Le Verdon, a port at the mouth of the Gironde. It was clogged with ships, one of which Conrad hoped would take him back to England.

Veronica had dropped Conrad and headed south. This far from Paris, the roads were navigable, and she reached the Atlantic resort by teatime. Biarritz was the kind of place that served tea for its many English visitors.

It took Veronica no time to confirm that the duke and duchess were staying at the Hôtel du Palais. At the reception desk Veronica demanded to see the duke, introducing herself as the daughter-in-law of Lord Oakford. The message came back that she should wait, which was what she had expected. She lit a cigarette, and observed the clientele. It was surprising how many English people had chosen to take a holiday in France in the middle of a war which was going so badly. Good room rates, Veronica supposed.

A man sat down opposite her. 'Theo!'

'Actually, my name is Petar Šalić,' said Theo. 'I'm a Yugoslav businessman looking for my wife who is trying to flee France.'

'Are you now? Well, I'm very pleased to meet you. You're the spitting image of a friend of my ex-husband.'

'Do you know where Lord Oakford is?' Theo asked.

Veronica glanced at Theo. 'Perhaps we should go for a little walk?'

They wandered through the hotel to a door leading out into gardens overlooking the Atlantic and the beaches. It was a lovely afternoon; the sun had lost some of its midday strength and the breeze from the sea brought the smell of salt and the sound of surf into the garden.

'Well?' said Theo.

'You know who is staying here?' said Veronica.

'I do,' said Theo. 'The Duke of Windsor. Lord Oakford is on his way to Biarritz to persuade him to go back to England to take the throne. And I am here to stop him.'

Veronica pulled out a fresh cigarette. Theo lit it, shielding the flame from the sea breeze. Should Veronica trust Theo? Conrad did. He had been dead right about the invasion date when they had met in that café in Holland. This was no time to be cautious; Veronica decided to trust her instinct. And her instinct was to trust Theo.

'Lord Oakford is dead. He died on the road somewhere south of Tours. You are right: he was on his way here to get the duke to Britain.'

'How did he die?'

'Shot by mistake by a lunatic Englishwoman.'

'Constance Scott-Dunton?'

'That's her. She's dead too. Shot by a perfectly sane French lady.'

Theo paused to think through what he had just heard. 'Where's Conrad?'

'I hope he is on a boat from Bordeaux to England to warn the government that Henry Alston plans to overthrow them.'

'And you? What are you doing here.'

'My plan is to try to persuade the duke not to go to England.'

'How are you going to do that?'

Veronica told him her idea.

Theo listened, nodding. 'Not bad. But I think we need something more. Something to do with Wallis.'

Ten minutes later, Veronica returned to the hotel lobby. A hotel flunkey of medium rank, under-manager or something, was searching for her in a state of mild agitation. He showed her up to a suite on the third floor, opened the door and announced her.

Although Veronica had met the duke two or three times in the past, he was more recognizable from the newsreels. Short, with a slender figure, thick golden hair and a small upturned nose, he was in Veronica's estimation pretty rather than handsome. His wife looked thin, tired and grumpy.

But the duke stood up and gave Veronica one of his charming smiles. Veronica curtsied.

'We've met, haven't we?' the duke said. 'You're Isobel Haldeman's sister?'

'That's right, sir,' said Veronica. 'I stayed with my sister only three nights ago.'

'What a shambles,' said the duke. 'I'm glad I'm out of Paris. I felt in the circumstances I should be with Wallis. Would you like some tea?'

He poured Veronica a cup from the tray on a coffee table. The sitting room of the suite was large with a view over the Atlantic waves. Wallis was embroidering something and ignored Veronica entirely. She did not seem happy.

'I believe you were expecting a visit from Lord Oakford, my father-in-law?' Veronica said.

At this, Wallis looked up.

'Yes, I was,' said the duke, carefully.

'I'm afraid he can't make the journey himself, so he sent me instead.'

'Oh, yes? And does he have a message for me?'

'He does,' said Veronica. 'He says there is no need for you to return to England, sir.'

The duke glanced at his wife. They were both frowning. 'That's odd,' said the duke. 'I would have thought that given the current circumstances in London, Oakford would be recommending I fly over there at once.'

Veronica shook her head. 'No need, he says. He was quite firm about that.'

'Did he say why not?'

'Not to me, he didn't. Sorry. Can't help.'

'Strange,' said the duke.

'Surely you must have some idea?' said the duchess witheringly.

'None at all,' said Veronica, summoning all her confident ignorance. Then she stood up and looked out at the ocean. 'Sir? Would you mind showing me your balcony?'

Another glance between the duke and his wife. It was a pretty unsubtle way of demanding to speak to the duke out of Wallis's presence, but it worked.

The duke opened the windows and he and Veronica stepped out on to the balcony. She was horrified to see that it overlooked the garden where she and Theo had just been talking.

Veronica leaned on the railing, with the duke next to her. They stared out over the beach and the Bay of Biscay. The surf created enough noise to drown out their conversation from the woman waiting inside.

'Your Royal Highness,' Veronica said, 'I have a personal message to add to that of my father-in-law. You may not be aware of this, but there are some misguided men in London who want you to return to England and become king again. They hope to lead a government which will make peace with Germany and become a strong ally of Hitler.'

'Really?' said the duke.

'There is another group of men, senior figures of the aristocracy and their sons, twelve good Englishmen in all, who have sworn to shoot your wife, should you do that.'

'I beg your pardon?'

'You won't know who they are. They are the kind of men who find themselves close to the king and queen, if the duchess were to become queen. There is nowhere in England she would be safe. Probably not in France. Perhaps if she were to shut herself up in a *Schloss* in Germany she would be protected. But that wouldn't be much fun, would it? Your wife locked up in a castle, while you sat on a throne alone?'

The duke looked shocked. And angry. 'Who do you think you are, threatening me like that? Get out! Get out now!'

'Of course, Your Royal Highness,' said Veronica, dipping a quick curtsy as she returned inside. She curtsied again to the duchess and scampered out of the room.

She hurried out of the hotel to her car, or rather her sister's car. She had lied comprehensively to the Duke of Windsor from beginning to end, and she thought she had done it rather well, with some help from Theo. Now for some honesty: she had promised to return the Cadillac to her sister. No point in hanging around; it would be nice if she could get to Paris before the Germans.

As she turned the car around in the street, she saw the good-looking Yugoslav businessman sitting outside a café opposite. He raised his hat to her, and she gave him a little wave.

Then she drove north out of town.

Fifty-Four

Extract from Lieutenant Dieter von Hertenberg's Diary

26 May

> We have penetrated the old ring of fortifications around
> Calais and are in the town. The British won't last much
> longer.
>
> General Kleist arrived, but this time he congratulated
> our efforts. First time I have seen him since he bawled out
> Guderian. He acknowledged me and we had a friendly
> conversation, but I can't forgive him for the way he treated
> my commander.
>
> At last the halt order is rescinded and we are allowed to
> attack Dunkirk.

Calais, 26 May

Colonel Rydal ducked as the first Stuka peeled away from its
formation and dived. The scream was chilling, but the British
soldiers had learned that the Stuka's bark was worse than its bite.
Hell came and went amid a deafening cacophony of sirens and
explosions, but providing you were in cover, you were nearly always
all right. It was the sniper watching your position who was more
likely to pick you off the instant the Junkers 87s had flown off.

They were in Bastion No. 1, just to the north of the elegant Gare
Maritime, which was now crawling with German infantry. The

bastion was part of the sixteenth-century fortifications of Calais, which could hold out against the English siege cannon of the time, but not modern German artillery. Or tanks, for that matter.

After nearly nine months of patient preparation, action had come thick and fast. The battalion had been sent from Suffolk to Southampton and then across the Channel to Calais, where they were ordered to cover the possible withdrawal of the British Expeditionary Force. It was pretty clear to Rydal when his orders were explained to him that it was unlikely he or any of his men would be returning to England. They seemed to be going in rather the opposite direction to everybody else, but he knew his men would do their duty.

And they had. They had fought bravely and well for three days, but they couldn't last much longer. Across the harbour, Rydal could barely see through the dust and smoke to the medieval citadel where Brigadier Nicholson was holed up. Between the two positions were German infantry and tanks. Nicholson had refused to surrender, on the basis that every hour they could hold out was an hour longer other soldiers could be evacuated from Dunkirk, just to the north. Soldiers who could defend Britain from invasion.

A shell thudded into the breastwork just below them.

'There's another tank in range, sir.' It was Lieutenant Dodds, who had acquitted himself well in battle so far. 'Have a look, sir.'

Rydal peered over the parapet. There was indeed a German panzer squatting in the street belching fire at their position. And another. And another. Rydal had abandoned the last of his anti-tank guns in the Gare Maritime. There was nothing he or his men could do apart from wait to be pummelled into submission.

A bullet whistled past his ear and struck stone behind him. The German infantry were getting closer all the time.

'I could take some men and try to disable it, sir,' said Dodds. 'Those houses to the left are still unoccupied.'

Rydal swept his binoculars towards the street Dodds pointed to. He could see grey figures crouching and running barely fifty yards away from them.

'They would be occupied by the time you got there.'

Colonel Rydal scanned the devastated town. The Germans on three sides were closing in. There were Germans above him and the sea behind. There was nowhere to run. It was time.

'Mills, get me Brigade,' Rydal said to the wireless operator. He would inform the brigadier that he was about to surrender. He wondered who among his officers spoke German. De Lancey. He could have used de Lancey these last three days.

'Mr Dodds, organize a white flag.'

The look of disappointment, almost shame, on Lieutenant Dodds's face as he looked at his CO touched Rydal. 'Yes, sir,' he said.

Dodds pulled himself to his feet.

And a bullet ripped out the back of his head.

Fifty-Five

Extract from Lieutenant Dieter von Hertenberg's Diary

27 May

Calais taken yesterday with thousands of prisoners of all nationalities.

Moved north to attack Dunkirk, but given another order to hold off. Why? It's a mystery. We could see a mass of ships off the coast – not just Royal Navy warships, but also little civilian boats. They are taking the British Army off the beaches. It is so frustrating! Unless we do something now, they will get away!

Who knows how many British soldiers have escaped?

Pall Mall, London, 27 May

The Civil Servant was waiting in Alston's favourite corner in the club library. He looked uncharacteristically flustered.

'I don't have long, I must be back in Downing Street in half an hour,' he said.

'What's happening?' Alston asked.

'Halifax has taken the gloves off. He is arguing for sending peace feelers out through the Italians. He's also asking the Italians what it will take to keep them out of the war. He's pushing hard in the War Cabinet.'

'And how is Winston taking it?'

403

'He's pushing back. Chamberlain is supporting Churchill for now.' Chamberlain was important. Although Chamberlain's reputation with the general public was low, the Conservative Party still respected him; most of them regretted ditching him for Churchill. 'Halifax is threatening to threaten to resign.'

'Threatening to threaten?' said Alston.

'You know what I mean,' said the Civil Servant. 'Halifax will never take the direct route when an indirect route is possible. But he means it.'

'Excellent!' said Alston. Churchill would not survive a minute without Halifax's support.

'The two of them are talking in the Downing Street garden as we speak. And there's something else.'

'Yes?'

'Churchill is going to ask Chamberlain if he objects to Lloyd George joining the government.'

'Lloyd George will refuse,' said Alston. He had discussed timing with the old fox; Lloyd George had no intention of being co-opted into a failing government. Halifax had lost his nerve. Chamberlain had lost the country's confidence. Hoare was ambassador in Spain. There were no other major politicians in British politics. Apart from Lloyd George. They would have to turn to him for Prime Minister, and Alston would be right there with the old man.

'Now, I must be going,' said the Civil Servant.

'Thank you for keeping me so well informed,' said Alston.

He sat alone in his leather armchair in the library, thinking. Tomorrow or perhaps the day after, Churchill would fall. The twenty-ninth would be the day to act. But where was the Duke of Windsor?

Alston hadn't heard from Lord Oakford, or from his travelling companion Constance, since they had left Paris four days earlier. Alston's sources at the Foreign Office had told him that the duke had arrived in Biarritz. Perhaps something had happened to Oakford and Constance on their journey across France? A delay? An accident?

He hated the idea of something happening to Constance. He depended on her so much for things his wife couldn't give him, or his political friends for that matter. When his triumph came, he wanted to share it with her. He wasn't quite sure how that would work, but there had been prime ministers with mistresses before.

The thought excited him.

There was the duke to think about. It would be much better for Oakford to persuade him face-to-face that he should return to England, but if Oakford hadn't made it, then Alston would have to risk a telegram.

He shifted to a writing desk in the library and composed something brief and unambiguous.

'SIR YOU ARE REQUIRED URGENTLY AT HOME STOP LEAVE 28TH STOP PLANE WAITING FOR YOU AT BIARRITZ AERODROME STOP ALSTON'.

Wiltshire

It had been a long, long voyage from Bordeaux, and it wasn't over yet. Conrad had managed to get a place on a cargo ship from Durban which had diverted to Bordeaux to pick up passengers. The ship had room for sixty passengers, but there were at least three hundred on board. Conrad found himself a few square feet of deck on which to lie.

The journey had taken thirty-six hours. The ship had dumped its passengers in Falmouth, before continuing its scheduled voyage to Liverpool. From Falmouth, Conrad had had to fight for a place on a train to Exeter, and then on to London.

He had had plenty of time to think. About his father, most of all. How was he going to tell his mother what had happened? She was a brave woman, but Millie's death had hit her hard. And of course he would have to tell her his own part in his father's death. He hoped she wouldn't blame him; she knew Lord Oakford and his pig-headed determination to achieve peace at any costs better than anyone else.

And his father had been foolish, typically foolish. He was living proof that a pacifist could be brave; he had been willing to sacrifice his life for what he believed in. Indeed willing to dare his son to shoot him. What kind of father was he?

A courageous, stupid, fanatical, bad-tempered, principled, treacherous father. That's what kind.

How could Conrad live with a dead father like that?

How could he live without him?

Of course, as Veronica had pointed out, Conrad was now the new Viscount Oakford. Conrad didn't want the bloody title. It was his father's. Or Edward's. As far as Conrad was concerned, even bloody Reggie could have it; he'd love to be lord-of-the-bloody-manor. Conrad just wanted his family back.

He had hastily discussed with Madame de Salignac what to do with his father's body. She had suggested burying him in the local village churchyard. Conrad had agreed, but on condition that Constance Scott-Dunton was buried somewhere else, anywhere else, just not next to his father. He imagined taking his mother there after the war. What he couldn't imagine was what kind of country France, or Britain for that matter, would be when the war eventually ended, and whether that would be in several years' time or just a couple of weeks.

He remembered Veronica urging him to shoot his father. He could forgive her that: she understood why he was hesitating and was urging him to do what she believed was the right thing. He wasn't sure about her working for McCaigue, although he believed that she had been duped by the major. He wondered whether she would be successful persuading the Duke of Windsor to stay in France. A tall order, but Conrad had learned never to underestimate his wife.

He had grabbed a copy of *The Times* at Exeter station. Rumours that the Allies had surrendered Calais were false. The French were counter-attacking near Amiens. Back in England, pig clubs would come to the aid of small rearers in time of war and housewives were advised to move kitchen cabinets nearer to the stove to save labour.

Conrad wondered whether his battalion was still twiddling its thumbs in Suffolk, or whether it had been ordered to France as Colonel Rydal had anticipated. Perhaps they were fighting the Germans at last. If so, it sounded as if they would be lucky to get back to England in one piece. He should be with them.

And what of Anneliese? How would she be taking captivity? Conrad had hoped that McCaigue would get her out of prison. Much more likely, he was keeping her inside.

He missed her. He felt a sudden, almost overwhelming desire to hold her. To talk to her. To stroke her hair.

But now he was on a train jolting and juddering its way towards London, he couldn't think about his mother, or Anneliese, or even returning to his unit. Somehow he had to convince the British government that it was in imminent danger. But whom could he talk to?

Not McCaigue, obviously. Van almost certainly wouldn't listen to him and would alert McCaigue. His mother, perhaps. She knew people, but she was back in Somerset. It would take too long. Also she was German and therefore bound to raise doubts.

What of his father's friends? Many of them were powerful people. But Conrad had no idea which, if any of them, were involved in Lord Oakford's plotting. Or which were also friends of Sir Henry Alston.

There was his father's old school chum Lord Halifax. Conrad had met him on a number of occasions, and he was sure Halifax would remember him. He was also as convinced as he could be of his integrity and loyalty.

But not his initiative. Halifax was an expert at doing nothing.

There was one man who might listen to him, and if he believed Conrad, who would definitely act. He had listened to Conrad once two years earlier. The trouble was, he would be hard to reach, especially in these times.

But he was Conrad's only hope.

Fifty-Six

Extract from Lieutenant Dieter von Hertenberg's Diary

28 May

Fighting near Dunkirk. We can see hundreds of British ships evacuating troops, thousands of troops. If only we hadn't been forced to halt, we would have bagged the lot of them!

Later given the order that we are to be relieved by XIV Corps. Guderian is to be given his own Panzer Group, which of course he deserves. It will be good to stop fighting for a few days, but we can't sleep yet. Our new Panzer Group headquarters is 200 kilometres away. Maybe once we get there we can have a few days' rest. We all need it.

Eighteen days since the offensive started. Who would have thought that eighteen days could be so vital? We have achieved more in those eighteen days than the German army achieved in four years in the last war.

Maybe peace will come now.

Downing Street, London, 28 May

Winston Churchill listened to Duff Cooper, the Minister of Information, argue the case for honesty about the latest news from the continent. It was dire. That morning the King of the Belgians had surrendered. Calais had fallen the day before, Boulogne the day before that; 11,400 men of the BEF had been evacuated from

Dunkirk so far, leaving behind a quarter of a million more waiting. The French wanted to discuss peace with Germany. They were defeated and they knew it.

Over the weekend the Chiefs of Staff had circulated a dispiriting paper entitled 'British Strategy in a Certain Eventuality', that eventuality being the fall of France. The report concluded that if the Germans won complete air superiority, there would be little the Royal Navy could do to prevent invasion.

But Britain wasn't defeated. Not yet. Not according to Churchill.

Churchill was presiding over the War Cabinet, the small group of five men who ran the war day-to-day: himself, Lord Halifax, Neville Chamberlain and the two Labour ministers Arthur Greenwood and Clement Attlee. While the discussions focused on the details of the war, the unspoken question hung in the air. At what point should Britain admit defeat?

The question had become very close to being spoken the day before, when Lord Halifax had argued that the British should open discussions with the Italians. Afterwards, in the Downing Street garden, Halifax had threatened to resign and Churchill had been forced to apologize and beg him not to. Churchill could not allow the government to be seen to be split on the issue of peace and war.

The Prime Minister studied the adversary sitting opposite him. Halifax had a long, lugubrious face of high-minded seriousness. He prided himself, with justification, on his pragmatism, on his rational mind, on his ability to weigh pros and cons dispassionately. Britain was losing the war and Halifax felt that the War Cabinet should discuss what to do about it.

The trouble was that Halifax had no imagination and no sense of history, both of which Churchill knew he had in spades. Instinct told him, history told him, that at this vital moment it would be fatal to show any sign of weakness. Britain was an island that had not been invaded for a thousand years; it had a glorious history of defending freedom; it had a parliamentary democracy that was the admiration of countries everywhere; it had the greatest empire the world had ever seen. All that was the work of centuries; Churchill would not give it up without a fight.

But he couldn't defend it single-handedly either. He needed the support of the War Cabinet, of the Conservative Party and of the British people. And he was weak. He had only been Prime Minister for eighteen days, and in those eighteen days the Allied armies had been routed. No one blamed him directly. But Halifax's quiet appeal to hard-headed pragmatism in a dire situation was difficult for Churchill to counter.

Conrad perused *The Times* as he waited in an ante-room in 10 Downing Street. He was interested to see no mention of Calais that day, apart from a tiny piece stating that French sources in Paris claimed the town was still probably in Allied hands. It was half past eleven; Conrad had been waiting since ten. His demand that he must meet the Prime Minister with urgent news from France had met with scepticism, but when he had identified himself as Lord Oakford's son, he was at least admitted.

A Civil Servant approached him.

'I understand you wish to see the Prime Minister, Mr de Lancey?'

'Yes. I have some urgent news from France.'

'As you can imagine, the Prime Minister is very busy today. Perhaps you could tell me and I can pass it on?'

'No. I must see him myself.'

'I'm afraid that won't be possible.'

Conrad had been expecting this. 'Just tell Mr Churchill I'm here to see him and he can decide if he wants to meet me. Remind him that I saw him at Chartwell two years ago with an important message from Germany.' That had been that the German officers were planning to overthrow their Führer. 'Tell him this message is even more vital.'

'I will tell the Prime Minister and we will be in touch with you,' said the Civil Servant. 'Can you give me details of where we can reach you?'

'I can wait here,' said Conrad. 'The Prime Minister really needs to hear this as soon as possible.'

'I am sorry, Mr de Lancey, you will have to leave.' The Civil Servant glanced at a moustachioed policeman at the door of the ante-room.

Conrad argued for a few minutes longer, but it was clear he was getting nowhere. In the end the policeman escorted him firmly but politely to the door and out into the street.

Conrad stared desperately at the door of Number 10. 'I have to tell him. I have to tell him somehow,' he said to the policeman, because he was the only person there. 'The future of the war depends on it.'

The constable, who was a large, comfortable man in his fifties, examined Conrad. 'I shouldn't say this, sir, but the Prime Minister often lunches at the Admiralty. You might catch him there later on.'

Halifax bided his time. The War Cabinet broke up with Churchill promising to make a statement in the House of Commons preparing them for bad news from France. They agreed to meet again at four that afternoon, when Churchill was sure Halifax would make his move.

Churchill pulled Neville Chamberlain to one side and asked him if he would agree to inviting Lloyd George into the cabinet. The ostensible reason was to strengthen government unity. Lloyd George was known to be defeatist; he had spoken of Hitler in admiring terms in the past, had been opposed to the war and had argued for peace intermittently since its outbreak. But if the worst came to the worst, Churchill preferred the idea of his old political partner Lloyd George taking over from him than someone like Oswald Mosley.

The success of Vidkun Quisling in usurping the Norwegian government in April had shaken Churchill and was one of the reasons why he had sanctioned locking up Mosley and Maule Ramsay. But they could always be let out of prison again once Churchill had gone.

Neville agreed to Lloyd George. Churchill then went off to lunch at the Admiralty to work on his speech to the House. He was still lodging there, having allowed Neville and his family to stay on at 10 Downing Street.

The food, and especially the wine, fortified him and, clutching a newly lit cigar, he left the Admiralty for Parliament in slightly better spirits.

'Prime Minister! Prime Minister! May I have a word?'

Churchill glanced at the young man trying to attract his attention. He recognized him. 'Mr de Lancey?'

'That's right, sir,' said Conrad. 'I must speak to you.'

Churchill grinned. 'If I stopped and talked to everyone who wanted to speak to me, I'd never get anywhere.'

'What I have to say is more important than the message I gave you at Chartwell two years ago.'

Churchill frowned. He was intrigued. He had liked de Lancey. They had talked then not only about his German friends' plans to remove Hitler, but about history and about bricklaying. Those days, which had seemed so dark at the time, now seemed a period of tranquil unemployment. How he would love to be working on his kitchen-garden wall at Chartwell and chatting to this young man!

'What is it, de Lancey?'

'We need to talk privately, sir.'

'I'm afraid that's impossible,' said Churchill. 'I'm on my way to speak in the House.'

'I have become aware of a plan to replace you as prime minister,' Conrad said. 'My father was involved, I am ashamed to say.'

'Your father!' Churchill was surprised. Although Lord Oakford's pacifism, even defeatism, was well known, Churchill had always held him in high regard. 'Who else?'

He noticed de Lancey glance to see who was within earshot. Just Churchill's detective and a uniformed policeman. 'Henry Alston. And the Duke of Windsor.'

Churchill considered the young man in front of him. Could he be speaking the truth? He had done so at Chartwell in the summer of 1938. Churchill's instinct was that he was doing so now. The duke was a worry, and Churchill had never trusted Alston.

'See me in the House of Commons this afternoon.'

Churchill made his speech and then met the War Cabinet at four o'clock in a room in the Commons. Halifax went on the offensive immediately. He opened proceedings by stating that Vansittart had learned that the Italian government was prepared to act as mediator between Britain and Germany. The question was now firmly on the table. Should Britain discuss peace with Germany?

Halifax's logic was persuasive. There could be no harm in seeing what terms would be acceptable to the Germans. And Britain would achieve much better terms before France was knocked out of the war and Britain's aircraft factories had been bombed than after.

Persuasive, but wrong. Churchill made the point that once negotiations had been opened with Germany it would be impossible to back away from them and still maintain the defiance necessary to win the war. Nations that go down fighting rise again, but those that surrender are merely finished. Besides, Churchill believed the chances of Germany offering decent terms were a thousand to one against.

The War Cabinet wasn't swayed one way or the other. Churchill adjourned the meeting to speak to the wider Cabinet, saying that the War Cabinet would reconvene at seven.

The Outer Cabinet met in Churchill's rooms in the Commons, without the presence of the other War Cabinet members, including Halifax. It had become common practice for one or other of the members of the War Cabinet to brief the rest of the government on what was going on, but Churchill insisted on doing this particular briefing himself. The Outer Cabinet consisted of twenty-nine ministers, half Conservatives from Chamberlain's government, half new men.

Churchill gave it his all. He said that it would be foolish not to consider discussing peace with Hitler, but that the peace terms would probably be harsh, involving giving up the fleet and naval bases. Britain would become a slave state and a puppet government would be set up by Hitler under Mosley or some such person. He concluded by saying that of course, whatever happened at Dunkirk, the British would fight on.

He had thrown in the last remark as a casual observation, but it was the key question. Would the British government fight on?

They would. Quite a few rushed up and patted him on the back. There wasn't a voice of dissent.

Churchill was buoyed by their support, but he knew it would count for nothing if Halifax succeeded in pushing for peace in the War Cabinet. Everyone respected the towering figure of the Foreign Secretary, even Churchill himself. Unless he could win Halifax round, the war was lost.

So Churchill would find a way of winning him round.

Conrad watched Churchill's speech to the Commons from the Strangers' Gallery. It was grave. Belgium had surrendered. Things were clearly going badly in France, although the Prime Minister wasn't specific about exactly what, promising instead to speak to the House at the beginning of the following week. He warned of 'hard and heavy tidings'.

The House listened intently, and there were brief speeches of support from a Labour and a Liberal MP, but none from any Conservatives. Conrad wondered if that was a bad sign. The Conservatives were in a majority and it was they who would dump Churchill if he was going to be dumped.

Conrad picked out Sir Henry Alston's disfigured face on the benches behind the Prime Minister. The scarring made it difficult to read the MP's expression at distance, but Conrad was confident that it would show nothing more than outward loyalty and sincerity. Conrad was half hoping he would see either Lloyd George or Alston speak, but of course that was not part of the plan. They were waiting for their moment.

Churchill hurried from the chamber and Conrad left also. He

made his way to the Prime Minister's room in the Commons and told a clerk there that Mr Churchill had asked to see him. Then he waited in the corridor. At one point he saw the Civil Servant striding rapidly towards him. Conrad bent and tied his shoelace. Fortunately, the Civil Servant was too preoccupied to recognize him.

A string of Cabinet ministers filed past him in glum silence. A short time later they emerged from Churchill's room chatting to each other. There was a buzz of barely suppressed excitement. Whatever the Prime Minister had said to them, he had said it well.

'Mr de Lancey. The Prime Minister will see you now.'

Conrad entered the Prime Minister's spacious room where he was shown to a sofa. Churchill occupied an armchair next to him and lit a cigar. He looked worried. He jabbed his cigar at Conrad.

'You have ten minutes, Mr de Lancey. Tell me more about this threat.'

So Conrad told him. About Sir Henry Alston and his plan to subvert the British government to concede its country's independence to Hitler, without the British people even realizing what was happening. About how Lloyd George would become Prime Minister and the Duke of Windsor would become king. About powerful figures in the press, the army, the civil service and Parliament who would support this new government. About a Major McCaigue in the secret service who was in Alston's pocket. About how Conrad's own father had been sent to France to fetch the Duke of Windsor and had died on the way in murky circumstances.

Churchill puffed at his cigar thoughtfully. 'It's exactly what I fear most,' he said. 'A coup by stealth rather than by fascist mobs on the street.' The cigar glowed. 'What proof do you have that Lloyd George and the Duke of Windsor are involved?'

'No direct proof. Just what I have told you.'

'Do you know whether they are knowing accomplices? Or are they compliant dupes?'

'I have no idea, sir,' said Conrad. 'My impression is that Alston keeps his plans very close to his chest. He likes to manipulate people if he can, rather than tell them openly what he is about.'

Churchill grunted. He stared at Conrad for a full minute.

'Wait here, de Lancey,' said Churchill. 'I would like you to repeat all this to the Foreign Secretary. You have no reason to think that he is involved?'

'None,' said de Lancey.

Churchill summoned Lord Halifax. Within a couple of minutes the lean frame of the Foreign Secretary appeared at the door. He was six feet eight inches tall, very thin, with a left hand that took the form of a black clenched fist with a thumb on a spring. A birth defect, not a war wound. Despite the hand, Lord Halifax was a good shot, as Conrad had witnessed once on a grouse moor in Yorkshire.

His eyebrows shot up when he saw Conrad.

'Do you know Mr de Lancey, Edward?' said Churchill.

'Indeed I do,' said Halifax.

'He has something to tell you,' said Churchill.

Halifax frowned. 'We don't have much time, Prime Minister.'

'I know that, Edward. But listen to him. Just for ten minutes. Listen to him.'

Conrad repeated to the Foreign Secretary what he had told the Prime Minister. Halifax listened closely, his face registering ever-deepening shock. Afterwards he asked more or less the same questions as Churchill had.

'I find this very hard to believe,' he said, when Conrad had finished.

'Do you?' said Conrad.

The lines in Halifax's long face deepened. 'Maybe not,' he said. He stood up and went to the window, which overlooked the Thames. He spoke with his back to Conrad. 'I find your father's actions particularly disappointing. I know him . . . I knew him well, most of his life. We were at Eton together.'

'I know,' said Conrad.

'I'm sorry about what happened to him. I would have said he was a good man, a great man.'

'Except for this,' said Conrad.

'Yes,' said Halifax. 'You know we might lose this war, de Lancey?'

'Yes,' said Conrad. 'But isn't it better to lose it on the battlefield or in the Channel or in the air than in the back corridors of Westminster?'

'That's what the Prime Minister thinks,' said Halifax. He shook his head. 'What they are up to is treason pure and simple. I cannot be part of it.'

'No, sir,' said Conrad.

The War Cabinet met again at seven o'clock. Churchill told them of the enthusiastic reaction of the Outer Cabinet to his proposal to fight on. He reiterated that he was not in favour of making an approach to Germany at the present time.

He turned to his Foreign Secretary. Lord Halifax looked thoughtful. But he said nothing.

The conversation turned to whether and how to make an appeal to the United States.

It was decided. Britain would fight on.

Conrad stood in the square and turned back to look up at the Houses of Parliament, the place where his father had spent so much of his time over the previous ten years, and, if France fell, the one place where democracy would live on in Europe. Conrad had done all he could – he had persuaded Churchill and he had persuaded Halifax. It was up to them to deal with Alston and his co-conspirators and to fight the war to its end.

Conrad knew there was a good chance that the end might mean defeat for Britain. But after all the turmoil and confusion of the previous year, the prevarications of the phoney war, the loss of his sister and his father, and the imprisonment of Anneliese, there was one thing of which he was certain: it was a war that had to be fought and he had to fight it.

'Dave, what did that Veronica woman say to you, when you were outside on the balcony?'

The Duke of Windsor glanced at his wife, who was trying on earrings for dinner. They were in the bedroom of their suite. She had made a point of not asking him about Veronica de Lancey, but she couldn't resist any longer.

'Oh, it was nothing, darling,' said the duke.

That didn't satisfy her. He should have known it wouldn't. 'It can't have been nothing! Did you see how fast she bolted?'

The duke sighed. Time for a little lie. 'You know how these young women can be? You would think that now we are married and with you actually sitting inside, she would have known better. It's extraordinary! So I sent her away with a flea in her ear.'

Wallis's eyes flicked up from the mirror. The duke knew she was considering whether Veronica de Lancey might be a 'good friend' from the old days. But she wasn't, and Wallis knew it. She let it drop.

The duke left the bedroom and moved through to the sitting room. He lit his pipe and went out on to the balcony to watch the sea. He fished out the cable he had received from Sir Henry Alston in London the night before and quickly reread it.

Then he struck a match and lit the corner of the telegram, letting the ashes scatter in the soft Atlantic breeze.

EPILOGUE

Summer 1940

It was seven o'clock in the morning when the bell rang in Alston's flat in London. He pulled on a dressing gown and went downstairs to answer it. He was still drunk from the copious amounts of whisky he had put away the night before when he had heard that Constance had been killed a week earlier in France, together with Lord Oakford.

There were four policemen at the door: two detectives and two uniformed constables. They were arresting him under Defence Regulation 18B. They asked him to get dressed, pack a few things and accompany them.

Alston wasn't surprised. He invited them in, and then went through to his bedroom. Before the constable following him could stop him, he had grabbed the revolver which he kept in his bedside drawer, turned it to his temple and pulled the trigger.

Hundreds of other men and women were rounded up that morning and in the following month, including many members of the Right Club and the British Union of Fascists. But none of the senior members of the government, the armed forces or the civil service whom Alston had courted were imprisoned, nor the dukes and other aristocrats who had sympathized with him and Freddie.

Major McCaigue was helpful in identifying who needed to be kept under observation; it turned out that he had cultivated useful sources within Alston's conspiracy. He stuck by his assessment that Conrad de Lancey was a Soviet spy and by his decision to send de Lancey's ex-wife to keep tabs on him. Although de Lancey had Churchill's support, McCaigue ensured the SIS kept an open file on him. A reliable man in a crisis, Major McCaigue.

A fear of a 'fifth column' of foreign spies and British Nazi supporters swept the nation, a fear shared wholeheartedly by the Prime Minister. In addition to the Britons suspected of sympathy with the Nazis, thousands of Germans and Italians were interned, including most of the Jews who had escaped to Britain from Germany and Austria. Anneliese was released from Holloway, only to be rearrested with her parents a week later. She and her mother were sent to Huyton near Liverpool, and her father was despatched to the Isle of Man.

Theo returned to Germany from his mission in Spain. Joachim von Ribbentrop mourned the loss of his star protégé, Otto Langebrück, on a dangerous mission in enemy territory. Intelligence from the Abwehr suggested that British spies had been responsible for Langebrück's death in an attempt to keep the Duke of Windsor away from Britain.

Theo's intelligence duties switched to Britain, which was natural given his education there. He read with great interest Abwehr intelligence reports of the collapse of Alston's plans and of his suicide, and that the Duke of Windsor had decided to drive to Antibes from Biarritz instead of returning to England. With the defeat of France, invasion of Britain was becoming a real danger. But Admiral Canaris had Theo working on exaggerated reports from southern England of the number of British divisions available and the strength of their secret fortifications: armoured cars lurking in the bunkers of the golf courses of St Leonards, a catacomb of gun emplacements underneath the hill at Rye. These the admiral passed on to Hitler with gloomy assessments of the likely failure of a German invasion attempt. Theo was pleased to see his chief gradually moving towards his own position on where his true loyalty to his country should lie.

The Duke and Duchess of Windsor travelled first to Antibes, and then, when France fell, on to Madrid and Lisbon. Concerned that his inclinations were known to be pro-Nazi and that he might become a focus for intrigue, Churchill forbade the duke from returning to England, and ordered him to take up a position as Governor General of the Bahamas, well out of the way.

Joachim von Ribbentrop sent Sturmbannführer Schellenberg to Lisbon to try to persuade the duke to remain in Europe, or if that failed, to kidnap him. Schellenberg offered the duke fifty million Swiss francs, and frightened him with claims that the British secret service was planning to assassinate him on the ship to the Bahamas. Echoing Venlo, Schellenberg suggested that the duke and duchess go on a shooting holiday at a forest on the Portuguese border, from where they could be easily spirited into Spain. They could wait there until they were needed in England.

The duke and duchess prevaricated, but eventually the duke's friend and legal adviser Walter Monckton flew out to Portugal and persuaded them to leave Europe. They set sail for the Bahamas on 1 August, where they languished for the remainder of the war.

On 27 August 1940 a notice appeared in the Forthcoming Marriages section of *The Times*:

LIEUTENANT VISCOUNT OAKFORD AND MISS ROSEN. The engagement is announced between Lieutenant Conrad William Giles, second son of the late Viscount Oakford, G.C.V.O., V.C., M.C., and Lady Oakford of Chilton Coombe, Somerset, and Anneliese Gisela, daughter of Dr Werner Rosen of Douglas, the Isle of Man and Mrs Hilde Rosen of Huyton, Liverpool.

AUTHOR'S NOTE

How much of this novel is based on truth?

It's a fair question, and one that is surprisingly difficult to answer. But I shall try. The historical sources cannot be trusted. The main players had reputations to protect; governments had a war to win. Conspiracy and cock-up walk hand in hand through a jungle of lies, rumour, gossip and fabrication. Conspiracy theorists and many conspiracy novelists love the idea of cold, super-intelligent plotters driven by a thirst for power. There may have been one or two of these around in 1940, like the fictional Sir Henry Alston, but most of the actors were driven by fear, vanity, prejudice and panic.

Nowhere is this more obvious than the vexed question of whether the Duke of Windsor was a Nazi spy.

The idea for this novel first came to me after reading Martin Allen's stimulating book *Hidden Agenda*, which makes the forceful case that the Duke of Windsor willingly passed secrets about the French defences to the Germans in the hope of securing a role as King or President of a pro-German Britain. The problem is that some of Mr Allen's sources are suspect, such as a letter purporting to be from the duke delivered to Hitler in November 1939 by Charles Bedaux. A fascinating article by Ben Fenton in the *Financial Times* in 2008 points out that twenty-nine forged documents have been *inserted* into the Public Record Office at Kew, and that these have all been used as source material in three books by Mr Allen. Five of them were cited in *Hidden Agenda*. It is the only known case of documents being inserted rather than removed from the PRO. At the time of the writing of the article they had only been accessed by Mr and Mrs Allen and by the

Foreign Office and MI6. There was a police investigation, but it was dropped. Martin Allen denied any knowledge that these papers were forgeries. Despite this mystery, much of Martin Allen's argument is supported by more reliable sources quoted elsewhere, and in my mind, many of his points still stand.

The British Establishment was torn over how to treat the Duke of Windsor's story. On the one hand, they wanted to vilify the man who had given up the throne for the love of a divorced American woman. On the other, they wanted to preserve the reputation of the monarchy. Thus, signs of cover-up are everywhere. Anthony Blunt was sent around Europe in the years immediately after the war in search of German documents relating to the duke. That's the same Anthony Blunt who was spying for the Soviet Union and who, unlike fellow spies Philby, Burgess and Maclean who were publicly accused as soon as they were discovered, was allowed to continue as the Surveyor of the Queen's Pictures until he was eventually exposed in 1979.

In September 1954, fearful of leaks by the Americans, the Stationery Office published messages sent by the German ambassador at The Hague in early 1940 to his bosses in Berlin informing them that the Duke of Windsor was unhappy with the British government and willing to impart information on Allied war plans. In 1954 these revelations provoked outrage in Parliament: Captain Kerby, Member for Arundel and Shoreham, asked Sir Winston Churchill, the Prime Minister, why such clearly false allegations had been published by Her Majesty's Government and whether an apology had been made to the Duke of Windsor. The Prime Minister assured the House that the duke had not raised any objections to the documents' publication and that the Prime Minister agreed with the duke that the German ambassador's allegations would be treated with contempt. 'They are, of course, quite untrue.' Yes, Prime Minister.

But there are some 'facts' on which most historians and biographers can agree, and by listing them baldly, the picture becomes a little clearer.

The Duke and Duchess of Windsor were married at a chateau belonging to Charles Bedaux in 1937. The duke pointed out the weaknesses in the French lines around Sedan in reports to the British general staff in late 1939. The duke dined with Charles Bedaux several times in Paris in autumn 1939. Charles Bedaux visited the Netherlands in the winter of 1939 and 1940 where the British secret service became suspicious of him. The German ambassador to the Netherlands thought the Duke of Windsor was unhappy with the British government and might provide intelligence to the Germans. The Germans changed their invasion plans to attack through the Ardennes rather than central Belgium. Charles Bedaux is mentioned in the Abwehr files as one of their 'V-Men'; that is, an agent. In 1942 he was arrested by the French in Algeria, and shipped to America, where he committed suicide in 1944 while waiting to be tried for treason. From 1939 to 1940 British intelligence became increasingly concerned about the loyalty of the Duke of Windsor. In the summer of 1940, Winston Churchill, one of the duke's most loyal supporters when he had been king, insisted that the duke take up the post of governor general in the Bahamas. According to a paper drafted by Lord Lloyd at the time, this was because of fear of the duke's well-known pro-Nazi attitudes and the possibility of intrigue growing up around him.

There is an absence of conclusive documentary evidence of the duke's treachery. But there is ample evidence that documents relating to the duke have been hidden or destroyed by the British government.

Was there a conspiracy to overthrow Churchill's government and replace it with a pro-German puppet government? Another difficult question. There were many Establishment figures who wanted to end the war in 1939–40. These included Rab Butler, Lord Tavistock, Lord Beaverbrook, Richard Stokes, Samuel Hoare, Oswald Mosley, Captain Maule Ramsay, General Ironside, David Lloyd George and, in late May 1940, Lord Halifax. Some simply believed any war was wrong. Some wanted to win the war, but believed facts had to be faced: it was better to negotiate peace terms rather than lose it. And some admired Nazi Germany and preferred her as an ally rather than an enemy. All considered themselves patriots. Some, like Lord Oakford in the novel, were confused by these differing motivations.

The role of Lloyd George is an interesting one. Although seventy-seven, he was the most viable alternative to Churchill, Chamberlain and Halifax as Prime Minister, and indeed had served as such in the First World War. He had visited Hitler in Germany and the Duke of Windsor in the south of France and declared himself an admirer of both. According to his secretary, as quoted by John Lukacs in *Five Days in London*, the reason he turned down a position in the War Cabinet in the summer of 1940 was that he 'was not going with this gang. There would be change.'

In France in June 1940, Marshal Pétain became the leader of a French government based in Vichy, which collaborated with Germany. Although vilified by history, at the time the 84-year-old soldier was seen as a true patriot, and a hero of the Great War. If Pétain could become President of Vichy France, it is not beyond the realms of possibility that Lloyd George and the Duke of Windsor could have been prepared to lead an equally subservient Britain.

Something was going on. I don't know what it was – it may be that no one still alive does – but *something* was going on.

Sir Henry Alston, Lord Copthorne, Lord Oakford, Major McCaigue and Constance Scott-Dunton are fictional characters, although they share many traits with real pacifists and pro-Nazis of the time. There were many men and women who were pro-Nazi in 1938 and genuinely realized the error of their ways in 1939, such as poor Lord Redesdale, Nancy Mitford's father, who concluded that 'abroad is unutterably bloody and foreigners are fiends.' He fell out with his still pro-German wife, and removed himself to a Scottish island where he died a broken man. Without proper evidence I am reluctant to accuse real individuals such as him of treachery, so I have preferred to create fictional equivalents.

The Abwehr, the German secret service, was consistently

opposed to Hitler before and during the war. Admiral Canaris was arrested for his part in the plot to assassinate Hitler in 1944 and was executed in 1945. The implications of what it means if a nation's secret service is opposed to that nation's government in war have not to my mind been fully explored, although Richard Bassett's book *Hitler's Spy Chief* makes a start. The 'little W.C.', as Canaris called himself, was a big admirer of 'the great W.C.'. Theo is a fictional character, but representative of a number of young German lawyers who became involved in the opposition to Hitler, including Fabian von Schlabrendorff, Peter Bielenberg, Adam von Trott, Hans-Bernd Gisevius and Helmuth von Moltke.

Any novel set in the Second World War presents the writer with a seemingly unending list of books to read, but it is worth mentioning the most useful ones here. On the Venlo Incident there are accounts by Sigismund Payne Best (*The Venlo Incident*) and Walter Schellenberg (*The Schellenberg Memoirs*). Both were spies, and hence professional liars, and both had reputations to protect. The two sources conflict, and while trying to reconcile them I realized that it was possible not only that one was right and one was wrong, but that they could both be incorrect. This was an important lesson for all sources on this subject. Dieter von Hertenberg's diary entries are based on General Guderian's account of the Blitzkrieg in *Panzer Leader*. The patrons of the Russian Tea Rooms and other dodgy pro-Nazis are described in *Patriotism Perverted* by Richard Griffiths. The intricacies of French and German war plans are untangled in Ernest May's *Strange Victory*. The precarious position of the British government in May 1940 is the subject of John Lukacs's book *Five Days in London*, and is thoroughly addressed in Andrew Roberts's biography of Lord Halifax, *The Holy Fox*. Philip Ziegler's *King Edward VIII* provides a sober antidote to Martin Allen's *Hidden Agenda*, and Sol Bloomenkranz's e-book *Charles Bedaux – Deciphering an Enigma* comes close to doing just that.

I have tried to tamper with historical events as little as possible, but in the interests of novelistic clarity, I have made some minor manipulation to dates. For example General Guderian was given

the order to take up a new command on 29 May 1940, not 28
May, and the duke fled Paris for Biarritz a little later than 22 May.
Also I have simplified the tangle of security organizations which
reported to Heydrich – the Sicherheitsdienst, the RHSA and so
on – to 'the Gestapo'.

Finally I would like to thank a number of people for their help:
Robin Reames, Hilma Roest, Lisa van de Bunt, Theo Kes, Kate
Howles, Sander Verheijen, Richenda Todd, my agent Oli Munson,
and Nic Cheetham and his colleagues at Head of Zeus. I also need
to thank my wife and children for putting up with a husband and
father who has spent much of the last couple of years hiding from
the twenty-first century in his own little phoney war in Holland
and France seventy-five years ago.